"I need an assistant for the weekends only. Your main priority would be typing my handwritten book," he said, turning to stride across the room to stand next to the lit fireplace.

"You write by hand?" she asked, unable to hide her amazement and forgetting the reason for her visit.

"Yes," he said, his voice deep.

"And you've finished your new book in the Mayhem series?" she asked.

"So, you're familiar with my books?" he asked, his attention locked on the crackling fire.

Samira wished she could see his face. She felt almost like he was hiding it from her intentionally. "Yes," she finally answered. "My favorite is *Vengeance*."

He grunted.

She eyed him. There was something so powerful but still sad about his stance. The way he moved. The way his stare was downcast. She was surprised at how strongly she needed to know what gave him such a demeanor. It, plus the dark interior of the home and neglected exterior, was all so mysterious—maybe even more so than one of his novels.

The man was an enigma. How could someone so abrupt and insolent write with such emotion and rhythm that she was forever transformed by his words? The two did not match.

Niobia Bryant is the award-winning and national bestselling author of more than thirty works of romance and commercial mainstream fiction. She has twice won the RT Reviewers' Choice Best Book Award for African American/Multicultural Romance. Her books have appeared in *Ebony*, *Essence*, the *New York Post*, *The Star-Ledger*, *The Dallas Morning News* and many other national publications.

"I am a writer, born and bred. I can't even fathom what else I would do besides creating stories and telling tales. When it comes to my writing I dabble in many genres, my ideas are unlimited and the ink in my pen is infinite." —Niobia Bryant

Books by Niobia Bryant

Harlequin Kimani Romance

A Billionaire Affair
Tempting the Billionaire
The Billionaire's Baby
Christmas with the Billionaire

Visit the Author Profile page
at Harlequin.com for more titles.

NIOBIA BRYANT
and
CAROLYN HECTOR

Christmas with the Billionaire
&
A Tiara for Christmas

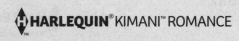

HARLEQUIN® KIMANI™ ROMANCE

ISBN-13: 978-1-335-47099-7

Christmas with the Billionaire & A Tiara for Christmas

Copyright © 2019 by Harlequin Books S.A.

Christmas with the Billionaire
Copyright © 2019 by Niobia Bryant

A Tiara for Christmas
Copyright © 2019 by Carolyn Hall

Recycling programs for this product may not exist in your area.

Printed in U.S.A.

HARLEQUIN®
www.Harlequin.com

CONTENTS

As always, for my mama, my guardian angel,
Letha "Bird" Bryant.

CHRISTMAS WITH THE BILLIONAIRE

Niobia Bryant

Dear Reader,

Welcome to the last Passion Grove romance. This is bittersweet. I'm happy to tell the fiery love story of Lance and Samira—especially with its slight take on the *Beauty and the Beast* theme—but it's hard to leave the little town behind. I will cherish the memories of four ardent love stories: Alek and Alessandra, Chance and Ngozi, Naim and Marisa and now Lance and Samira. And don't forget the secondary romance of Roje and Lulu woven throughout the series.

So I hope you'll enjoy following the romantic journey of Lance, the reclusive author with more grumpiness than grins, and Samira, the billionaire heiress who wants love, career and a vibrant social life.

It's a story you don't want to miss. I promise.

N.

www.NiobiaBryant.com

Chapter 1

"It is end of day, Samira."

Life is all about balance.

Samira Ansah believed in that mantra and was determined to achieve it. So, when her virtual assistant gave her its daily reminder, she allowed herself just a few more moments at her desk looking over a report from one of the brand associates that she supervised as the growth strategist for the Ansah-Dalmount Group. Ambitious, she loved her work for the billion-dollar conglomerate, particularly since her late father, Kwame Ansah, had been one of its founders. She was determined to be equally successful in work, play and love. Balance.

She exited the document and then logged out of the ADG network before she rose from her desk to walk to her slender lone window in the corner. New York's autumn skies were darkening, the lights across the metropolitan area illuminating the windows of towering buildings, the streetlights and headlights of the many cars moving at a slow pace in the congested traffic below. She found it exhilarating. Of all the places she'd lived and all the places she'd seen as she'd traveled around the world, New York was one of her faves, because the vibe was hard to match.

Samira turned from the window of her modest office, tucking her jet-black, nearly waist-length hair behind her ear before she pulled on her lined trench coat. After retrieving her black leather Fendi purse and a Dolce & Gabbana garment bag from the hook on the back of the door, she left her office without a look back.

The large office the three members on her team shared was already empty. She was always the first to arrive and last to leave by design. The heels of her designer shoes clicked against the marble floors as she took long strides, made easy by her tall height. She reached the wood-paneled elevator before the reception desk, turning to look around.

The corporation operated around the globe, including in Milan and London, but New York was its headquarters. ADG owned the twenty-five-story building but leased out all but the top four floors, with the co-CEOs occupying the extravagant two offices on the top floor with their own private elevators. The majority of the small glass-enclosed offices were empty as the time neared seven. It was on this twenty-second floor where the lion's share of ADG employees were housed. The worker bees. Those driven by pure hunger to succeed. Many who wanted not just a paycheck but to climb the ranks of the company and lay claim to one of the executive offices on the upper floors that came with larger space, better views and priceless executive assistants.

Samira wanted that as well.

Although she was an heir to the Ansah fortune, which made her wealthy, Samira's ambition was to help run the billion-dollar conglomerate. Business was in her blood. Her grandfather, Ebo Ansah, began a financial services firm in Ghana in the 1950s that grew significantly in the mid-1960s, providing a very respectable living for his wife, Kessie, and their four children. His eldest son—her father, Kwame—grew up under the tutelage of his father and was anxious for his opportunity to enter the family business. They expanded the financial services offered to their loyal clients and grew their business. Life was good, and with the Ansah men working together doggedly, it became even better. Upon Ebo's passing in the early 1980s, Kwame took over the running of the business, aggressively acquiring smaller banks and insurance and investment firms to catapult himself to wealth and prominence. When the opportunity arose in 1987 to join forces with Frances Dalmount, a business competitor from England, he accepted with the intent to use their combined resources to take on other business ventures. The Ansah-Dalmount Group was formed, eventually becoming one of the most successful conglomerates in the world with its business umbrella covering financial services, oil, hotel/resorts/casinos, telecommunications and, most recently, shipping.

Samira was just a teenager when her beloved father was killed in a plane crash. She was a daddy's girl and took his death hard. The years had passed, but her pain and regret lingered. As she entered college and majored in finance, she was determined to help cement her father's legacy by working alongside her two older brothers, Alek and Naim. Alek was the heir to the proverbial throne, and her brother Naim, who was just as qualified to lead, had worked his way up the ladder from the marketing department to become president of the telecommunications arm.

She was determined to have similar success.

Already, she'd overcome the usual gender hurdles. She'd slain Alek's outdated misgivings about women in business—whether they could measure up or stick to the job in the same way men did—and she'd been inspired by the tenacity and work ethic of his wife, Alessandra. And it had been her sister-in-law who gave her the shot her brother had not.

"I want to work for the firm my grandfather created from nothing and my father helped shape into a billion-dollar corporation. I want in at ADG."

Samira remembered the moment when she'd stiffened her spine, notched her chin and presented her résumé to Alessandra with more confidence than she actually felt. She was thankful for the brilliant businesswoman who had become her sister-in-law. Like Alessandra, she wanted to be one of the rare women of color to become a top executive and to create opportunities for others like her, wanting the corporate glass ceiling shattered once and for all. Lately, she had been pondering starting a blog to help other women who aspired to enter corporate America by highlighting women in business and offering career and education advice.

Ding.

She turned as the wood-paneled door to the elevator opened and stepped inside the lift, pressing the button for the penthouse. The ride was smooth and quick. Within minutes she was striding off the elevator and past the empty reception area to the wide marbled hall leading to Alessandra's suite of offices. The automated glass door leading into the outer office opened upon her approach.

"Good evening, Ms. Ansah. Go right in," Alessandra's executive assistant, Unger Rawlings, said.

Samira gave the tall and slender man a soft smile as she continued past his desk to enter the spacious office taking up almost half of the entire floor of the building. The nearly 360-degree view of Manhattan through the floor-to-ceiling windows was spectacular. The open floor plan was breathtakingly beautiful and sleek at over three thousand square feet, with twenty-foot ceilings with skylights, a private spa bath, a small kitchen, an exercise room, a lounge area with a grand fireplace, a library and an outdoor terrace.

Over the years since she claimed her spot as co-CEO of ADG, Alessandra had made the space that once belonged to Samira's father her own.

"Hello, Ms. CEO."

Alessandra paused in sliding folders inside her red leather briefcase and offered her a warm smile. "Hello. Date night?" she asked.

"Yes," she said, coming to a stop before her desk. "Thanks for letting me use your bathroom. I'm meeting someone for dinner and would rather not make a trip home to change."

"Someone?" Alessandra asked, tucking her sleek bob-cut hair behind her ear, the diamond of her extravagant wedding ring sparkling brilliantly with the gesture.

"Norman. Stockbroker. Tall. Gorgeous. Funny," she supplied, her eyes sparkling as she held up crossed fingers.

To date, Samira had been unlucky in love, and she wanted to change that. She was single and happily dating after her college boyfriend ended things because he no longer wanted to be in a relationship. Samira was of the school of thought that what was not meant to be shouldn't be forced, and she took the breakup in stride, determined not to give up on love. For her, happily-ever-after meant falling in love, starting a family and thriving in business. She wanted it all.

The last of the shelves of books lining the wall swung open, and her brother Alek walked in from the long, windowless concrete hallway that ran along the back wall of the boardroom and connected his office to that of his wife. He smiled at them both, looking very *GQ* in his tailored suit and polished handmade shoes. He moved to Alessandra's side, setting his own briefcase on the desk before sliding his arm around her body and pressing a kiss to her temple.

Samira stroked the garment bag tucked over her arm as she eyed two successful business magnates running a billion-dollar business and their family together with both brilliance and love.

Alek's eyes dipped down to the garment bag and tote she carried. "What are you up to tonight?" he asked, his British accent acquired from their London upbringing still as present as her own.

"Minding the business that pays me, big brother," she quipped, giving him a playful wink.

"Funny. I thought I paid you," he returned as his wife looked on at their spirited sibling jibing.

Samira chuckled. "For my work. *Not* my business."

"Touché," Alek said, inclining his head.

"I'm having dinner at Daniel," she supplied as she turned on her heels to move toward Alessandra's private en suite bathroom.

"On East Sixty-Fifth?"

Samira nodded.

"Order the foie gras–stuffed quail. It's really good."

"Will do," she said as the frosted automated door to the spa-like bathroom opened as she neared.

"We're headed out. Be safe," Alessandra called out behind her.

"I will, and tell Aliyah that Aunt Mira will see her this weekend," she said, rushing into the bathroom for fear of being late.

Not the best impression on a first date.

Quickly she undressed and twisted her hair up

under a shower cap, oblivious to the elegant surroundings as she started the water and stepped beneath the rain showerhead.

"That feels good," she said to herself, wishing she had more time to enjoy the spray of the water against her skin.

Twenty minutes later, with her makeup freshened up and her body smelling of her favorite Hermès 24 Faubourg perfume of ylang-ylang, orange blossoms, jasmine and iris, Samira made her way out of the office and toward the elevator. She felt decadent in a satin-trimmed lace dress with corset boning that clung to her curves and revealed just enough of her skin to tempt and tantalize.

And later, as she finally entered the elegant Upper East Side eatery and was led to the bar, she smiled as Norman rose from the stool and presented her a white cosmopolitan with an orchid in an oversize sphere of ice.

"You remembered," she said, accepting the drink and the warm kiss he pressed to her cheek.

"Most definitely," Norman assured her.

She'd mentioned the delicious drink in passing when they first decided where to have their dinner date.

Nice touch.

She slid onto the stool he held out for her, taking a sip of her drink before setting it and her clutch atop the bar in front of a backlit wall filled with shelves of liquors. "So, tell me more about yourself, Norman," she said, crossing her long legs and drawing his eye.

They'd met through an online dating app. Samira was not only an employee on the rise at ADG but also one of the heirs to the family fortune. Being a billionaire heiress made her cautious about whom she chose to have in her life, and the app allowed access to a wide dating pool while still keeping a good chunk of her life—and her wealth—to herself. The last thing she was looking for was fake love fostered by a desire for a billionaire lifestyle. The money she received via her share of the family trust and her shares in ADG made her career more of a passion than a necessity.

As he talked of his life, Samira listened intently, sizing him up and finding he might very well fit in her life. He was smart, well-spoken, attractive and groomed. She was surrounded by power couples: Alek and Alessandra; her brother's best friend, Chance, a self-made tech billionaire and his wife, Ngozi, a powerful attorney; and her other brother, Naim, and his wife, Marisa, also an heir to the wealthy Dalmount family, who was creating her own destiny through her own chocolate business. Power and passion.

Each woman was a wife, mother and shrewd businesswoman.

I can have it all, too.

I will *have it all.*

Emerson Lance Millner's daily ritual was set in stone, and he liked it that way.

With a soft grunt, he awakened. He reached for his iPhone and checked the time, already knowing it was somewhere around 3:00 a.m., as it always was when he rose. Setting the phone back down on the night-stand, cloaked by the darkness of the early-morning hours, Lance moved his frame to sit up on the edge of the king-size bed. He forced himself not to think of just how empty the large bed was even with his over-six-foot height and broad build.

His grief was the norm for him as well.

He rubbed his eyes with his hands before stretching his arms high above his head and then rising to his feet. He waved his hand over the base of the lamp to softly illuminate his master bedroom. Nude, he strode across the polished hardwood floors to enter the walk-in closet/dressing room and continued through to the rustic-styled bathroom. He reached inside the tiled glass-enclosed shower to turn the water on to steaming hot before brushing his teeth at the double sink, avoiding his reflection in the copper-framed mirror that accentuated the wood walls.

In the shower, he faced the opposite wall and closed his eyes, enjoying the feel of the hot water pelting against his shoulders, back and buttocks. These days it was the only way his body was touched. He kept himself isolated and alone, suffering in silence and only finding the smallest bit of joy in his work.

Not in love.

Not in a family.

Not anymore.

Lance winced as pain radiated across his body, and he tilted his head back to wash away his tears beneath the spray of the water. Three years had not dulled his heartache or lessened his anger and regret. They were his new normal.

He finished his shower and stepped out of the glass enclosure with the steam swirling outward as well, surrounding his frame. He reached for a plush chocolate-colored towel and dried every inch of his body vigorously, giving his face just one hard press with the cloth before dropping it into the chute behind the door where it would land downstairs in a hamper inside the laundry room.

Without looking in the mirror, he brushed his close-cut hair and walked back inside the closet/dressing room area, moving past the shelves and racks of tailored designer clothing he no longer favored. Not for years. Instead, he chose a pair of jeans, a thin long-sleeved T-shirt and lightweight boots and grabbed one of a dozen boonie hats he owned to fold and shove in the rear pocket of his pants once he was dressed.

He paused before turning to eye the clothes that lined the other side of the massive closet. His gut clenched as he allowed himself to stroke the skirt of a sequined crimson dress. Most days he was good at ignoring all the things left behind.

Clearing his throat, he freed the cloth and rushed from the closet, swinging the door with one hard shove to slam it closed.

Wham!

The noise almost surprised him.

His house—his rustic eight-bedroom, nine-bathroom, mansion—was always so quiet.

Lance's footsteps echoed against the hardwood

floors as he left his bedroom and used the metal-framed elevator at the end of the hall to go up one flight. He opened the wrought iron gate to step directly into the oversize attic he long ago had converted into his office. Here the dark wood, vaulted ceilings, large skylights and abundance of shelves stuffed with books gave him the inspiration he needed to create. Here the lights stayed on like it was the hub of the house.

He pulled the cap from his pocket as he moved across the room to his large ebony desk. Tossing the hat on the corner of the desk, he sat in his mahogany leather chair and held the edge to roll forward. With movements that were almost automatic, he turned on the eighty-six-inch television on the wall but placed it on mute, turned on the desk lamp illuminating a perfect circle of light down upon the college-ruled notebook and extra-fine-point pen that sat upon it. Last, he put his phone on Do Not Disturb and synced it to the speaker sitting on the edge of the desk before pulling up Meek Mill's album *Championships*.

He glanced at the time. Four a.m.

Right on time. Just like always.

He picked up the pen and tapped it against the edge of the leather blotter of the desk as he reread the last few pages of his crime fiction novel to regain the pace and rhythm of the story before putting pen to paper. For the next two hours, he got lost in the latest crime-solving adventure of his protagonist. The feel of the pen scratching against the pad was addictive, and he allowed himself to get lost in a world of his own creation.

For him, the computer felt like a middleman blocking him from the emotions he poured into his writing. He knew it was a mind thing, but it was his process. His comfort. He had no plans to even try to do it differently.

Thankfully his millions of loyal readers enjoyed his stories as much as he found pleasure in creating them, making him a very wealthy man. A very lonely, isolated, wealthy man.

He paused and flexed his head toward his left shoulder and then the right.

Lance had always had a love for words, starting when he was a child fascinated by reading books and getting lost in stories. With the dissolution of his parents' marriage in his teens, he turned to writing to create a world where he felt more in control than he did in reality. He began with short stories and novellas that he would only share with close friends but soon developed and completed his first book. He was first published at the age of twenty-one and won major book awards for his debut novel. When his second two-book offer from his publisher was made via his agent, Lance officially became a full-time author, and his career only grew with each new book release.

It had been eleven years and five bestselling books translated into a dozen or more foreign languages.

Coming to the end of the twentieth chapter, Lance dropped his pen atop the notebook and worked the fingers of his left hand to relieve the tightness caused by his extensive handwriting. Eight pages. Just another twenty or so and the first draft of *Danger* was done.

He frowned deeply as he turned and looked down the length of the attic at the smaller desk with an all-in-one touch-screen computer sitting there. Unused and uncared for. Lance disdained it and normally relied on his personal assistant to convert his handwritten text to type.

Unfortunately, he was in need of a new one. His fifth in the last two years.

He checked the time. Seven a.m.

Right on time.

Lance rose from his chair and moved around the desk to one of the windows in the room. Like every other in the massive house, it was covered by blackout curtains, which he moved aside with his hand just enough to peer out at the sun, now high in the blue skies above the heart-shaped lake that served as the center of the small, affluent town of Passion Grove, New Jersey.

No sign of rain.

"Good," he muttered, shifting the curtain back before he retraced his steps to the desk to grab his hat and pull it over his head, being sure to lower it over the top portion of his face. He left his phone on the desk and made his way across the attic to the elevator, riding it down to the first floor.

His strides were long and his steps echoed through the dimly lit, empty house. There was no staff. He preferred the solace even if he knew the majority of the house was sorely ignored and in need of organizing and dusting. Most of his time on the lakeside estate was spent fishing or holed up in his office writing.

He entered the large chef's kitchen, pausing just long enough to grab a bottle of water from the Viking fridge and a container of spicy sesame stick, mini pretzel and almond mix. He left the kitchen and entered the mudroom, tugging on his beloved safari-style jacket before grabbing his fishing rods, bait and tackle box. After opening the door and pausing in the portal to take a deep breath of fresh and crisp fall air, he continued down the paved walk leading across the yard to the pier, where his all-black twenty-five-foot bass boat was docked on the water.

Lance swapped his fishing equipment for the bright neon life vest, pulling it on before untying the vessel and using his foot to launch the boat and then apply the throttle. For safety, especially boating alone, he connected himself to the kill switch via an extendable cord to disable the motor in case he fell off the boat. He accelerated forward until he reached the center of the lake and dropped the anchor. As he baited the hook with an earthworm and cast his line, he spotted two figures jogging around the lake. As they did every morning.

It was the attorney and her billionaire husband. The tech guy. She used to run alone every morning, and then one day he joined her and it had been the two of them ever since. He'd read in the local newspaper, the *Passion Grove Press*, about their marriage and well wishes for a happily-ever-after.

Lance grunted in derision. *Good luck with that.*

They both waved as they jogged. He grimaced as he jerked his hand up in the air in return.

Ignoring them, he gently wiggled his rod to move the bait and attract one of the perch or striped bass swimming below. At the tug of the line, he leaned back, tightened his grip on the rod and gave it a jerk upward to lodge the hook in the fish's mouth. With ease, he reeled in his catch and freed it from the hook before dropping it into the boat's live well. That was the only one he would keep, clean and then give away or freeze. He switched to a barbless hook in preparation of properly releasing the rest of the fish he would catch back into the water with minimal damage.

A fisherman who didn't eat fish. That irony was Emerson Lance Millner.

He was the only regular fisher in the town. Most residents enjoyed the lake for swimming in the summer or skating upon in the winter months soon to come. He looked around at the serene surroundings after he baited and tossed his line again. He was glad the early-morning hour kept the residents away. Later in the day, after school was done, teenagers would fill the lakeside benches, picnic areas and pergolas while enjoying the music that would blare from the surround-sound system.

He would be long gone and back inside his home, leaving them to it.

Not that he didn't love the small town of Passion

Grove. The residents knew him well and gave him the space he craved. The fishing gave him solace. He found all the streets being named after flowers nonsensical, but the beauty of the town was undeniable, with its large estates set back from the pristine streets, wrought iron lampposts and oversize flower pots on each corner. The convenience of upscale living devoid of the fast pace of larger cities was ideal with a population under two thousand and fewer than three hundred homes, each on an average of five or more acres.

Passion Grove was his home and had been for the last five years, and there was no changing that any time soon, even though he owned land and properties elsewhere.

He fished for the next few hours before steering his boat back to his dock. He wanted to continue, but his desire to write was stronger…and his hunger even stronger than that. In the mudroom, as he washed his hands, he quickly pondered walking to the town's main street area for a pastry and strong cup of coffee from the bakery, La Boulangerie, but instead, he made his way to the kitchen to clean the fish in the copper apron farmhouse sink before vacuum sealing it. With his hat still on his head, Lance opened the fridge and found it lacking.

He wasn't much of a cook and usually ate pre-cooked meals sold at the Gourmet Way, the specialty grocery store in town. His stomach growled as he reached for a bowl of egg salad, opening it and holding it to his nose to sniff out its freshness. With a shrug of one shoulder, he set it on the slate countertop and reached for a bag of nutty whole wheat bread. He checked that as well, found no mold and made himself two heaping sandwiches, cutting each in half.

Turning with saucer in hand, Lance paused at a clear and vivid memory of better days. Smiling faces. Soft touches. Loving hugs. Laughter. Family.

He closed his eyes and tightly gripped the saucer. The silence mocked him, pushing him to a dark place he fought hard to escape on a daily basis.

Needing an escape, he rushed across his spacious home and onto the elevator, feeling relieved once he was inside his office. He cleared his throat as he took his seat and bit off a big hunk of his sandwich. And then another and another and another, chewing and swallowing without tasting and savoring.

Just going through the motions. A lot of his life felt that way since…

Brnnnnnnnnng…

Lance looked over at the cordless landline phone on the edge of his desk but didn't bother to answer it. He only used the number for business. He glanced at the time on his phone. It was near 10:00 a.m. Like clockwork, he started his second wave of writing at the same time every day, and anyone who knew him well knew that.

Brnnnnnnnnng…

He grunted and took another bite of his sandwich before swiveling in his chair and opening the small fridge behind him to remove a bottle of fruit punch.

"Leave a message." His recorded voice echoed into the air. Gruff and rough.

Beeeeeep.

"Lance, pick up. I know you're in that office listening to me. It's rude and you know it."

It was Annalise Ray. His longtime literary agent, who knew his writing habits inside and out.

"*Leave* a message," he repeated, setting the bottle down on the desk and reclaiming his pen.

"Okay, *fine*, Lance," she said, her soft tone amused. "Let me know when you want to advertise for a new assistant and I will handle that for you."

He reached to press the button to answer the call on speakerphone. "I'm ready," he said.

Annalise chuckled. "So I was right," she said, sounding victorious. "Hello there, Mr. Millner."

Lance clenched his jaw. He had no time for pleasantries. "Let's find one that lasts longer than a few months," he said.

"One what?" she asked.

He drew his fingers into a fist. He could clearly envision the petite woman sitting behind her large desk, legs crossed, with a smile on her face as if she had all the time in the world to chat with him. Annalise was a big talker. Lance was not.

"Assistant, Annalise," he said, wishing he'd never picked up the call.

"Yes. Right. Yes," she said, clearing her throat. "This time I'll line up qualified applicants for you to meet with, and then you choose for yourself."

His brows deepened as he thought of having to

speak to a ton of strangers, but they furrowed even more at the idea of having to continuously select a new assistant when one either quit or was fired. With a breath, he said, "You're right. Thanks."

"No problem, Em," she said, using her nickname for him.

The line went quiet.

He tensed. The pattern was familiar.

"Listen, Em," Annalise began.

Just like always.

Lance was well aware that she wanted nothing more than to elevate their relationship from business to pleasure. Her hints and gentle nudging over the years had become hard to ignore.

"Maybe this weekend I can drive down to the estate, cook you a Southern meal like my grandma taught me and we can review the résumés together," she suggested, her soft voice hopeful.

"*No*, Annalise…but thank you," Lance added, not meaning for his rebuke to be too harsh.

More silence.

"They would want you to be happy, Em, not just surviving or getting by, but *truly* living."

Lance closed his eyes tightly and released a little breath. So clearly, he envisioned them both smiling at him. One with the love of a woman for her man and the other the adoration of a daughter for her father.

His heart literally ached as a pain radiated across his chest, and his grief nearly swallowed him. It felt just as deep and unwavering as it did three years ago when he lost his wife and his six-year-old daughter. His family. The loves of his life.

In his midtwenties, he'd married his childhood love, Belle, and settled into a happy life as a writer and husband. The birth of his daughter, Emma Belle, was the highlight of his life. Fatherhood had been key for him. He was very hands-on and loved her dearly.

"Em? You still there?" Annalise asked.

He didn't answer her. His thoughts were locked on the loss of his family.

In the time since they'd left him behind, Lance had withdrawn from the world, barely leaving his estate and clinging to the anger he felt at their deaths. He tried his best to rebuild his life but found it hard to not be consumed by grief that made him sullen and disgruntled. He knew he was considered a recluse, and he welcomed the clear field everyone gave him when he did venture off his estate.

Writing and fishing were his sanctuaries.

"Em?"

He cleared his throat and picked up his pen to tap against the edge of his notebook at a rapid pace. "Annalise, I really need to get back to work," he said, using his free hand to shift the hat he still wore low over his face. "Just line up a list of appointments in two weeks, here at the estate, and I'll select a new assistant."

"Okay, but, Em—"

"Annalise, *please*," he stressed. "Let me be, damn it." His shoulders slumped with regret, "Annalise—"

The sound of the dial tone echoed into the air.

He reached and hit the button to end the call on his

end before dropping his pen and sitting back in his reclining chair as he wiped his hand over his mouth.

Lance felt remorse for his harshness, but he also felt Annalise was wrong to press him to move out of his grief on her terms. He knew she wanted more from him than he was willing to give to anyone. Love and a new relationship were not a part of his plan.

Memories of his time with his Belle and Emma were more than enough.

Chapter 2

Samira was a woman on a mission.

She climbed from behind the wheel of her custom rose-gold metallic Mercedes Benz GT and pulled her fluffy silver fox jacket closer around the black turtleneck and leather jeans she wore with thigh-high boots. She left the car parked on the paved brick street and walked around the vehicle to stand on the sidewalk as she eyed the expanse of land before her. All twenty acres were beautifully manicured and gloriously empty.

Just prime for the picking.

"It's perfect," Samira whispered into the late-fall winds before turning to eye the length of Baby's Breath Lane in Passion Grove.

Large gardens with faded remnants of spring and

summer blooms stretched to the left and right with not an estate in sight for blocks. The cleared land served as the dead end to the street. Not much traffic. No residents to be disturbed.

"Perfect," she repeated.

Just as she had since she first spotted the property two weeks ago, she could visualize a luxury boutique hotel built on the land. One of more than twenty she had mapped out as a part of her initial rollout plan for the hotels/resorts division of ADG. It was just the type of expansion idea to fast-track her from a mid-level position to upper management.

There was talk around ADG that Jake Cooley, president of the hotels/resorts division, was hinting at retiring in the very near future. Samira wanted his position and had worked privately during her personal time to come up with a solid business plan to expand the division by selling larger, underperforming resort properties and setting up small luxury boutiques with much less overhead. She'd done the research, run the numbers, constructed a firm rollout plan and even personally searched and scouted new sites around the world for each of the twenty properties she wanted to build. She'd identified each possible problem that could financially or logistically affect the project and now felt prepared to deliver her business plan to her brother and sister-in-law to gain their approval.

The last minor setback?

Getting the owner of location twenty to show any interest in selling.

Samira owned a glamorous duplex apartment in

the same posh Manhattan apartment building as her mother, but with the influx of Ansahs into Passion Grove over the years, she found herself in the small, affluent town more and more. Alessandra and Alek and her adorable chubby-cheeked niece, Aliyah, lived here. Her brother Naim and his wife, Marisa, with her soon-to-be a year-old nephew, Kwesi. Even her brother's best friend, Chance Castillo, whom they all loved like family, had moved to the small town with his wife, Ngozi Johns-Castillo.

Passion Grove was an it spot to live for the young and affluent. All the luxuries without the hustle and bustle of a large metropolitan area.

The *perfect* locale for a luxury boutique hotel.

Unfortunately, every attempt she'd made to reach out to the owner about an interest in selling the land was rebuffed. Using public tax records, she discovered an Emerson Millner to be the owner.

She reached for her iPhone from her back pocket and pulled up his contact info now saved in her phone. *Perhaps the third time's the charm.*

Samira paced on the street as the line rang several times. The fall winds were beginning to creep through the warmth of her fur.

"Yeah," a male voice said, gruff and filled with his annoyance.

"Mr. Millner, this is Samira Ansah, sir—"

"Again?" he asked, his tone reprimanding.

She closed her eyes and squeezed the bridge of her nose between her slender fingers. "Yes. Again," she added, stiffening her spine and notching up her chin. "And I *still* would like to speak with you about the land on Baby's Breath Lane."

He just grunted and said nothing else. "Shocker, Mrs. Ansah."

Samira held the phone from her face and looked down at it in bewilderment. The man was uncouth. *Keep it cool, Samira. Do not lose it. You need him.*

"Ms.," she supplied.

"Excuse me?" he asked.

"It's Ms., not Mrs.," she explained.

He grunted. "If you remain so dogged, it will never be Mrs."

She arched a brow even as she bit down on her bottom lip to still her tongue from giving him a sharp retort that she was well-known for. She could easily think of a few:

"Does a man with your temperament have a Mrs.? I doubt it."

"If it took marrying a man like you, I would stay single. Forever."

"My life doesn't rotate around the opinions of a man like you."

And those were polite and lacking the profanity needed to really put him in his place.

"Perhaps I should call back at a better time," she said after putting the call on speakerphone, finding his deep voice grating so close to her ear.

"Or *not* at all," he offered, his tone sardonic.

She stiffened. Her childhood days of etiquette training restrained her from giving him a lecture on decorum. Instead, she released a small and soft laugh that was forced. "Enjoy your day," she said, deciding to let it go at the moment. "I apologize for interrupting—"

Click.

Her mouth fell open in shock. "No, he did not," she said, even though she knew he absolutely had.

Shaking her head, she gave the land one last look as she walked back around her vehicle and climbed into the driver's seat. "Butthole," she muttered as she started the ignition and accelerated forward smoothly to make the short drive to Alek and Alessandra's estate. "Absolute complete butthole. Period!"

What could possibly make one human being so dang grumpy?

She tried to visualize Mr. Emerson Millner. His voice was that of a man far younger than seventy years or more, even though his demeanor said otherwise. She chuckled at a vision of a wizened, elderly man with a bent figure and fingers as twisted by arthritis as his mouth was with derision. "Grumpy Grouch," she muttered, continuing her drive to Dalmount Lane, named after the one-of-a-kind hybrid rose Alessandra's father had commissioned in honor of her mother.

The private mile-long length of paved street led to the sprawling twenty-five-acre Ansah-Dalmount estate, where Alessandra and Alek had set up their home together once they wed. She slowed to a stop before the twelve-foot-tall wrought iron gate and lowered her window to enter her personal pass code to unlock it. Moments later the gates rolled open. It was another half mile down a tree-lined paved road before the three-story, twenty-four-thousand-square-foot stone French Tudor came into view. She eased past the six-car attached garage with the security office above it before following the curved driveway to park in front of the mansion.

Samira was still thinking of Grumpy Grouch with a shake of her head as she climbed from her car and climbed the steps. The mega-mansion was heavily staffed, and by the time she reached the elaborate front door, a uniformed maid was already holding it open. "Thank you," she said, removing her fur and handing it to the young woman before following the sound of the voices coming from the family room. As she came to a stop in the doorway, she looked at the dozen people assembled in the grandly decorated room.

Alek and Alessandra were talking in front of the massive fireplace, sharing a smile and a long look that spoke of naughty thoughts. Samira's mother, LuLu, was regal as ever in a dark purple head wrap trimmed in gold, remaining true to her Ghanaian heritage. Marisa fed Naim a decadent treat crafted from her homemade chocolate recipe that was well sought after by local bakers and candy makers. Alek's best friend, Chance Castillo, a self-made tech billionaire, and his wife, Ngozi, a top criminal attorney, were feeding each other hors d'oeuvres in between sharing loving kisses as she sat on his lap. Alessandra's aunts Leonora and Brunela, both in their mid- to late sixties, were resplendent in vintage Chanel dresses and jewelry as they shared a playful champagne toast and giggled about something together.

Thoughts of her being the only Dalmount or Ansah heir to be alone rose as she eyed the loving couples again, but she pushed aside any envy and entered the room. Samira was happy to see them all. A gathering at one of Alek and Alessandra's homes—in Passion Grove, New York, London or otherwise—was commonplace, whether for the upcoming Thanksgiving and Christmas holidays, birthdays, or an upscale barbecue just because they enjoyed each other's company. *"Ciao famiglia. Scusa se sono in ritardo."* Samira apologized for her tardiness in smooth Italian, walking into the room and drawing everyone's attention.

They all greeted her warmly as she moved about the room greeting everyone with a hug and kiss to the cheek, beginning with her mother and ending with both her brothers. Moving over to the bar, she poured herself a glass of sparkling water and sipped from it as she stared off outside the tall patio doors at the sun casting a glow against the manicured lawn.

How can I convince the grouch to sell his land?

"A dollar for your thoughts."

She smiled and eyed her brother Naim over the rim of the glass as she took another sip. "The going rate was a penny," she quipped.

"The Ansahs do everything big," he said, looking tall, dark, bearded and handsome with his white teeth gleaming against his deep brown complexion.

"Yes, we do," Samira agreed, setting down her

glass and taking his snifter from his hand to pour two fingers of his favorite scotch into it. *"Normally."*

Naim looked pensive. "Anything I can help with?" he asked.

"If only it were that easy," she said, reaching to squeeze his free hand.

"Work or pleasure?" he asked.

"Definitely work," she admitted. "My last date spent most of the night talking about *his* accomplishments."

"To impress or to equate?" Naim asked, crossing one strong arm over his chest.

She arched a brow. "I'm not sure. Good observation, though," she said, admitting that dating a strong, educated woman who was a billionaire in her own right could be intimidating and make a man feel the need to prove himself worthy…which still made him the wrong man for *her* regardless.

"So, what's the problem?" he asked, ever concerned about his little sister.

Samira took another sip of her water as she eyed her brother. She was far closer to him than to their older brother, Alek. Their nearness in age and the feelings of being overlooked in business by their father were something they shared.

"I'm working on making my big move at ADG," Samira finally admitted. "It's my turn."

He opened his mouth, and she held up one slender finger. "And no offers of help. Wearing lipstick, heels and skirts does *not* equate to needing assistance."

Naim bowed his head slightly in acknowledgment

to both her education and her tenacity, traits they shared.

"I'm just having a hard time connecting with someone I need to finalize my idea," Samira said, her eyes squinting a bit as she thought of Emerson Millner. Annoyance rose in her quickly.

"Connecting?" he asked, looking confused.

The sounds of tiny running feet echoed along the floor, and moments later her niece, Aliyah, burst into the room, full of smiles and joy. The preschooler went barreling toward her grandmother LuLu, who scooped her right up into her arms. Naim and Marisa's nanny, LuAnn, held their son, Kwesi, as he promptly dropped the bottle he held and squealed, "Mama!"

LuAnn set him on the floor, and he instantly crawled at a quick pace over to where Marisa had squatted down to pick him up into her arms and nuzzle her face against the sweet softness of his neck.

Everyone laughed as Kwesi giggled, tossed his head back and sighed like all was right with the world.

"Oh, my Chocky-Wocky," Samira sighed, using her pet name for him because of the deep brown complexion he'd inherited from Naim.

"Hey, Uncle Naim. Hi, Auntie."

Samira looked down into Aliyah's angelic face, her heart bursting with love for her niece as she stooped to meet her at eye level.

"Hello, beautiful," Naim said with warmth.

"You left me for last. Did you forget your auntie?" Samira teased.

"No," Aliyah laughed as she reached and pressed her hand to Samira's cheek.

She cared nothing about her flawless makeup as she enjoyed the warmth of her niece's hand on her face. "I don't know," she teased. "Maybe I shouldn't FaceTime you so much and visit more often."

"Face-to-face *is* better," Aliyah said before leaning in to lightly rub her nose against Samira's.

It was her turn to giggle. "Yes, it is," she agreed.

Samira then frowned as she stroked her niece's cheek and rose to her full height. "Face-to-face is better," she repeated softly as Naim scooped Aliyah up in his arms to toss into the air and catch as she squealed in delight.

She pulled her iPhone from her pocket and swiped up her info on Emerson L. Millner. All the properties he owned in the county were public record, and there was just one other address listed in Passion Grove outside the land in which she was interested.

Dare I?

She put the address into the GPS on her phone. It was less than ten miles away.

"Humph."

Samira nibbled at her bottom lip and tapped the tip of her boot against the hardwood floors as she weighed her options. *Face-to-face is better.* And she wanted her answer once and for all.

Plus, she was *very* curious about Mr. Emerson L. Millner. "The Grumpy Grouch," she muttered under her breath.

Curiosity would have to kill the cat.

"I'll be back," Samira said, striding across the room.

"Samira, *où vas-tu*? *On va déjeuner!*" LuLu said, her French flawless.

She stopped and turned at her mother's question about where she was going when they were about to have lunch. Nearly every eye in the room was on her. She gave them a smile. "I have something work related to handle. I should be no more than an hour or so. Everyone enjoy lunch," she said, maintaining her normal poised demeanor.

"Work related?" Alek and Alessandra said in unison.

"Work related?" Aliyah mimicked her powerful parents.

"Chinese wall. Remember?" Samira reminded them of their insistence to never bring work home so they could maintain some balance between family time and working together all day as co-CEOs of the conglomerate.

The couple shared a look.

With a slight tilt of her head, Samira turned and quickly strode from the room, retracing her earlier steps back to the front door. She moved so quickly she didn't retrieve her fur and instantly regretted it as a fall wind whipped around her, lifting the ends of her waist-length weave. She climbed beneath the wheel of her car, feeling comforted by the heat of the seats and the car from her automatic start.

As she followed the turn-by-turn directions verbalized by the GPS, she wished she had on a more professional outfit but didn't want to chance a drive home to her Upper East Side apartment in Manhattan. She might lose her nerve and just resort to the phone calls and emails that were fast becoming futile. If one of her staff handled the grouch, she might have more patience, but that was impossible with her holding close to the vest her entire plan for using luxury boutique hotels to revitalize the hotels/resorts/casino division.

She turned down Aster Drive and pulled to a slow stop on the street in front of the massive cabin-styled mansion on the lake.

"You have reached your destination."

"Have I?" Samira asked, her eyes taking in the forlorn-looking place in the distance. At every window, the curtains were dark in color and closed. Because winter was nearing, the trees were bare of leaves and the spacious lawn in need of cutting. No flower boxes at the window. No potted plants or topiary on the porch. No garden. No holiday decor. There were no vehicles in sight. There were no signs of life.

She frowned a bit, half expecting a large tumbleweed to blow across the yard, pushed by the fall winds.

She retrieved her phone to double-check the address but turned to look over her shoulder as a small red compact came driving up the paved road. *Is that his car?* Samira extended her arm to wave the car down. It pulled to a stop, and she bent at the waist to look through the passenger window at a tall and thin young woman with short curly reddish-brown hair and glasses. She smiled and lowered the window.

"Hi," she said. "You're here for the interview, too?"

Interview?

"It's here, right?" Samira asked, hiding her confusion as she pointed her thumb toward the mansion.

The young woman looked forward through her windshield at the house and then back at her. "That's what Ms. Ray said, right?"

Ms. Ray?

Samira nodded. "Right," she said, rising to her full height and walking over to her car. She paused. "Good luck."

"Thanks. You, too," she said, before accelerating forward.

"Interview?" Samira said as she climbed back in her car and closed the door before speeding up the drive toward the house that was set far back from the street.

So the house isn't empty.

Samira pulled her sports car to a stop on the stone-paved courtyard. If it was at all possible, the house looked more lonesome up close. It was in need of the tender loving care and attention that would make the sprawling home majestic.

She looked on as the other woman climbed from her car. "Oh wow," Samira said, drawing it out as she took in the short skirt and high heels, and a blazer nearly bursting as her full breasts pressed against the button.

"An interview for *what*?" she asked herself aloud.

The woman, who looked to be in her early twenties, climbed the stairs slowly and rang the doorbell.

Samira lowered the window of her car as one of the large double doors that was trimmed in metal opened. Her heart pounded as she fought to see him. She failed.

"Good afternoon, Mr. Millner. I'm here to interview for the personal assistant position," she said, extending her hand.

Personal assistant?

"Thank you for your time, but absolutely not. Have a good day."

Samira gasped in shock as moments later the door closed shut. She cringed in dismay before she cleared her throat and summoned up all her determination as she climbed from the car. "What happened?" she asked, reaching the other woman just as she opened her car door.

She shrugged one shoulder and chuckled. "He took one look at these—" She began waving her hand across the air in front of her breasts. "I guess he didn't want to be distracted."

Samira gave her a weak smile. To be honest, the outfit was wholly inappropriate for a job interview. He wasn't wrong, but he was rude. And insolent. And grouchy.

So damn grouchy.

"Excuse me," Samira said, gripping the car door to keep the other woman from closing it. "What exactly does he do? Why does he need an assistant?" she asked.

"Some big-time writer... Lance Miller or Muller."

Samira's heart pounded. "Millner? *He's* Lance Millner?" she asked.

The woman shrugged. "I guess," she said before giving a little jerk that freed her door from Samira's hand before she soundly closed it.

Samira was stunned at the revelation.

Her downtime outside work and dates and family was reading. Her genre of choice was crime fiction and mysteries, and her favorite author was Lance Millner. "Wait. What?" she asked, knowing her face was incredulous.

Lance Millner lived in Passion Grove?

Lance Millner was Grumpy Grouch?

Of course he was. Emerson L. Millner and the *L* was for Lance.

How the hell did the dots not connect?

She didn't know whether to be excited to meet him, worried to reveal her intention to him or disappointed to discover her favorite author was an a-hole.

"Are you here to see me or not?"

Samira stiffened in surprise at his voice from behind her, but she quickly released a breath and stiffened her spine as she turned. "Yes, I am—"

The doorway was empty.

She wished for something to kick. Anything. A ball. A rock. The imaginary tumbleweed she envisioned bounding across the property.

His head.

The thought of his head flying across the sky made her smile as she crossed the courtyard and climbed the wide steps to the front door. He was standing just inside the foyer. The shadows of the dimly lit space covered most of him. She could tell he was tall and fit in the black V-neck T-shirt he wore with denims, but it was the bucket hat he wore low over his face that she found vaguely familiar. She could barely make out his face, except for his strong jawline, dimpled chin and full mouth.

Her eyes lingered there for a moment, finding the man nothing as she imagined. Nothing at all.

She took another step closer. "Mr. Millner—"

"I'm sure Annalise explained to you that I need an assistant for the weekends only. Your main priority would be typing my handwritten book, updating my social media accounts and running errands," he said, turning to stride across the room to stand next to the lit fireplace.

"You write by hand?" she asked, unable to hide her amazement and forgetting the reason for her visit.

"Yes," he said, his voice deep.

"And you've finished your new book in the Mayhem series?" she asked.

"So, you're familiar with my books?" he asked, his attention locked on the crackling fire.

Samira wished she could see his face. She felt almost like he was hiding it from her intentionally. "Yes," she finally answered. "My favorite is *Vengeance*."

He grunted.

She eyed him. There was something so powerful but still sad about his stance. The way he moved. The way his stare was downcast. She was surprised at how strongly she needed to know what gave him such a demeanor. It, plus the dark interior of the home and neglected exterior, was all so mysterious—maybe even more so than one of his novels.

The man was an enigma. How could someone so abrupt and insolent write with such emotion and rhythm that she was forever transformed by his words? The two did not match.

"I assume since you're here you made Annalise's round of cuts," he said.

Annalise? As in Annalise Ray?

"Absolutely," she lied, completing winging this unexpected interaction.

"I like that you don't talk much."

She pressed her lips together.

"Do you want the job?" he asked, crossing his strong arms over his chest.

She didn't miss the way the thin material stretched with the move. "Wait. What?" she asked, forcing her attention from his fit form framed by the light of the fire and onto his words.

A billionaire heiress working as an author's weekend assistant. The thought actually made her smile.

But I would get a first read of his new book.

The smile widened.

And maybe a better chance to get to know him and just what his reservations are about selling the land.

She contemplated all the pluses and minuses of the ruse. Some work related.

Samira eyed the fine lines of his taut body and her body instantly responded to him.

Some not.

"Yes or no?" he asked, his tone brusque.

Is this crazy? Am I?

"Yes, Mr. Millner, and thank you," she said.

Will this work?

"Good. Ms…?"

She opened her mouth but closed it as she almost supplied him her real name. He might very well know the Ansah name. "Samantha Aston," she lied, pulling the name out of the air.

Ding-dong.

She briefly looked over her shoulder at the front door at the sound of the doorbell.

"Your first duty is sending away all the other applicants," he said, turning and leaving the room with long strides.

What the hell have I gotten myself into?

Chapter 3

Two weeks later

Lance slowed down his run on the treadmill, clocking in at five miles as he decelerated to a brisk walk before eventually coming to a stop. He grabbed the towel hanging over the padded handlebar and wiped the sweat from his bared upper body before draping it around his neck. In the winters, running replaced fishing for relaxation. Motion to help forget the darkness of his life outside of the moments he sank himself deep into the world he created in his novels.

He showered and completed his morning rituals, dressing in a sweater and denims, leaving his feet bare. Grabbing one of his dozens of bucket hats, he pulled the oversize headwear on as he left his suite and made his way down the long hall. He was about to step on the elevator when a distant noise from downstairs made him pause. He turned his head and cocked it, listening for the noise again.

He frowned as it sounded off again and turned to walk back down the length of the hall and down the wooden stairs at a rapid pace. After letting her in this morning, he'd thought his new assistant was upstairs in his office, typing away and awaiting his arrival. He came to a stop in the doorway of his massive kitchen.

He was wrong.

Samantha looked up from pouring a glass of orange juice and smiled at him. "Good morning, Mr. Millner," she said.

His frown deepened.

The curtains were all open and admitting light. The round table in the nook was set with a vase of fresh flowers in the center. There was a plate of food awaiting him with the folded paper beside it atop a stack of typed pages. When she opened his fridge to replace the juice, he found the shelves fully stocked.

The hell?

She eyed him as she moved back to the table to pull his chair back.

He shifted his gaze from hers. She was so direct. So unapologetic. Always. Her demeanor was not like that of any other assistant he had.

"I ordered you breakfast, and I have the next fifty pages typed and ready for you to edit," she said, pulling a red fine-point Sharpie from her back pocket to sit atop the pages.

His eyes darted from the open curtains and beaming sunlight to the flowers, table and pages of his manuscript. "I don't eat breakfast," he said before striding across the room and picking up the newspaper and pages, ignoring the fresh fruit, pastries and bagels with smoked salmon and cream cheese.

"Are you a vampire?" she asked when he strode away.

He paused in the doorway but did not turn. "Excuse me?" he asked.

"You seem to be afraid of sunlight, and I wondered why is that?"

He scowled. "And you seem to do everything except what you're hired to do," he countered.

"Not true," she volleyed back. "And you know it."

He frowned. She was right. She did her job exceptionally well. It was the extracurricular butting into his life that he could do without.

He turned. She was sitting at the table, calm as she pleased, spreading cream cheese onto her bagel.

She glanced up at him, tucking her long hair behind her ear before taking a small bite. "I am ahead of schedule with the typing—loving the story, by the way—and I did *more* than everything you asked," she supplied before wiping the corners of her mouth with a napkin.

So refined. Graceful even.

"You're welcome," she said, inclining her head and just barely hiding a smile behind the glass of juice from with she sipped.

Lance grunted and turned again to walk away, not

slowing his barefooted steps until he reached the elevator and rode it up to his attic office. The fact that his stomach grumbled annoyed him further. Normally he didn't eat a full meal until lunch. He actually wished he'd eaten the bagel.

Ten minutes later when she entered the office, he barely glanced up from the pages he was reading and making notes on until she silently set a plate with bagel and cream cheese on the corner of his desk. She then just as silently claimed her seat at the other end of the large space. When he dropped his pen and reached for the bagel, he heard her chuckle as he took a bite.

Lance barely noticed his new assistant and pointedly ignored any attempts at engaging him in conversation. He was content that she was competent to transcribe his handwriting, run errands, answer emails and keep up with his social media accounts. She rarely got in his way as they stayed on their opposite ends of the attic.

Very often he even forgot she was there.

He liked it that way.

He turned and retrieved a bottle of juice from his mini fridge, twisting the cap to open it.

Pop!

After a long and satisfying swallow, he set the bottle down and reached for the newspaper, deciding to take a morning break before his day even really began. Not his normal routine. He grunted at that as he flipped the page and reached for his bagel. His hand stopped midway as he picked up the paper and leaned in closer to it as he stared at a photo.

His gut clenched.

There was an article on a local charity event with a photo of the billionaire Ansah and Dalmount families. He looked at the face of one of the women in the photo, then down the long length of the office at his assistant with her mouth slightly ajar and her chin tucked in her hand as she read from his notebook. Samira Ansah. The very same Samira Ansah who was reaching out to him about purchasing his land on Baby's Breath Lane.

He recalled her seemingly innocent questions about properties. Questions he avoided.

But a billionaire heiress working as his assistant? For what gain? It all made no sense.

He scowled.

Samira Ansah and Samantha Aston. Very similar. Too similar. Almost one and the same.

Can't be. That wouldn't make sense.

His heart pounded as he looked back at the picture of the woman in a glamorous, strapless red dress that glowed like fire against the deep mocha of her smooth complexion. "Samantha," Lance called down to her, even as his writer brain conjured up a thousand different scenarios to explain it all.

She looked up from the notebook with reluctance, pressing one slender finger against the page as if to mark her place. "Yes?" she asked.

Again, her grace and composure stood out to him. He blinked and looked at her. Really looked at her.

She—Samantha or Samira—was in her midtwenties, with flawless skin as dark as chocolate and wide almond-shaped eyes framed by long natural lashes. Her pug nose and full mouth were centered by her rounded chin. Jet-black hair framed her face, flowing long and thick to her waist. The woman really was quite exquisite.

Like an African goddess.

His heart pounded in his chest, surprising him.

"Yes, Mr. Millner?" she repeated.

What are you up to...Samira?

He squinted. "Never mind," he said.

She looked curious for a moment before returning her attention to her work.

Lance tapped his keyboard to wake up his computer and logged in to the banking website. After a quick search, he realized she never cashed the weekly paychecks he gave her.

And then he remembered the sports car she drove the day of the interview. He felt foolish for the clear signs he'd missed.

He was being duped by Samira Ansah, the billionaire heiress. He grunted. Now he had the upper hand. He leaned back in his chair, setting one ankle on the knee of the other leg as he turned the chair to peer down the long length of the room at her.

Time for some fun...

"Samantha, could you walk down to La Boulangerie for me?" Lance asked.

"Walk?" she asked.

Humph.

"Yes, I would like a dozen chocolate turtles," he said, steepling his fingers together under his chin.

"I was almost done with this chapter," she said.

"It can wait."

"I don't think it's open yet," she reminded him as she rose to her feet.

She was tall and shapely, with a long-sleeved T-shirt and wide-leg jeans emphasizing that. As she walked toward him, he forced his eyes away from her, feeling suddenly nervous.

He glanced at the time on his watch. "You're right. While you're waiting for it, if you could grab my leaf blower from the garage and clear the courtyard," he said, sitting forward and turning back to his desk to pick up his pen and focus on the manuscript before him.

He felt the warmth of her presence as she came to a stop by his desk. His sudden nervousness both surprised and annoyed him. It felt like a betrayal. Gritting his teeth, he paused in his reading. "Yes?" he asked, without looking up at her.

"I just wanted to make sure we're on the same page," she said.

He squinted, just hearing the slightest hint of an English accent.

"A walk to the bakery *and* leaf blowing?" she asked, her tone tinged with annoyance.

For the first time in a very long time, Lance felt the desire to chuckle. He bit the inside of his cheek to keep from doing so. "Exactly," he said.

She turned and walked across the office to the elevator.

"And," he began.

She paused in the now-open entry of the lift.

Her silhouette was distracting.

Lance looked away from the temptation, his grip tightening on his pen so hard that he feared he would snap it. "After that, if you could take a couple of fish out of the deep freeze, thaw and clean them," he said, feigning nonchalance.

"I thought you didn't eat fish?" she asked.

True.

"It's not for me," he said, offering no further explanation.

"And the typing?" she asked.

"That needs to be done as well...of course," he added.

She turned with one finger pointed and vibrating as if she could barely contain her emotion.

"Yes?" he asked calmly.

Her supple mouth, lightly painted with a peachy gloss, opened and closed several times, but finally, she pressed her mouth shut and hit the button for the elevator to descend.

Good.

Lance wasn't one for games of any kind, but if she wanted to play, he would be the master.

Bzzzzzzzzz...bzzzzzzzzz...bzzzzzzzzz...

As she stood in the center of the courtyard, Samira turned off the vibrating noise of the leaf blower and reached for her iPhone from the back pocket of her jeans. *"Bonjour, Maman,"* she greeted her mother, reverting to her mother's preferred language.

"Bonjour. Où es-tu, ma poupée de chocolat?" LuLu asked.

As her mother asked where she was, using her childhood pet name—Chocolate Doll—Samira smiled. She turned and looked up at the mansion, scowling a bit at the fall sun beaming in her eyes and the sudden closing of one the attic's curtains. *"Mon propre enfer spécial,"* she replied.

"Your own personal hell?" LuLu asked in English. "What does that mean, Samira?"

"I'm fine, and I'll explain later," Samira said, knowing her family's curiosity had to be piqued because she had spent the last few weekends not in their presence.

LuLu's pause was palpable. "Tonight," she insisted after some time.

That one word was enough. LuLu Ansah was a loving and giving mother but also a formidable one. All three of her children gave her the respect she demanded after just a stern look or even a soft demand. *"Ce soir,"* she repeated in French.

"Je vous remercie," LuLu said, thanking her.

Samira was still staring up at the window as if paused in time and caught him when he opened it and looked down at her. She could just barely make out his hard frame and that ridiculous hat he wore all the time. He was more vigilant about his hats than LL Cool J.

Does he shower in it?

There were odd moments of her workday when she thought of that hat and smiled at the vision of taking all his headgear and tossing them into a fire blazing so strong and hot that it would melt the sun. They would all go up in flames.

Poof!

She tilted her chin up. He remained in the window, his arm raised as he held the curtain back. Watching her. She didn't look away even as her heart galloped and she felt the pulse at the base of her neck pound. In truth, even with his silly hats covering the top portion of his face, there was something in the way Lance Millner moved that drew her eye. With the power and presence of a sleek animal. It was magnetic. And the allure of his writing was an added level of magnetism she could not deny.

"Alessandra is supposed to contact the paper to get a digital copy of that picture," LuLu said.

"Huh? What picture?" Samira said, turning away from the window when Lance did the same.

"Samira, I emailed you a link to the news article the newspaper in Passion Grove did on the ADG charity event last week," LuLu said. "We've done plenty of press, but I really liked the photo of the entire family the photographer took that night."

Samira pinched the bridge of her nose. She loved her mother—absolutely adored her mother—but she could care less about one a dozen family photos she took every year at random events. "*Maman*, can I call you back? There's a fish or two calling my name," she quipped, thinking of the those in the sink thawing that she still had to gut and clean.

"Fish?" LuLu said. "Samira, what is your life these last couple of weeks?"

She turned, still carrying the leaf blower, and walked back toward the house, climbing the steps two by two. "Tonight. Remember?" she reminded her softly.

LuLu released a sigh that communicated her complete frustration with her daughter. "Okay."

"Au revoir, Maman," she said.

Samira ended the call and had taken a dozen or more steps into the immense living room before she stopped in her tracks, her body rigid. She gasped as realization dawned. "Photo in the paper," she said, closing her eyes at the memory of Lance calling out to her in the office upstairs and staring at her when she looked up as he held the morning paper in his hand.

He knew.

And he'd given her menial tasks to punish her.

"That asshole!" Samira gasped in anger this time, dropping the leaf blower onto the floor and sending a few leaves floating up into the air as she took long strides fueled by her fury.

With each step to the elevator and then every foot it crept upward to the attic, her anger grew. The pacing did nothing. Pressing her fingernails into her palm barely registered. All signs of lip gloss were erased as she licked and bit at her mouth. And by the time she stepped off the elevator and glared at Emerson Lance Millner, her body was heated with contempt.

He barely spared her a glance. "The fish ready?" he asked.

She cocked her head to the side a bit and arched a brow. "Funny, because your little stunt has me as hot as fish grease, *Lance*," she said, with mocking emphasis as she dropped the formality of "Mr. Millner."

He dropped his pen and wiped his large hand over his mouth and chin as he leaned back in his chair. "That was the goal, *Samira*," he volleyed back, his voice dark and a bit ominous.

She chuckled acerbically and released a small sigh as she spread her legs and pressed her hands to her hip. "You're lucky my goal isn't to leave my foot planted deep where the sun doesn't shine!"

"And you're lucky I don't have you arrested," he growled, picking up his pen with an angry jerk.

"Arrested? For *what*?" she snapped, storming across the room to reach him.

"Criminal impersonation," he supplied with ease. *Is that a thing?*

"What's your deal, Grumpy Grouch? What's your angry vibe about? Are you perpetually constipated or you're just in a bad mood for *absolutely* nothing?" she snapped, feeling what little patience she had completely snap. "Or maybe these stupid hats you wear are cutting the circulation to your brain."

"Are you seriously upset with me when you're the one who invaded my life?" he asked, shaking his head as if amazed by her.

He had a point, but that only frustrated her more.

"While, I, on the other hand, gave you duties for the same job you scammed to get."

Samira opened her mouth and then closed it.

"I don't know your motivation in lying to me, but I'm positive you will never own that land."

"Then we have nothing else to discuss, Mr. Millner," she said.

"Ever," he inserted.

She released a breath and closed her eyes for a second to keep from throwing back a retort. "You're right," she admitted. "I invaded your life, and I apologize for that. It was my goal in first coming here. I had no clue when I came that Emerson L. Millner and Lance Millner the writer were one and the same. I just couldn't pass up the chance to get a first look at the new book from my favorite writer. I came for the land, but I stayed for the book. I apologize for lying to you."

His body tensed, but no words came.

Samira threw her hands up in exasperation. "*Say* something," she insisted.

"Ever," he reminded her.

She gasped in shock. "Are you serious right now?" she asked.

"Goodbye, *Miss* Ansah," Lance said, a hint at his earlier dig at her marital status.

Oh, to hell with you!

Without another word she turned and strode away from him to step onto the elevator. She hit the button to descend without turning to face him again. Through pursed lips, she released a long, steadying breath, hoping to release the anger, embarrassment and nervousness she still felt.

"I'm positive you will never own that land."

She'd gambled and lost.

It wasn't until she was halfway across the living room toward the front double doors that she remembered she'd left her key fob behind on her desk in her haste to leave. With a roll of her eyes at her own forgetfulness, Samira turned and headed back to the elevator. She could only imagine his upset at seeing her face again.

No early access to the book. No purchasing of the land.

"You screwed the pooch on this one, Ansah," she admonished herself as she stepped back onto the elevator.

She felt much calmer during this ride up to the attic then she had the last time.

The elevator slid to a stop, and through the gate-like door, she saw Lance look up at her. She gasped in surprise at him without his hat and the jagged scar across his brow and a small part of his forehead. Her mouth was ajar and her heart raced like crazy as she realized his hat was to keep the disfigurement hidden. "Lance," she began, her eyes taking in the remainder of his face. His broad features softened by his mouth and his eyes. Big, bright, beautiful brown eyes surrounded by lashes fuller than her own.

"Get out!" Lance roared, whirling to give her his back and hide his scar from her once again.

She literally jumped at the ferocity of his tone, and

her chest ached at the shame he so clearly felt. "I'm so sorry. I came back for my key," she explained.

He stepped over to the desk and grabbed his hat to shove on his head, his back still to her. His form was rigid.

Samira opened the gate and quickly walked down the length of the attic to snatch her key fob from where it sat near the corner of the desk. Her retreat was even faster. She spared his rigid frame just one last look before stepping onto the elevator.

"Never come back here," he said, his voice deep, dark and foreboding.

She hung her head as she closed the gate. "Trust me. You have nothing to be ashamed of," she told him with absolute truth as she pressed the button and stepped back. "Nothing at *all*."

Just before the lift descended, she saw him turn a bit, offering her his profile. She soaked it in. Enjoying every line of his face and his body as he disappeared from her vision.

Long after she left his sprawling estate and returned to her own apartment on the Upper East Side, Samira was haunted by Lance's scar and questions of how he'd been marked in such a way. Although she promised her mother an explanation for her recent disappearances, Samira didn't go up to her apartment in the same upscale luxury building that night, nor did she answer her phone calls. Her thoughts were as full as the day's events. She had so many questions that only Lance could answer.

"That's not happening," she muttered aloud, taken back to the anger he'd displayed at her.

Samira made herself a large pitcher of Orgasm, a cocktail of amaretto liqueur, crème de cacao coffee bean and vanilla liqueur, and triple sec. Lately, it was the *only* climax in her life. With a sigh, she poured herself a large flute of the creamy drink as she crossed her spacious all-white living room in the center of the apartment to reach her owner's suite—as a woman with dark skin and heritage direct from Ghana, she refused to call it a *master* bedroom.

Having stripped off her clothes, Samira strode nude into her bathroom, where she drew a bath. While she waited for it to fill, she sipped her drink and enjoyed its warmth spreading across her belly. She treated herself to a long soak in scented hot water with her head resting against the rim of the claw-foot tub. Clearly, she remembered the sight of Lance. His scar had surprised her but did not distract from his appeal. She smiled a little, thinking he favored Lyriq Bent, the handsome actor from the movie *Acrimony* and Spike Lee's *She's Gotta Have It* TV series.

She released a soft little moan in the back of her throat and then a long breath through pursed lips as she bit her bottom lip. The warmth she felt between the plump lips of her shaven womanhood had nothing to do with the heat of the water. Nothing at all. She loved his mouth. Just soft and full. The kind she'd kiss and nibble on for hours on end or love to have pressed against her intimacy, suckling at her core until her juices covered his lips.

Just fine. All man. Strong. Grown. Fit. Powerful presence. All of it. Just sexy as hell.

The scar would never be commanding enough to distract from that.

But what happened to him?

She wondered that long after the water cooled and her glass was empty. After she got out of the tub, she dried off, slipped on one of her silk robes and made her way back to the bar in the corner to refill her drink. As she sat in the windowsill overlooking the New York night traffic with her long hair over one shoulder, she had to fight the urge to call him and tell him again he had nothing to hide or be ashamed of.

Her curiosity about Lance Millner led her to searching for info about him on her iPad. Her efforts were futile. As his assistant she was already familiar with his website and social media accounts, so she skipped reviewing those. Interviews and articles about him all focused on his writing career, but nothing personal. His privacy was closely guarded—that wasn't surprising. The only clear takeaway was that several years ago the interviews and articles stopped. His headshots were not updated.

His secrets were his to keep.

That night as she slept, snuggled deep beneath the monogrammed crisp cotton sheets and plush down comforter of her king-size bed, Samira dreamed of Lance. Kissing him. Being kissed by him. Revealing what was beneath his clothing. Having him nude and hard above her. And in her. Over and over again.

* * *

The next day thoughts of her sexy dreams haunted her throughout her workday.

"Have you heard the news?"

Samira sat up in her chair and erased the wicked smile on her lips as her brother Naim came striding into her office. Thoughts of Lance's head buried between her open thighs vanished. Regretfully. "What news?" she asked, removing her oversize red computer glasses.

He picked up her spectacles and held them in front of his face to study and look through. "When did you start wearing glasses?" he asked, his English accent more pronounced than her own.

"They're computer glasses to prevent eyestrain," she explained, reaching to take them from him. "The news? Remember?"

"Jake Cooley officially announced his retirement in thirty days," he said, hitching up his tailored pants as he sat on the edge of her desk.

"No," she said in disbelief, arching a perfectly shaped brow.

"Yes," Naim emphasized with a toothy grin that was as charming as he knew it to be.

Samira crossed her arms over her chest and leaned back in her chair.

"You ready, sis?" he asked, holding out his fist.

She made one of her own and tapped it against his. "*Damn* right," she assured him.

The Passion Grove land was a no-go, but that morning she'd finalized another property purchase in Short Hills, New Jersey, to replace it. Her report was ready, and so was she, to step into Cooley's shoes as president of the hotels/resorts division. Biting her bottom lip, she slid on her glasses and logged on to her computer to print the report off. Twice.

Naim looked on as she picked up her phone and dialed an extension. "Hello, Mr. Ansah," she said, playfully winking at her brother as she placed the call on speaker and replaced the handset.

"Samira?" Alek said, his deep voice seeming to fill the moderately sized office space. "Why the formality, little sister?"

"I would like to schedule an appointment with both you and Mrs. Ansah-Dalmount today to discuss a very lucrative business proposal," she said, her voice firm and no-nonsense.

Naim gave her a nod and a thumbs-up.

The line was quiet very briefly.

"You aiming for the hotels/resorts division, huh?" he said, demonstrating his trademark intuition.

She was proud of him as her big brother and as one of the well-respected leaders of the billion-dollar firm.

"Absolutely," she assured him.

"Mrs. Ansah-Dalmount and I were scheduled to have lunch together. Why don't you join us here in my office at one o'clock?" he asked.

"See you then," she said.

"See you then, Ms. Ansah."

Now all she had to do was prove herself ready to Alek and Alessandra, who would be nothing but professional in the meeting. Co-CEOs and not her sibling and sister-in-law.

"Samira Ansah, president of the hotels/resorts division for the Ansah-Dalmount Group," Naim said. "Good luck."

Samira smiled with the ease.

The title sounded right.

Chapter 4

Two weeks later

It was a little over a month until Christmas, but signs of the season were everywhere, with the vibrant decorations, lights, Christmas carols and abundance of Santa Clauses panhandling for the holidays.

Lance hated it. Christmas meant good cheer for most, but for him, it was a reminder of everything he missed most in the world. Passion Grove during the holidays was a Christmas extravaganza. Manhattan was a hundred times worse, and he was ready to get away from it all, retreating to his estate where not one sign of Christmas existed.

That was a real joy.

Only a meeting with his publisher and editor could

draw him to the city, and those were few and far between.

He adjusted his shoulders in the tan wool coat he wore over a burnt-orange cashmere sweater, dark denims and weathered cognac leather boots. It had been a long time since he'd worn anything other than his fishing clothes. Although everything was tailored to fit him, he felt uncomfortable. Especially the brim. He wore the wide-brimmed fedora tilted on his head to hide his scar.

Lance blinked away the memory of the car wreck that had caused the deep wound requiring layers of stitches to close. Thankfully the elevator slid to a stop and his focus became forward motion as he stepped off and made his way to the receptionist desk.

"Good afternoon, sir. Welcome to ADG. How may I help you?" the blonde receptionist asked with a smile of her ruby-red lips that went from polite to sultry when she looked up at him.

"Lance Millner for Samira Ansah, please," he requested.

"*The* Lance Millner?" she asked.

"Probably not," he lied, feeling uncomfortable and gripping the edge of the tall counter as he fought not to turn and stride away.

"If you'll have a seat, Mr. Millner, possibly *the* Lance Millner, I'll let her know you're here," she said.

He gave her a short nod and turned to bend his frame to sit in one of the dozen chairs lining the wall across from her.

He hadn't done a book signing or event of any kind

since the accident. Thankfully his readers were loyal and focused on the books and not him. This trip to Manhattan was a rarity, but he had been unable to deny himself. He was on a mission.

For the first time in a long time, something other than his writing held his interest.

Lance turned his head and did a double take at Samira, who was leaning against the receptionist's desk looking at him. She wore a winter-white wool dress that clung to the curves of her body and was brilliant against the dark hue of her skin. Her hair was pulled back from her face into a low ponytail show-casing her eyes and high cheekbones. Dark gloss covered her lips.

His gut clenched.

This poised, confident and graceful woman was the full manifestation of the person he'd only caught glimpses of when she'd worked for him. This was Samira Ansah the billionaire businesswoman, and she was radiant. Nothing in him could deny that.

Lance rose and walked toward her, pushing aside the feelings of embarrassment from the day she saw his disfigurement. He'd wished at that moment he had the power to disappear in a cloud of smoke like Houdini. For him, it had been completely horrible. He felt hideous. So ashamed.

"Trust me. You have nothing to be ashamed of. Nothing at all."

Her words had come to him over and over again ever since.

He couldn't explain why he believed her words had been heartfelt and not just to placate him.

When he came to a stop before her, the scent of her sultry perfume reached him. She looked up at him with her big brown eyes, and her head tilted to the side.

"Surprise, surprise, Mr. Millner," she said, her voice soft.

"I had a meeting in town, and I thought it was time we talked," he returned.

Samira looked away from him for a moment. "Okay. I owe you that," she said, standing tall before him.

He was more than six feet. With her heels on, her head came just to his mouth. He was surprised by this sudden urge to place a kiss on her forehead.

It wasn't the first time he'd had such thoughts about her. Grimacing, he pressed his lips together until they felt thin.

"Follow me," she said, turning and walking down the tiled hall with ease in her ridiculously high heels.

Heels that showed off her shapely legs and drew his eye to the hypnotic back-and-forth motion of her hips.

Lance forced his eyes upward. Soon she stopped before a door and opened it, standing in front of him to wave him in with one hand.

"You look very nice," she said, once he passed her to enter.

"Same."

She chuckled. "Why does it sound like you had to pull that from your guts with a crowbar?" she asked.

He found her office mediocre and the view nearly nonexistent. Not at all what he expected from one of the heirs to the Ansah fortune. "This is *your* office?" he asked, knowing he scowled.

"Yes," Samira said, coming to claim her seat. "Now, how may I help you?"

Lance sat down in one of the chairs in front of her desk. He bent his leg and set his ankle on his knee. "Tell me why you lied to me," he demanded, rubbing his clean-shaven chin with his hand as he bit down on his bottom lip.

He saw her eyes dip down to take in the move before she cleared her throat and looked away.

Wait? What?

That nervousness he felt in her presence crept up on him.

"As you know, I was interested in the purchase of the land you have in Passion Grove—"

"For?" he asked, as he wished the scent of her perfume didn't reach him, seeming to nudge him. Tempt and taunt him.

Samira picked up a pair of glasses and began working them in her hand. "To use as a commercial property," she said.

"I was right not to sell it to you, because I like Passion Grove as is," Lance said.

It was well-known the city council maintained a strict ban on commercial enterprises to keep the small-town nature of the community. It was one of the appeals of the town for him.

She nodded and turned her supple mouth downward as she shrugged one shoulder. "No worries," she said. "I found a new location."

"Good for you," he said.

"*Great* for me, actually," she stressed. "I was well aware of the steps it would take to get the city council to approve the land for commercial use. Although I was willing to tackle that and win, actually, now it's one less worry on my plate."

I missed her.

He'd convinced himself that he wanted to intrude on her life the way she invaded his, but in truth, her presence around the house for the few weekends she'd been there had left more of an imprint on his solitary existence than he realized.

"I said it before. I'll say it again. I came for the land, but I stayed for the book."

Lance looked to her. "You lied," he said, his tone accusatory.

"Yes," she agreed. "To learn more about you. To see why you wouldn't sell land you are not using. To try and figure you out. Yes, I lied."

"I didn't appreciate it."

"But you're none the worse. The work was done—including sending me on a fool's errand to the bakery and having me play yardman," she said, splaying her hands.

"And if I just implanted myself in your life, would you be as nonchalant?"

"Like today?" she asked.

"Exactly."

She set the glasses down and rose to come around

the desk, leaning against it with her legs crossed at the ankle.

The scent of her perfume intensified.

"Sorry to disappoint, Mr. Millner, but I'm actually very pleased to see you...especially after the way things ended."

Her eyes locked with his, and although Lance hid it well, pure awareness shimmied over his body. Samira Ansah excited him, and as much as he felt his desire for her was a betrayal, he couldn't seem to help it. Although he had been off the market for years, he was still a man well aware of when a woman desired him as well.

"Trust me. You have nothing to be ashamed of. Nothing at all."

It was his turn to clear his throat as he shifted his frame in the seat.

Brrrnnnggg.

"Excuse me," Samira said, turning slightly on the desk to pick up the phone. "Yes?"

He tipped his hat back just enough to stroke the scar he hated so much as he fought not to watch the curvy lines of her body so close to him. If he opened his legs a bit wider, his knee would stroke her leg.

He hungered for the seemingly simple touch. He was so tempted to go for it.

"The board wants to see me?" she said sounding excited as she rose to her feet. So unlike her normal composure. "Now? I'm on my way up."

Pulling his hat back down, he rose to his feet just as she turned to face him. They were inches apart.

She gasped a bit in surprise.

He didn't move one bit as his eyes searched her face. Her mouth.

She's beautiful. Her skin dark as night and still, somehow, radiant like gold.

"I have to go," she said, whispering as if she had lost her breath as well.

With reluctance, he stepped back. "So… I'll stay out of your life and you stay out of mine," he said, futilely trying to claim anger and failing.

"Agreed," Samira said, her eyes unable to hide her confusion before she turned and walked to the office door to pull it open wide. "Goodbye, Mr. Millner."

"Am I being dismissed?" he asked as he reached her.

"I think you dismissed yourself, and I'm acquiescing," she said, the epitome of refinement even at her young age.

"Goodbye," Lance said, stepping past her to leave the office.

He took a dozen or so steps before he stopped and turned. He was surprised to find her still standing in the hall just outside her door watching him. No words came as his body reacted to her, confusing him further. She gave him one last wave and entered her office, closing the door behind her.

He grunted as he turned and strode down the hallway to the elevator, wondering if he'd truly seen the last of her.

The heart-shaped pond that was the centerpiece of Passion Grove was pretty during summer, beautiful in the spring, warm and inviting in the fall, and simply majestic during the winter. Unblemished snow coated the branches and surrounded the trunks of towering trees. The lake was frozen over, and the rays of the winter sun glistened upon the ice. Many of the townspeople were enjoying their weekend, having snowball fights or ice skating, including the Ansah and Dalmount crew.

Through the clear vinyl window of their portable heated tent, Samira smiled at each of her brothers holding her niece Aliyah's hand as they gently pulled her across the ice on her little skates. *"Ma petite-fille n'a pas peur de rien,"* LuLu said, pulling her fur hat down over her ears.

"No, she is not," Samira agreed with her mother—Aliyah wasn't afraid of anything.

"She reminds me of you, *ma poupée de chocolat,*" LuLu added, leaning over to gently knock her daughter's shoulder with her own. "You are fearless, Madam President."

Samira was still awaiting word from the board on the position. They'd called her into their meeting to make her presentation and to be questioned in lieu of an interview. She'd yet to hear anything about their decision. "I hope," she said. "No interference, *Maman.*"

"For what? None is needed. You are worthy," LuLu said, her eyes determined as they locked with those of her daughter.

Samira appreciated her support and confidence in her. It was equal to that she had for her sons.

"That really could be a beautiful home."

Samira looked to Alessandra where they sat at a folding table before following her line of vision to the rear of Lance's lakeside home. It looked empty. She smiled a little thinking of the weekend hours she'd spent in his home with him, feeling that same lifelessness. It was a home of darkness and despair.

Why is that?

That question plagued her at odd moments of the day. She was so curious as to why Lance had lost his smile. She wanted *him* to tell her his secrets.

"It fits him, though," Alessandra said.

"He is definitely *not* a people person," Marisa added before taking a sip of her warm drink as well.

"Doesn't look like a long walk," LuLu whispered to her, locking her gaze on the sprawling house as well. "If nothing else, get answers to your questions. At the same time, you might be able to help him by offering to listen to his troubles."

Samira had finally filled her mother in on the details of her dealings with Lance Millner. All of them. Including her unending curiosity about his life and why he chose to live it in isolation.

The nightly dreams of kisses and long strokes she'd kept to herself.

It had been nearly a week since he surprised her at the ADG offices. Even with the days that had passed, she clearly recalled the thrill she felt when the receptionist announced he was there to see her. And how desire reigned when she'd walked up to the reception area and spotted him sitting there groomed and still grouchy.

But handsome as hell.

"Samira, remember the time you were at the bakery and you two collided?" Marisa asked. "You were looking down at her phone and walking in while he was walking out. And then bam!"

Samira's nodded. "I forgot about that," she said, remembering that brief but harried moment she and Lance had shared over a year ago...

"I'm sorry," she'd said.

"You should watch where the hell you're going," he'd said before brushing past her and leaving the bakery with long strides.

Samira walked up to Marisa, standing behind the counter where she sold her handmade chocolate treats. "What a grouch," she said, scowling.

Marisa laughed as she turned the sign on her counter from Open to Closed. "Aww, the right woman could put a smile on his face," she said.

"Who would even bother trying?" Samira had asked.

Blinking away the memory, Samira looked back at his house, feeling a literal pang of hurt for him. Following an impulse, she rose to reach for the short black hooded fur she wore with fitted denims and thigh-high riding boots. "I'll be back," she said, pulling her fur-lined calf-leather gloves and knitted hat from the pocket.

"Where are you going?" LuLu said.

"To check on Lance the Grouch," she said before turning and exiting the tent.

The change in temperature was intense. She pulled

her hood over her head and pressed her gloved hands into the deep pockets of the jacket as she trekked the cleared path surrounding the lake and up the walkway to Lance's back door. With a breath that instantly chilled in the air, she knocked and rang the doorbell.

The ring around the doorbell turned electric blue.

"What part of goodbye forever is this?" he said via the intercom on the doorbell video system.

"Let me in, please," she said.

The light faded, and moments later the knob turned before the door opened and he filled the entry.

She looked him up and down, shaking her head at his normal garb and one of his bucket hats in place on his head. "Cinderfella is back to the norm, I see," she said, stepping past his tall body into the mudroom.

Samira turned at his silence to find him peering out toward the lake. "It's for more than fishing," she said, the sounds of laughter and squeals of glee reaching them.

He made a noise before stepping back and closing the door. "What do you want?" he asked.

"Civility would be great, but since I know that is beyond you, I wanted to first apologize again for my duplicitous behavior regarding that land," she said, feeling his presence overwhelm her in the contained space.

"You don't have to impress me with big words because I write books," Lance said, folding his arms over his hard chest.

Samira took a sharp intake of breath. "Stop being an asshole…is that basic enough for you?" she snapped before turning from him and massaging the space be-tween her eyes with her fingers.

"A little too basic," he muttered.

Samira whirled and pointed a finger at him. "What is wrong with you?" she wailed. "Why are you on a path of destruction to make sure no one gets close to you? Why do you live in this dark, desolate-ass place? Why are you so grouchy and ill-tempered? Why are you hiding away from life? And why are you ashamed of that scar?"

"None of your damn business," he said, his tone insolent as he walked past her to leave the mudroom and enter the kitchen.

Samira gritted her teeth and followed behind him reaching for his arm to grip. "I'm making it my busi-ness," she insisted when he turned to look at her hand and then at her.

"Why?" he roared, leaning over until his face was close to hers.

They stared each other down. Both with their chests heaving and their short breaths blending in the brief space between them.

Samira gave him a soft smile and felt the warmth fill her eyes. "Because I care," she said with honesty. "I truly give a damn and wonder about every question I asked you. I see you alone in this world, and it both-ers me. It breaks my heart a little. I see past the wall you put up. It's there in the way you write. I refuse to believe someone so angry could write so lyrically—you have moved me to tears in your books. I want you to see what I see, Lance Millner, because you are one beautiful man, scar and all."

He released an annoyed breath and waved his hand dismissively as he turned from her. "You're full of it," he muttered, snatching open the fridge to remove a bottle of beer.

"No, you are," she said, walking over to take it from him, twist off the lid and take a deep swig.

"I am?" Lance snapped, splaying his hands in disbelief at her taking his beer before he turned to pull another from the fridge.

Samira nodded. "You're willing to share stories as long as they are made-up and not your truth," she said, dragging her finger along the length of the counter, surprised to find it clean.

"You don't know a damn thing about my life," he said with coldness.

"Exactly," she agreed, moving to the bay windows of the breakfast nook and looking up at dark clouds rolling in from the distance.

"Exactly?" he repeated.

She looked over her shoulder at him. "The fact that I know nothing about your life is my point exactly," she explained.

"Get out."

"No," she said, turning to face him.

He frowned, she could tell from the downturn of his lips. "So you're intruding on my life…*again*?"

"Someone needs to, so it might as well be me," she said, walking back across the room to stand before him.

"Get. Out."

She shook her head. "No," Samira said, turning just long enough to set her unfinished beer on the large island before she removed her fur and set it there as well before facing him again.

He reached up in a flash and snatched his hat off. The wound was lighter than his medium brown complexion and nearly four inches long, crossing his forehead and the top of his eyebrow. It was jagged and uneven. Angry looking. The sign of trauma.

"Welcome to the freak show," he said, his words biting.

"Hardly," she drawled, being sure to show nothing but nonchalance.

His face became incredulous.

Samira reached up to stroke his face.

He flinched and jerked his head back before she could land her touch as he replaced his hat.

She shook her head. "I promise it's not as bad as you have convinced yourself it is," she said, her voice soft as her eyes searched his. "And not at all worthy of you closing yourself off from the world, Lance."

She reached for him once more.

This time he quickly gripped her wrist, blocking the move.

Their eyes locked again.

The house darkened a bit as the clouds passed over above. A second later thunder snapped loudly, flashing light. Emotions were high and his annoyance with her was clear—but so was the flash of desire she saw in his eyes as they fell on her mouth. Some energy more vibrant than the storm brewing outside crackled between them.

Samira felt breathless as a desire to taste his mouth filled her until she was heady.

To hell with it.

She took a step forward that brought their bodies together and raised up on her toes in her boots to grab the front of his sweatshirt and kiss him with all the passion she felt for the brooding man with a body as rock hard as his will to be alone. She gasped in his mouth when he opened it to allow her tongue to lightly touch his own as his hands gripped her hips.

He tasted of goodness. Heat. Excitement.

"Lance," she exhaled, easing her hands up around his neck to softly stroke his nape.

She felt him shiver. She did the same. She was so lost. And it was *so* good.

"No!" Lance said, sounding tortured and reproachful of them both as he broke the kiss and stepped back from her.

Samira's lids were half closed and her heart still pounding as she swayed a little from being freed from their intense connection.

"I don't want you here," he said, motioning his hand toward the door with a quick jerking gesture. "I don't want any of this. I don't want you."

Her embarrassment stuck in her throat as she turned from him and grabbed her fur, knocking the beer bottle over by mistake. The sound of the glass crashing against the floor echoed as she raced from the kitchen and into the mudroom to fling the rear door open. The rain falling was steady, the skies were darkened and the cold was chilling. She paused just long enough to jerk on her fur as she quickly walked down the path.

Her foot skidded across an ice patch and she hollered out as her body went up in the air and then down onto the pavement with a loud *thud*. She grimaced and released a heavy breath as she moved to a sitting position.

She looked ahead and saw the family's tent and their vehicles were gone. She looked up at the turbulent skies and didn't blame them for quickly seeking shelter.

Frowning a bit, she leaned up to reach in her back pocket for her phone. There was a message from her mother telling her to call to have one of the family's on-staff drivers pick her up from Lance's and to stay out of the inclement weather. "Shit," she swore, shivering from the rain drenching her body and the cold nearly turning it to ice upon her.

She looked back. Relief and surprise washed over her as she saw Lance rushing out of the house toward her.

Chapter 5

Samira wrapped her arms around his neck and buried her face against it as Lance stooped to pick her up in his arms. She shivered uncontrollably, amazed at how quickly the cold had affected her.

"Hold on, I got you," he said, his chin nestled against the top of her hat-covered head and the ends of her long hair whipping up in the wind.

"Thank you," she whispered to him as he carried her with ease.

She felt relief when they reached the mudroom and he nudged the door closed with his foot before continuing into the kitchen and then across to the living room. Her teeth nearly chattered as he set her on her feet in front of the roaring fire. It felt delicious, and she closed her eyes, enjoying the warmth as she out-stretched her arms to splay her hands.

"Be right back," Lance said, quickly striding down the hall and soon returning with a stack of plush folded towels and blankets.

"S-s-s-s-so c-c-c-cold," she said, shivering from the soaked clothes clinging to her body.

He shook his head. "I didn't know you walked here. I should have taken you home," he said, drop-ping the towels onto a nearby distressed-leather chair. He held up the blanket in front of her. "You have to come out of those clothes. I'll get something for you to wear while I dry them, and then I'll take you home."

"You don't have a car. You're always walking," she said over the edge of the blanket as she removed her drenched fur to drop to the floor. It took effort with her slightly throbbing fingers to undo the button and zip of her jeans.

Lance's head was turned as he looked into the fire. "My garage is full," he said.

It was a four-car garage. "Oh," she said, her eyes skimming his profile.

His jawline, so square and masculine, begged to be kissed. Licked. Enjoyed.

She bit her bottom lip and looked away from him, avoiding the sultriness of stripping, undressing as the fire crackled and lit their bodies with a warm golden glow. Still, her body's pulse points went on high alert. Racing. Pounding. Throbbing.

Behind the blanket, she bent to unzip and remove her boots one by one before peeling her skintight denims and socks off to add to the growing pile. She looked down at her sheer bra and panties, still slightly damp against her body, but decided to keep them on. "All done," she said.

Lance draped the blanket around her, looking down at her.

The light of the fire warmed his brown eyes. She couldn't turn away and didn't try, remembering their kiss. The heat and passion. Something in his brown depths let her know he remembered it as well.

Lance Millner confused her. His vibe said yes even when his mouth said no.

He stepped back and picked up her dripping-wet clothing. "I'll dry these," he said. "The fur I'll hang up, but you'll need to take it to a furrier to have it dried properly."

She nodded, licking her lips as she watched him retreat. Alone, she twisted the blanket around so that the front edges were held closed with her hands. She looked behind her before sitting in the other leather chair, extending her bare feet toward the fire and enjoying the heat. She took one of the towels and dried the ends of her hair before snuggling deeper into the chair, resting her head against it and closing her eyes as she waited for the last of her shivers to fade.

She didn't know how much time had passed when he returned with an oversize T-shirt, her phone from the back pocket of her jeans and a steaming cup of tea. His movement awakened her, but she left her eyes closed, feeling some of her earlier embarrassment return. She even released a low snore, enjoying his care and concern but needing a reprieve from his steadfast refusal to admit he desired her.

She could tell he set the items on the log-shaped table beside her. When he walked away, she peeked with one eye at him leaving the room. She closed it when he returned with another blanket that he placed on her. When he remained standing beside her, she had to force herself not to hold her breath.

"I am fascinated by you, Samira Ansah," he admitted. "I wish I wasn't, but I am."

She opened her eyes and locked them with his, seeing his shock that she wasn't, in fact, asleep.

He moved to walk away, and she reached for his wrists, locking him in place and unknowingly opening her blanket with the sudden movement. "Lance," she said, imploring him to surrender.

He looked down at her lace-covered body and then shifted his gaze away. "Let me go, Samira," he said.

She shook her head. "I can't," she said.

The fire crackled into the silence that followed.

"You honestly are a beauty, not a beast, Lance. Why don't you believe me?" she asked, tugging his arm to pull him down onto his knees between her open legs. As she removed his hat, she leaned forward to press a kiss to his cheek. Then she stroked his scar lightly with her thumb as they stared at one another.

The mood was hypnotic.

She saw his struggle against his desire for her just before she saw him relent to it and lean in to take her mouth with his own as he brought his hands up her bare thighs and then around to grip her buttocks. She gasped into his mouth as she inched her body to the edge of the chair and pressed herself to him. Her body reacted to him in a way she had never experienced before. Shivers. Excitement. Racing pulses. Anticipation. Pure pleasure that hardened her nipples and caused the fleshy bud nestled between the bald lips of her intimacy to throb and ache.

"Samira, Samira, Samira," he moaned against her mouth before dipping his head to warmly suckle her neck.

Her body jerked in sweet torture as she brought her hands up to grasp the back of his head. She flung her own head back and released a breath that was filled with her desire. "Yes," she sighed, relishing in the sexy haze pushed forward by the fire. It was everything. All things. She was heady. Lost.

And when he curved his strong back to press his face to her cleavage, planting heated kisses there, she released him to reach up and grab the back of the chair as she placed one leg over each arm of it.

Lance leaned up to look down at her, shaking his head in wonder at the sight of her nearly nude body in delicate lingerie that barely hid her from his eyes. "Damn," he swore, lowering his head to suck one taut brown nipple into his mouth through the sheer brassiere.

Samira rolled her body and closed her eyes, giving in to his skill. The light flickers of the tip of his tongue against her nipples alternated with a deep sucking motion made her wet. Aching. She moaned, hearing how it sounded pulled from deep inside her where he was a stoking a fire that warmed her in a way the fire could not.

Lance yanked the lace down beneath her breasts, freeing them and allowing him to taste her without a barrier. He moaned deeply and she felt the vibration of it against her flesh as he sucked as much of her into his mouth as he could.

She cried out as she hotly bit her bottom lip.

Lance opened his eyes, looking at her with her nipple locked in his mouth as his tongue deliciously circled it. And there in the brown depths, she saw the wildness. The savageness that had been released. The man who desired her. Wanted to ravage her. Please her. Be inside her.

She could hardly wait for *that* moment. That connection. She was hungry for that. Him. *It.*

"Let me see it," she demanded softly, sure that her eyes were as wild as his. She was gone. There was no turning back.

This—them—was going to happen. She hadn't realized just how badly she wanted until right then. She was thirsty and seeking to be quenched. Hungry and needing to be fed. Inch by inch.

He smiled wolfishly before freeing her nipple, leaning up to remove his shirt.

She reached to stroke the hard contours of his chest and abdomen as she rolled her hips.

Lance undid the button and zipper of his jeans, jerking them down below his buttocks and freeing his hardness. He held it at the base as he rested on the chair between her open legs.

"Oh…*oh*…okay. Okay. Oh, okay," she said in won-der, at a loss for words as she admired the length, the width, the curve, the slightly darker hue than the rest of his body, and the soft hairs curling around the base like a bush.

"Touch it," he commanded thickly, looking down at it and then up at her.

She obeyed with no hesitation, taking him into her hand to stroke him from the root to the smooth tip. Slowly. Deliberately.

He gasped and grunted, flinging his head back as he deeply bit his bottom lip.

She tapped his hardness against her core. It was solid and weighty. "Shit," she swore, feeling a little fear that he might be too big for her.

Lance grabbed her hand, stopping her strokes of his flesh. "What's wrong?" she asked.

"I don't want to nut," he admitted, wrapping an arm around her waist as he buried his face against her chest.

She stroked his thick tip one last time and felt his prerelease wet her hand. She grunted at the thought of him having no control. She loved it. "Kiss me," she pleaded.

He shifted his body and did so, gently sucking the tip of her tongue as they waited for his climax to sub-side. She wrapped her legs around his waist as she trailed her fingertips across his broad back, drawing goose bumps and shivers that made her feel powerful.

With one last taste of her mouth, Lance kissed his way back to her breasts.

She reached behind herself to undo the clasp, extending her arms upward to remove her bra and fling it away from them. "Take off my panties, please," she whispered to him, lowering her feet to the floor to lift her buttocks from the chair.

Lance's eyes seemed to darken in color from brandy to hot chocolate as he slid his thick fingers beneath the edge and worked them down over her hips and then down her legs. He picked them up once they hit the floor by her feet and eyed her hotly as he pressed them to his face.

She smiled with a little grunt at the back of her throat. "Smell good?" she asked, letting her eyes soak in being able to see his beautiful face, scar and all.

"Damn good," he moaned.

She set her legs back up on the arms of the chair and eased her hands down her body, patting her core. "It tastes even better," she promised.

"Let's see," he said, moving back on his knees to lower himself.

"Let's," she agreed as she moved her hand to the back of his head to gently guide him forward.

His kissed each thigh first before stroking her bud with his tongue with featherlight flickers. He sucked the throbbing bud into his mouth with a dangerous one-two motion like he was pumping her.

Samira cried out, grasping her own breasts as she felt warmth spread from her core and down to heat her toes. "I'm coming," she gasped, arching her back as tiny explosions burst inside her.

Lance moaned deeply as he deepened the sucking motion.

She fought to be free of the pleasure, afraid she would pass out from her clit being so sensitive, but he locked her in place with his arms and licked at her wildly. "Please," she whimpered, pushing her hand against his forehead.

Lance released her with one final kiss before he gripped her knees and used his hips to guide the tip to rest at her intimacy. "Ready?" he asked.

Samira nodded as she released a long breath through pursed lips.

That vibe—their energy—intensified as he slid inside her, spreading her, filling her inch by inch as he captivated her with the intensity of his eyes. And when he filled her so completely that the base of his shaft pressed against her clit, she winced and shuddered loudly. "Oh damn," she cried at the feel of him.

"You wanted it, Samira, then get it," he said, playfully taunting her.

Never one to deny a challenge, she wrapped her legs around his waist and shifted to the edge. She sat up and pressed her upper body against his hard one and gripped his shoulders as she suckled his neck and worked the walls of her core against him. He grunted and tightened his entire body. She chuckled softly against his neck as she kissed her way up to his ear lobe. "You want it. Now get it," she volleyed back in a hot little whisper before licking his earlobe.

And he was off. Stroking deep within her. Beneath the feet she crossed over his buttocks, she felt them as they clenched and released with each thrust that felt like a jolt of lightning inside her. Intense. Raw. Wild.

They kissed deeply, with passion, as she worked her hips to sex him just as hard as he worked her. Their rhythm was perfection. Back and forth. Fast. Sometimes slow. Always hot and deep. The heat of the fire and their chemistry drew sweat from them, coating their bodies and slickening their moves against each other.

Samira was lost in him. Just gone. And didn't give one damn that she was.

Lance had been hungry for it all. The connection. The intimacy. The concern for him.

He bit down on his lips to keep from telling this remarkable woman, who had somehow broken through his shell, that he'd needed this. And he hadn't even known it until the dam in him had been broken.

It had been years since he allowed himself to desire another woman. And he did. He wanted her. Just her. Other offers had been made. Other women had tried and failed. He had not lied when he spoke of his fascination with her. Her spunk and grace. Her ability to be so normal in the face of being a billionaire heiress. Even her subtle shade that someone with lesser intelligence had missed. And then just her. Her beauty. The darkness of her skin. The shape of her hips as they swayed in countermotion to her arms as she walked. Her style. And yes, even her tenacity. The same grit that led her to infiltrate his life with a lie but had kept her still playing the part of assistant even when it meant doing grunt work.

He was simply impressed with her. This intelligent, beautiful young woman who walked as if she wore a crown and knew that her regality rested not in her wealth but her connection to the motherland.

He fought it. He lost. He wanted her. He wanted no one else to have her.

And now in this heated moment before his fireplace, on the edge of his favorite leather chair, he mated with her with an intensity that shook him. He fought not to tremble. Or roar. Or come too fast from his excitement and appear inept.

Lance brought his hands up to clasp the sides of her face. He stroked her cheekbones with his thumbs as he tilted her chin up and kissed her with every bit of the passion she aroused in him. "I'm getting it?" he asked, his eyes dazed as he watched her. "Huh? Tell me. Say it."

Samira nodded. "You got it. Damn it. You *got* it," she said.

He chuckled before deepening their kiss and easing his hands down her back to grip her buttocks, enjoying the feel of the soft flesh as he delivered stroke after stroke inside her. He looked down between them, hardening at the sight of his tool glistening wet from her.

She gasped, and her fingers gripped his shoulders. "I felt you get harder," she said.

"And I feel you throbbing against me," he whispered.

"Like that?" she asked, tightening the muscles of her walls down upon him. Gripping him.

Lance closed his eyes and rested his head against hers. "I'm trying so hard not to come, Samira," he warned her, his tones low and warm.

"Oh, I feel how *hard* you're trying," she mused, kissing his mouth.

He released a low chuckle before getting serious again. "And would you like to feel how hard I am when I come?"

Samira gasped as she felt his inches swell inside her. "As long as you come *with* me," she whispered to him, her eyes sexy and filled with mischief.

Utterly fascinated.

Lance captured her mouth with his own as he wrapped an arm around her waist and then leaned back on his haunches, bringing her body with him. She placed her feet on the floor on either side of him and gripped his shoulders as she began to circle her hips against him, sending her core up and down the length of him.

Lance was lost in her eyes, loving the flare of the roaring fire reflected in the dark brown depths as she rode him. The movement of her body. The back-and-forth sway of her breasts. The way she bit her bottom lip and flung her head back in pleasure. The feel of her clasping and releasing his hard inches as her wetness slickened their strokes. He reached behind her for the edges of her long hair and twisted it around his fist, tugging gently to tilt her head back and expose the smooth lines of her neck to him. He sat up to suckle right where her pulse throbbed against his tongue and tried his best not to get so caught up that he left a mark.

She rode him to the edge, and all he could do was hold on to her as his body felt the sweet anticipation of the release. He was ready for it. There was no turning back.

"I'm gonna come," he whispered against her neck, wincing as the first hot shot of his come filled her.

Samira arched her back and rode him harder. "Me, too," she gasped up into the heated air.

He felt her tremble against him, her body jerking with each white-hot spasm.

They cried out together. Roughly. Loudly. Uncaring.

With his arm back around her waist, he shifted their bodies again until she was pressed down upon the rug and he was delivering hard and deep thrusts as he looked down into her face and soaked up the pleasure he saw with an intensity that shook him. He grunted with the last of thrusts, both pleased and disappointed for his explosive ending. He could stay in her forever. Lost in her heat and tightness.

Samira released shallow breaths as she reached up to stroke his face. He shifted his face from her when she touched his scar. She lightly gripped his chin and forced his face forward to look at her. "Not with me. Not anymore," she insisted softly.

Her request was not easy. For so long he'd barely looked at the scar or even himself. It had been years. To him, he did not see his true self but rather some disfigured version of that being that was a reminder of his pain. His loss. His devastation.

He opened his mouth to explain that but refrained. He wasn't ready. Not yet.

Samira lifted her head from the floor to lick at his mouth. He held her neck in his hand to support her as they shared languid kisses. The feel of her plush body beneath him as she massaged the backs of his thighs with her soft heels sparked him again, and he was surprised when he hardened inside her. At her deep, guttural moan, he knew she felt his arousal.

He hid his face against her neck. He was self-conscious. It had been so long since he'd allowed the door to his sex drive to open. So very long. "I'm sorry," he whispered in her ear.

Samira slid her feet up to his buttocks and locked her legs to push him deeper into her.

His clenched his fist and lightly pounded it against the floor. It took everything in him not to stroke inside her. Get lost inside her. "You tender?" he asked, aware of his size.

"Yes," she admitted, pressing kisses to his shoulder.

He raised his head to look down into her face. Her eyes were hot and dazed with desire. His inches got harder.

She gasped as she tilted her head up.

"You want me to stop?" he asked, feeling tortured.

"No," she moaned. "No."

He laid his arm beneath her head to protect it from the hardness of the floor and eased his other hand beneath her to arch her buttocks as he began to glide inside her. Slowly and not too deeply.

"Yes, yes, yes," she sighed over and over.

Utterly fascinated.

He couldn't take his eyes off the chocolate beauty. She had awakened something in him he swore he didn't need. Just the touch of her hand to his scar made him feel that it faded away. She saw it. Saw him. And still wanted him. Still thought him attractive. Still desired him.

Lance pressed kisses to the corner of her beautiful mouth before lightly biting her chin as he continued to deliver slow strokes that were just as devastating as fast pumps. Maybe more so.

There on the floor by the fire, they made love.

He allowed himself some freedom. Some happiness. Goodness. For once in a long time, he thought of nothing but the moment. There with Samira. In her. Making love to her. Surrendering to her heat. Cloaked by her tightness.

And as they looked in each other's eyes and shared gasps of pleasure and softly whispered words of praise, they came together again. He fought to maintain the steady back-and-forth of his hardness inside her, not wanting to rush or make their climax furious this time. To enjoy the way they made each other feel. Just achingly satisfying.

"Samira," he moaned into her open mouth as he filled her with the last of his seed and felt his spasms as she drew it from him with ease.

"Shit," Lance swore.

She smiled, just slightly, with her eyes half closed.

With one last kiss to her delectable mouth, he rolled them over until her body was nestled atop his. She rested the side of her face against his chest, and he turned to look into the fire as he dragged his fingertips back and forth across her lower back, unable to resist touching her.

She fell asleep before he did, but fatigue soon came, and in the last moments before he closed his eyes, he took note that her body fit perfectly against his.

Samira awakened first, smiling at the low rumble of Lance's snore that echoed inside his chest. She raised up to look down into his face, loving how relaxed he seemed. So unlike his brooding self.

That's what good sex will do for ya.

With a kiss to his chest, she attempted to ease his strong arm from around her body.

"I'm your ride home," Lance said, his voice still thick with sleep. He tightened his arm around her body.

Samira chuckled. "Yes, you are," she reminded him, looking down into his handsome square face. "And I need that ride. My mama and family know I'm here, and I refuse to let them know *all* of my business."

He eyed her. Studied her. "Okay," he said, kissing her mouth before he freed her.

Samira rose to her bare feet, reaching for the blanket to cover her nudity.

Lance rose as well, his member long and thick as it swayed across his thighs as he moved. With a shake of his head, he reached for the blanket and gently tugged it from her grasp to fling onto the chair.

Samira arched her brow as she pretended to cover her breasts and the plump clean-shaven vee between her legs with her hands.

He smiled, passing by her with a light slap to her buttocks as he left the living room.

Alone, she took a breath as she looked at the chair where their coupling had begun. Her cheeks warmed, surprised at herself. At her wild abandon.

I had sex with Lance Millner.

Mind-blowing.

She needed a moment to take it all in. Away from him. Never had she made love with a man with whom she was not in a relationship. This one-night stand— or however it could be categorized—was not her norm. She didn't regret it. Not at all. But she wanted to understand why on that day she was okay with being different.

She picked up her phone from the table by the now-scandalous chair. She dialed her mother's cell phone.

"I presume all went well," LuLu said as soon as she answered the call.

"I waited out the weather," Samira said. "Where are you?"

"About to leave Alek's," she said. "Roje has to go into Manhattan and offered to drive me so I wouldn't have to disturb Mandridge."

Roje was once the long-time driver of Alessandra's

father, Frances, and then became Alessandra's upon his death. Mandridge was the Ansah family driver. Samira didn't care which chauffeur was driving—she was ready to get home, luxuriate in her jetted tub and figure out just whom she had become on that day.

"Good. Have him pick me up from the lake," she said.

At the silence, Samira held her phone from her face to ensure that the call had not failed. "*Maman*, you there?" she asked.

"Yes. I'll have Roje pick you up. We're leaving now."

"Okay," Samira said, curious about her noticeable pause. She ended the call.

"Your clothes are dry, but your fur isn't."

She turned as he walked back into the room and enjoyed the contoured lines of his body and the sway of his dick as he carried her clothing to her.

Absolutely no regrets.

The bud between her lips throbbed at the thought of how he'd made her come. How explosive. How dramatic. How thrilling. Just satisfying. Addictive.

"Thanks," she said, taking the clothes and still-damp fur from him.

"You want to shower first?" Lance asked.

She shook her head. "I'll take a hot bath as soon as I get home," she said, beginning to get dressed. "The car taking us back to Manhattan will pick me up from the lake."

"You sure? I would have taken you," Lance said.

"No need for two trips to the same building."

"You live with your mother?" he asked.

She shook her head and made a face. "Same building. Different floors."

"I'll be back," he said, striding across the room and up the stairs.

She eyed his hard buttocks and then smiled at his member dangling between his legs as he took the steps two at a time. By the time he returned, fully dressed in his normal garb of jeans, T-shirt and one of those hats, she was dressed as well, holding her fur by the hood. He handed her a parka with a fur hood.

"Wear this since your fur is still wet," he said, some of his gruff tone returning.

She eyed it. "Your coat will dwarf me," she said even as she took it from his hand.

He shoved his hands into the pockets of his jeans and frowned as he looked into the fire. "It's not mine," he said.

Whose is it?

But she refrained from asking him that aloud. She eyed him as she pulled the coat on and could see he was already withdrawing into himself.

Perhaps he needs some time as well.

"Thanks. I'll get it back to you," she said.

He nodded.

She studied his profile beneath the rim of the cotton hat and saw more of the man who shut out the world and not the man who just made love to her with such intensity that she was still rattled.

"Goodbye, Lance," she said.

He remained staring into the fire.

"Lance," she called over to him again.

He looked over at her, but his eyes were distant, and for a moment it seemed he'd forgotten she was there. "Huh?" he said.

"I said goodbye."

He shook his head as if to clear it. "I'll walk you out," he said.

She followed him out of the living room, across the kitchen and to the mudroom. He opened the door and the winter winds blew in, carrying flakes of loose snow with them. Thankfully the rain had ceased. He reached to pull the hood of the parka over her head.

Samira reached up and grabbed his wrist before he released his light grip on the hood. "Thank you," she said.

He said nothing, but there was warmth in his eyes as she looked up at him.

Saying nothing else, Samira opened the door and left him, sure the cold would freeze the damp fur as she made her way down the paved path around the lake and toward Alessandra's vintage black 1954 Jaguar MK VII sedan. She was careful not to slip and fall again during the brief walk.

She looked back once she reached the car, where Roje stood holding the rear door open for her. Lance still remained in the doorway watching. She gave him a wave and climbed onto the butter-soft leather seat next to her mother.

"Is there a reason we couldn't pick you up from the front door?" LuLu asked.

"This was easier," she said, not revealing she didn't

want her mother to insist on meeting Lance. She knew if they'd pulled up to his front door, LuLu Ansah would have expected him to come out and greet her.

Bzzzzzz.

Samira pulled out her cell phone and smiled. Lance had air dropped her his phone number. As Roje drove away, she looked back at his log-cabin mansion, which suddenly didn't look quite as desolate anymore.

Chapter 6

One month later

"Congratulations, you are being offered the position of president of the hotels/resorts division."

Samira felt her eyes light with fire as she nodded her approval and then went around the entire table and shook the hands of the board members as she bestowed her thanks. "And any word on the proposal for luxury boutique hotels?" she asked before reclaiming her seat at the table and crossing her legs in the wide-leg crimson jumpsuit she wore with a dramatic structured cape that stopped at her upper arms.

Several board members eyed either Alessandra or Alek. They sat at opposite end of the conference table. Her sister-in-law bowed her head as if to give Alek leeway to speak first.

"We will be moving forward with the luxury boutiques next year. We have discussed it, and we all agree that we'd prefer your attention be given to learning the ropes, reviewing, selecting new staff. Getting acclimated to the job before tackling such a big venture," Alek said, leaning back in his chair as he tapped his pen against the table.

Samira nodded and offered each person in the room a cool smile as she decided which side she landed on with flight or fight. *I am an Ansah. We fight.*

"Please know that I am honored to accept the position, but I believe to be completely effective as the president of hotels and resorts that is my duty to express my concern with your decision," she began.

Alek and Alessandra shared a look.

"I don't want to come into the position to clean up or correct someone's possible missteps. I want to guide the department in an efficient, logical, money-making direction, and these boutique hotels will do just that. I've done the research. I ran the numbers. And above all… I am trusting my instincts. My *gut*," she insisted, locking eyes with these men and women who held her future at ADG in their palms. "Instincts bred from heritage, my education, my tenacity and my work for the last few years as the senior market strategist for this global company."

One of the board members cleared his throat. "Miss Ansah—"

She held up her hand. "Ms.," she corrected and then softened her firm tone with a smile. "Let me finish first, please."

He nodded and splayed his hand, giving her the floor.

"In a different scenario, had this proposal been given to you all, it would have been forwarded to me or one of my team members to analyze, to dissect and to offer my opinion on its viability. This is a winner. *This* would have received my thumbs-up. *This* will rejuvenate the division. Offer something different. Make *money*," she stressed, leaning forward to tap her index finger against the desk as she spoke. "That's not my ego speaking, ladies and gentlemen, that is my experience. I ask you all to reconsider, and I'll leave you to do so. And when you do change your minds, because you trust someone who was your lead strategist less than five minutes ago, I'll be one floor down in my new office."

There was no more to be said, so she rose and took her leave with long confident strides that made her feel like a hybrid of Queen Nefertiti, Harriet Tubman, Maxine Waters and Oprah Winfrey.

As soon as she closed the double doors of the executive conference room, Samira leaned against them for a moment and allowed her knees to weaken. "Yes!" she said, punching her fist into the air.

Would her last-minute rally for her proposed project work? Who knew? The board was infamous for shelving a decision until the next monthly meeting. She knew their ultimate goal was to make the best decisions for the Ansah-Dalmount Group in order to maintain the legacy and financial health of the goliath in international commerce that her and Alessandra's fathers started.

As she rode the elevator down one floor alone, she allowed herself a celebratory two-step and body roll. "Yessssssssss!" she sang as she snapped her fingers to imaginary music.

Ding.

She regained her cool composure just before the doors slid open. She paused a step at finding a tall and slender Middle Eastern woman in a skirt and blouse awaiting her with a tablet in hand and a poised smile in place.

"Hello, Ms. Ansah. I am Assi Aoun. I have been assigned as your new executive assistant," she said, her accent pronounced.

Samira stepped off the elevator and extended her hand. "Welcome to my team, Assi," she said.

"Your office is right this way, Ms. Ansah," the young woman said, extending her hand in front of them.

"Are you psychic?" Samira asked as they walked down the wide length of the hall. "Or…"

"I was appointed to you this morning, and I've spent the time getting it ready for you as instructed. Someone called to let me know you were on the way down," the woman said as they came to a stop before a glass-walled office midway down from the corner offices.

"I had all of your things packed up and moved

here, including your purse, coat and phone," the woman said.

Samira was more focused on her office. It was three times the size of her old one, with glass walls and a large desk.

"Is that Veuve Clicquot?" she asked, also enjoying the large bouquet of flowers beside the ice bucket of champagne.

"Of course. I thought you would want to celebrate your new position," Assi said, reaching to open the door. "Ready?"

Samira took a breath. "I was *born* ready," she asserted.

Lance read the final lines of his manuscript on the screen and nodded his approval. His agent had taken the remaining handwritten pages and ensured they were typed by one of her employees. Since the full document was emailed to him a week ago, he had done two revisions. He was satisfied. The book was complete.

As always, he felt a mix of relief and melancholy.

His fingers tapped away on the keyboard as he attached the document and emailed it to both his editor at the publishing house and his agent with nothing more than the words "All done.—L."

There were rounds of edits to come to prepare the book for publication in nine months, but for now, his time was his alone.

Nothing to distract me.

He closed his eyes and tilted his head back. He frowned at the silence he usually treasured.

That's new.

Lance rose and moved to the bar to pour himself two fingers of scotch—a tradition when he finished a book. He needed normalcy, especially with all the newness in his life. All of the change. Taking a sip of his drink, he made his way to the elevator. His stomach grumbled in hunger. He debated making himself dinner or walking down to Main Street for a hot take-out meal from the Gourmet Way. "Or I could have the food delivered," he said aloud as the elevator slowed to a stop on the main level.

"Congratulations!"

As he stepped off the elevator, Lance frowned at the four people assembled in his living room with bunches of glossy balloons floating up toward the towering beamed ceilings. His eyes landed on his mother, Helena Michaels-Millner, first. "When did you arrive from South Carolina?" he asked, still locked in place.

She chuckled as she came to stand before him, and she bent her fingers to beckon him to bend down to her petite height. He immediately obeyed, and she pressed kisses to his cheek. "An hour ago. I've been here for every book you've finished, and a wellness retreat would not change that now," she explained. "Cheer up, Grumpy."

He made a face as he thought of Samira.

What's your deal, Grumpy Grouch?

How could he forget that his mother called him Grumpy as well?

"Good job, son," his father, Lawrence Millner, said, coming over to soundly pat his back. "I can't wait to read it."

Lance eyed his parents as his agent, Annalise, looked on from where she sipped champagne by the fireplace. His parents had long ago divorced when he was in his teens, a rupture brought on by his father's refusing to release his beliefs on free love they both acquired in the '60s. They were both free spirits who had him in their forties. From his mother, a retired college professor, he inherited his smarts. From his father—a respected poet and painter—his creativity.

They still got along and were friends, having put aside any grief with each other to coparent before it was called that by society. They were quirky and at times odd, but he loved them.

"Thank you, Pops," he said.

"I want to read it, too, Lance!"

His mother and father moved apart to reveal Law, his five-year-old-brother from his father's relationship with one of his "life sharers"—of which he had a few.

Lance stooped down before him and held his pug nose between his fingers to wiggle. "One day, Lawrence Millner Jr.," he promised.

Law laughed and patted his cheek before he ran over to jump and try to touch the balloons.

He genuinely smiled at his little brother's exuberance.

"Sounds good to have a little one around here, doesn't it?" his father asked.

Lance stiffened.

"Lawrence," Helena said calmly.

"Says the man who is seventy years old with a five-year-old," Lance drawled. "Chances are, Pops, I'll have to pay child support to his mother when you go on to the Great Beyond, *so*…"

"Lance," Helena said, her tone still peaceful.

Lawrence chuckled as he rubbed his bald head. "You damn sure will…and like it," he said.

It was hard to stay annoyed at either one. Instead, Lance moved beyond them and walked over to Annalise by the firelight.

"I would offer you a glass of champagne, but I see you're already celebrating," she said. "To another bestseller *and* early talk of an option for the movie rights."

Lance scowled.

Annalise smiled as she tossed her waist-length blondish dreads over her shoulder. They suited her shortbread complexion and freckles. "Em, do you not enjoy making us both lots and lots of money?" she asked.

His frown deepened.

Annalise sighed and reached to grab his hand.

He stiffened.

She grasped it tighter, refusing to let go. "Em, I hate to sound like a broken record, but there are so many opportunities that you let slip by you. So many chances to grow and to expand and to be happy… *again*," she said.

He looked down in her eyes and saw that her words were about more than the work, that she had convinced herself that she was the solution to his grief. He loved her as a friend, respected her as an agent and trusted her judgment, but he would never see her as a mate. He knew then he had to tell her the truth.

"She's right, son," Lawrence added from where he had stopped to pick up Law and attempt to raise him high to reach the balloons. He winced and released a small little cry and set him back down.

Lance strode across the room and lifted his brother with ease high into the air. Law opened his little arms wide and gathered a bunch of balloons close to his chest as he giggled with the sweet abandon of a child. Something deep inside Lance warmed at the sound of it. It was immediately replaced with the all-too-familiar sting of loneliness and sadness.

Would it ever end?

Ding-dong.

Samira arched a brow as she finished putting on her diamond chandelier earrings in front of the large oval mirror in the foyer of her apartment. She'd change out of the jumpsuit she'd worn earlier in the day and the jewelry went perfectly with the sequined black top that exposed one shoulder. Tucking her thick ebony hair behind her ears to highlight the jewels, she stepped over to the door and opened the black metal cover of the peephole. She gasped at Lance standing on the other side of the door.

"Surprise," he said, biting back a smile.

Her heart raced as she flung the door open wide to step right into his waiting embrace. No words were spoken as they kissed with all the passion and promise stoked during the week since they last saw each other.

Samira broke the kiss, aware they were nearly in the hall of her upscale building. "Hey," she whispered up to him.

"Hey," he responded, his eyes twinkling.

She took his hand and led him inside her apartment. The door had barely closed before he pulled her back against his body and kissed her again. Slowly. Their moans echoed in the air around them.

"I missed you." He spoke against her throbbing lips as he held her face with both hands.

"Good," Samira said.

Since their first coupling on the floor of his home, they'd spent as much time together as they could, relishing in their chemistry and passion at his home. He rarely left his estate and had only spent the night at her apartment once.

"Congratulations on your promotion, Ms. President of Hotels and Resorts," he said, his voice as warm as the twinkle in his eyes.

Samira's smile was bashful. Lance made her feel that way. Soft and compliant. "Thank you," she said. "I can't believe you're *here*. I thought your family and Annalise were there."

"When you called me earlier today to tell me you got it, I just wanted to see you and celebrate with you," he said, reaching into the pocket of his overcoat to withdraw a bottle of champagne. "So I came as soon as they left."

She took the bottle and held it to her chest as she

reached up to wipe away her gloss from his lips. Just the very sight of him and being near him made her feel warm inside, like she glowed from within. And there were many times, whether they making love, enjoying a furious romp or just talking with each other, that there was a look in his eyes that said he felt that same warmth.

"Just how did you want to celebrate?" she asked, leaning to set the champagne bottle on the gilt French baroque console by the door before she began to undo the button and zip of her matching sequined pants before kicking off her Louboutins.

His eyes smoldered. "It's your big day. You decide," he offered, removing his coat and kicking off the polished leather shoes he wore.

"Yes, but you finished your book today," she reminded him before pulling her shirt over her head. "You have reason to celebrate as well."

Lance eyed the sight of her small but plump breasts in her strapless lace bra as he unbuttoned his cotton shirt, exposing his hard chest covered with fine hairs. "You do have a point," he said, tossing the shirt onto the pile forming beside him.

"That's not all I have," she said, removing her delicate lace panties to twirl the perfume-scented garment on her index finger before gently tossing them over to him.

He caught it with one hand. "I got a match for it," he said.

"A match?" she asked.

"And it's the perfect fit," Lance said, draping the panties on his shoulder as he removed his pants.

She eyed his erection in his snug black cotton boxers and arched a brow. "Perfect?" she asked, thinking of his size and how each time he entered her she felt every bit of him pressing and stretching her walls. Every. Bit. The inches. The width. The curve. He had enough for himself and a little more for someone else.

Lance chuckled. "You adjust to it well," he commended her, removing his boxers. The waistband got hung up on the tip of his hardness.

"I try," she said, eyeing him as he reached for the brim of his hat. "Leave *that* on."

He tipped his head to her in agreement.

Samira turned and drew the long length of her tresses over one shoulder to lightly tickle her belly. He crossed the short distance to reach her. The feel of his warm fingers against her skin as he undid the clasp of her bra caused her to gasp and shiver. Once the brassiere fell to the floor, he brought his blunt fingers around to cup her globes, and she tilted her head back against his chest as she reached behind him to clasp the sides of his hard buttocks. He lightly bit her shoulder as he eased one hand down to palm her intimacy. A gentle squeeze placed pressure against her clit, and she cried out in pleasure.

The ring of her cell phone echoed in the air.

She stiffened.

"Forget it," he moaned against her neck.

The ringing continued.

Lance turned her body, lifting her up against him

as they kissed, and he took two large steps to press her body against the wall. There was something so intimate and close about their faces being shaded by the brim of his hat as she pressed one hand to his cheek and clutched his strong back with the other.

The cell phone's incessant ringing ended, and her landline began.

She broke the kiss. "My mother," she said, knowing no one used that line but the person who insisted she have it. "I better answer. Next there will be knocking on the door."

She crossed her arm over her chest to hold down her breasts as she raced across the living room to the lone cordless phone located on its base in her home office. *"Bonjour, Maman,"* she said into the phone, a little out of breath.

"I thought you were headed up, Samira," LuLu said.

"I am. Give me a few more minutes and I'll be there," she said, turning in the dimly lit room as Lance's sizable figure shadowed in the doorway.

"Other people's time should be respected, Samira, and you know that," LuLu said, before ending the call.

Samira set the phone on its base.

"Is everything okay?" Lance asked.

"My mother is throwing a lavish dinner party to celebrate my promotion today," Samira said, crossing the room to reach him.

"And I interrupted," he said. "I'm sorry."

She looked up at him with her head tilted a bit to the side as she reached up to stroke his scar with her thumb. "Tonight would be a great time to meet my family and celebrate with me."

He shifted his head away from her touch, shaking his head. Denying her. "No, Samira," his said, his voice low but insistent.

Her disappointment assailed her. This debate over his isolation was not new. He refused to leave the safety and seclusion of his estate while Samira felt her social life withering because her choices were going alone or not going at all.

"Lance, I know there is so much more than I know about you…and I've been patient with your privacy, but I want you to share moments, things and events with me. You know that. I've never pretended to want anything else," she said, leaning against the wall outside the office with her hands behind her as she looked up at him, trying to reach his level of under-standing with her eyes.

"And should I sit in your mother's house and dis-respect her by wearing my hat all night?" he asked.

"Or," she stressed, "you could remove your hat and not be self-conscious anymore."

He eyed her.

She returned his look.

"Or," he said, "you can go and enjoy your fam-ily. I'll hang out here and start outlining a book idea I have to keep busy until you get back."

Samira reached out to wrap her hand around his member, gently pulling down on it. "Will you be naked when I get back?" she asked, lifting her chin as she eyed him.

He hardened as she stroked downward on his inches. "Don't start something you don't have time to finish, Samira," he warned.

She lowered her body until she was kneeling before him. With a look up at him meant to be coquettish, she drew his smooth tip into her mouth and gave him several slow sucks.

Lance's knees buckled, and he reached out to press his hands against the wall as he hung his head between his extended arms to look down at her. "Samira," he said, his voice tight.

With one last kiss and lick, she freed him before rising. "To be continued," she said over her shoulder before walking away and leaving him hard.

"Damn," he swore.

"Serves you right for leaving me alone to attend yet another event," she called from the foyer as she began to pick up her discarded clothing and get dressed.

"I'll make it up to you."

As she stepped into heels, she looked back to find him leaning against the entry. She eyed him, enjoying his sculpted body and the promise of pleasure offered by his inches, but the smile she gave him was slightly forced because it covered the disappointment stinging her chest. *"Again,"* she said softly. Adamant.

She moved to pick her clutch and keys from the table by the door.

"Samira—"

"I'll see you in a little bit, Lance," she said, pausing in the entryway after she opened the door. "It's all good."

But it wasn't. Not at all.

His secrecy and seclusion were a big issue. She wanted to know the reason for it all, but she'd decided that her days of searching online or gently probing him with questions were over. Only Lance held the key to the door locking away his secret. His pain. His reclusiveness. She wanted the truth, but she was tired of games and subterfuge and would only accept his truth from him or move on from him without it.

She left the apartment but paused to lean back against the closed door, because she hated the doubts beginning to rise of having any real future with the reclusive Lance Millner.

"It's all good."

A week later, Lance stood before the door to Samira's apartment reminding himself of those words she'd said to him when he declined to attend her celebration dinner. She'd smiled, but hurt and disappointment had filled her eyes and her voice, speaking a truth that she did not fully articulate with her words. Some innate desire to protect her from hurt and harm had touched him in a way that he had not felt for another person in years. It both surprised and alarmed him.

That night when she came back to her apartment, they'd had sex. It had been perfunctory. Routine. That was a first. Good but not great. Not explosive. Chemical. Passionate. The ending hadn't been quite as happy.

He missed their connection. For days after, his

mind went back to that night. He felt unsettled about it. The thought of not having her in his life did not sit well with him—which annoyed him. But he wasn't ready to let her go—which scared him.

Through the door, he heard the very faint sound of lively conversation and Christmas carols playing. He raised his fist to knock but paused it midair. Awaiting him was his woman and her family at a small Christmas party she was having just to introduce him.

Lance released a breath.

He would never admit to the anxiety gripping hold of him at that moment. He wanted nothing more than to turn and flee. He was concerned about how he would be viewed. That insecurity was so different from the confidence he held before...

He closed his eyes, wincing as memories of the car wreck replayed. He could hear the screech of tires and the loud boom of the crash as the cars collided. Years had passed, but the memory was clear and vivid. The aftermath had left him crippled with grief, and he felt it rising in him in waves.

"Shit," Lance swore, stepping back from the door and fighting not to give in to the desire to snatch off the bow tie he wore with his all-black tuxedo and a black fedora.

Wiping his mouth with his hand, he turned and took long strides toward the elevator at the end of the wide hall. Relief was already conquering his anxiety and fear.

He stopped, feeling less than.

That's not me. That not who I want to be. Not anymore.

He turned and looked down the length of the hall at her door. He smiled, knowing his arrival would make Samira happy. That mattered to him. He enjoyed her in his life. In and out of his bed. She was a bright spot in the darkness. She was light and goodness. She was the healing he hadn't even realized he needed.

With a lift of his shoulders and a roll of his head, Lance mustered up the courage still brimming in him and made his way back to her door. Back to Samira.

Knock-knock.

His heart pounded. He felt like a high school kid. The thought of that made him smile a little.

The door opened, and there she stood looking radiant in sequined, claret-colored wide-leg pants paired with a sheer long-sleeved shirt of the same shade that exposed the strapless velvet bra she wore beneath it. Her hair was pulled back into a low ponytail, and her makeup was dramatic and appealing.

She looked beautiful, and his heart raced in response to her. "You made it," she said, reaching for his hand to pull him inside to kiss him.

"I'm not taking off my hat," he said as she wiped her maroon gloss from his mouth with her thumb.

"This is *my* house, purchased by *me*, and you don't have to," Samira said, her eyes twinkling with the happiness he knew she would feel at his arrival.

He removed his cashmere topcoat and handed it to the uniformed servant patiently standing nearby. "I'm starving," he admitted.

"For me or for food?" she asked once the butler had moved away to hang up his coat.

"Both," he said.

"Ooh. Dinner *and* dessert," she said.

"Exactly," he said with promise.

"Don't make me rush my family out of here," she said, taking his hand and leading him into the living room.

He enjoyed the feel of her fingers wrapped around his as they came to a stop. As her family rose to their feet and turned to face them, he allowed himself a moment to take in the winter wonderland decoration. The reminder of the upcoming Christmas holiday was another level of anxiety he hoped to avoid. Swallowing over a lump in his throat as he pushed memories of Christmas past, Lance raised his hand in a wave he already knew came off as awkward. "It's very nice to meet you all," he said, trying his best to remove the usual brusqueness from his tone.

But then that felt unnatural. Un-*him*.

He flexed his shoulders.

Samira wrapped her arm around his and squeezed his bicep with her hand. "Lance, let me introduce you to the gang," she said, pulling him about the room before each person. "My mother, LuLu. My brothers, Alek and Naim, and their wives, Alessandra and Marisa, respectively. And this is my brother from another mother, Chance Castillo, and his wife, Ngozi."

Lance air-kissed the cheeks of the women and firmly shook the hands of the men, who then promptly guided him away from Samira and their wives to gather around him by the bar.

"Preferred drink?" Alek asked.

"Beer, actually," he said.

Alek motioned for the server.

"You have to try Ghana beer," Naim said, seeming warmer and more open than his older brother. "I wish I'd known beer's your preference. I would have brought you some."

"Samira keeps some here for me and brought me some for my house when she—"

The rest of Lance's words faded as three sets of eyes suddenly gazed at him with frowns before they shared a look.

"Chinese wall, man," Chance said. "Some things just shouldn't be shared."

"Agreed." Lance accepted the opened bottle of beer and glass from the tray the server held.

"Let's talk books or some shit, man," Alek said before taking a swig of his drink.

Chance and Naim laughed. It broke the tension.

"Go easy," Samira called over to them in warning.

Lance gave her a reassuring smile as if to say, "All is well."

She gave him a big, broad and beautiful smile, and his gut clenched, but he wondered what Pandora's box he had opened by agreeing to the dinner party. How many more times would he have to step out of his comfort zone and attend social gatherings with her? Things were going well enough, but what if they were just too different to make it work without someone making a great sacrifice?

What *if* they just weren't right for each other?

Ding-ding-ding.

"I just wanted to thank you all for being here, especially since we're all leaving in the morning for our annual Christmas in the Swiss Alps," Samira said. "Tonight is very important to me, and I appreciate you all making time for Lance and me. Cheers to the holidays, family and new friends."

"Cheers," everyone said, raising their glasses in a toast before taking a drink.

"And dinner is ready," Samira added, waving Lance over to her.

He joined her as she slipped her arm around his and they led her family toward her dining room.

"I know we agreed six weeks was a little soon to do family trips, but I am going to miss you, Mr. Millner," Samira said to him, for his ears only.

"Same here, beautiful," he assured her.

He paused at the entrance.

The room was a winter showplace, complete with a lit fireplace that was adorned with an elaborate garland and tiny Christmas trees on the mantel. The smell of fresh pine was heavy in the air. There were trees of varying sizes in every corner. The table was adorned with ornately wrapped presents as centerpieces.

It all saddened him.

"Daddy! Daddy! Wake up. It's Christmas!"

Lance cleared his throat at the recollection, feeling

that all-too-familiar wave of pain, grief and regret. He shifted his shoulders in the jacket of his custom tuxedo. There was still so much to overcome. So much he didn't share.

"You okay?" Samira asked, nudging him forward. *"Don't you love Christmas, Daddy?"*

He used to. Not anymore.

Lance moved to hold the chair at the head of the table by which Samira stood. Never had he wanted so much to be back on his estate away from anyone. "Yes," he lied, ready for the night to end before it even truly began.

Chapter 7

Five months later

Samira yawned behind her hand as she reviewed a report on underperforming resorts owned by ADG across the world. Using her stylus, she made notes on the large tablet before removing her computer glasses and pinching the bridge of her nose as she stretched once more. She was exhausted. Late nights at work and early mornings with Lance before trekking back into the city were wearing her out.

She looked at her office, now decorated in sleek charcoal with bronze lighting fixtures and pops of fuchsia accents. Like the job, she had made the space her own. She swiveled in her chair and looked out the glass wall at the metropolis in the summertime. She was able to see her reflection in the glass wall, and the look on her face was pride. Three months ago, the board had approved her plan for the luxury boutique hotels, with the first rollout in Kauai, Hawaii. Today one of her management staff had flown to the main island, known as the Garden Isle, and finalized the purchase of the property she'd previously scouted the year before. The tentative grand opening was not for another two years, but Samira was excited nonetheless.

"Excuse me, Ms. Ansah," her assistant said via the intercom.

Samira whirled in her chair. "Yes, Assi," she said.

"You have a guest," the woman supplied.

"It's your mother, beloved," LuLu added, her voice now filling the room.

Samira smiled. "Come on back, beloved," she said, already rising from her seat.

LuLu soon entered, looking like an African queen in tailored gray pantsuit with a kente cloth head wrap in a rich maroon shade, which stood for Mother Earth. That was apropos, because LuLu Ansah was the consummate mother figure. Loving but firm when needed. Filled with wisdom and guidance. Respected and cherished. Truth and love personified. Since the death of her husband, she had truly become the backbone of the Ansah clan.

Samira's eyes fell on the black leather picnic basket her mother carried. "Lunch?" she asked.

LuLu smiled as she came to a stop in the center of the spacious office and looked around with an approving nod. "Yes, of course. For all my children," she said, her accent pronounced.

Samira's stomach grumbled as she came around her bronze-trimmed L-shaped glass desk to give her mother a quick hug and kiss on her high cheekbone as she took the posh picnic basket from her. "What did you make?" she said, setting it on the round glass dinette set with a frosted bronze-trimmed base and charcoal parson chairs.

"Abenkwan and fufu," LuLu said as she set her oxblood tote on the sofa and removed her fur to join it. Her mother lived in Manhattan but rarely ventured to the ADG offices. She'd made her seafood stew of tilapia, shrimp, crab meat, eggplants and okra cooked down in tomatoes and palm oil with lots of spices.

Samira stiffened before she moved to the adjoining bath in the corner of the office and washed her hands. She looked at her reflection in the round mirror over the pedestal sink. In her eyes, she could see her wariness.

This impromptu pop-up was about more than food.

Samira gave herself a look before turning and leaving the bathroom. Her mother had already removed the large plastic containers and dinnerware from the basket to set the table. "Your homemade ginger drink, too?" she asked, eyeing the glass bottle of the nonalcoholic drink made with ginger root, lime and peppercorn. Also her favorite.

Oh, this is serious.

She sat down at the table and crossed her legs as her mother served up the food. Fearing she would not enjoy the conversation, she refrained from rushing it so that she could at least get a good bite of fufu dragged in her stew first. She maintained her silence even after they had said grace over the food.

"How's everything with Lance?" LuLu asked, casting her a brief side glance before she reached with her right hand to break off a piece of the round dough. She shaped it into a ball and pressed an indent in the middle with her thumb before using it to scoop up some of her stew in the bowl.

Déjà vu.

Lance. Same topic. Different day.

"A one-sided relationship is not a happy place, Samira," LuLu said.

Samira chewed her food and wiped her fingertips on the linen napkin, but her mind was on Lance and the truth of her mother's words. It had been just six months since they began their...

What?

Dalliance? Affair? Friendship? Relationship?

No such boundaries had been set. The only thing Samira knew for sure was she enjoyed his company, rejoiced in their sex and longed to know more about the secrets that kept him walled off from everyone—even her. At times, she felt like he was feeding a hunger in her with crumbs of his time and attention and not a full meal created by openness and devotion.

At her mother's silence after that, Samira looked to her. The faraway stare in her eyes both surprised and confused her.

"Trust me on this," LuLu added with a touch of sadness.

When she glanced over and found Samira's steady gaze on her, she smiled and reached for her daughter's hand. "Be clear on what you want, and if you're not getting it, demand it," she stressed. "I just want to make sure you have the tenacity and fight for yourself—your heart—that you have in business. You wanted this office and this position and you got it. Keep that same energy in life and in love, *ma poupée de chocolat*."

Samira gave her a smile she hoped was reassuring as she raised her mother's hand to her mouth to press a kiss to the back of it.

"Compromise is important in any relationship—be it a mother with a child or a spouse with a spouse," LuLu said. "But I see you changing so much of who you are to be with him, and that worries me."

She was right. Samira the social butterfly had vanished over the months. She couldn't remember the last time she had lunch with friends or went dancing. She even chose to be with Lance over family, tucked away inside his seclusion from the world. Lost in him.

And I still do not know why.

She thought of his scar and the occasions he awakened from sleep startled and panicked. He would sit on the side of the bed and she would wrap her arms around him from behind and press kisses to his shoulder blades until the pounding of his heart eased under the hand she pressed to his chest. She would ease him through it, but he never revealed the cause. Never let her in.

LuLu smiled. "I know my children as well as I know myself," she said. "I know you all *better* than I know myself. I want more for you. Be a little selfish. More than I have the courage to be."

She extended her mother's fingers inside her palm and looked down at her ring finger, smiling when she spotted the tiny mole by her cuticle. Her smile faded at the unshed tears glistening in her mother's large eyes. *"Maman, qu'est-ce qui ne va pas?"* she asked, gripping her hand with her own.

LuLu blinked away the tears. "I'm okay. I just want you to have love, Samira. All the love the universe owes you, *ma poupée de chocolat*," she whispered.

Samira nodded, stroking the back of her mother's hand as she gazed out the window and released a heavy breath filled with thoughts she'd had way before her mother had given voice to them.

"Is this your owner's suite?"

Samira and Lance lay on their sides in the middle of the bed with the sweat-soaked sheets barely covering their naked bodies as they spooned with their arms extended and their fingers entwined. Her question was unexpected.

Lance was pressing a kiss to her nape, but he stiffened at her question.

Since they began their relationship, they'd spent a good bit of it on his estate…in the same bedroom.

"No," he admitted.

It was her turn to become rigid.

Lance closed his eyes. He wasn't surprised when the warmth of her body moved away from him on the bed. He rolled over onto his back, folding his arms behind his head as he opened his eyes to watch her rise. The summer moon was bright and cast a glow over her brown body. Her curves were outlined like a silhouette. Her hair swayed gently against her lower back as she moved.

She was magnificent.

"Is this where you sleep when I'm not here?" Samira asked, turning to face him.

Lance reached out to touch the lamp and softly illuminate the room. "No," he admitted, unable to lie to her.

Their eyes met and locked.

"Your life. Your secrets. Your past. Now your bedroom," she said, giving him a soft, sad smile that matched her eyes. "What else are you keeping me out of?"

Pain radiated across his chest and clenched his gut. "Samira, there is a difference between secrecy and privacy. I have no secrets," he assured her.

She looked pensive as she glanced away from him and then back again. "Then let's go to bed in your room, Lance," she said, walking about the sizable room to pick up her discarded clothing.

He shook his head and sat up in the middle of the bed. "No," he said firmly.

She turned with her clothes gathered to her chest in her arms. "I'm here *a lot*. More than I'm home," she said. "*But* it's front or back door straight to your kitchen. Front or back door straight to your office. And of course—of course—front or back door straight to this room that I thought was your room, but it isn't. You have me well trained, sir. Good job. Where's my Scooby snack?"

Her chuckle was short and bitter.

"Samira, please don't," Lance stressed.

"Don't what? Ask questions? Wonder? Feel foolish? Feel slighted or disrespected?" she asked. "Don't *what*, Lance?"

He rose from the bed, snatching up the sheet to wrap around his waist.

Samira pointed toward his groin. "You're keeping that from me now, too," she snarked. "Oh no, of course not. Then we would have nothing. Right?"

"That's not true and you know it," Lance said, his voice hard.

"Do I? How? Am I psychic?" Samira asked. "Or *maybe* when you screw me and plug your dick into my body I'm suddenly connected to your thoughts. Um, *sorry*, it doesn't work that way."

"You're being crude."

"And you're rude. Sue me."

They fell silent, turning away from each other. Only the sounds of their breaths filled the air.

"How did you get the scar?" she asked.

"I don't like talking about it," he admitted.

"Or the bad dreams? Your seclusion? Your darkness? None of it, right?"

"Right," he agreed.

Samira nodded with her lips turned downward. "If you want me to stay here tonight, I will only do it in *your* room," she said, looking away from him and down at the floor.

Lance eyed her.

She looked up, and whatever resistance she saw in him made her shake her head. She set her clothes on the edge of the bed and began getting dressed. "I, uh, have to go to Milan for business. I leave in the morning," she said, avoiding looking at him.

He had to ball up his hands to keep from stopping her.

Tell her. Talk to her. Trust her.

But he couldn't. The last thing he wanted from her was pity, and the last thing he wanted for himself was one more person privy to his pain and trying to convince him to move beyond it.

"I need a break anyway," she said, stepping into her shoes. "I need to figure out if this 'situationship' is best for me."

He hung his head, thinking perhaps a little time apart was what they needed. She walked to the door and opened it.

"When will you be back?" he asked, unable to help himself even as he felt relief.

"Back home? Soon," she said, never turning around. "Back to you? I don't know. Maybe never."

He felt gut punched.

She left without another word.

Two weeks later

Samira stepped out of her heels as soon as she entered ADG's elegant two-story penthouse apartment in the heart of Milan, the financial capital of Italy. She poured herself a glass of Château d'Esclans Garrus rosé wine and carried it up the wrought iron stairs to the roof garden. At the doorway, she paused to take in the panoramic views of the historic Piazza del Duomo, the main square of the city. The sight of the gothic cathedral against the blue skies and white clouds was stunning, made even more so as the sun set and deepened the blues, painting the clouds with shades of orange, lavender and red that radiated against the 356-foot bronzed statue of the Virgin Mary atop the building.

She crossed the rooftop and took a seat on one of the patio lounges, happy that the leaf-covered walls on the sides offered privacy from neighboring buildings but the views of the city were unobscured. After a long day at the Milan ADG offices, and dreading another night missing Lance as she lay in bed, this time was important to her peace of mind.

It had been two weeks since she requested last-minute permission from Alek and Alessandra to work out of the Milan office. She'd pulled the family card and they'd obliged her, but her work ethic had not diminished. In fact, she worked harder, utilizing modern technology to properly manage her division and attend meetings. She knew it couldn't last and she had to get back to New York, but for now, the distance between her and Lance was needed.

The man took her breath away.

And I needed to breathe.

Emotions rose and brought tears with them. She closed her eyes as they raced down her cheeks. Foolishly she had gotten too deep with Lance when he didn't show the signs of getting as deep with her. She wasn't upset about entry to his master bedroom. The bedroom was just a symptom of a bigger problem in their relationship. His loyalty and his heart rested with another woman.

And that hurt.

"A one-sided relationship is not a happy place, Samira."

"No, it's not," she whispered, using the side of her hands to wipe her tears.

Still, she missed him. His rare smiles. His bashfulness about his scar. The deep timbre of his voice when he spoke her name. The time they spent in each other's company just reading or relaxing, not speaking any words. The feel of his snores vibrating against her breasts as she held him from behind as they slept. The passion of his loving. The look on his face when she made him climax.

"Damn," she swore in a whisper, feeling a tingle at the thought of that.

Her cell phone rang. She took another sip of her wine before sitting it on the table beside her lounge and picking up her phone. A FaceTime call. She made sure her face was tear-free and plastered a smile on before answering.

"Auntie Mira!" her niece, Aliyah, exclaimed as soon as her little face filled the screen.

"Hello, *ma poupée de chocolat*," she said, using her mother's pet name for her on her niece.

"Kwesi, say hi to Auntie," Aliyah said, placing the phone in front of him.

He reached for it and patted the screen as he smiled and laughed.

"Hello, Chocky-Wocky!" she exclaimed as his nanny held him face forward in her arms.

Aliyah joined him on the screen. "We miss you," she said, her Afro puff covering part of his face.

Kwesi squealed and reached for it with both chubby hands.

"Arrête!" Aliyah snapped for him to stop in French.

The phone dropped as the nanny worked to free Kwesi's grip on Aliyah's hair. It was total mayhem and Samira knew she was homesick because even the chaos was familiar and she missed them still. Her heart swelled for the little chocolate cherubs she loved as if they were her own.

"Kwesi!" she said sharply into the phone, knowing he could hear her even if their phone was pointed to the ceiling as it lay on the carpeted floor.

Moments later Aliyah picked up the phone and her face reappeared on the screen with her one of her puffs a little deflated and her brows furrowed in annoyance. "Kwesi is *bad*!" she proclaimed, obviously perturbed.

Samira bit back a smile as she rose from her seat and moved to lean against the railing. People milled about the plaza, competing with the pigeons for space. The wind whipped her hair across her face. She tucked the strands behind her ears, and her line of vision fell on a bright blue taxi turning the corner and pulling to a stop a little way down from her apartment building.

"When are you coming home, Auntie?" Aliyah asked.

"Soon," she said, about to turn from the railing.

She paused when the door to the taxi opened and a tall, broad-shouldered figure exited the rear of the vehicle. She smiled a bit thinking he reminded her of Lance.

Especially with that hat on...

Samira did a double take. Her heart pounded wildly. She leaned a little more over the railing as she looked down at the man accepting the suitcase his driver pulled from the trunk. Suddenly he looked up. She gasped and accidentally released her phone as she looked down into the face of the person who'd been her distraction for the last six months of her life. "Lance," she whispered, her surprise making her light-headed.

"Bye-Bye, Auntie!"

Samira looked down in horror as her iPhone free-fell and her niece's face on the screen was too far away to see her any longer.

"Shit!" she swore, thankful the street was empty as it crashed to the ground and shattered.

Samira turned and crossed the roof to reenter the penthouse. Her feet lightly slapped against the stairs as she came down them and moved across the stylish foyer to the front door. She refused to let the many questions she had about Lance's sudden arrival in Milan overtake her. She didn't want to make presumptions. He would have to fill in the details of who, what, when, where, why and how.

As her personal elevator connected to the penthouse opened, she looked across the ornate lobby and through the glass revolving doors just as Lance entered the building. She was a collection of raw nerve endings as she watched him striding toward her. He looked handsome in his linen shorts and matching V-neck tee with a cotton bucket hat. Her eyes missed nothing. Not one detail. It all was so familiar. And missed.

He came to stop before her and handed her the phone.

She reached for it. "Thank you," she said.

He caught her hand in his.

She shivered from his touch as she looked up to him, imploring him for the answers to all her questions.

"You are everything I didn't know I needed until you were gone," he said, his thumb lightly stroking her pulse and probably feeling it race.

"Lance," she whispered, shaking her head as if to deny him when all she wanted was to leap into his arms and kiss the night away.

"Samira."

She looked up at him, and the warmth in his eyes was there, weakening her knees and her resolve before he even said the words. She gulped in air as the all-too-familiar breathlessness returned.

"I *love* you," he said, his voice deep and seeming to vibrate with the emotion.

"I just want you to have love, Samira. All the love the universe owes you."

She tilted her head to the side and reached up with her free hand to stroke his cheek. "You are everything I didn't know I needed until I left," she whispered up to him, stroking his bottom lip with her thumb. "But—"

He shook his head as he turned it to press a warm kiss to her palm.

"Do you love me?" Lance asked, his vulnerability exposed and raw.

She nodded and smiled up at him. "With every bit of my heart," she admitted with no shame.

Her soul glowed at the relief filling his eyes, and she knew that his admission of love had been a huge breakthrough for him.

"Then it's time," he said.

"Time? For what?" she asked.

"To tell you everything."

Her eyes widened.

Finally.

"Okay," she said softly.

Lance smiled as he looked down at her feet. "You're barefoot," he said.

She looked down at them as well, feeling happy and nervous in his presence, as she wiggled her crimson-painted toes atop the handmade Italian porcelain tile floor. She squealed as he slipped one arm around her waist and picked her body up against him until her feet floated above the floor. She wrapped her arms around his neck, enjoying the scent of his cologne and the feel of his hard body pressing against hers.

Their faces were aligned and they inhaled each other's breaths as they stared at one another.

With no words spoken—or needed—Samira pressed a hand to his cheek as she leaned in to taste his mouth. Slowly. She savored him with grunts of pleasure as he kissed her in return with a hunger that made her heated.

"Voi due siete bellissimi insieme!"

Samira smiled against his lips before she looked over at the suit-clad middle-aged concierge looking over at them with warm eyes from his desk across the lobby. *"Grazie*, Agostino," she thanked him.

"What did he say?" Lance asked, pressing kisses to her jaw.

"He said we are beautiful together," she translated.

He looked to Agostino as well. *"Grazie,"* he repeated.

"You ready?" she asked when his eyes rested on her again.

"Are you?" he asked.

"Absolutely," she stressed. "I want to know and to love all of you, Lance."

He nodded and looked beyond her toward the elevators. "Six?" he asked.

"One for every floor, but the last one on the right is for the penthouse so it's all mine."

"Of course," he said with a chuckle.

She snuggled her face against his neck and enjoyed his smell—his closeness—as he carried her with one arm and used his free hand to pull his suitcase behind him. "I can't believe you're here," she whispered near his ear when they stepped onto the lift.

"I should have been here sooner. I missed you, and this is a conversation long overdue," he admitted.

"I'm anxious to hear whatever you have to share with me."

"I hope you still feel that way after we talk."

She raised up to look at him. "I hope so, too," she said, unable to be anything but honest with him.

"I'm not a serial killer," Lance drawled.

Samira arched a brow. "My instincts would have told me to stay clear of the angry man by the lake who was stacking dead bodies in his basement," she drawled. "My gut *never* lies."

The elevator doors opened. He stepped off and crossed over to the wide double doors of the apartment.

"And your gut hasn't told you anything about me that you felt I wasn't telling you?" he asked.

"Definitely," Samira said, tapping his shoulders for him to release her.

He set her down on her feet. "Like?" he asked.

"Most times I felt you were grieving a loved one and thought you were cheating on them," she said matter-of-factly, grabbing his hand and turning to lead him over to the living room.

She frowned a bit when he didn't budge from his spot by the front door.

"I do."

Samira turned back to him, gripping his hand tighter when she saw the grief in his eyes. "Lance," she whispered, stepping close to him to stroke his face with her free hand.

He closed his eyes and leaned his face against her touch.

"Oh, Lance," she sighed. "That was so cruel of me. I'm sorry it came out so flip. I'm so sorry," she whispered up to him, with waves of hurt and self-reprimand flooding her.

He reached for her and pulled her body against his as he lightly settled his chin atop her head. "Belle was my childhood love," he began, his hand on the small of her back. "We were friends who fell in love. We married after my first book was published, and we were *happy*."

Married?

She refrained from the many questions that flooded her at the news of his marriage. Her instincts that she trusted so very much told her to let him speak. Let his words flow freely. The truth would be revealed in due time.

She closed her eyes against his chest, feeling the rigidness of his stance and wanting to lead him to the sofa but knowing the way they stood shielded the emotions he may reveal on his face from her. She accepted that, understanding the ways of a man.

"When we had our daughter, our Emma Belle, she was the highlight of our lives."

Daughter? Was?

Samira cringed, feeling dread fill her from her toes to the top of her head. She bit her lip to keep from asking any questions, wanting his story to flow from him freely without interruption. She did caress the back of his hand with her palm.

"Three years ago, we were all in the car coming from dinner," he said, his hold around her body tightening a bit as if bracing them both for the rest. "Our car was hit by a drunk driver."

The torture in his voice sent a ray of true pain across her chest.

"I was the only survivor, Samira," he said, the words broken by his emotion. "I lost my family, and I felt like I didn't deserve to live."

She freed his hand to wrap both arms around his chest and held him tightly as his body shook with his pain and his grief. She understood so much, and although she was happy he'd finally shared this huge piece of his life with her, she had regrets for making him relive the pain of it all. The same way the scar was a constant reminder of the tragedy for him.

There was so much to process, but at that moment her only desire was to hold him and try to love on him through his grief.

Chapter 8

One week later

"Dance with me."

Lance looked up at Samira. He sat at a small round table in the corner of an offbeat cocktail bar in the middle of Milan that had more character than space. She wore a short sheer peach floral sundress and heels that added six inches to her height. She smoothly did a little salsa move to the Spanish music playing and extended her hand to him.

She was hard to resist. The soft smile on her face and the warmth of her eyes drew him in.

That was Samira, and he loved her.

He popped a piece of cheese from the charcuterie tray into his mouth before he slid his hand into hers and accepted her invite, amazing himself that he was willing. From the look in her eyes, he knew he surprised her as well. Right there, in a tight little space between two tables, Lance took the lead and pulled her body to him with a hand to the small of her back as he matched her mini-salsa steps with rhythm.

"You can dance?" she asked in amazement as he raised her hand and spun her before tilting her backward into a small dip.

The crowd applauded and whooped it up at them.

Lance and Samira laughed together as he lifted her upright and kissed her. She wrapped her arms around his neck as the music slowed, and they began to sway together in a spot truly no bigger than a two-foot-by-three-foot square. He forgot about the crowded hole-in-the-wall bar and got lost in her as she lightly stroked his nape with one hand and gripped the back of his shirt with the other. He still was uneasy out of his shell, but having Samira there constantly urging him to step beyond the boundaries he put around himself made it easier.

He gently lifted her up against him, and Samira looked down into his face as the crimson and blue lights of the club swirled across their bodies.

"Fai l'amore con me," he said in the Italian command she'd taught him over the last week.

Her eyes smoldered at his request for her to make love to him. *"Tutta la notte, se vuoi,"* she returned, dipping her head to draw his bottom lip into her mouth.

All night long, if you wish.

Without another word spoken, he lowered her to the floor, took her hand and led her through the crowd out of the club.

Samira ran her fingers through her hair as she sat in the back seat of the chauffeur-driven company car taking her from the ADG offices to the corporate penthouse apartment. Hers had been a day filled with meetings and a few small mishaps with the Hawaii development that left her drained and in need of downtime. She smiled, thinking of Lance awaiting her as he had every day that week since his arrival.

The car pulled to a stop before the converted villa and Samira gathered her clutch and briefcase as the driver left the vehicle to come around and open the door for her. *"Grazie, Signor Luca. Buona serata,"* she said to the elderly man, thanking him and wishing him a good evening.

Samira looked up, and just as he had been every evening when she arrived, Lance was in the rooftop garden looking down awaiting her arrival. She smiled up at him, her heart already pounding in anticipation.

"Sei innamorato," Luca observed.

You are in love.

She looked at the elderly man, who was shorter than her by several inches. *"Sì, proprio così,"* she admitted to very much so being in love.

"Un cuore felice è meglio di una borsa piena," Luca said.

A happy heart is better than a full purse.

She smiled at him. *"Questo è molto vero,"* she said, agreeing that that was very true.

He glanced up at Lance and then back at her. *"Vivi con passione. Ridi di cuore. Ama profondamente."*

"Live with passion. Laugh out loud. Love deeply," she said, translating his words.

"Sì. Sì," he said. *"Buonanotte, Signorina Ansah."*

"Good night," Samira said in return before turning to cross the pavement and enter the building.

With a smile and wave to the concierge, she hurried across the lobby to her elevator. The ride was thankfully quick. The front doors were already open, and she dropped her purse and briefcase on the table by the door as soon as she entered.

Lance awaited her, bending to press a kiss to the corner of her mouth before turning to walk back to the living room. "I finished ten pages on the new book today," he said, sitting on the sofa and picking up his leather-bound notebook and pen. "I'm hoping to finish this scene before we head out for dinner."

At her silence, he finally looked up, and his eyes widened.

Samira stood before him nude except for her heels, having undressed as she followed him into the room. She came over to him and pushed the notebook beside him onto the sofa before motioning with her hand for him to remove his pants.

He did.

She straddled his lap and stroked his inches to hardness as his hands came up to grip her soft buttocks. Rising up, she grasped the sides of his face and kissed him as he guided his length inside her with one swift and deep upward thrust. And then another. And another.

"Yes," she gasped, letting her head fall back and feeling the edges of her hair tickle the top of her buttocks.

He moaned in pleasure, easing one hand up her back and guiding his mouth to her breasts to suckle one of her taut brown nipples.

Samira gripped the back of the sofa and rolled her hips against him, sending her core up and then down his inches and causing the hard and thick base of it to strike against her clit, driving her toward a climax. She craved it. The release. The explosion deep inside. Getting lost in pure pleasure.

She needed to come. With him. On him.

As the first white-hot waves washed over her, she cried out. Rough and loud. She didn't care. Lance held her body close, suckled at her nipples wildly, stroked deeply inside her and joined her in euphoria with a moan that rumbled deep in his chest.

They pursued that high without a care to their fast-pounding hearts and sweat-soaked bodies, drawing it out for long, aching moments that were mindless—the moments countless—until they were sated, drained and spent.

The last two weeks in Milan had been some of the best moments of his life. Exploring the city and getting lost in the abundance of art and history with Samira at his side, savoring foods rich in flavor, absorbing beautiful landscapes as she leaned her body back against his, or even just resting in her apartment after she got off from work and they shared their days with each other.

At times, he felt he didn't deserve her. His guilt and grief remained, but they were not as all-consuming and intense. The stranglehold on his life was lighter.

He could breathe.

Lance reached for Samira's hand where they sat aboard the private jet together preparing for their flight from Milan to New York. She was reading a report on her tablet and talking on her cell phone, but she gripped his hand tightly and gave him a look as if she knew—with those instincts of hers—that he needed her at that moment.

He didn't know what he'd done to deserve two great loves in his life or what he'd done to suffer such great losses.

And if he was honest, there was a thin thread of fear that he would lose Samira as well.

Like Belle.

Like Emma Belle.

"I love you," Samira mouthed.

He gave her a warm smile and tipped his hat with his free hand before he raised their entwined hands and kissed the back of hers with a silent prayer that his luck had changed for the better.

Samira sat on a swinging cedar rocker bench on the large deck of Lance's home. They had been back from Milan for a few days, and he had invited his tiny tribe over for dinner to meet her. He was frying fish for his guests and having grilled chicken for himself. There was his father, Lawrence, a charmer who couldn't help but flirt—even with his thirtysomething girlfriend, Koi, at his side; his mother, Helena, a peaceful spirit with a soft voice, the only wildness about her being her shoulder-length Afro of curls; his agent and friend, Annalise, who clearly wanted pleasure more than business; and his little five-year-old brother, Law.

She was just happy to meet them and know that Lance had people in his life who cared for him as well.

"He's hasn't looked this happy in a long time."

Samira looked up at Helena standing beside where she sat, offering a new glass of rosé wine. She took it, setting her empty glass on the table beside her. "Good," she said. "He told me about his wife and daughter."

Helena claimed the seat next to her on the bench. "Tough times," she admitted, cradling her own glass of wine in her wrinkled hands. "Grief can be all-consuming. Lord knows we all struggled after the accident, but he finally seems to be breaking through to the other side of it, where you learn to accept and learn from it even if you never completely heal from it."

"I couldn't imagine going through it…for any of you," Samira added, acknowledging the woman's loss as well.

"Like I said…tough times."

"I like my fish fried hard, son," Lawrence said, his voice seeming to bellow into the summer night air.

Samira looked to the tall, bald-headed seventy-something man with his arm wrapped around his date's waist. "Question?" she asked.

"Fire away," Helena said.

"That doesn't bother you to be here with him and her?"

"We've been divorced since Lance was a teenager, but we had him in our forties and we shared a lot of years together. More good than bad, actually," Helena said, crossing one leg over the other in the floor-length caftan she wore. "We were of that '60s mind-set of free love and happiness by any means, but when we had Lance—and we were older—I didn't want him to be of that same mind-set. Suddenly *I* changed the rules, and Lawrence didn't want to adjust. I took my ball and didn't want to play anymore, and we decided to let the marriage go and live our lives separately."

Helena paused to take a sip of her wine. "When you have shared more than twenty years of your life with someone and you accept that you are just not right for each other anymore, then it should end well. No anger. No bitterness. No war. We share a son. We've shared loss. And now in our elder years, we share a friendship—a *platonic* friendship," she added. "And now we laugh about his exploits and failing body parts and life. He was my one great love, and now he is my best friend. So, no, none of *that* bothers me."

She liked Lance's mother. She was so calm. So peaceful. So unbothered.

Samira eyed Lance as he lifted his bucket hat enough to wipe at the sweat on his brow with a paper towel before balling it up and tossing it away into the nearby receptacle. She squinted a bit when his agent said something to him and lightly touched his arm as he continued frying up a huge batch of fish and hush puppies. Then they both laughed.

"Don't worry. Lance looks like his father, but he has my loyal heart," Helena assured her.

She had been watching as his agent, Annalise, a shortbread cutie with waist-length blondish dreads and freckles, found yet another reason to touch him. "She's pretty," Samira said, crossing her legs in the strapless emerald-green jumpsuit she wore.

"Prettier than her have tried to catch his eyes over these last few years," Helena said. "You succeeded."

Samira took a sip of her drink as she forced herself to look at the lake in the distance and away from the man she loved and a woman who obviously wanted his adoration.

"I'm happy to meet you, Samira…the woman my son so obviously loves," Helena said, nudging her shoulder with her own.

Samira followed her line of vision to find Lance's eyes steadily on her. Butterflies seemed to flutter in her stomach. He raised his glass in a toast to her, and she did the same.

Annalise looked up at him and then over at her, following his line of vision.

Samira saw the understanding fill the woman's face before it was replaced with respect and perhaps a touch of regret. The two women shared a look before Annalise raised her glass to her as well as if to surrender her one-sided fight for Lance.

"I feel silly," Samira admitted to his mother.

"What you feel is love, and when it's the right kind of love ain't *shit* wrong with that," Helena said.

"Nothing at all," Samira agreed.

"Turn it up, Daddy. Pleeeeease! That's my favorite song."

As they sat at a red light, Lance smiled over at Belle sitting in the passenger seat of their Lamborghini crossover, then in the rearview mirror at their daughter sitting in the middle of the rear seat securely strapped in her booster seat. Her face was so like his own. His mini-me save for her mother's dimples and curly hair.

He used the volume control on the steering wheel to turn up "Watch Me (Whip/Nae Nae)" by Silentó.

Emma Belle instantly began singing along to the catchy tune and doing the dances along to the music with all the abandon a lively six-year-old could have.

"Probably too much sugar in her dessert," Belle said with a laugh.

"A double scoop of ice cream with all the works will do that," he said.

"You had ice cream, too, Daddy," Emma Belle said.

He looked over his shoulder at her. "You know what? I sure did," he said, seconds before he began to whip and nae nae, too.

"You had a little scoop, Mommy!"

"I did," Belle agreed.

She joined them in singing along to the song and dancing in her seat.

He winked at her before he turned to look back at Emma.

"Lance!"

He whirled around just as the bright lights of an oncoming car glared into his eyes.

Boom!

Lance awakened, startled. He sat up straight in bed as he exhaled in puffs through his mouth and fought hard to erase the sounds of metal meeting metal as the SUV hit them head-on and sent their car—their world—toppling over into a series of flips down the highway and landing on the roof. The dream was over, but he was still deep in the clutches of the nightmare.

"Shit," he swore, moving to sit on the side of the bed. "Shit. Shit. Shit. Shit. Shit."

"Lance," Samira said, shifting on the bed in the darkness to ease her arms around his back so she could hold him tightly from behind.

He reached for the hand she had pressed to his palm and held it tightly as he waited for normalcy to reign.

She pressed her lips to his spine. "It's okay. It will be okay," she said, and he felt her whispers blow against his skin.

"I miss them," he said aloud as pain tightened his throat. "I hate the way that they died. I hate it."

"I know you do," she said. "I never met them, but I hate it, too. I really do hate that happened to them."

He looked back over his shoulder and although he

couldn't see her face, he knew there was nothing but truth in her words.

He tilted his head back until it rested against the top of hers.

"Tell me about them," she said, more whispers that caressed him. "Talk about them. Remember them with me. *Please.*"

"You're the best mommy and daddy in the world."

He smiled at the memory of Emma Belle jumping into the middle of their bed between him and Belle. As he allowed himself to think of them—remember them—more memories came flooding back. Big moments. Little details. All of it. For years he had forced himself not to think of them.

As Samira continued to hold him, he began to talk to her about his Belle and Emma Belle long into the night.

"Did I ruin your fishing?" Samira asked as she and Lance walked together down Main Street for lunch at La Boulangerie after a lazy Sunday morning of fishing on the lake.

He chuckled. "It was…different," he said. "It was your first time, right?"

Samira flung her head back and laughed. "Um…*yeah*," she said, looking up at him. "And probably my last, if you have your say."

"Fishing is my solace. My peace," he explained.

"And *my* headache, so you can have all the peace and solace on your boat that you want, Lance," she said.

He looked relieved.

She stepped in front of him to jump up a little and kiss his mouth. He picked her up by the waist until their faces were aligned. "Will you miss me when I go home tonight?" she asked as she set her hands on his shoulders.

The weekend was coming to an end, and she had an early-morning flight to Paris for business.

"Of course," he assured her.

"Good," she said.

They shared a brief but heated kiss before he set her back down on her feet.

"Passion Grove really is a beautiful town," she said as they both checked for oncoming traffic before they crossed the street.

As they stepped up onto the curb, the town's police chief, Harley Ransom, was climbing from his cruiser and crossing the sidewalk to climb the porch steps of the Victorian home that had once served as the town's mercantile during the early days of its creation in the 1900s. For the last fifty years, it had served as the small town's police station.

"Good afternoon, Chief," Lance said pleasantly to the portly man as they passed him.

"Huh?"

Lance paused and looked back at him with a hint of a smile. "I said, good afternoon, Chief," he repeated.

Harley looked perplexed by the salutation.

Samira covered her mouth with her hand to refrain from laughing at the man's comical expression.

"Uh…um…uh…hello. Uh…good afternoon," he said.

Lance tipped his hat and turned to continue on his way with a whistle.

"You almost gave the man a heart attack just by being cordial," she said, sliding her arm around his.

Lance chuckled. "Let's rile up some more of my neighbors," he said.

For the next block, he made a point of speaking to every person he passed. Many returned the favor, but a few that were familiar with him and his usual bad temperament were unable to hide their shock.

His eyes were lit with humor as he held the door to the bakery open for her to enter. "I really was a grouch, huh?" he asked.

"Are you *just* realizing that, my love?" she asked, arching of her brow.

"I knew. I didn't care," he admitted with a shrug of one broad shoulder.

"And then?" she asked as they got in line in the Parisian bistro–styled bakery.

Lance stroked her chin with his thumb. "And then came you, Samira Ansah," he said warmly.

"Oh, you do have a way with words, Lance Millner."

A week later Lance entered the walk-in closet/ dressing room of his master suite and passed through it to reach his bathroom. He turned on the lights and looked over at the copper-framed mirror above the double sink. With a slight grimace, he padded bare- foot over to it but kept his eyes down on the sink.

His book *Danger* was being released in less than ninety days, and his publisher's marketing and PR team were in full publicity mode, wanting to secure television and magazine interviews, book signings, blurbs, and panel discussions. Since the accident, he had not agreed to any public appearances. His team was aware of that, but with every new book, they extended the offers. The truth was, the more reclusive he became, the more media outlets vied to book him.

How could he do appearances when he still felt uncomfortable with the scar and the questions he knew it would evoke?

"Trust me. You have nothing to be ashamed of. Nothing at all."

He patted his hand against the edge of the sink and shook his head with a slight chortle as Samira's compliment came back to him. She was the only person, outside of his doctors, to see his scar. To really see him. The person he hid from the world—even from his family and friends. And Lord knows she had no aversion to it. It had done nothing to quell her desire for him. She would look him in the face, kiss him, express her love for him as if the scar was not there.

He reached up and removed his boonie hat, letting it fall onto the vanity. For the first time in three years, Lance looked up at his reflection. His eyes focused on every zone of his face except the scar slashing across his brow. He'd lost weight—that he knew from the fit of his clothes—but he hadn't realized his face had become leaner over the years. He actually liked it.

He touched the scar as he finally let his eyes settle on it. It ran from the side of his forehead and down across his brow. He'd been given fifteen stitches to repair the deep wound. The scar remained. It wasn't as protruding as he remembered, but it was there all the same. Where the glass had cut him, the hair of his brow had never grown back, and the scar created a pale slash through the rest of his medium brown complexion, pulling his lid at the corner tighter than his other eye. He hated it.

His readers reached out via email and his various social media accounts to let him know they wanted their books signed and to see him personally. But he knew they wanted to see the face in his headshots, not the scarred oddity he'd become.

"You honestly are a beauty, not a beast, Lance."

He closed his eyes and shook his head trying to free himself of Samira's voice. "It's easy for her to say," he drawled.

Bzzzzzz. Bzzzzzz. Bzzzzzz.

Lance turned from the mirror, removing his phone from the pocket of his navy cotton pajama bottoms as he pressed his buttocks against the sink to lean against it. A FaceTime from Samira. She was with friends from college in the city for an epic girls' night out—as she put it. He reached behind him for his hat and slapped it on before he answered.

Her face filled the screen. Her hair was pulled back into a ponytail, and her makeup was glamorous. "Are you in the bathroom?" she asked.

"Are you?" he asked, hearing the muted thump of bass music as he looked at her background as well.

"Yes. I wanted to call you and let you know I'm

good. I know you worry about me when I'm out," she said.

He did. He was working on not letting his fear of losing her make him a certified nut. Her recent trip to Paris had been a true test of his will. "Thank you, but I won't relax until I get your call or text that you're home," he admitted.

"I know and I will," she promised.

"What are you wearing?" he asked as he walked out of the bathroom and through the dressing room.

She panned the phone down to show the strapless sequined rose-gold jumpsuit she wore with strappy metallic heels. "You like?" she asked, moving to stand in front of the mirror to show off the view of her plump buttocks in the wide-leg pants as well.

"Hell yeah," he said.

Samira jiggled her rear a little before placing the phone back in front of her face.

"Are you having fun?" he asked.

"I am. It was good to get out, dance and have a few strong cocktails with friends."

"I agree."

They fell silent.

"Is that the elusive master suite?" she asked.

Lance stiffened. "Uh...yeah. Yup. It is," he said, looking around.

They still used the in-law suite downstairs. He just couldn't accept being intimate with her in the same bed he'd once shared with his wife. "Samira—"

"Listen, Lance, thank you for letting me into your heart," she said, her eyes serious. "I know that it wasn't easy with everything you've been through and… I feel honored that you made room for me in your life."

Her words were understanding, but there was some emotion he couldn't gauge that clouded her eyes.

He sat down on the bed and rested his head against the padded leather headboard. His eyes were sad. "Samira, you knew some of this wasn't—*isn't*—easy for me," he said.

"Right, I did know that," she said with a smile that was vacant from her eyes.

"Samira, I love you—"

"I know," she said, cutting him off. "I better get back to the girls before they think I left. I'll text you when I get home. 'Bye."

The call ended.

Lance dropped his phone onto the bed and reached for his hat to ball into his hand and throw across the room.

Chapter 9

Three months later

Samira couldn't sleep.

She picked her phone up from beside her on the bed and checked the screen. It was after midnight, and she had to get up early in the morning. It had been ten months of their relationship—really not that long. Definitely not enough time to ask a man to sell the home he once shared with his family because she felt out of place when she was there.

She didn't know the right thing to say or to do. She wasn't even in total control of her own feelings or sure she had a right to feel them. Her emotions were varied. Hurt. Disappointment. Even jealousy. And then such guilt at what she felt was her own pettiness considering the loss of both his wife and child. *Will he ever love me like he loved Belle?*

She winced. It felt heartless to think and even more cruel to ever say.

She thought of him losing his child, and she was ashamed. She couldn't imagine how that felt. Her father's life had been taken in an airplane accident many years ago, and Samira missed him still. Cried for him still. Wanting nothing more than him to be there still.

Samira sat on the side of the bed and reached for the martini glass to sip her creamy Orgasm drink. "I have to get out of my own head," she said with a breath.

She pushed her feet into her bed slippers and reached for her black satin robe to cover the matching black silk slip with fuchsia lace trim. As she tied the long belt of the kimono-style robe, she left her suite and made her way through her expansive apartment to her kitchen, deciding to use the rear halls since she was in her nightclothes. She grabbed the key chain from the drawer nearest the rear door. On it was the key to the back-door lock and a small can of Mace.

She trusted no space completely, no matter the zip code or per capita income.

Holding up the hem of her gown to keep it from dragging against the tiled floor, Samira made her way down the narrow, brightly lit hall to the stairwell. The bottoms of her slippers slapped against the concrete steps as she easily climbed two levels. She reached for the door out to the rear hall of the floor of her mother's apartment.

"I need to talk to my mother...*and* have a bowl of

strawberry fool," she said aloud, ready for the delicious Ghanaian dessert of fresh strawberries and wine folded into heavy whipping cream.

She came to a stop in the open doorway. "What?" she softly gasped as she eyed her mother, LuLu, and Alessandra's longtime chauffeur, Roje, in a heated embrace as they shared a kiss that was obviously loving.

Samira was stunned, and she cringed at watching another man be so familiar with her mother like her father used to be. Her father, with whom she had been very close. *"Maman?"* she said, unsure of which of her emotions to give priority: anger, sadness or disbelief.

She walked down the hall as they shared a look before both turned to her. She shook her head as her mother closed her robe to cover the silk and lace gown she wore. She frowned at the comforting hand the man placed on her back.

"I'm sorry," he said to her. "I didn't want it to come out like this."

LuLu glanced up at him with a soft smile. "It's okay, my love. It was time for the truth to be revealed," she said before resting her concerned eyes back on her daughter.

"My *love*?" Samira squawked. "The truth? What truth?"

Roje pressed a small kiss to LuLu's temple. "Call me," he said, before giving Samira a nod and walking past her to eat up the distance of the hall and reach the door to the stairwell.

Samira turned to watch his exit before whirling back to face her mother, but her door, still ajar, was empty.

She rushed inside, closing the door behind her as she watched her mother move about the large kitchen preparing coffee. "I thought Daddy was the great love of your life?" she asked, coming to stand by the island.

LuLu lowered her hands to the white marble countertop as she stiffened. "Never question my love for your father," she said.

"That's hard to do with a man sneaking out the back door of your apartment in the middle of the night," Samira returned, coming to stand by the marble island.

LuLu turned. "Not just any man, *ma poupée de chocolat*," she said. "We have been together for nearly a year—"

Samira recoiled.

"We are in love," LuLu continued.

Samira turned from her.

"And we are getting married."

With that, she whirled around with her eyes wide. "You have got to be kidding!" she spat.

LuLu held up her hand and gave her daughter a steely-eyed stare. "Respect me. Always," she said, her tone hard.

Samira laughed bitterly. "Request of me what you demand for yourself, *Maman*, because falling for the schemes and machinations of a chauffeur doesn't reek of respectability."

"Is that who I raised you to be, Samira? Because if so, I am disappointed in myself," LuLu said, her voice soft.

"*That* disappoints you?" she said, knowing she was being snide.

Anger and hurt were her fuel, and that was a dangerous combination.

"Follow me," LuLu said, leaving the kitchen with the hem of her silk robe rising a bit from the floors.

With reluctance, Samira followed her mother through her five-thousand-square-foot postwar apartment. They came to a stop before her wall of original Ghanaian artwork and artifacts. The streetlights glowed and cast a bluish light through the French doors of the adjoining terrace.

"*Assois-toi!*" LuLu demanded.

Samira obeyed her mother's command and sat down on the low-slung gold leather couch, but her emotions stood firm.

"Did you know I was a painter?" LuLu asked as she stood there eyeing each piece of artwork. "From the time I was a toddler, I loved to paint, and my parents encouraged me in any way that they could. All through school. Lessons with notable artists. I graduated from the National School of Fine Arts in Paris. My second year there, I even had one of my paintings in a collection at a gallery. I was considered gifted. More so, I simply loved my art, and the time I spent in Paris attending school was a highlight."

Samira looked on as her mother lightly touched the frame of a realistic painting of a young girl crying. "No, I didn't know that," she said. "Why don't I know that?"

LuLu looked back at her over her shoulder. "Because I became devoted to being a wife and a mother," she said simply. "And no one cared about my life before then. Not even me."

It was hard to deny the sadness in her mother's voice.

"Maman—"

LuLu shook her head as she turned back to the wall. "I am a good mother. I was a good wife," she said, reaching again to stroke the painting. "For the first time in a really long time, I am putting myself first. I'm choosing *me*. I'm choosing to be happy."

Samira looked away from her mother. "Can't you just paint something?" she asked, knowing she sounded childish and petulant.

LuLu threw her hands up in exasperation.

"No. Nope. Nah," Samira said, rising to her feet and walking away.

"Samira!" LuLu called behind her.

She stopped in the hall, dimly lit by sconces. "No, *Maman*," she said, shaking her head. "Absolutely not. This marriage will *not* happen."

"You're being a hypocrite, Samira," LuLu said, calmly sitting on the sofa her daughter had vacated.

"How?" she asked, feeling perturbed.

"Lance."

Samira looked down at the polished floors as she allowed her body to lean back against the wall.

"So he deserves to fall in love again after losing his spouse?" LuLu asked. "But I don't?"

Damn.

"It's not the same," she insisted.

"Different rules for your mother than your lover, huh?"

Samira pushed off the wall and thought of her own fears about her Lance and just how deeply both his love and his grief for Belle ran. She sat down on the floor at her mother's feet. "This is about more than love," Samira said, closing her eyes at the feel of her mother raking her fingers through her hair like when she was young. "Roje is a chauffeur. What are you going to do—take him to charity events after he gets off duty driving Alessandra? Or let me guess, he'll quit working, right?"

LuLu's hand disappeared. "You got those instincts you love so much from me, you know?" she said.

She bent her legs and rested the side of her face atop her knees.

"Roje and I are not clueless to the differences in our stations in life, Samira. He wants nothing from me or any of you. We have agreed that any wealth or items your father left to me will go to you and your brothers upon my passing. Even this apartment, Samira. I am not foolish. He is not an opportunist."

Hearing that freed some of the tensions from her neck and shoulders.

"But if I had to leave this all behind," she said, waving her hand around the elaborate multimillion-dollar apartment, "then I would at this point to be with him."

"Un cuore felice è meglio di una borsa piena," Samira said, thinking of her driver in Milan, Luca.

A happy heart is better than a full purse.

"Assolutamente," LuLu sighed in Italian, absolutely agreeing.

"But will you move?" she asked her mother.

LuLu tsked. "Of course not. I love my apartment. I've been here since a little after your father passed," she said with a dismissive wave.

Samira smiled at that.

The hand returned. "I loved my husband, and for a long time, I wondered if I ever would be happy without him," LuLu said. "I am happy again, Samira. Roje makes me happy. He loves me, and I love him."

Samira closed her eyes, lost somewhere between her anger at her mother and wanting to know more about this new phase in her life, because the parallels between her mother and Lance could not be denied.

"Will you forget Daddy?" she asked, her voice soft as she remembered her closeness with her father. No one denied that his lone daughter had been his favorite.

"Never," LuLu said emphatically.

"Is Roje just to replace him?" she asked, speaking to her own fears again.

"That would be impossible, *ma poupée de chocolat*," she said with softness. "For me…or for Lance."

Samira said a silent prayer that her mother was right.

The next day LuLu eyed her family as they sat in the family room of Alessandra and Alek's mansion. She was nervous. The night before, when Samira had happened upon the truth of her relationship with Roje, it had not gone well. Her sons might take the news twice as badly. Nevertheless, the time had come to be honest with them, because she had not hesitated when Roje proposed to her as they made love over a week ago.

A year after the tragic death of her husband, Roje had happened upon her during a moment of gloom and had made it his business to cheer her up. Long into the night, they'd talked and laughed. And when they shared that first hesitant kiss, her surprise had quickly faded into the desire she felt for him the entire night. For a little while, she forgot her grief and got lost in the most intense passion.

"That night I left a piece of my heart with you that I will never get back, LuLu." She smiled, remembering him telling her at ADG's golden jubilee celebration, four years after their one night together.

"So did I, Roje."

Her admission had been the truth. LuLu had never forgotten his compassion or his passion that night. She had wanted more of both but denied herself and him because of her obligations to her children, to the dynasty her husband helped to create, to her marriage of more than twenty years, to class and her age.

But Roje never gave up on them. Never.

She touched her fingertips to her lips at the memory of him kissing her with passion in the rear garden of Alek and Alessandra's home. It had taken all her might to deny her feelings and run away. But then one day she'd stopped running and turned to him. Enjoyed him. Loved him.

And still, he'd pushed for more than stolen moments.

"As long as we pretend we're not in love, right? Like we're near strangers and not lovers, LuLu?"

Nearly two years ago, she'd known she wanted him as not just her lover but also her family. She had felt so conflicted as she stood near him in the private waiting room of the hospital as the entire family awaited news of Marisa's emergency caesarean. Their hands had briefly touched and their eyes locked as he handed out the coffee he brought for everyone. All of the love they felt for one another passed between them without a word spoken, and she had wanted nothing more than to feel his strong arms around her and to have him hold her close to ease her fears.

Enough was enough.

It's time to claim my happy.

"What's going on?" Alek asked, the last to enter the room and claim his seat on the sofa beside his wife.

LuLu eyed her sons and their wives before resting her gaze on Samira. She felt foolish seeking understanding from her. It was clear from her closed expression that her daughter had none to offer.

"I have some wonderful news," she began, rubbing her hands together where she stood before the unlit fireplace.

"What is it, *Maman*?" Naim asked, his eyes just as warm and charming as ever.

And so LuLu began to tell her children and their spouses of her sadness and grief after their father's death. But as she began to tell them of her newfound love and happiness, she had to stiffen her back and notch her chin just before she revealed that it was Roje.

LuLu winced as her sons both hit the roof.

She calmly answered every one of the same questions Samira asked the night before.

"Why are you so quiet?" Alek barked at Samira.

"I had *my* conniption last night," she replied smoothly.

"Last night!" both men roared.

LuLu rolled her eyes.

"Besides, *Maman* pointed out that I'm currently in love with a widower, making my argument against this union hypocritical," Samira said, crossing her legs and holding up her hands. "Y'all have to troubleshoot this."

LuLu did not miss the look Marisa and Alessandra shared before both began to manage their husbands. *Thank God.*

"Wait," Alek said, holding up his hand to stop the melee as he eyed his wife. "The night Naim saw Roje leaving my mother's apartment last year, you said you sent him there to pick up papers."

Alessandra looked uneasy.

Both Alek and Naim threw their hands up in the air and swore.

"I did not lie. I was managing a truth that was not mine to tell," Alessandra said.

The melee resumed.

LuLu looked beyond her family, to where Roje stood in the doorway quietly watching them, distinguished in his work uniform of black suit with a black open-necked shirt. He was tall and strong, bald and handsome, and made all the more charming by his silver goatee and dark brown complexion. Looking at him gave her peace as she smiled at him with all the love she had for him in her eyes.

"*Maman*, why are you tickled?" Naim asked.

They all swung their heads to follow her line of vision resting on Roje.

He came into the room and cleared his throat as he stood by her side. "I understand your difficulties in being comfortable with our relationship, but I believe—and I'm sure you do as well—that the majority of your conversation can be had outside the company of your mother," he said, giving each man a stare that matched their own. "We will leave you to it, and when we are all ready to have this discussion with nothing but respect for each other, we will rejoin you."

LuLu eyed her children and their expressions of surprise and some annoyance.

The roles had just changed. This was an employee—a well-paid one—who had just claimed his role as the future husband to their mother. He placed a hand to her lower back and guided her out of the room ahead of him.

LuLu loved it. One of the things she adored about him was his strength and insight. He was the epitome of class and grace—even under fire. And she was going to spend the rest of her life loving him for who he was without concerns for who he was not.

Samira drove her Benz through the streets of Passion Grove from the Ansah-Dalmount estate to Lance's property. It was early October, and the signs of fall and

Halloween decor were on full display—cornucopias and jack-o'-lanterns on steroids.

Soon fall would transition into winter—the season when she and Lance had begun. "A year," she said, turning her vehicle onto the drive leading to the expansive log cabin–styled mansion.

Time was flying.

As she parked in the courtyard, she stayed in the car and looked out the driver's side window at the residence, taking note that it looked just as lacking in love and life as it had when she first saw his home. She couldn't help but wonder if her effect on his life was as minimal as her attempts to have him liven up his home. Open the windows. Draw the curtains. Buy live plants. Add color.

Stop mourning.

One of the front double doors opened, and Lance filled the entry.

Smiling at him, she climbed from the car and dug her leather-gloved hands into the pockets of her full-length multicolored tweed coat gathered at the waist with a matching belt. She wore it with vintage jeans and heels. The wind whipped her hair around her face as she took long strides to jog up the steps and reach him.

"I made some hot chocolate," he said, bending to kiss her mouth.

She pressed a hand to the side of his face and deepened the kiss with a moan of satisfaction.

"That bad?" Lance asked, closing the door once she stepped into the foyer.

She had already filled him in on her discovery of

her mother's relationship last night and the family meeting LuLu had called for that evening after work.

Samira removed her coat and gloves to hand to him. "The only word for the last twenty-four hours is *chaos*," she said as he hung up her coat and then led her into the living room. A large mug sat on each small table beside the duo of leather chairs before the lit fireplace.

Lance waited for her to kick off her heels and take her seat before he sat as well.

She picked up the cup and let it warm her palms before she took a sip, enjoying the feel of the steam rising against her face. "*With* amaretto," she sighed at the taste of the almond-flavored liqueur.

"How did it go?" Lance asked after a few moments of silence only broken by the crackle of the fire.

"Alek was caving when Roje and *Maman* left. He's more upset about the deceit then he is the relationship," she said, before enjoying another sip. "Naim is the most upset. He feels it's a betrayal to our father."

"And you?"

She looked over at him. "Me? I'm a hypocrite," she admitted, casting her gaze away from him and into the fire. "How can I not want for her what I want for you?"

At his silence, she looked over to find him looking into the fire as well. "Grief is lonely. You never imagine being left alone by the person you love. You never really comprehend till death do us part until…death."

She pushed past the unease she felt. "I can't lie that the look on my mother's face when she saw Roje was pure peace," she said, remembering the smile. "Why wouldn't I want that for her?"

If she was honest, they looked good together.

"Coming from someone who thought he would never fall in love again, it's a good thing," he said as he looked to her again. "*You're* a good thing."

"But am I *enough*?" she asked impulsively.

He eyed her, but there was a definite pause, as if he was gauging the impact of her question. "For?" he asked.

Samira closed her eyes and released a stream of air through her pursed lips, accepting at that moment that within the realm of her relationship, she was insecure. That did not sit well with her. Not well at all. "You know what? That was a ridiculous question," she said. "I am enough. A woman should never rely on someone else to designate her worth."

"And do you think I've done something to bring on any insecurities?" he asked.

"Intentionally? No," she admitted, looking around at his home.

"What does that mean?"

She eyed him. "Nothing," she said with a shake of her head as she reached for her hot chocolate.

"Something," he insisted, rising to his feet to stand before her chair. He extended his hand to her.

She eyed it but did not take it. "Oh no," she said, chuckling.

"What!" he exclaimed.

"A hug and then a kiss and then suddenly it's long strokes all night long and a bunch of moaning when we come together," she said. "You know it and I know it."

His hand remained. "Sometimes a hug is just a hug," he said.

She wrinkled her nose at him as she finally slid her hand into his and allowed him to tug her to her feet. She wrapped her arms around his waist and leaned back to look up at him.

"What have I done—*unintentionally*—to make you feel insecure?" he asked.

She slid her hands down into the back pockets of his jeans. Playfully she squeezed his buttocks.

Lance shook his head.

"I didn't say I wouldn't be the one to initiate sex," she explained.

"Samira."

She didn't look at him. Instead, she pressed her face against his chest as she looked into the flames.

He held her tighter, resting his chin atop her head. "What's going on?" he asked.

For so long she had put aside her questions and doubts, not wanting to be insensitive. "Are we really doing this now?" she asked.

Lance stiffened. "What have I done—unintentionally—to make you feel insecure?" he asked again.

Say what needs to be said.

"How long are you going to punish yourself for your wife and daughter passing?" she asked.

Lance released her.

They shifted away from each other. Not even the fire could warm the sudden coolness.

Samira crossed her arms over her chest and

glanced over at him. "I am your enabler," she said, turning to him.

His jaw tightened, and his shoulders straightened. "You make me sound addicted," he said, his voice low.

"To your grief? Maybe so, Lance," she said.

He eyed her in disbelief.

"I know you lost your family, and that's the toughest thing you will ever have to face and get past one day, but you're the ghost, Lance," she said, spreading her arms as she did a semiturn in his living room. "Look around you. No pictures. No sunlight. No plants. No color. No joy. No holidays. It's a damn portrait of suffering and damn despair. You're just a faded version of yourself."

"You don't know me," he roared.

"Do you?" she asked calmly in the face of his anger. "Do you remember who you were before the car accident? Do you want to?"

He strode over to his bar and jerked up a decanter of some brown liquor to pour himself a healthy share into a glass. "I guess you think my anger is a sign of something else?" he asked as he dropped cubes into the glass.

"I don't know. I'm not a therapist," she said.

He frowned. "No shit, Sherlock," he drawled condescendingly.

"Welcome back, Grumpy Grouch," she said.

Lance set the glass down on the bar. His stance softened as he turned to face her. "I love you, Samira," he said.

"I absolutely believe that," she said, her heart racing. "I love you, too. So much. This is not about the present. It's about the future—our future—and what it will look like."

Slowly he walked over to her.

"Would you bring children into this bleak life?" she asked.

He stopped.

Her breath caught.

The crackle of the fire filled the silence.

"Samira," he said, his face was bleak.

A real chill raced over her body.

"I don't want to have more children," he said.

She'd never known her heart could beat so fast. "What?" she asked.

He took a step, and she shook her head. He stopped.

"That would have been nice to know before this moment," she said, her voice monotone as she tried to imagine finding love, maybe even one day marrying, but never having children.

"Samira," he said.

She moved quickly to the closet and grabbed her coat to pull on. "At this moment I realize my mother is courageous for being able to move on beyond her grief," she said, as she tugged on her gloves. "So, I thank you for *that*."

Long strides brought him to her side, and he reached for her wrist before she could open the door and flee. "Samira, please," he begged, pulling her body to his and pressing kisses to the side of her face.

"Please what?" she asked, leaning back to look up at him. "Please give up your dreams of having a family? Please choose you over having children? Please forgive you for keeping another one of your secrets? Please enjoy living in the shadow of your guilt and grief? No."

She kissed him, allowing herself to enjoy the feel of his mouth and the rise of his ardor as they clung to one another. "Lance," she said, easing her hand down onto his chest to push him back from her. "I'm giving myself thirty days to get over you. I'm giving you the same thirty days to get your shit together or leave me alone for good."

He reached to twist his hand in her hair and jerk her close to him once more. "Don't do this again," he said, alluding to their last break when he followed her to Milan.

"Hugs. Then kisses. Then long strokes all night long. No," she insisted, pushing out of his embrace. "Do not call me. Do not come to me. Do not look for me. Do not contact my family to reach me. Thirty days. Either you're all in or all out, Lance."

With that said, she rushed from the house before he could see the first of many tears fall.

Chapter 10

Two months later

"Happy holidays, Ms. Ansah!"

Samira gave her assistant, Assi, a hard glare as she passed her office on the way to her own. She fought the urge to mutter, "Bah humbug"—but just barely. She paused in the doorway at the sight of a large poinsettia on the corner of her desk.

Assi ran into the back of her, and Samira glanced back at her over her shoulder.

"Sorry," the woman said with a slight wince.

Samira continued into her office and picked up the plant to hand back to Assi. "Have you confirmed the travel plans with my mother?" she asked, removing the sleek caramel-colored camel-hair coat she wore over a formfitting leather dress in the same shade.

"The car will pick you, your mother and Mr. Roje—"

"Just Roje," Samira said, removing her computer glasses from the ostrich-leather eyewear case to slip on before she logged on to her computer. "Actually, I don't know his last name. I guess I should find out, since they're to be wed in three months."

"Okay," Assi said. "Your driver will be downstairs at 9:00 a.m. sharp. Your luggage has already been shipped ahead and arrived at Mr. and Mrs. Ansah's chalet in the Swiss Alps."

Samira nodded, wishing she didn't dread the annual family holiday trip. Lance had forever changed Christmas for her—and not for the better. She allowed herself to think of him and took great comfort in the pain of hurt and disappointment being less sharp than it had been when her thirty-day deadline came and went two months ago.

Work had become her new lover.

"I uploaded the video interview with Ms. Burns this morning," Assi said.

Samira found her first smile of the day. "Thank you, Assi," she said.

Her conversation with Ursula Burns, the first African American woman to be CEO of a Fortune 500 company, was just the debut she needed for her new blog/initiative to encourage young African American girls to aspire to join the growing ranks of powerful black women in corporate America. She planned such conversations once a month, and next on her list was Alessandra.

The formation of her nonprofit offering scholarships to women of color looking to acquire their MBAs was receiving a lot of press. That was a bright spot in the last few months.

I just knew he was coming back to me.

"Coffee or tea, Ms. Ansah?"

And I was wrong.

"Ms. Ansah?"

Samira blinked and looked up at Assi, pushing away a memory of crying until her eyes were puffy because of her heartbreak. "Yes?" she asked.

"Would you like coffee or tea this morning?" Assi asked again.

"Hot chocolate, actually," she said.

"Right away."

As Assi departed the office with the Christmas plant in hand, Samira thought of the last time Lance made her the same drink. It seemed like a lifetime ago.

"I'm giving myself thirty days to get over you. I'm giving you the same thirty days to get your shit together or leave me alone for good."

"Knock-knock."

Samira looked up at Alessandra, striding into her office looking beautiful in a bright orange silk blouse paired with a matching leather pencil skirt. "Good morning, sis," Samira said, removing her spectacles.

Alessandra claimed one of the seats in front of her, lightly tapping a rolled-up magazine she held against the edge of the desk. "I watched the interview you did with Ursula. It was excellent. You really are good on camera," she said. "Funny. Smart. Insightful. A mini Oprah."

"Thanks."

"But that's not the reason I'm here," she admitted, unrolling the magazine she held to set in front of her.

Samira looked down at the national weekly celebrity magazine. "What's this for?" she asked curiously as she eyed Rihanna on the cover.

"Follow the sticky note," Alessandra said, crossing her legs as she settled her body in the chair.

Samira felt a little apprehension. "I'm not really into celebrity gossip," she said as she opened the page. "Hell, I hate when *we* make the press—"

Alessandra smiled. "Looks good, doesn't he?" she asked.

Samira pressed her now trembling fingers to the headshot of Lance on the glossy page. "Really good," she whispered, taking in how ruggedly handsome he looked as he smiled proudly without a care for his scar. So confident and sexy.

"It's nice to see him *without* the hat."

"For the whole world to see without the hat," she said in awe.

"The interview is good, too," Alessandra added with an arch of her brow. "I think you'll agree."

Samira nibbled at her bottom lip, with her heart pounding and her nerves shot, as she read the interview with speed. He was promoting his newest release, *Danger*.

"'Lance Millner, who is just as well-known for being a recluse as for his literary accomplishments, explains the reason he stepped out of the public eye several years ago,'" Samira read aloud.

She gasped. Lance opened up about the car accident, his wife and daughter's deaths, and his scar, all leading to him becoming solitary.

"'The love of a good woman and therapy helped me overcome it,'" she read aloud.

The love of a good woman...

So that's why he never came. He'd fallen for someone else.

That hurt.

She closed the magazine and pushed it across the desk toward her sister-in-law as she put on a smile. "I'm happy to see Lance doing much better," she said, reaching for her glasses and blinking to keep even one tear from falling.

Alessandra pushed the magazine back toward her. "Why do you look as if you're smiling while constipated?" she asked.

She smiled harder, seeing the shadows of her cheeks rise beneath her eyes.

Alessandra recoiled and held up her hand. "No, you are giving off Joker from *Batman* vibes right now," she drawled.

Samira stopped smiling. "Joaquin Phoenix or Jack Nicholson?" she asked.

"A little of both," Alessandra emphasized with a shiver.

Samira playfully winced before she laughed softly. "That was a smile to keep from crying," she admitted, removing her glasses yet again.

"Crying for what?" Alessandra asked. "Lance loves you. He worked through his issues. He's made some major changes. It's time for your happily-ever-after."

"I'm truly happy for him," she said with honesty. "But I am not the woman he's talking about, and that's…okay. I haven't heard from him since the night he told me he didn't want children, so I am not the woman he loves anymore."

"Aw, Samira. I'm sorry. I thought maybe you reconnected recently."

She shrugged her shoulder. "Definitely not."

Alessandra eased her hand across the top of the desk to reach for the magazine.

"It's fine. Leave it," Samira said, turning to her computer. "I am still a Lance Millner fan and I am ordering a new copy of his book right now. I typed the first half, and I want to see how it ends."

"Too bad real life can't be written with the perfect ending like a book," Alessandra said, leaning forward to extend her hand.

Samira took it and gave it a squeeze. "Says the lady with the perfect ending to her love story."

"Not perfect, but good because of love, respect, hard work and lots of compromises," she insisted.

Assi walked in. "Excuse me, ladies," she said. "Ms. Ansah, I have your hot chocolate. Ms. Ansah-Dalmount, would you like something?"

Alessandra rose with a shake of her. "No, thank you," she said. "Samira, I will see you in the morning for our flight."

After the women left her alone, Samira immersed herself in work, distracting herself from the thought of Lance finding his happy with someone else. She failed at it so many times, having to tell herself, "Move on, Samira," and "Focus" to get back on track. Throughout meetings and conference calls, her sadness about Lance was there, pulsing beneath the surface.

Later that day her fingers paused on the keyboard and she glanced over at the magazine.

The love of a good woman...

She closed her eyes and rested her head in her palm. "Shit," she swore as the tears welled up.

She couldn't stop them, not anymore.

"I loved him," she whispered, reaching to the edge of her desk, where a white leather box held tissues, to quickly snatch a few before leaning back in her chair and dabbing at her eyes.

I love him. Still.

"Damn."

She whirled in her chair and looked out at light snow falling on the city. In the windows of the office building across the street, she could make out tiny lit trees or Christmas wreaths in the windows for those celebrating the season. "Merry Christmas to me," she muttered. "Thanks so much, Lance."

"You ready?"

Samira looked up to find her mother, Alessandra, Marisa and Ngozi entering her office. She cleared her throat as she balled the tissues up and tossed them into the wastepaper basket by her desk. "Hello, *everyone*," she said. "Ready for what?"

LuLu opened her closet and removed her coat and pocketbook.

Marisa and Ngozi gave Alessandra a meaningful stare.

"Fine," she said to them, before turning back to Samira with a smile. "Lance has a book signing in Manhattan tonight, and we all thought this is your opportunity to say whatever you have to say to him."

Ngozi held up both her hands. "In a public place."

"In case he wants that old thing back one more time," Marisa chimed in.

"No hugs, kisses and then long strokes," LuLu added drily, motioning with her hand for her daughter to rise.

"Y'all told *her* about that?" Samira asked, jerking her thumb toward her mother, who was now sliding her coat up her arms as if she were a child.

The women all shrugged, as if they couldn't help themselves.

Samira accepted her bag from her mother. "I don't have anything to say to Lance," she lied. "What if his new woman is there? What if I embarrass myself letting him know I even care that he moved on so quickly and publicly proclaimed his love for her when I had to slow-walk his ass to even leave his estate?"

"That sounds like some things that need to be said," Ngozi offered.

"And we're all here to support you in saying goodbye one last time," Marisa added.

Goodbye.

"He didn't even say goodbye," she said softly, mainly to herself. "Neither did I."

"Let's go, *ma poupée de chocolat*," LuLu said, leading the way out of the door.

Samira was a bundle of tight nerves and anxiousness as they all made their way to the elevator and then down to the lobby. Her mother's chauffeur-driven SUV awaited them at the curb. She was surprised to see Roje holding the door for them.

"I thought you retired?" she asked.

He chuckled. "I did. I'm not chauffeuring. I'm driving my fiancée," he explained, turning to hold the passenger door open.

LuLu smiled up at him before she scooped up her full-length mink and climbed in with the regality of the queen of England.

Samira barely gave it a second thought as she slid onto the rear seat beside Marisa with Alessandra and Ngozi on the third-row seat behind them. Soon they were being driven through the streets of Manhattan. She had no clue what the other women discussed to occupy their time.

She began to pant and pursed her lips to focus on exhaling and inhaling before she passed out.

This is crazy.

"Retouch your gloss, Samira," Marisa said. "And catch those flyaway hairs."

"And the purpose of putting lipstick on a pig headed to slaughter?" she asked, even as she opened her bag and removed her compact mirror and tube of lip gloss.

"Let him see what he's missing, dear," LuLu smoothly supplied from the front seat.

Samira caught Roje giving her an encouraging but worried smile in the rearview mirror, and she surprised herself by smiling back as if to let him know she was okay. She had to admit that she liked that he was concerned.

"It's right up ahead," Roje said.

Samira nodded as she eyed her reflection in the lit mirror to apply a fresh coat of a peachy shade. *You are crazy.*

She snapped the compact closed.

Roje double-parked. Through the windows of the big bookstore, she could see the large crowd in attendance to hear her Lance. *No. Not yours anymore.* Still, she was proud of him.

As the women all climbed from the vehicle and entered the brightly lit store, Samira's eyes went to the rows of seats facing a small stage with a podium. Annalise introduced Lance to thunderous applause, and Samira felt breathless as he stepped through a door and stepped onstage. Sans hat. He looked good. Really good.

Damn good.

"Good evening, everyone," Lance said into the mic attached to the podium.

She looked up at him as he glanced about the crowd with a warm smile.

"Thank you so much for coming out into this weather to see me. I truly appreciate it. I really do," he continued.

Samira pressed her hand to her chest and felt the pounding of her heart. "Do you see *him*?" she asked, turning around. She frowned to find none of the women still behind her in the crowd.

"Hi, Samira! It's good to see you."

Annalise.

Instantly she remembered the night the woman had so clearly worn her feelings for Lance on her sleeve. Perhaps she had finally won him over. She turned with reluctance. "Hello, Annalise," she said, barely able to muster any niceties into her voice.

The woman's expression became guarded. "Um, this is for you," she said, handing her a copy of Lance's hardcover book.

Samira eyed it as she strode away from her. It wouldn't fully close. She opened it.

Taped to the dedication page was a beautiful diamond ring beneath the words *Marry me.*

"Wait. What?" she said, touching the ring as her face filled with confusion.

And then she saw the dedication: *For Samira. Forever. For always. For love.*

She felt light-headed as she looked up. His eyes—those delicious brown eyes—were on her. Waiting. Assessing.

"I hope you all excuse me for just a moment while I handle some important business before we start the reading," Lance said, and then he stepped down and walked up the middle of the aisle to reach her.

Every person in the packed area turned to watch them, and murmurs floated through the crowd.

Lance pulled her close to him and lifted her body up a bit. "I had a lot of shit to get together, and I needed more than thirty days," he whispered near her ear. "Counseling helped, but I would not come back to you until I was ready to love you the way you deserve, Samira."

Samira closed her eyes and brought her hands up to press against his strong back.

"I thought you were done with me until Alessandra called to cuss me out for how she *thought* I treated you," he continued. "She also revealed you still loved me."

Oh, Alessandra, thank your nosy heart!

He released her with a kiss to her neck and then knelt before her.

Gasps and sighs swelled in the air. Flashes from phones of the attendees and the cameras of the press began to pop like crazy.

He took the book from her and removed the ring before reaching for her trembling hand. "I love you, Samira," he said. "Thank you for pushing me to be a better man. To be happy. To find the colors. I want to share the rest of my life with you. I want to have beautiful babies with you. I want you to be my wife."

"Awwwwww," several women sighed in unison.

I'm the one he loves. Me.

Samira stroked his cheek with her free hand. "I love you," she admitted. "I am speechless."

"Just say you'll marry me."

She nodded and used the back of her hand to swipe away an emotional tear. "I will," she whispered to him.

"She said yes!" someone exclaimed.

Lance rose and grasped the sides of her face as she rose up on her heels to meet his mouth. The crowd erupted in applause. Their kiss was brief but filled with their hunger and the familiarity of their unique chemistry. She suckled his tongue with ease, getting lost in him.

"That's enough, you two, you're in public."

Samira's eyes widened in shock as she broke the kiss at the sound of Alek's voice. She whirled to find the entire Ansah and Dalmount squad behind them. Quickly she hugged each one as Lance and everyone in attendance patiently waited. Her mother. Alessandra's aunts Brunela and Leonora. Alessandra, Marisa and Ngozi. Chance and his mother, Esmerelda. Her brother Alek, who held her niece, Aliyah, and then her brother Naim, who corralled a squirming Kwesi. And finally, Roje.

"Don't forget us."

Samira whirled again, and happiness lit her face as she squeezed Helena and then Lawrence to her before bending to plant a juicy kiss to Law's cheek.

"Let's get this book signing finished so we can celebrate," Lance said, reaching for her hand.

"Me?" she asked as he pulled her behind him toward the stage.

"Yup. You're not leaving my side," he promised her.

Lance reclaimed his spot at the podium, and Samira accepted the seat Annalise offered her.

"Congratulations, Samira," she said with warmth.

"Thank you," she said, feeling remorseful.

It must have shown in her eyes, because the woman gave her hand a brief but tight little squeeze before they both focused on Lance.

After the book signing and dinner with both their families, they returned to Lance's home, where, just inside the foyer, he lifted her up and turned to press her back against the wall as he kissed her deeply. Hungrily. And he was starved.

"God, I missed you," he moaned into her mouth.

Samira turned her head to break their connection. "Wait, we need to talk," she said.

"But—"

She lightly touched her fingertips to his mouth, stopping him. "Please," she insisted.

Lance nodded even as he shook away her touch and pressed light kisses to her cheek.

"Therapy?" she asked.

"Not done with it. At all," he added. "But it helped. You were right. I needed the time apart to get my shit together, even if it meant taking the chance to lose you. I had to find me."

Her eyes searched his. "I thought you gave up on us."

"I thought the same about you," he returned, feeling vulnerable.

She stroked his scar. "Yes, but Alessandra had to get involved?" she asked.

He saw her doubts and hated them even as he understood them. He'd had some of his own with each day that had passed during their separation from each other. "Alessandra accelerated the plan, but she didn't create it," he insisted. "I was coming for you, Samira. I purchased the ring a month ago."

She lightly bit her bottom lip, and that made his inches harden.

"Good," she said.

"Good."

"My family leaves for the Swiss Alps in the morning," she said with a wince.

"I know."

"Now what?" she asked.

"You invite me along," he said simply, with a face like "duh."

Samira chuckled. "You celebrate Christmas now?" she asked.

"Hold on," he said, with an arm around her waist.

She wrapped her legs around him and gripped his shoulders as he turned to stand in the entry to the living room. It was dark.

"Watch this," he said, extending his arm to hit the light switch.

He watched her face closely as she gasped in surprise at the abundance of colorful, brightly lit Christmas decorations. The works—a huge tree. Garland on the mantel. The sounds of soulful Christmas carols playing. Christmas scenes tucked away on tabletops. Colors galore.

He loved the sight of it all reflected in her eyes.

This was what Christmas meant to him again. Spending it with someone he loved who cared for him just as deeply.

"You like it?" Lance asked.

She nodded. "When you get your shit together, Lance Millner, you *really* get your shit together," she said, hugging him around his neck and enjoying the warm and spicy scent of him.

"Uh-oh," he teased, pressing kisses to her neck.

"What?" she asked as he carried her deeper into the living room.

"Hugs," he said.

He pressed his mouth down upon hers. "Kisses."

"And long strokes," they said in unison.

Samira awakened with her head on Lance's chest as they lay with limbs entwined atop the thick rug in front of the lit fireplace. His snores blended with the crackle of the logs in the firebox. She leaned up on one elbow to look down at him. She could hardly believe the day's events. She had found her happily-ever-after.

With a smile, she looked around at the festive Christmas decor as Teddy Pendergrass serenaded them with "This Christmas (I'd Rather Have Love)." She held her hand up and looked at her ring. "So true, Teddy," she whispered.

"You happy?"

She looked down to find Lance's eyes open and watching her. "Absolutely," she said.

He pressed her down onto the carpet and turned over to settle himself between her legs. "I will never get enough of you," he said, rolling his hips to slide his growing hardness against her leg.

Her eyes heated as she arched her back and presented her hard nipples to him to suck. He quickly obliged, drawing a raw, strangled cry from her that only hinted at her desire for him. "Lance," she gasped, clutching at his strong shoulders.

He kissed his way up from her cleavage to her neck as he slid his hand beneath her to lift her buttocks. She spread her legs wide and shivered as he used his strong hips to guide the smooth tip of his dick to her core. She licked hotly at his mouth before he deepened the kiss with a moan and thrust his hardness inside her.

"Ooh, that feels so good," she whispered.

He smiled down at her as gave her the last inch with a hard thrust.

She cried out. "I feel you," she gasped.

"And how does it feel?" he asked as he lightly bit on her chin.

"Hard."

He raised one of her legs up to rest at his shoulder and bent his own as he began to circle his hips, easing his length inside her with long tantalizing strokes.

"You're the gift that keeps on giving, huh?" she asked, her eyes glazed as he quickened the pace of his thrusts, each one more powerful than the last when he struck against her fleshy bud.

"Damn right."

"Merry Christmas to me," she said with a sultry smile.

She tilted her chin up and deeply kissed the man she loved before they both roughly cried out, clinging to each other as they gave in to their explosive and hot climaxes.

Epilogue

One year later

"Happy six-month anniversary, Mrs. Millner."

Samira smiled as she woke to Lance pressing warm kisses to her shoulder where they lay spooned in the middle of their king-size bed. Their bodies were nude, and the feel of his skin pressed against hers was the best way to wake up.

She glanced back at him over her shoulder with a slight arch of her brow. "I remember someone once said I would never be a *Mrs*." She reminded him of his earlier insult with the hint of a smile.

Lance chuckled. "He was a bitter and angry fool," he said, his breath whispering against her neck.

She shivered as she turned to lie on her back and

look up at him. "And now?" she asked, stroking his strong jawline.

"Now he's happy again," he said, his warm eyes locked on hers before shifting down to her belly, rounded with their child. Their daughter. Emmerson Ansah Millner.

"Just three more months," she said as he pressed his hand against the roundness.

Samira covered his touch with her own and looked over at the lit Christmas tree filling the corner of their suite in Naim and Marisa's chalet in the Swiss Alps. The twinkle of the white lights in the fading darkness as morning came was beautiful—even more so as she envisioned next Christmas.

"Do you think Emmerson will love Christmas as much as I do?" she asked.

He chuckled. "Impossible," he drawled.

"Right," Samira agreed.

He fell silent.

"Hey," she said softly.

Lance looked down at her.

"You good?" she asked.

He smiled and nodded. "I'm good," he reassured her, his eyes offering warmth because she understood holidays were still a bit difficult for him.

He was free of the fog of his grief and guilt, but she knew he missed them, and she would never ask him to hide that from her.

"Good," she said, raising her head from the pillow to press a kiss to his dimpled chin.

Six months ago, on a beautiful golden beach in Accra,

the capital of Ghana, Samira had wed Lance surrounded by their family and friends. The ceremony had capped off a week of the Ansahs, Dalmounts and Millners enjoying the West African country, reconnecting with her parents' family, savoring the food and strengthening their connection to their ancestry.

It had been everything she wanted and more. Something right out of a fairy tale. Magical, even.

Afterward she and Lance honeymooned on a secluded tropical island in the Maldives for another week before returning to Passion Grove to check on the building of their new estate on the land on Baby's Breath Lane. They'd moved in just a few weeks ago upon the completion of its construction and interior decoration.

She smiled to think of how badly she'd wanted the land for business, and but now it would be the foundation for her home. Her family.

"We better get downstairs," Lance said, sounding reluctant as he bent his body to quickly suckle one of her taut nipples into his mouth before he rolled away and rose from the bed.

She eyed his nudity as she did the same, promising herself a tryst with her husband after breakfast. "*Maman* promised you bofrot this morning," she said, speaking of the fried doughnuts he'd fallen in love with in Ghana.

"And they are best fresh out of the grease and not in your brother's or Roje's greedy hands," he said, quickly tugging on pajamas before striding into the adjoining bath.

Samira smiled, loving how close Lance had become to her family. Gone was the awkwardness and his isolation. He was one of the family, just as she had come to love his parents and little brother. She pressed a hand to her stomach and couldn't help but smile as she let it sink in that she really did have it all. Love, family and career. It had been worth every bit of the fight.

* * * * *

Kimber licked her lips in response before she could come up with a verbal challenge. "Only if you think Mrs. Claus wouldn't mind."

"This Santa is single." To prove it, Dario lifted his left hand and showed his naked ring finger. "Are you up for the position?"

"Highly unlikely that's going to happen," Kimber said. "This elf doesn't compete with the helpers in Santa's village."

"Aw, don't be like that," said Dario. He hopped down from the carriage and loomed over her. She wasn't intimidated at all, not like he was trying to be intimidating. He just wanted to call her bluff. "You're the only elf for me. But if you play your cards right, you could be sitting beside me next Christmas."

Kimber pressed her hand against his chest, in part to stop him from leaning forward for a kiss, which he was known to steal from her. A few she gave up, especially when she purposely stood under the mistletoe in her apartment.

"I doubt that as well," said Kimber, "but I will take you up on the offer for a ride back to the apartment."

"Great." Dario reached down to wrap his arms around her waist. Before she had the chance to protest, he'd placed her on the red cushions of the sleigh.

Having your story read out loud as a teen by your brother in Julia Child's voice might scare some folks from ever sharing their work. But **Carolyn Hector** rose above her fear. She currently resides in Tallahassee, Florida, where there is never a dull moment. School functions, politics, football, Southern charm and sizzling heat help fuel her knack for putting a romantic spin on everything she comes across. Find out what she's up to on Twitter, @Carolyn32303.

Books by Carolyn Hector

Harlequin Kimani Romance

The Magic of Mistletoe
The Bachelor and the Beauty Queen
His Southern Sweetheart
The Beauty and the CEO
A Tiara Under the Tree
Tempting the Beauty Queen
Southern Seduction
A Tiara for Christmas

Visit the Author Profile page
at Harlequin.com for more titles.

A TIARA FOR CHRISTMAS

Carolyn Hector

I would very much like to dedicate this book to one of my dearest friends, the badass cancer-kicking middle-school teacher Mrs. Larina "Mickey" Cornelius.

Acknowledgments

To my friend Kaia Alderson-Tyson, my #DestinDiva, who thought of me in a tiara-making video a long time ago, which sparked Dario's hobby. Thanks, girl!

And I would like to thank the fabulous authors who came before me like Beverly Jenkins, Brenda Jackson and Kristan Higgins. Their constant kind words and actions of support have meant the world to me.

Dear Reader,

It's time for the final crowning!

A Tiara for Christmas is the last book in the Once Upon a Tiara series with the closing of the Kimani line. It's been a wonderful ride and I thought I'd end it with the girl—now grown-up—who stole our hearts (and a dress) in the first book of this series: Miss Kimber Reyes. I love a good friends-to-lovers trope. I thought it would be great to give Dario Crowne, bachelor party-boy heartthrob, a taste of his own medicine by sending him to friend-zone hell.

A Tiara for Christmas is my tenth book with Harlequin Kimani. It has been such a wonderful journey. I thank you all for taking the time to step into my world by reading and supporting my books.

Best,

Carolyn

Prologue

Was it a crime to find Santa sexy? Kimber Reyes picked up the pep in her step down the cobblestone streets of downtown Southwood, Georgia. In her defense, this Santa in particular wore a red jacket with the sleeves ripped off and the buttons undone. One could imagine the bulging muscles of Santa's biceps hadn't fit in the velvety material. Kimber wrapped her green vest a little tighter and buttoned it just under her breasts for the perky effect. Instead of wearing the felt flats with brass bells and the curved tips at the toes for holiday spirit, Kimber had switched into her black heeled sandals to better show off her Santa-inspired pedicure.

Dario Crowne's back was turned as he fiddled with whatever was in the giant red Santa sack in the back of the custom-designed sleigh. Twin cream-colored horses stood in front of the sleigh with their heads bobbing up and down at the sight of Kimber rounding the corner. She guessed they were on edge after spending the early part of the evening being fawned over by the hundreds of children excited about a visit from the North Pole.

"Whoa, whoa, whoa," Santa Dario called out, turning to grab the black leather reins.

Their eyes met. Kimber smiled past the butterflies in the pit of her stomach. It wasn't like this was the first time she'd laid eyes on Dario. For heaven's sake, she saw him less than half an hour ago. The faux white beard now hung around his neck, revealing the dark five-o'clock shadow across the tawny hue of his chiseled jawline. The fact he'd worn no shirt under the Santa jacket drove her insane with wanton ideas. Flat dark hair covered his navel and abs, disappearing down into the black belt of the suit.

"What did you say?" Kimber asked with a raised brow. She stopped at the side of the sleigh.

Dario leaned over and offered Kimber a lopsided hundred-kilowatt smile. "I said whoa, not ho."

"You're funny," Kimber said, rolling her eyes.

"And you're the sexiest elf I've seen all day."

"Considering there were elves from the seniors center as well as the high school football team," she said, "I'll take that as a compliment."

"You should." Dario extended his hand for her to take. "C'mon up. I'll take you back to your place. I left my car at the farm. You can ride back with me."

Every time Kimber came back home to Southwood, Dario took it upon himself to escort her wherever she needed to go. Kimber didn't mind. She liked
driving around in the classic muscle cars he and his
brothers restored. Truth be told, she hated driving
down some of the streets in town, especially the one
where her parents had died over six years ago. At
least when someone else drove, she could close her
eyes for a moment.

"In the sleigh?" She cocked her head to the side.
Dario had been a busy man today, passing out presents at the children's wing at the hospital on top of
everything else. The kids had all received gifts—in
green wrapping for boys and red for girls, but a red-
and-white-striped box with a big white bow on it appeared to have been left behind.

It was on the tip of her tongue to inquire about it,
but then Dario's grin deepened, revealing an undeniable dimple that peeked through the dark mask of
facial hair as he answered her question. "That's up
to you."

Kimber licked her lips in response while she came
up with a verbal challenge. "Only if you think Mrs.
Claus wouldn't mind."

"This Santa is single." To prove it, Dario lifted his
left hand and bared his naked ring finger. "Are you
up for the position?"

"Highly unlikely that's going to happen," Kimber
said. "This elf doesn't compete with the helpers in
Santa's village."

"Aw, don't be like that," said Dario. He hopped

down from the sleigh and loomed over her. She wasn't intimidated at all. He just wanted to call her bluff. "You're the only elf for me. And if you play your cards right, you could be sitting beside me next Christmas."

Kimber pressed her hand against his chest, in part to stop him from leaning forward for a kiss, which he'd been known to steal from her. Although she'd given a few up, like when she purposely stood under the mistletoe in her apartment.

"I doubt that, as well," said Kimber, "but I will take you up on the ride."

"Great." Dario reached down to wrap his arms around her waist, lifting her onto the red cushions of the sleigh.

Kimber clapped her hands together with excitement. In response, Dario raised a brow.

"What?" Kimber felt the heat of her blush touch her cheeks. "Can't a gal be interested in a horse-drawn carriage?"

"Sure. Okay, it may take a minute to get out there."

Kimber shrugged her shoulders. "Cool with me. You know Charlotte and Richard just got engaged."

Dario nodded and took hold of the reins again. "I heard. Good for them."

"True, good for them, but those two have been celebrating every chance they get. And don't get me wrong, I love that they're together, but I did come back to the apartment so I could study for exams. Instead, I feel like I'm back in my dorm room."

"Well, you know me," said Dario. "Whatever it takes to spend time with you, I'm down."

Even though his eyes were on the road, Kimber rolled her own again. Dario wasn't known as a playboy for nothing. Bold women in the street now waved and called out Dario's name. Some even extended their pinky and thumb up by their ears to tell him to call. If Dario noticed, he didn't let on. He kept his eyes on the road in front of him and guided the sleigh through the town.

There weren't a lot of people on Main Street. Probably a good thing, Kimber thought, considering his open jacket flapped in the wind. She sidled closer to Dario for warmth.

"I have a blanket back there if you'd like," he offered.

"I'm good, unless I'm making you uncomfortable."

Dario shook his head quickly. "Nah, I like this. Your little girly hands around my biceps."

"If you bend over to kiss your muscles, I'm hopping out."

Tightening his arm so those muscles flexed under her hands, Dario bellowed a deep laugh that caused the horses to take quick steps forward. "You're the only woman offended by my hard work."

"This—" she dug her nails into his skin "—is hard work?"

"Ouch, and yes."

"I am sure your fans love your dedication." Kimber sighed.

"Again, the only person I'm concerned about impressing is you."

They fell into a lull of silence when the horse's hooves stopped clicking on the streets and thumped against the clay road through the forest, heading toward the farm. A full moon tried to peek out from behind the pine trees and the bit of cloud cover in the lavender sky. A cool wind crept through the air. Somewhere in the distance, someone had a fire going.

Thankful they could avoid County Road Seventeen, the road most traveled by everyone, Kimber cuddled closer to Dario. "Thanks for being a good sport today and dressing up as Santa. Even if you did it without a shirt on."

"Hey, I kept my jacket buttoned until the end," Dario defended himself.

"And the sleeves? I suppose they ripped off when Miss Britney and one of the mothers were fighting over you." Miss Britney was notorious for hitting on every hot man, single or not. It wouldn't be so bad if she wasn't an elementary teacher.

Dario looked down to face her. "Miss Britney and Andrew to be exact."

Kimber couldn't help but laugh. "Okay that doesn't surprise me." Andrew, her aunt's right-hand man at Grits and Glam Studios, had very good taste, after all.

"Does this mean you're giving me the benefit of the doubt?" Dario bumped his shoulder against hers.

"No, there was another coat you could have put on," said Kimber, pushing back.

"I was already getting ready to leave," he replied, "so I didn't see the point."

While it made perfect sense, Kimber could imagine if the incident had happened earlier in the afternoon, Dario would still have finished the day wearing the sleeveless coat. In the last two years before she left, she'd given up trying to keep it at the friendship level and dabbled in the occasional kisses here and there. A man like him did not settle down—which was perfect, since she was the type with no relationship goals.

As she reflected on their months of uninhabited flirting, Kimber realized the wheels of the carriage had stopped moving. When she glanced up at Dario, she half expected him to be looking at her. Instead his gaze was focused ahead on the opening in the parallel oak trees in the distance, adorned with twinkling white lights strung up to warn motorists about nearby deer. Without need for an explanation, she knew exactly what had caught his eye.

Instead of the usual spectacular Southwood golden sunset, the sky had turned bright red. Strips of thick white clouds floated against the crimson background.

"It's a candy cane sky," Kimber announced. "Let's take a selfie." She pulled her phone out of her elf costume's pocket.

Dario covered her hand with his. "I'm not taking a selfie. Let's just enjoy the sky."

"You're such a fuddy-duddy," she argued. "I'm taking one with or without you." She turned for the perfect pose. After finding the right angle she snapped the photo with Dario's back. "You're dressed as Santa but you're truly the Grinch."

"Yet you wouldn't have it any other way." Dario leaned back and kissed Kimber's shoulder. She happened to capture that on camera also.

"Whatever." Kimber shrugged. She glanced at the time in the upper right-hand corner of her phone.

Dario nudged Kimber's side. "You still haven't heard about that internship?"

She shook her head and tried to ignore the disappointment rising in her chest. If she got the call, she'd be working down in Miami at the headquarters of MET, Multi-Ethnic Television, as a junior correspondent. She could work anywhere, but this was the dream. "No. Today was the last day for them to call."

"They'll call."

"It's after five. I doubt it."

Dario reached around and lifted Kimber back until she leaned into his lap. Kimber let out a squeal but let her body be moved. "I've got something to help you celebrate the call."

"We can't celebrate," Kimber protested. "It's bad luck or something."

"Then how about this," said Dario, lifting her hair off the shoulder close to his massive chest. Through her half-closed lids she understood why Dario was such a sought-after man. He had a way of making a woman feel dainty and feminine. She watched him lick his lips. "We can call this a Christmas present."

Kimber swayed close to his face. "It's Christmas Eve. Still too early."

"Woman." Dario sighed. He dropped his hand from her shoulder.

Chills ran down her spine. He leaned forward, and taking the cue, Kimber crossed the ultimate line. She pressed her lips against his. For a man who oozed masculinity, his lips were soft and succulent. When he drew his head back in surprise, panic raced through her veins as she realized this might not have been what he meant by a present. "Oh my God," she exclaimed. "I'm so…"

Anything else she wanted to say died on her lips. Dario's hand slid to her backside. His other hand reached around her torso and caressed her face. Their tongues touched and his minty taste filled her mouth. Liquid pools of desire soaked her to the core.

Eager, Kimber maneuvered herself to straddle his lap. Her hands caressed the hard muscles of his bare arms, the veins in his biceps under her fingertips. The red velvet pants did nothing to hide the bulge of his erection against his thigh, and Kimber's heart raced with excitement. The green felt material of her costume tore as she spread her legs to wrap around his waist.

Dario leaned forward and feasted hungrily on Kimber's neck. The warmth of his breath tantalized her being. Kimber locked her ankles around him when he stood up and changed positions. The seat back dropped and she found herself lying down. Dario stood long enough to rip the Santa jacket off his body. Kimber lifted herself to her elbows and cocked a sandaled foot against the edge of the seat, and a gasp left her lips when he reached for the black buckle of his belt.

A wild look filled Dario's coppery eyes while he kept his focus on her thighs. He reached into a small pocket of his pants to extract a foil packet. Apparently a man like Dario never traveled without protection. His hand gripped her extended leg and pulled her toward the edge of the seat. The movement caused what remained of her skirt to roll up higher, exposing red panties with a bow on each hip. In a matter of seconds, he'd torn one side of the flimsy material. The rip of the fabric didn't even faze her. The only thing she wanted was him.

Dario slid the red pants over his narrow hips and brandished exactly what she'd felt through the fabric. The cool air of dusk filled her lungs. The anticipation while he slipped on the protection nearly killed her but when he grabbed her by the other ankle and positioned himself between her legs, it was well worth the wait.

The skittish horses shifted, causing the carriage to rock.

Dario pulled Kimber up by her lower back with his left forearm and she arched her spine for a better fit. Her inner walls hugged him like a glove. Kimber's hands gripped his shoulder blades and pulled her mouth to his neck and he moaned against her collarbone when she nibbled his earlobe. As the sun disappeared behind the pine trees, Dario made love to every inch of her body. Her toes ached from curling so many times. They'd definitely crossed the friendship line now, and for once in Kimber's life, she found herself imagining how perfect life could be with one man.

Satiated for the time being, they rode together in silence toward the stable. Once they came out of the forest, Kimber's phone began to ping and ping and ping again. For a moment she was confused and irritated by the disturbance to her afterglow. Unraveling her hand from the crook of Dario's elbow, she slid her finger to check her messages flipping it off camera mode. Three missed calls and five text messages. Best to start with the voicemails and then read the messages.

Kimber put her phone on speaker and hit Play.

"Ms. Reyes, this is Rory Montgomery calling from MET Studios in Miami. We are reaching out to see if you can get to Atlanta to cover a speech at the governor's mansion at six. We understand this is last minute but after going through our list of intern applicants we realized this would be the perfect introduction to the MET network."

Kimber's heart sank. It was after seven now.

"Kimber, where are you? Pick up your phone."

That message came from her aunt Amelia. The five text messages were from her aunt, as well. The final voice mail on her phone broke Kimber's heart.

"Ms. Reyes, this is Rory calling again from MET. We apologize for the last-moment request and hope we're able to connect next time. We'll call if something should come up again."

Kimber turned her face up to Dario. His mouth

opened for what she assumed was an apology. She held her hand in the air.

"Forget it. If I hadn't been out here with you, I would have had the perfect job."

"Kimber, that's not fair. How was I to…"

She held her hand up again. "Save it. Maybe you don't want to put your business degree to use in whatever it is, urban development, because you'd have to grow up and quit partying all the time. But I worked my ass off in school and now I just lost the best internship possible. I gotta get out of here."

Chapter 1

Eleven months later...

It took a few minutes for Kimber Reyes to cram herself and her rolling suitcase into the already crowded elevator, even longer if you counted the time she'd been standing there on the seventy-second floor waiting for one of the elevators to arrive. There'd been no scientific proof that Dubai's tallest building had begun to sway, but the longer Kimber waited, the more she was sure she felt it.

The others crammed into the compartment from previous floors had not been pleased to be joined by Kimber and her luggage. When the doors opened, a gentleman in a silver suit in the back-left corner had sighed heavily. The man in the Stetson beside him had clenched his jaw as he focused on Kimber standing there.

She'd just smiled smugly and waited as Stetson man and suit man squeezed themselves against the back wall to make room. The women on the elevator, however, didn't give much ground, and one huffed audibly when Kimber's phone began to ring as soon as the doors had closed behind her. Kimber reached into a deep pocket of the long-sleeved black maxidress decorated with red roses and pulled out the pink-bedazzled device. She'd set the ringtone to "Jingle Bell Rock" just after Thanksgiving last week when Uncle Stephen had sent a photo of her aunt Lexi and aunt Amelia doing their own rendition of the festive song.

"Hey, Aunt Lexi," Kimber said cheerfully. Her mood had already lifted at the sight of Lexi's smiling face in the saved-call ID photo.

"Did I catch you at a bad time?"

Kimber gave a side-eyed glance to her left and then right. "No, not at all," she lied. "What's going on? I was just getting ready to head to the airport."

"What time does your flight leave?" Lexi asked. "You're coming back home, right?"

Gnawing on her bottom lip, Kimber shook her head. "I have a few stops I want to make before returning for the holidays."

"Oh."

The single word, more like a disappointed sound, told Kimber everything she needed to know. Something was the matter. "What's wrong?"

The elevator shot down a few more floors before

the doors opened again. Kimber's stomach trembled along with it. Less than ten years ago, she'd received the horrific news that her parents had died in a stupid car crash while avoiding a deer on County Road Seventeen back home in Southwood.

"Nothing's wrong, per se," began Aunt Lexi. "Things would be much better if you were to come home sooner than Christmas Eve. Preferably in the next twenty-four hours or so."

"What?"

"I just proposed a Christmas pageant at the Christmas Advisory Council and I would love it if a few of my former belles could stand with me. You're available, right?"

"What do you mean by *available*?" She didn't have to ask really, Kimber thought with a pout.

"Single belles, single belles," Lexi sang into the phone, "single all the way."

The punishment for not being married in Southwood was being appointed an official errand runner and party planner. It was a high price to pay but Kimber wouldn't trade it for the world. She never wanted to settle down with anyone. She knew Lexi didn't have a lot of options because everyone Kimber knew was married now and probably busy over the holiday season. "Great. So what you're saying is, I'm a loser."

"I'd never put it like that," said Lexi.

"Well, you know I love you and I'll do whatever you need."

"Great. I've checked the flights. There's one leaving in two hours. I'll order the ticket now and leave it in your name."

Kimber took a deep breath. That meant in twenty-four hours she would find herself face-to-face with the man who'd sent her running from Southwood. *Dario Crowne*. The thought of his name made her knees weak.

"Sure," Kimber said sweetly. "You know I'd do anything for you."

"Great. I'll see you soon."

Kimber disconnected the line at the same time as the elevator doors opened on the ground floor. It took her as long to get out as it had taken her to get situated in there. At least, until struggling with getting the wheeled luggage to move forward she realized the Stetson dude held on to one side.

"Allow me to help," he drawled.

"Help? You're the one causing the problem," Kimber huffed and gave her suitcase one hard yank. She stumbled in her black sandal stilettoes but caught her balance. "No thanks. I've got this."

The man looked beyond Kimber's frame, then held his hands up in surrender before backing away. She sighed in relief. While the cowboy was hot, she didn't have time for a fling before heading back home. Besides, there was no other man Kimber could imagine touching her like…she grimaced, hating the man.

Thankfully, something shiny caught her eye—a small child wearing a gold-colored crown with red "rubies" on the points.

One of the main reasons Kimber had taken the

Miss International Pageant Beauty Beat job in Dubai was to uncover the mysterious designer of the sweet donation of tiaras around the hospitals in South Georgia. Between her experience with pageants and her degree in journalism and linguistics, she'd been a shoo-in for the reporter position at the blog, posting and updating the latest pageant news.

In the pageant industry, a few designers created platinum crowns set with Swarovski crystals as prizes for the winners. As Miss Florida International Sweetheart, Kimber had encountered many such treasures during her travels around the nation.

Kimber believed in giving back to her community. When her parents had passed away, it felt like everyone in Southwood and the surrounding cities came out to support her and her sister, Philly. She'd paid it forward by volunteering at Four Points General Hospital where she worked in the children's wing, brightening up the kids' days.

Just over a year ago, a box of beautifully crafted handmade tiaras had appeared in the hospital just in time for the pageant event Kimber was organizing for the girls in the long-term wing. No one knew who'd left them. There was no note or sign of where they'd come from. They'd just appeared, and the craftsmanship was amazing. Shortly after initially seeing the crowns, Kimber had started spotting people wearing them on Instagram. Kimber wanted to give one of the beautiful tiaras to her aunt Lexi. She owed everything to her uncle Stephen's wife. If it hadn't been for Lexi,

Kimber was sure she'd have ended up some entitled brat, shoplifting for the thrill of it.

A young American mother reached for the little girl's hand before she had a chance to leave the concierge desk. Kimber could spot an American a mile away. They were usually dressed in more revealing clothing than that of the local women. Kimber loved her bodycon dresses as much as the next woman, but Dubai was not the place to wear them, out of respect.

It took Kimber a moment to move. Her eyes focused on the way the mother reached for her daughter, all the while talking to the man at the desk. A lump formed in her throat, recalling the way she would step too far from her mother as a child. She couldn't explain the telepathic way Kimber had known to take her mother's offered hand as a child, even when her mother wasn't looking. By the time Betty died, Kimber had been too cool to hold her mother's hand in public. She regretted that the most. Sniffing, Kimber took a deep breath and focused on the family in front of her. The little girl with the tiara skipped away from the gold fish pond over to her mother's side.

Kimber dragged her bag behind her and made her way to the mother-daughter duo to get the scoop on where she'd purchased the tiara. Whenever she thought she was on to something, her palms itched. And her palms itched right now. The closest Kimber had come to the tiaras, besides the local beauty queens back home, were the budding beauty queens from some of the cities she visited while in the Dubai area. No one she spoke with could recall where the tiaras came from. Kimber began to wonder if it was a conspiracy to keep from exposing the designer.

Kimber had the tiaras inspected and learned the jewels were not real but a step above Swarovski and cubic zirconia that made up some tiaras. These man-made crystals were manufactured by the Assadi Association and were also sold at Assadi Jewelers here in Dubai. Kimber understood that the Crowne family back in Southwood had a connection to Aamir Assadi, a sheikh from this area with an American education. It would make sense for Kimber to ask the Crownes what they knew about the mystery tiaras and Aamir, but she wasn't exactly on speaking terms with the Crownes at the moment. Things with Dario had ended so awkwardly, she wasn't sure how to broach the subject—especially since it'd been a while.

"Excuse me," Kimber said, gently tapping the mother on the shoulder. "I don't mean to interrupt your check-in, but I was hoping I could ask you a question."

The American lady turned around and smiled, clearly happy to recognize the familiar accent. "Oh, thank God, you can ask me anything you like if you'll get this man to understand I have a reservation for this afternoon, and I want to check in early. I'm getting nowhere."

Having stayed there several times already, Kimber knew the concierge, Omar, spoke and understood English well. She pressed her lips together and gave him a look. Omar returned the look with a raised eyebrow. Mentally she got it. The American lady wasn't being friendly. Kimber switched to Arabic. "Stop playing, Omar. I need to ask this lady a question."

"What's the English word for obnoxious?" Omar asked back.

"Fine." Kimber sighed. "I'll make sure you're my special guest when I come back for the next pageant."

Satisfied with that, Omar handed the woman her keys and smiled sweetly.

"Thank you," the woman responded. "Now what was it you wanted to ask me?"

"The tiara," Kimber replied, glancing down at the young girl. "Did you get it locally?"

"I guess you can say that," the woman answered. "My husband works at American Hospital Dubai and these were under the tree for the sick kids."

The little girl didn't look sick one bit, but who knew? She may have healed well. "I'm sorry. Looks like she's on the mend."

"She isn't sick. She just wanted a crown," said the mom. "So we grabbed one."

Listening at the desk, Omar snickered loud enough for Kimber to hear. She narrowed her eyes in his direction. Kimber turned her attention back to the mother. "Thank you very much for your time. Merry Christmas to you both."

"Anytime," said the woman. "And if you're looking to make your own, I noticed there's a jewelers right across the street."

"What are the odds?" Kimber wondered out loud. "Thanks again."

Kimber dragged her bag behind her and headed

out the revolving doors into the bright sunny afternoon. What were the chances she'd find what she was looking for right in front the whole three months she'd been here? Dario Crowne popped into mind. Again.

The idea of going home must really be getting to her. Ah, but if she were there, the weather would certainly be different. It was December and here she was in Dubai, wearing a thin dress. Southwood this time of year might not ever see snow but she'd have on a thin sweater, at least. Hiking her purse higher on her shoulder, Kimber inhaled the warm air.

"Are you leaving us already?"

Kimber glanced up at Kal, the doorman, and flashed him a smile followed by a pout. "Alas, my time here has come to an end, at least for now."

"My days will be less bright," Kal replied. "Are you heading back home?"

"I am," Kimber answered.

"We're going to miss seeing your pretty face around here," Kal added quickly.

"I'll miss you guys, as well." Kimber thought fondly of Kal's counterpart, Raheem, who worked the evening shift. Kal stepped to the corner and raised his hand for a taxi, but Kimber stopped him. "That's okay, I'm going to run across the street for a minute before I head out."

Kal held up the traffic so she could cross the busy street and head toward the building the American had mentioned. The thirty-story tower didn't stand as tall as its neighbor across the street but maybe it did hold something more powerful than the hotel. The secret to the tiaras.

As she entered the building, a breeze of air conditioning was a welcome contrast with the temperature outside. Flying while sweaty was not something Kimber wanted to do. It was bad enough when other people did it; she didn't want to be a hypocrite.

Kimber scanned the directory of names, reading the English version next to the Arabic. She found a jeweler on the third floor and headed toward the elevator, but not before noticing the Assadi last name in English. Her heart began to race. Her journalistic senses were telling her she was on to something. Confident, Kimber pressed the elevator button and took a deep breath. She was about to uncover one of the biggest stories in her pageant career.

"You're looking pretty soft there." Dario cocked his head to the side for a better view on his laptop's monitor of his twin brother "How much did you eat while you were at Dom's?"

Wiping his hand down the face similar to Dario's own, Darren frowned, then groaned. "I ate everything, including the baby's food."

Their older brother's wife, Waverly Crowne, had recently given birth to a baby girl, Maddie, and Dario couldn't wait to hold her and also see her siblings, his niece and nephew. Twins Justin and Ariana were three, a fun age. The Crowne family had gathered for Thanksgiving while Dario was still away in Dubai working on an urban planning proposal, which he'd turned in this morning. Biting the inside of his cheek, Dario picked up a green tennis ball and tossed it in the air. He hated the idea of missing out on family time.

"Are you trying to show me how fit you are?" Darren asked with a droll sigh. "I swear I can see your heartbeat in that tight-ass shirt you're wearing."

"I am just pointing out that you look like the Before ad in a gym membership, while I am the result of fine fitness." After making a catch, Dario chuckled and flexed his biceps as further proof through the fabric of his gray-striped oxford shirt.

"Whatever," Darren said. "I'll hit the gym tonight."

"If you wait, I'll be there after dinner. I need to make sure we retain our title as Kings of the Rocking Around the Christmas Ring at Christmas Chaos this year." Dario scanned the contents of the manila envelope on his desk and checked all the signatures. His cellphone sat upside down on the desk, ignored as it buzzed away.

"Yeah," Darren grumbled, "don't remind me. I've already caught the fire department jogging through the town like a military troop, cadence and all."

Two years ago, Dario and Darren had created the twisted underground holiday, Christmas Chaos, held at their older brother's ranch house. It was a Yuletide-themed mashup of *American Gladiator* and *Fight Club*. Rule number one: tell no one about Christmas Chaos. They invited most of the single parents they knew, some they'd dated, so they could take out their frustrations during candy cane duels, obstacle races and on the Santa piñata. It had become more competitive when they invited the guys they hung out with at the gym. Some of the guests weren't even parents, just alone at Christmas. There was a lot of aggression for parents to work out when they didn't have their kids over the holiday break. Dario and Darren didn't have children of their own, but they were single. Christmas Chaos was a way to get everyone together and have fun.

The black rectangular phone continued to vibrate against the solid black oak wood desk. A red light blinked on his office phone, and through the window of his closed door, he could see that his secretary, Ilaria, was pressing her face against the glass to peer inside.

Darren blinked and looked upward. "Is someone trying to get in touch with you?"

"I think so."

"I can let you go," offered Darren.

Dario had been out of the country for almost a year, but he'd made sure he made time for his family. That meant no interruptions, and typically his staff adhered. "I'm not sure, hang on a second." Dario turned his attention away from the laptop and waved Ilaria into his office.

"Sir," Ilaria said meekly, "I know this is your family time, but you said to interrupt you if it was a particular emergency."

"I did?"

"Sir." This time Ilaria cleared her throat, then stretched her dark eyes wide. "She's here."

"Who's here?" Darren asked through the monitor.

Not sure whether to answer him, Ilaria shifted her feet from side to side. "Miss Reyes."

Dario's heart lurched in his chest. The last time he'd seen her, she'd made it clear she needed to focus on her career. Guilt still riddled him for causing her to miss that phone call for the internship she wanted. But what caused him more pain was how she'd left without looking back or saying goodbye.

"Kimber Reyes?" Darren repeated. "She's in Dubai?"

"She's been in the area for a while, working on a string of beauty pageants," Dario answered too quickly. He cursed himself for letting out that bit of information.

Darren laughed and shook his head. Dario's misery over his first heartbreak annoyed his twin and their sister, Alisha. "Even overseas you're weak for her."

"Shut up, it's not like I've seen her," said Dario, flipping his brother off with his right hand, just out of Ilaria's sight. "Ilaria, where is she?"

"She's downstairs at the jewelers, inquiring about the crystals."

Great, Dario thought with a groan. Kimber was on the hunt for answers. Answers he wasn't ready to give her just yet.

Last year, Dario had brought Kimber and her Miss Southwood crew up to Four Points General Hospital to get the kids to participate in a mock pageant show. The dude who was supposed to supply the tiaras upped the cost at the last minute. Since Dario was good with his hands, he'd gone into his garage, welded a few crowns together with materials he had around the place along with a few "gems" from his sister's costume jewelry.

It wasn't like he'd never fixed things for kids before. Despite the wealth the Crowne family had now, their upbringing was filled with ramen meals and disappointment. Dario and Darren got by with a football or basketball, but Alisha was often teased for not having the same toys as her friends. She had one fashion doll.

As a child, Dario put together cars, built homes and fastened together crowns out of scraps of metal. Their father, however, did not care for Dario spending his time building things for dolls, even if it was for his sister. Dario had always enjoyed the sense of accomplishment from the time he received his first building blocks to his first model car. His father called them "man things," even though he never did anything around the house. To get his point across, John Crowne often took his belt to Dario's backside to make a man out of him. But seeing his sister smile was worth the beatings. And getting Kimber to smile had been important too. He'd gone back to the hospital with Kimber the following visit, carrying boxes of dresses. When he had a moment alone, Dario had set the prototypes tucked in one of the boxes, down on the bed of a girl who was about to be discharged. Kimber was so in love with the crowns and the gesture he was sure he'd won brownie points, at least until he realized he never left his name on the box.

He'd come very close to taking responsibility, but

there was something about the pure joy on Kimber's face that day. It was like she'd witnessed a Christmas miracle, and he didn't want to rob her of any of the magic of that moment. That, combined with how pleased the little girls receiving the gifts were, had influenced him to continue to make them and had them delivered anonymously, maintaining the mystery and magic.

He was man enough to admit he was going to great lengths to try and impress Kimber, even if he wasn't taking any of the credit. She was the only woman to make Dario regret the bad-boy reputation he'd had when he joined his brother and sister in Southwood. She'd seen through his charming grin and called him out on his BS. It was probably the reason he'd been so in love with her. They'd had more than a moment that last Christmas before Kimber broke everything off to focus on her career. She had some nerve blaming him for messing up her internship when she ended up landing a perfect position after all.

Darren took advantage of Dario's silence. "Why is she there looking at crystals, Dario?"

Dario pushed away from his desk, grabbing the clicker to open the cabinet hiding the pyramid of monitors positioned to view various spots around the city to study traffic flow and pedestrian congestion in order to see how he could improve the city. The one in the center captured the image of the lobby and front entrance. He rewound the recording, and sure enough, Kimber sauntered—she always sauntered—into the lobby and strolled right over to the listings.

"She's inquiring about the jewels," Ilaria went on, "and wanted to know who has been buying them in bulk and where they were shipped to."

"Is she talking about the crowns you make?" Darren's voice came from the laptop. "Dude, you still haven't told her?"

"Should I tell her we'll send someone down there to answer her questions?" Ilaria asked.

"Hell no," Dario said quickly. "Stall her while I get out of here."

"Dodging Kimber?" Darren laughed. "It's a Christmas miracle."

Dario moved around the desk. "The miracle will be you being able to walk once I'm done with you in the octagon when I get back tonight." With that, Dario disconnected the face-to-face call and chuckled to himself.

"Sir?" Ilaria stood, wide-eyed and confused.

"I'm heading home a little earlier than planned, Ilaria," said Dario. "Go ahead and shut the office down and have yourself a nice paid break until I get back after the New Year."

For the first time in Kimber's life, no amount of flirting or batting her lashes got her past the support staff at the closed gates at the Dubai International Airport. Kimber's little mission to find the buyer of the jewels had been fruitless, and on top of everything else, she'd missed her flight. On any other occasion, Kimber wouldn't have minded reverting to her original plan to return home later in the week, but this was for Lexi. And Kimber owed Lexi everything.

Defeated, Kimber considered going to relax in the Zen Garden or heading over to the private lounge for a drink to help her decide what to do next. The latter won. Hiking her purse up, Kimber headed toward the bar. She stopped when she spotted a familiar figure commanding attention. A wave of women parted down the corridor, then stared at the back view of the man walking toward her dressed in a fitted dark blue suit.

A second wave flowed through Kimber then. Shock and then jealousy. All these women and a handful of men dared to lustfully stare at him—her man. Or who might've have been her man. Kimber stood with her hand on her hip and the corner of her bottom lip between her teeth as he approached, waiting for him to acknowledge her presence. When he did as she expected, their eyes met. There he was. In the flesh. Her Dario Crowne.

Kimber offered him a shy smile. Their last parting hadn't gone so well. After an evening of pure bliss, she'd left him. The whole point of hanging out with Dario had been his reputation around Southwood. It was no secret he didn't want a commitment. Neither had she, which was what had made their friendship perfect. Kimber wasn't going to fall for his swagger and he didn't cave when she batted her lashes.

When they crossed the blurred friendship line Kimber had panicked. She'd needed space from him, but not out of regret. Her need for that internship intensified even more when she realized how deep her feelings for Dario might grow. She'd never wanted to settle down, be a mother or stay in Southwood. But Dario's kisses had had her rethinking everything she'd worked hard for. Instead of telling him the truth, that her feelings for him scared her, Kimber had told him she needed space to concentrate on her career. She'd thought he understood. But judging by the way his lips twisted now, from a smile to a flat, unfriendly line the moment he laid eyes on her, maybe he hadn't understood. Her heart quivered with disappointment. This was not her day.

"Kimber," Dario said with a cool tone in his deep voice.

Kimber pretended to shiver. "Dario, why so frosty?" She lifted her arms for a welcoming hug. "Oh my God, it's so good to see you." There was no mistaking the way he barely leaned over to make contact or the half-assed way his hands wrapped around her waist. Kimber had to lift herself up on the balls of her feet just to get a semi-decent hug. He smelled delicious, like spiced Christmas. A sigh of disappointment escaped her throat when he pulled away.

"I'm shocked to find you here," Dario said.

"I just finished a job with the Miss International Pageant."

Dario cocked his head to the side at her baggage. "And now you're on to the next. What is it? The Big Four?"

Beaming, Kimber pressed her hand against her chest. "Aw, you remembered."

"Are you waiting for your plane?" Dario nodded toward the gates. "I think you're in the wrong area. That's heading back to the States."

"I'm in the right spot," she replied. "I'm heading home, not to the next pageant."

"To Southwood?" Dario asked with wide-stretched dark eyes.

"That is home," Kimber said, nodding her head. "Lexi needs me."

His thick brow rose in concern. "Is everything okay?"

"Oh yeah. She is starting up a Christmas pageant and needs some help organizing. So I'm heading home."

"For the holidays?"

"Yeah." What was wrong with him? she wondered. "Where are you headed? Back to Southwood also?" Kimber pressed her hand against his sleeve and couldn't help but feel the bulge of his biceps. She bit her bottom lip for a moment. "You might be out of luck. The plane just left. Thankfully, I still have a flight booked for later this week, but I don't know how I'm going to break the news to Aunt Lexi. I promised I'd try to get there today but I was sidetracked by something sparkly." She didn't want to say what for fear of evoking an eye roll from him. Dario used to love teasing her about her collection of tiaras.

Dario let out a deep sigh. "I'll take you back."

Something about his words felt more like a forgiveness. Kimber scrunched her nose in his direction. "What?"

"To Southwood, Kimber. You need to get there, right?"

"Yes," she answered in a slow tone.

Dario nodded his head toward the empty waiting area. A half dozen uniformed flight staff walked through the silver barred door. The wide window gave a view of a sleek airplane.

"What's that?"

"It's your ride home, if you'd like."

Kimber blinked in disbelief. The Crownes made quite a pretty penny restoring classic cars. But owning a plane? As if Dario had read her mind, he sighed in annoyance. "The plane belongs to Aamir."

"The sheikh?"

"If it pleases you to know," said Dario, "fine, yes. Aamir Assadi's plane will take us back to Southwood and no, before you think about asking, he won't be joining us."

Kimber felt herself pull back from the bristle of his tone. Apparently the way they'd parted was worse than what she thought. The flirting banter they used to share was gone.

Licking her lips, Kimber swallowed her hurt pride. "Looks like this Christmas is starting off just right," she said with sarcasm oozing.

Chapter 2

Since he was the one who'd had Kimber stalled at the jeweler's, causing her to miss her flight, Dario couldn't help but feel responsible for making sure she arrived in Southwood in time to meet up with Lexi. That's who he was doing it for—Lexi, not Kimber.

Dario allowed Kimber to travel up the steps to the jet in front of him. Weak, his eyes traveled to her backside and his body responded in a typical adolescent way. Watching her hips sway from side to side, Dario told himself no man in the world would blame him for falling under Kimber's spell.

At least they were finally boarding. A change in the flight manifest had caused a thirty-minute delay. Now Kimber could have her pick of the seats and he could sit as far away from her as possible. No mile-high club here, he sniffed while watching Kimber's profile as she turned to face the seats. Her tongue darted out and licked the bow of her top lip. His body stiffened and beckoned him to touch her one more time.

"Nope," Dario said out loud before he could catch himself. An attendant at the back of the plane stopped what she was doing. He half smiled and raked his hand over his head. "Sorry."

"Is everything okay?" Kimber asked turning toward him.

Dario began to follow her farther down the aisle but stopped once enough space was between them and took a window seat to the left. He set his briefcase on the empty seat beside him. The long flight ahead gave him plenty of time to finalize his plans for the new school and tutoring center he'd been working on. Leaving early hadn't been wise, but a necessity.

"So, what's going on with you?"

The voice came too close to Dario's ear. He turned to find her peering over the empty seat beside him. "You should buckle up. We're going to take off in a moment."

"Dario, it's an almost twenty-hour flight. You can't be this cold to me the entire time and not talk to me."

Dario pinched the bridge of his nose. "I have a lot of paperwork to go over, Kimber."

Kimber clamped her hand down on his shoulder. He flinched at her touch. As if feeling the tension, she pulled her hand away. "Geez, it's that serious, huh?"

"What?" Dario turned in his seat to face her. Kimber's long, dark lashes fanned against her high cheek-bones. When she opened them, he recognized the true obliviousness behind her hazel eyes. In an instant, he realized what a jerk he'd been for being so cold to her. When she'd ended things, he'd had all the opportunity in the world to tell her he didn't want things to be over between them. His cowardice about admitting she'd hurt his feelings shouldn't have spoiled the friendship they did have.

It wasn't like he was one to acknowledge how he felt. His father had made sure he and his brothers never expressed their emotions—that was for the weak. Pushing all that behind, Dario curled his flatlined scowl into a smile. "I'm good. I'm sorry if I've been distant. I just have a lot on my mind. I shouldn't take my frustrations out on you. You have nothing to do with it," he lied.

"Like a job interview overseas?" Kimber smoothed her hands over his shoulder.

Thank God for the thick material masking the ripple of goosebumps she evoked. "Job interview?"

"Yeah," she said while her fingertips traced the lapel of his blazer. "I never thought you'd trade in your coveralls but I guess a man can't lie under a car forever."

Dario inhaled deeply. "And here I thought we'd spent some good times under a car."

Nodding, Kimber grinned and moved from around the seat behind to sit next to him, handing him his office work. *Of all the seats on this plane*, Dario thought again and then corrected himself. She was not to blame for their year-long radio silence.

"Oh my God," Kimber burst out and grabbed his arm. "I gotta tell you about how I was able to fix this Jeep's battery connector with a twist tie."

"That's not safe," Dario began.

"I know, but it got us far enough to get the car looked at." Kimber beamed and flashed a row of perfectly straight, white teeth. Her lipstick was red, the same color as the roses on her dress. He always wondered how she coordinated such a thing.

"Which beauty pageant were you off to cover?" He asked the question but knew the answer. Just because he hadn't been speaking to her didn't mean he hadn't kept keep tabs on her and made sure she was safe while in a foreign country.

Kimber pressed her lips together to think about her answer. "I was off to Miss Earth. We were scouting some of the local villages, which were putting forward their beauty queens, ya know. But when we stopped for gas, I noticed the clerk had a bracelet with those same ruby jewels from those mystery tiaras back in Southwood."

"I see," Dario said, calming the beat of his heart as it began to accelerate. He sat up and loosened the knot in the tie choking him at his throat.

"You remember how they mysteriously showed up at the children's hospital and around South Georgia, right?"

"I guess." He feigned boredom. "You're still asking about that?"

For a second Kimber poked out her bottom lip to pout. Her brows furrowed together in confusion. "Of course I am. There's a story behind them."

No story, Dario thought. He'd just wanted to do something nice without taking the credit. "Yeah, but weren't the tiaras dropped off anonymously? Do I even need to mention the keyword in that question?"

"So?" Kimber asked with all sincerity. She blinked and her long lashes fanned against her high cheekbones. "Someone that talented needs to be exposed."

"Why?" Dario responded quickly. He recovered with a cough. "I mean, don't you think if this person wanted to be found out, she'd have said something?"

"Or he," Kimber said with a knowing smile.

Dario's heart slammed against his chest. "You think a man made them?"

"I wouldn't rule it out," said Kimber, squaring her shoulders.

"It sounds as if you have an idea." Did she know it was him? If she did, why wasn't she asking him a thousand questions like the reporter she was? The plane began to taxi the down the runway and the flight attendant reminded them to buckle up until they hit altitude.

"I traced the jewels back to Dubai, and I was thinking, since you know Aamir Assadi, maybe you've heard something about it?" Kimber asked with a sly smile.

Dario just shrugged. "I doubt Sheikh Aamir has time to concern himself with something like that."

Kimber apparently remained unconvinced. "Well, I have all Christmas break to work on it."

"You say that as if you're not staying in Southwood after the holidays," said Dario, not sure why the idea bothered him. He'd left. Why couldn't she?

Kimber twisted her lips and shrugged. "Who knows what will happen? I'm having a blast doing what I do, ya know?"

"I do," he agreed with a head nod.

"But hey! At least we can hang this holiday."

As Kimber went on about how excited she was to spend Christmastime in Southwood, Dario allowed himself to be sucked back into Kimber's world. While he'd just vowed to himself not to hold on to his anger, that didn't mean he needed to fall head over heels in love with her again. Kimber had made it clear she had no desire to be in a relationship with one person.

It was ironic, because in the past, Dario had been the one to avoid settling down. And there was a long line of women back in Southwood waiting to get reacquainted with him. He glanced down at his phone to see a number of texts he'd missed from the single—and not-so-single—ladies in Southwood who'd apparently just received word he was coming back for the holidays.

The rest of the ride went as well as could be expected. After Kimber told him everything she'd been up to, she settled down, ate the provided meal—turkey sandwiches—and settled in to watch a movie on her tablet. At some point, Dario felt the weight of her head while she rested against his shoulder. Finally able to show some form of emotion, Dario smiled to himself.

Around midafternoon the plane began to descend onto the airstrip just outside of Southwood, Georgia. The runway was actually more often used for testing out the acceleration of the vehicles he and his brothers restored. It was a hobby that had turned into a lucrative business, Crowne Restoration. From the air, the landing strip appeared to be a giant P, with the curved part for testing tires in high-speed turns.

Out of habit, Dario peered out the window. An oversized garage stood at the end of the test track. Inside were thousands of chrome and steel tools, from wrenches, to saws, to power drills. Excitement pulsed through Dario's veins. A year was too long to be away from his toys.

Beside him, Kimber still rested her head on his shoulder. She'd filled most of the flight telling him about her travels. Dario enjoyed listening. At one point however, she stopped talking long enough to fall asleep. He wondered if he should wake her up. Behind the garage was a ranch-style home that sat on fifteen acres of land. A few cars were parked in the circular driveway. As the plane descended over the house, he noticed three truck beds filled with boxes, most likely for the Christmas Chaos party—something Dario did not want Kimber to know about. Fortunately, he recognized the long gold Cadillac that Lexi Pendergrass Reyes drove around town as it pulled into the circular drive.

"Wake up, sleepyhead," Dario whispered. Instead

of sitting straight up, Kimber did a cat stretch across him. Her forearms brushed against the zipper of his slacks. The slight gesture awakened his body. He pointed out the window. "I believe your aunt is already here waiting to get you."

"How did she know?" Kimber asked. "I didn't have the heart to tell her I missed the flight."

"I took care of it before we left," he said.

Suddenly Kimber smiled. "Funny, I was just dreaming about Aunt Lexi and the mystery tiara maker."

"Oh really?"

"Yeah, I realize there's another reason for me to find her or him." Kimber stretched once more before she rose from her seat. "I've decided I've got to get Lexi the best present in the world—a custom-made tiara."

Dario gulped. "Is that right?"

"Yep. And I won't stop until I find her," she replied. "Or him."

"I didn't expect to be able to drive just down the road to pick you up," said Lexi, interrupting the awkward silence after they entered the car.

Kimber hated the way things were between her and Dario. A year ago, he'd been one of her best friends. Before they took off from Dubai, he'd sworn there was nothing wrong between them but his hasty goodbye when they deplaned left her wondering. He didn't invite her or Lexi into the house for a drink or something to eat. Instead, he acted more like he needed them to hurry up and leave.

"Kimber?"

Blinking back to focus, Kimber shook her head. "I'm sorry, what did you say?"

"I was just curious about how you ended up flying home with Dario of all people." Lexi flipped her blond hair off her shoulders as she looked both ways before entering the tree-canopied two-lane road.

In all her travels, Kimber had missed this scenery, the flickers of sunlight shining through the trees. Tearing her gaze from the leaves, Kimber sighed. "I'm sorry. I missed the flight you booked for me."

"How?" Lexi gasped. "I thought you were on your way to the airport anyways."

"I know but I was distracted," Kimber started. Did she want to tell her aunt that she'd been distracted by something shiny? No, part of the reason Kimber had wanted to leave Southwood was to prove to her family she'd become a responsible adult.

Lexi shook her head and laughed, then reached over to tousle Kimber's hair. "Oh, Kimber, I've missed you so much."

"I missed you too."

"Tell me how you ended up on the plane with Dario. And are they making so much money now that they own a plane?"

"It belongs to a family friend," Kimber explained and then told her aunt about running into Dario at the airport and how he was kind enough to bring her home.

"You two were always so close," Lexi noted. "What happened?"

Hot, steamy, unadulterated sex, Kimber thought,

but decided not to mention that part to her aunt. "I needed to take a break from here, you know, focus on my career and all. I missed the opportunity for my internship, which led to this fabulous life of mine."

Lexi cut her eyes over at her niece. "Was it fabulous when you missed the last three Southwood holidays?"

In truth she did miss being home for the holidays, especially Halloween and taking her little sister and their cousins out trick-or-treating. Their neighborhood went all-out for the holiday with scary haunted houses and spiderwebs crossing from house to house. "I did," Kimber admitted, "but at least I can say I had turkey in Turkey last week."

"Oh, did the hotel do something nice for the American guests?"

"I'm not sure." Kimber shrugged. "Maybe someone from the pageant circuit felt sorry for me. Room service brought up roasted turkey, mashed potatoes and some dressing." There was no mistaking the eyebrow that lifted above Lexi's sunglasses. "And no, it was not the same as home."

"You're in luck. I happen to have a batch of cornbread dressing in the freezer for you."

"Thank God!" Kimber leaned back against the leather headrest. More of the suburbs came into view as the canopy road thinned out. "I've missed being back home."

"Good to know. And you've been missed here. The kids are cleaning their rooms just for you," said Lexi.

Kimber laughed. "That is so wrong. You know I don't care what their rooms look like."

"Hey, don't knock my motherly blackmail. I couldn't exactly get them to clean their rooms by not letting them join the annual Christmas cookie decorating contest this week."

After a good laugh, Lexi turned the car into the neighborhood Kimber had once called home. She'd always had mixed feelings about this place. Before her parents had passed away, Ken and Betty Reyes had fought often. Loudly and passionately. As a child, it had made her stomach roll with anxiety; she was never sure what to expect when she got home. Would she find them arguing in the kitchen or making out on the couch?

Kimber didn't think she'd ever want to settle down with one person, not if it meant fighting like that. Her uncles, Stephen and Nate, had showed her that couples could be happy long-term, but she still didn't trust her DNA. She was not meant to be in a monogamous relationship with someone. At the first sign of a disagreement she was sure to hightail it out of there. The men she dated all seemed to understand her stance and preferred it too. But Dario's tight-lipped smile at her twenty-four hours ago still stung. She'd been relieved when he'd said his mind was on work, but something still felt off.

The Cadillac slowed down and turned into the driveway of the Reyes home. Oh, the changes that had occurred. Kimber's eyes glanced up at her old bedroom window. She smiled to herself, recalling the frantic way her uncle had decided to install bars on her window specifically. Just because Kimber had foolishly decided to wear a rather adult dress to a party to impress an older boy at school, Stephen had gone all militant and barred her room, banned her from leaving the house and even had the nerve to try and take away her cell phone. At the time, he was a bachelor, clueless about technology and sim cards and young teenagers—and the drawer she had filled with phones. Kimber smiled to herself.

The front door burst open and banged against the four-digit house number. Three small children, two young boys and a girl, raced down the steps toward the car. A much taller and more mature preteen jumped off the top of the porch and outran the little ones to get to the passenger door. Kimber rushed out and screamed just as Celie had in *The Color Purple* when she was reunited with her sister, Nettie.

Even though she spoke with her sister via video-chat every week, there was nothing like holding her in her arms. The last time she'd physically seen Philly, the girl had been five inches shorter and still a tomboy. Judging by the sparkly lip gloss and red body glitter across her face, a lot had changed.

Everyone thought Kimber favored their mother, Betty, but her sister reminded her so much of their mom. That woman used to go overboard with the fun makeup. Kimber remembered helping her mom try to get her beautiful light brown eyes done up just right. They had been exactly the same color as Philly's. They also both loved to hug and right now, Kimber did not mind.

"You gotta promise me you'll never be gone so

long again," Philly cooed while Kenny, Angel and Victor wedged themselves between them.

Kimber reached down and embraced her cousins with big hugs that ended with her swinging them around in the air. After her parents died, she hadn't thought it was possible for there to be so much joy in the household. Her uncles and aunts were sure to make every day special for them. Uncle Nate had the special ability to transform homes. He used to live in the two-story home before getting married. Then he and his wife bought the property behind them, fenced in both homes to create a fortress with a swimming pool in between the houses.

The toddlers grabbed Kimber by the hand to show her the fun stuff they'd made for her. As they approached the house, Stephen clutched his heart as he stepped out onto the porch. In pure dramatic form he stumbled backward into the doorframe. "Is it truly my number-one niece?"

"Cute, *Tío*," Kimber said, feeling her heart fill with love.

"He's been so excited to see you," said Philly, coming up behind Kimber. "He's been in the kitchen all day."

Kimber took a step backward and shook her head. "Oh hell no," she blurted out.

"Swear jar," the toddlers chorused.

Giggling, Philly scratched her face. "Don't worry, he's just making beans and rice. *Abuela* has been on the phone with him most of the day making sure he stirs the pot."

"Is that my Kimber?"

Everyone turned toward the voice in the driveway. Lexi closed the door to her car and headed over to the black SUV where Amelia, Uncle Nate's wife, hung out the window.

"Speaking of stirring the pot," Stephen mumbled.

Kimber grimaced at him before crossing the surprisingly still-green lawn to greet the rest of the family. "Amelia," Kimber cried with joy. Kimber wasn't sure if she'd ever have learned to love journalism if it weren't for Amelia. The part-time producer for the MET Network had piqued Kimber's thirst for uncovering the truth her senior year in college. For four years Kimber had worked on her degree and exhibited her natural talent for investigative journalism.

"Oh, sweetie!" Amelia cried. "It's so good to have you home."

"Thanks, Amelia. It's good to be home."

"I finally know how Nate feels every time I'm off on assignment," said Amelia.

The man in question, Nate Reyes, appeared and swooped Kimber into a big bear hug. He was over six feet tall, looming, even with her in heels. Prior to the Crowne men arriving in Southwood, Nate had been the town heartthrob. Then he'd met Amelia.

"I've missed you, kiddo," he said after he set her back down on the ground.

"Be careful with her," Amelia fussed, swatting her husband on the arm. "An opportunity is opening up again. A field journalist."

Butterflies fluttered in Kimber's stomach. "Are you serious?"

"I wanted it to be a Christmas surprise for you, but

I thought it would be best to let you know now in case they want to try you out for a broadcast."

Kimber bit her bottom lip. She'd enjoyed her time covering beauty pageants for the last year. The circuit took her all over the world and she wouldn't have traded it for anything, but the shot at a job at MET would be outstanding.

"You're not going anywhere, are you?" Philly asked with panic in her voice.

Stricken with guilt, Kimber reached her arm out to embrace her sister. Philly clung to her side. "You're stuck with me," Kimber told her. *At least for the holidays*, she thought. She'd find time this month to break things down for her sister, explaining about not wanting to live in Southwood for the rest of her life.

"Have your uncles seen this?" Amelia asked, tilting Philly's face toward the sun.

Kimber's eyes followed to where her aunt looked. The red body glitter now appeared more like splotches. "What kind of glitter is that?"

"I didn't put glitter there," said Philly, pulling her face away. "What?"

Nate inspected his niece's face, as well. "Is that what I think it·is?"

Stephen came off the porch to see. "What are we looking at here?"

Amelia, Lexi and Stephen chorused, "Chicken pox."

"Why would you bother giving *her* a ride home? Does Aamir know you had her on his plane?"

A little teacup pig sniffed at Dario's ankles, drawing

his focus away from his sister's rant. Alisha Crowne did not care for many people in the world. Kimber Reyes definitely hadn't made the cut.

He sighed and sat up to scratch Hamilton, the family pig, under his chin, then shook his head at his sister in the kitchen of their family's downtown Southwood three-bedroom condo. With the way Christmas Chaos had grown, Darren had taken over the ranch house to make preparations and if Dario wanted any rest, he had to come here and endure his baby sister.

"Drop it, Alisha," Dario warned.

"You were pitiful to watch whenever she came into town during her college breaks, following her around like a lost puppy," Alisha continued. She slammed pots and pans around in the kitchen.

Dario sat up further to grab a thin slice of red pepper from the plate of crudités Darren had left for him, probably thinking there'd be some sort of twin connection where Dario would go along with this strict diet of no processed foods, sugars or alcohol with him. *Fat chance*, he thought, feeding the pepper to the pig.

"And that stuff is for you to eat, not Hamilton," Alisha went on.

"I'm not eating it. I've got a burger on the way." Dario picked up his cell phone to track the delivery service. "It should be here..." he paused to watch the footsteps of the delivery person in the parking lot "...any minute now."

"Good. That gives me a few minutes before you stuff your face to tell you about the job we have to do for Dominic."

At the mention of their older brother's name, Dario's interest was piqued. "What's going on?"

"Since you and Darren have destroyed the ranch house, Christmas is going to be held here this year," Alisha announced.

Excitement raced through him. Dominic had gotten married a few years back and now he and his wife, Waverly, had a set twins, Justin and Ariana, plus a new baby, Maddie. If Dario had been made for anything, it was to be the world's best uncle. Justin, a replica of all the Crowne men with his reddish-brown hair, already showed signs of being interested in the restoration craft. The tyke-sized toy Mustang model Dario had given him last summer for his birthday was already put together and painted. Much to her mother's dismay, Ariana also loved being in the garage and getting grease under her nails. Waverly would have preferred Ariana take after her mother and enter a beauty pageant, but the three-year old wasn't having it.

The thought of pageants brought Dominic's thoughts back to his beauty queen. He pictured Kimber seated at her family's table, giving them the details of how she'd tried to find the designer of the tiaras. He couldn't let that happen. What he needed to do was figure out a way to hang out with Kimber every day while she was in town just to monitor her investigation. And manage to not fall in love with her again.

As if following some odd little-sister intuition, Alisha slammed her hands on the table. "Are you even listening to me?"

"No," Dario admitted.

"We're going to have to get this place in Christmas shape for the twins."

"So do it." He sighed.

Alisha gritted her teeth together. "How am I supposed to do it? I can hang decorations, but I don't know the first thing about babyproofing. You guys did all that for me."

It was true. Because their father left the family when Alisha was still young, the boys had tried to help their mother whenever possible. Mary Crowne had worked three jobs just to keep a roof over their heads. Dominic worked from an early age until he got a scholarship he couldn't turn down. Dario and Darren did their share, finding jobs, as well. They all worked together to make sure Alisha never knew the struggle. Now he regretted going along with indulging her.

"It's about time you learn," said Dario. The doorbell rang and his stomach growled. He hopped up and trod across the hardwood floors to the door. "Thank God. I thought you'd gotten lost," he said, opening the door without looking through the peephole.

A young delivery boy stood there, a red blush across his face, holding a brown bag with grease stains on the sides. Rather than the bag being stapled closed with the receipt clipped to it, it was open. The smell of the burger wafted to Dario's nose. "Why is my bag…?" The words stuck in his throat when Kimber stepped out from behind the kid. She reached into the bag and extracted a long french fry. Steam rose from the center when she broke it in half.

"Sh-she said you wouldn't mind."

"I did," Kimber admitted. "You don't, do you?"

"There are consequences for eating a man's fries," Dario warned. He snatched the bag from the kid. "You better be glad I already tipped you."

Kimber draped her arm over the boy's shoulders, causing a deeper blush. "Which is why I gave him an extra tip for going along with it," she said.

Poor kid, Dario thought. He knew all about the effect she had on a man. "Whatever, thanks."

The delivery boy scatted down the hall toward the red exit sign. Kimber giggled and turned her head back to Dario. His heart thumped against his chest.

"To what do I owe the pleasure, Kimber?" Dario asked.

"Kimber?" Alisha grunted from the kitchen.

Kimber grunted. "She still hasn't moved out?"

Dario leaned against the doorjamb in the hopes of blocking the insult from making its way into the kitchen. As much as Alisha couldn't stand Kimber, the feelings were mutual. They were close in age but at different stages in life. Each judged the other for it. Breaking the tension, Hamilton came over to the door and licked Kimber's ankle. *Lucky pig*, Dario thought. "Didn't Lexi take you back to the house?"

"Chicken pox," Kimber said with a shrug.

The memory of being itchy and splotchy all over made Dario take a step backward. "You have them?"

"No—Philly." She gave her head a vigorous shake. The bun on top of her head came loose. As she combed her fingers through her dark hair, Dario felt the only thing missing was her doing it in slow motion with a fan blowing. He cleared his throat and focused on what she said. Her little sister, Philly, had just been diagnosed. "And since they can't recall my ever having them, they thought it was better for me to stay at Lexi's old apartment for a couple of weeks until the outbreak is over. The little ones may have it too."

"Oh, okay," said Dario.

"Yeah, so it looks like you've got a new neighbor for the holidays."

As the words sank in for Dario, Alisha came up behind him.

"Oh good grief," Alisha snorted.

Chapter 3

Kimber shuffled through her apartment in her fuzzy pink slippers and matching terry cloth robe on Wednesday morning after finally getting a good night's rest. The events of the last twenty-four hours played over in her head, and the cause of the restlessness was none other than Dario Crowne. Thank God her battery-operated boyfriend was in her suitcase. The humming sensation mixed with the incredulous face of her former friend had sent her into a much-needed sleep.

The sound of the grandfather clock against the wall ticked throughout her quiet apartment. Well, technically the place belonged to Lexi. She'd owned it before marrying Stephen and it just stayed in the family and came in handy when someone needed a place to stay. Kimber hated not being home with the family.

At least being in this apartment gave Kimber time to go over all the paperwork Lexi had handed her so she could get started on the Christmas beauty pageant. Thankfully, Lexi had started everything almost a year ago. Waiting to announce it to the council the other night had been smart. The town would have driven her crazy with contestants trying to get the upper hand.

Finding a comfortable spot on the couch, Kimber picked up the portfolio. Over the next few weeks, Kimber needed to secure the odds and ends of the pageant. They were going to hold it downtown at the theater. The stage would need to be set, and they'd need judging tables, backstage changing rooms, prizes for all the participants and of course, the trophies and tiaras. That last item reminded Kimber of her need to find out who was behind the mystery tiaras. Not only would getting a custom tiara made for Lexi be great, but it would be fantastic to have a few set aside for the runners-up at the pageant.

Kimber bit the inside of her cheek and sank further into her spot on the sofa. For some reason, her mind wandered back to Dario. Even though he'd said they were cool, there was something off about their friendship. Was he seeing someone now? Was that why he kept her at arm's length? It had to be serious if he was ready to push their friendship aside.

When she'd popped over to the Crownes' apartment, Kimber had half expected him to invite her inside. Instead, Dario never moved from the doorjamb. Had she lost her friend forever? Had their sleigh ride ruined their friendship? Kimber stretched her body out until her toes popped and curled. The simple movement reminded her of last year. Toes curling and everything. Despite her stance on relationships, Kimber had spent weeks after their tryst trying to get over him. She'd spent her entire life fighting relationships and then she was—one magical moment under a romantic sky had her rethinking everything. It was simple lust. That was all.

And now she wanted more. Perhaps that was the point of going over to his place last night. If Alisha hadn't been there, Kimber definitely wouldn't have turned down the opportunity to be with him again.

A rap at the door brought her out of her thoughts. Her heart flittered. She knew that knock. Dario. Could he sense her desire for him? Pulling herself out of the sofa cushions, Kimber headed toward the door and found him standing there, dressed in a pair of black baller shorts and a fitted black shirt. Sweat gathered at his brow and steam rose from the covered coffee cups from the shop down the street. Kimber smiled, happy he still remembered.

"Good morning," he said in his deep baritone voice. "I figured you might not have had time to pick up groceries, let alone some coffee."

Kimber opened the door farther and stepped aside so Dario could enter as she checked out his firm backside. *Damn*, she thought. He looked sexy as hell in a suit, workouts and naked too. Licking her lips, Kimber followed him into the kitchen where he set her drink on the bar. "So," she said, grabbing her cup, "you're just out and about delivering coffee?"

"Darren and I went for a run."

Excited, Kimber smiled. "How is he? Why didn't he come over with you?"

"He's crawling back into bed," Dario replied. "He hasn't been working out since I left."

The Crowne brothers were known for their fitness. They even had the local titles in the boxing ring down at the gym locked down. "How long have you been away?"

"Enough that he can't..." Dario cut off whatever he was going to say with a shake of his head. "Never mind. So what have you been up to all morning?"

"You make it sound as if it's the afternoon."

"Feels like it, I've been up since five. I'm still jet-lagged." Dario put a cup to his lips and she nodded, since she understood the tired feeling. "What have you got going on today?"

Kimber waved her hand toward the living room and her stack of binders. "A lot of pageant work, or at least, follow-up."

Dario nodded his head but said, "I have no idea what that entails, but sure."

"It's okay, you don't have to. What about you? I mean besides working out and getting sweat all over my kitchen floor?"

Taking a step to the side, Dario checked the white tiled floor. "I'm not."

"Your sweaty shirt is on my counter though," Kimber pointed out.

"So picky," Dario said, pulling his shirt over his head. "Better?"

Muscles rippled, sweat glistened in the light spilling into the kitchen. Kimber pressed her lips together to keep from licking them. "Rude," she mumbled.

"I can put the shirt back on."

"No—no," she responded too quickly. "I mean, whatever, you don't want to wear a sweaty shirt. I'm sure there's something here you can put on."

Dario frowned. "Pass. Are you busy inside all day?"

"Not this morning. I've got the Christmas Council this evening," said Kimber, "and before that I need to pick up a few deposits. Want to come and pretend you're my enforcer?"

"Sure, why not?"

"Well," she started, "because all the women in Southwood might be upset over you being out with me instead of making the rounds. I'm not sure if I'm up to having everyone mean-mugging me."

"You're not funny."

"Where is the lie?" Kimber teased him. "You can't tell me women weren't hanging out their windows with you and Darren running the streets this morning. How many hot meals do you think will be hand-delivered to your place?"

Dario drained his coffee. "A few casseroles were dropped off at the garage and now you've got this whole story going on in your head. You should write fiction."

The way he downplayed it made him look like an angel. But an angel did not have the sexual prowess Dario possessed. Kimber shivered and ran her hand over the back of her neck. "You forget we were close,"

Kimber reminded him, skirting across the thin line of friendship they crossed. "I was once hip-checked at the fair when standing in line for the Ferris wheel."

"And I didn't see some guy with a fifty-dollar bill ready to spend at your kissing booth last year?"

If Dario was trying to make a point out of the incident, it was moot. When that stranger put down fifty, Dario had broken out his black card and booked the whole afternoon with her. Proceeds went toward the local back-to-school drive. Kimber and Dario spent the afternoon hanging out being silly and practiced kissing—for viewing eyes' sake. It had been a win-win situation for Kimber.

Kissing Dario had been perfect. If only he hadn't made such sweet love to her last year that she'd gotten all in her feelings.

"Why are you staring at me like that?" Dario asked.

"Dang," Kimber hissed, hoping to cover her lust by rolling her eyes. "I was just staring."

Dario shrugged his shoulders. "Don't make things weird between us, Kimber," he said.

"I still feel like there's a big elephant in the room," she said. She took a sip of her coffee. "I hate that things changed between us."

"We're good, Kimber." Dario assured her with a half smirk. "I wouldn't be here now if we weren't."

Though he said it, she didn't believe him. "About last year."

"Save it," he said, holding his hand up. "You needed to focus on your future. I was the reason you didn't get that internship."

"I shouldn't have said you were the reason," Kimber clarified. "I wasn't in a place to take the call."

"Because of me."

"You didn't force me," Kimber confessed. She licked her coffee-scented lip. Her eyes grazed over his body once more. "I was a willing partner in all of it, everything that evening."

Dario's eyes flashed with excitement. "Why do I have the feeling I'm still the reason you made your decision to leave?"

"Dario," she began, setting her coffee cup down on the counter by the sink. "I was always planning on leaving Southwood. I grew up here. I can't stay here forever."

As he scratched the back of his head, Dario's biceps bulged. His barbed-wire tattoo stretched with his skin. Kimber had never thought of herself as a tattoo kind of girl. Most guys from Southwood participated in the rite of passage with a tattoo here or there but their contours on Dario's sculpted body covered him. He pressed his hand to his chest, right next to his heart and the tattoo of a jail door. Guarded heart.

"I didn't ask you to move in with me or marry me last year, Kimber," he clarified. "We only crossed a line we knew was coming."

"You think?" She challenged him with a lopsided smile, knowing it was the truth.

"I know." Dario returned the smile with a cocky grin. "I'm just stating facts. You hung out with me when you were home from college. I wouldn't mind hanging out with you again while you're here."

Bubbles rolled in the pit of her stomach. "I'd like that, Dario."

"It sounds like you're about to add a 'but.'"

"I am," she said, nodding. "I want to make it clear that I do not plan on staying here after the holidays. If things go my way, I may get that dream job with MET after all."

"Kimber, that's great news. We need to go celebrate. I heard Miss Vonna already has her new cupcake flavor."

Heat touched Kimber's cheeks; she was happy to have her friend back. They used to make sure they were first in line at The Cupcakery. And while she'd attended college a few hours away in Tallahassee, Dario and Kimber had made a pact to pick out a best-selling book to read and discuss when she returned to Southwood. Kimber missed riding around in the cars he and his brothers restored, belting out songs. Being back home with Dario by her side made getting through the holidays sequestered away from the chicken pox house bearable.

"Dark chocolate with a peppermint frosting and actual peppermint sprinkled on top," Kimber told him. "Philly already showed me—she was eating one when we video-chatted."

"What are we waiting for?" Dario asked, stepping forward.

"Uh, for you to take a shower and me to at least run a brush through this mane." To make her point, Kimber loosened her dark hair from the messy bun at the top of her head. She closed her eyes while shaking the tresses free. When she opened her eyes, she caught Dario's lingering gaze as well as his physical reaction through the mesh basketball shorts. Considering the electricity between them, Kimber wondered if it was possible to renegotiate the lines of a friendship.

Oblivious to the silence in Lexi's apartment, Dario rushed through the place in dire need of an ice-cold shower. He hated to admit how much he was going to miss the three-way shower in his apartment in Dubai. There, the water had blasted him from both sides of the shower walls and down from the ceiling, creating a fog that lasted all morning. Today, Dario didn't bother with the heat.

If he and Kimber were going to start hanging out together, he needed to get used to this. How did her just running her fingers through her hair turn him on? Why was he acting like he wanted to be just friends? And why in the hell did she still not want to be more than friends?

Dario had worked his ass off to become a respectable member of society—at least in Dubai. Not being visible there while Kimber was in town may have hindered him. People respected him. They listened to what he said. What she needed to see was how responsible he could be here in Southwood. He figured this was his second chance to make Kimber see the new him. But that meant she didn't need to know about Christmas Chaos.

It would make sense to cancel the whole thing but if he did, Darren would be pissed and blame Kimber for it. Speaking of his brother, Dario needed to give him a call to make sure he hadn't keeled over getting back to the house after their run that morning. Wrapping a towel around his waist, he crossed into his bedroom. The clothes he'd discarded cluttered the floor in front of his four-poster bed, including what he'd worn yesterday on the plane back to the States.

At some point during Dario's shower, Hamilton had pushed his way into the room and used some balled-up slacks as a bed. It surprised Dario to find the clothes still there. Typically, Alisha snagged things up to take to the cleaners. She was probably still mad at him for the whole Kimber incident.

"Alisha?" Dario called out before he reached for his cell phone. He was swiping to turn it on to call his brother when Darren's face appeared. "Hey, I was just about to call you."

"Twintuition," Darren chuckled. "I wanted to call you using video-chat."

"What's up?"

"I just needed you to see my face as I curse your ass out," said Darren. "My legs feel like jelly."

Dario laughed. "You need to curse out Dominic for letting you eat like a pig."

Hamilton squealed.

"Ham!" Darren shouted, which prompted the pig to leave the room. "Alisha left Hamilton with you?"

"You say that like she's gone out of the country," Dario noted.

"Uh, she did. She left me a rant last night about

how pissed off she is that you're right back with Kimber again."

Dario dragged his hand down his face. "We're not back together." *We'd have to have been together in order for that to be the case,* he told himself. "Tell me more about Alisha leaving. Where did she go?"

"Aamir called to see if you came in okay and then sent for the plane to go back to Dubai. Alisha hopped on and plans on staying there until Dominic and Waverly come back from Louisiana with the kids."

"Are you...?" Dario stopped himself. "What the...?"

"I take it you didn't know," Darren laughed at his brother. "I'll tell you what she said. Let's meet for lunch."

The doorbell rang.

"Company?" Darren asked him, peering at the phone as if he could see as Dario walked through the condo.

Dario prayed his brother was joking and he'd find Alisha on the other side of the door. They had a lot to get done in the apartment if they wanted to give the twins the best Christmas. "You got a lot of explaining to do," Dario declared, yanking the door open.

"Okay, but first I'm going to need you to put some clothes on." Kimber batted her lashes and licked her red lips.

"I see you're ready," he said, checking out the black Christmas sweater with a giant red-and-white swirled peppermint in the center that she wore.

"I take it we're not going to lunch," Darren said on the phone.

Dario had forgotten for a moment he was talking to his twin. "My bad."

"Hey, Darren," Kimber called out.

"Hey, Kimber," Darren returned the flirty greeting. "I'll let you guys go. Dario, it's messed up the way you're letting me hang." And he disconnected.

Kimber bit her bottom lip. "I'm sorry. We can grab a cupcake another time. I have some errands to run."

Dario's brow rose. "What kind of errands and how?"

"I can drive," said Kimber.

"But well?" he asked her with a grin, then ducked out of the reach of her playful punch in the arm.

"I don't suspect there's a lot of traffic to the hospital."

"C'mon in. I'll take you where you need to go."

Before stepping over the threshold, Kimber poked her head inside to look in both directions. "Where's Alisha?"

Damn, that was right. Alisha had left him to deal with all this Christmas decorating. He'd teased his sister for not knowing how to do it, but what the hell did he know? How was he supposed to make this place kid-friendly? Dario flagged Kimber in. She sidestepped a few half-opened boxes with Christmas wrapping paper leaning out the top. While he told Kimber about Alisha leaving the country, Dario concocted a plan. "I'll make a deal with you, Kimber. Help me out with making this place kid-friendly for Christmas, and I'll do you a solid by driving you around again like old times."

Kimber's hazel eyes lit up, igniting a fire in his soul. "Seriously?"

"Sure."

She flung herself into his arms, not caring about his still wet body. "Oh my God, that would be so awesome! I could totally use you and your brain to help me dig deeper into the mystery of the tiara maker."

"Oh yeah," Dario said over her shoulder, willing himself not to take a whiff of the peach scent of her hair. Working closely with Kimber would help him keep her off his trail. The last thing he wanted her to do was to discover he'd created them and not told her. If he was being honest with himself, he knew he should've just come clean at some point, but now he felt like he was in too deep. She'd never understand why he'd kept the truth from her all this time.

Kimber wiggled her body against his. "That sounds great."

Do not squeeze too tight, he told himself. *Do not notice how soft she feels in your arms*. But it was too late. His body reacted.

Kimber took a step back. Her lips parted. There was no hiding the full-fledged erection underneath the fabric of the towel. He owned it with a shrug of his shoulders. "I'm a man, Kimber."

"I see." She twisted a few strands of hair around her finger. "And I think we can work something out about that." Her eyes lowered toward his waist. "Something that would benefit the both of us while I'm here."

Well damn, Dario thought. How was he supposed

to say no to that? *Oh yeah, right. You're going to show her how mature you are now. A mature man isn't going to just jump at the chance to roll around in the bed with her...right?* Was it too late to ask Santa for strength?

"I don't know, Kimber," he found himself saying. "We'll see."

Chapter 4

*W*e'll see.

We'll see.

The words haunted Kimber for the next twenty-
four hours. How she managed to walk through the
Christmas aisles of the shops downtown with him
beside her, with his big muscular arms bumping up
against her skin, was beyond her. Kimber wasn't ig-
norant of the way the women welcomed his return
with open arms. Some of the church ladies dismissed
Kimber's presence. One woman even smacked Kimber in the face with her ponytail while turning her
back to her.

At The Cupcakery, Tiffani Carres wasn't the friend-
liest when she realized Kimber had walked in with
Dario. Kimber figured the abrasive welcome was more

out of loyalty to Alisha than anything else. Alisha and Tiffani were tight.

Instead of just showing up at Four Points General Hospital, Kimber set up an appointment for their Friday Fun Day in the children's ward. That gave her enough time to rally the local princesses and queens from Lexi's troupe for a visit filled with cupcakes and toys. She arranged for Miss Vonna, owner of The Cupcakery, to have a few dozen holiday specialties for pickup.

Leading up to the big meeting at the hospital, Kimber fulfilled her promise of helping Dario get his place set up for kids. That meant first going through all the old decorations they had. And when she said *old* decorations, she meant it. Dario's box of garland was filled with more tinsel off the string than on. They made lists of things they needed. She wondered why Dario didn't just decorate the ranch house, but his explanation about the private planes who used their airstrip in the back field made sense—for the most part. They'd been apart for a year. Dario may have changed in some ways, but in others, she still felt like she knew him. Something weird was up with his quick excuse about the house.

Perhaps she was still upset that Dario had rejected her proposal for the two of them to revisit their fling. He'd taken her comment more as a joke than anything else and brushed it off. At one point Dario would have pounced on the offer. If she didn't know better, she'd think he'd matured.

"We're here," Dario said, backing the red '92 Dodge

Viper into a visitor's parking space in front of Four Points General.

Kimber didn't realize she'd zoned out during their drive. Dario sat behind the steering wheel in an oatmeal colored cable-knit sweater. The neckline came up to his strong, square jawline. She licked her lips and forced herself to stare straight ahead. "It doesn't look like the Grits and Glam van is here yet."

"This baby does zero to sixty in under five seconds," Dario explained, patting the leather wheel. "Do you want to go in before they get here?"

Already unbuckling her belt, Kimber nodded. "I want to see if there's anyone who can help me access the visitors' records. I thought I'd start there with who may have signed in on the day the first tiara appeared."

Kimber adjusted her midnight black stockings over her knees. The color blended perfectly with her black suede ankle boots. She then straightened her black-and-white-striped skater dress, helping it fall into place. A four-point silver tiara perched on the top of her dark hair. She'd come to represent.

"You're still on that, huh?"

"Of course I am," said Kimber. "I am not leaving town until I know the name of that designer."

"Didn't you just tell me the other day you don't plan on being a lifelong resident of Southwood?"

Damn it, she had. "I meant figuratively, Dario. I want to put in an order for Lexi. Something about the tiaras spoke to me."

"Spoke? Kimber, they were just scraps of metal put together."

Kimber rolled her eyes. The doors slid open. He was a man. What did he understand about the crowns? No, she quickly took that back. Ernest Laing had tried to monopolize the local area with a stake in the tiara business. Kimber hated him on principle alone. He'd hurt Lexi years ago before she met Uncle Stephen. Ernest had passed on backstabbing and conniving ways to his daughter, Vera Laing. He and his wife would do anything to make sure Vera had an edge in beauty pageants, including bribing judges.

Kimber frowned and inhaled. The clean, antiseptic scent filled her lungs. People in the waiting room to the left looked up at the newcomers. A cable news show played on the mounted flat-screen television on the wall.

"Hi," Kimber said in a sugar-sweet drawl to the young man dressed in blue scrubs at the front desk. "I'm Kimber…"

"Kimber Reyes," he finished for her as a red tint stained his pale freckled face. "I went to high school with you. I was a few years behind, but everyone knew about you."

It took control for Kimber not to return the blush. "Oh yes, well, those high school days were something else, weren't they, Auggie?" She read the name off his garnet-colored badge to avoid Dario's piercing eyes.

"Tell me more about these high school days," asked Dario.

"We're on a schedule," Kimber noted. "I'm sure Auggie doesn't have the time."

"Well…" Auggie began.

"We don't," she said quickly. "We have an appointment with Dr. Ross over in the children's ward."

Auggie fiddled with the keyboard of his computer, then nodded. "They're expecting you. You can sign in there if you want." He pointed to a sign-in sheet on top of the desk.

It dawned on Kimber about signing in downstairs. "Auggie," she said sweetly, "how far back are your records?"

"What do you mean?"

Kimber tapped her fingernail on the clipboard. "These. I mean do you trash them after one night?"

"No, ma'am." Auggie gave his head a vigorous shake. "We keep everything for seven years. You looking for someone particular?"

Kimber shrugged. Dario stepped close behind her, his hand at her lower back, rushing her. "I'm looking for the mysterious tiara designer. Know any?"

"Can't say that I do, but if I hear anything, I'll let you know."

"Thanks," Kimber and Dario chorused.

Her boots squeaked on the clean floors as they walked toward the elevator. Kimber loved the hospital— not enough to be a doctor or to go into medicine, but she'd paired volunteer service with her pageantry. When she won Miss Grand Supreme at the Southern Style Glitz Pageant, Kimber witnessed how wearing the crown on her visits to the children's ward brightened their spirits. As she got older, she tried to come out every summer and winter.

"I've been away too long," said Kimber, dabbing

the corner of her eye with the pad of her thumb to keep her mascara from running.

Dario, his hands folded in front of him, nudged her with his shoulder. "You are here now, that's what counts."

"Sure, but I don't feel good about not having been here." Kimber let out a sigh. Four Points General was a long-term home for several children. Some of the parents stayed in the local communities of South-wood, Samaritan, Black Wolf Creek and Peachville. Hotels lowered their prices for the families. Everyone wanted to do their part.

The elevator stopped on the seventh floor. As soon as the doors opened, bright natural light from out-side greeted them. Her uncle Nate had had a hand in taking out the cold fluorescent light in the entry and some of the rooms. The alphabet carpet led to the main office where a group of young nurses waited for them to enter.

"Kimber!"

Thank God Nicolette was still there. Her former college classmate had gone through the nursing pro-gram at Florida A&M and they'd often shared rides back home. She had been there for parts of Kimber's wilder days. Now, seeing her with a pregnant belly, Kimber bet her partying days were behind her.

"Oh wow! Girl, hey!" Kimber cried, coming through the doors. Nicolette had been there last year when the tiaras first arrived. They caught up for a moment about what had been going on in their lives. Dario walked over to the window. Before the rest of the crew came up, Kimber wanted to get a little insight on the sign-in sheet. She leaned forward against the counter. "Say, Nicolette, I have a question."

Nicolette tore her attention away from Dario. "Yes, girl, you should go after that. He is fine."

"Who?" Kimber asked and followed her friend's gaze. "Dario?"

"Are y'all finally going to get serious?"

"Et tu, Nicolette?"

Smacking her on the arm, Nicolette shook her head. "You must have noticed his hotness. If I wasn't pregnant with Jackson's baby, I'd take a go at him."

"I'm going to assume horniness is a part of pregnancy?" The ladies shared a laugh. "But seriously, Nic, I have a question about something."

"Man, I can imagine what he looks like in a pair of gray sweatpants," said Nicolette.

If he heard, Dario didn't say a word. The man leaned against the wall beside a clay potted plant to read the screen of his mobile. Kimber didn't need to imagine what the man looked like in sweats. She'd seen him naked. But no one needed to know that.

"Nic!"

"Sorry, what's your question?"

"Do you remember last year and all the trouble we had with the tiaras from the Laings, when they wanted to charge us for the tiaras when everyone else donated stuff for the pageant?" The ensuing grimace gave Kimber her answer. "And then we had the other tiaras pop up?"

"Oh yeah, they were so elegant."

"I know, right?" Kimber agreed with Nicolette. "And I still have no idea who brought them here."

"Someone with access to this wing," Nicolette said simply. "Have you thought about going through the files? I think we have them—"

There came a ruckus from over by the window. Like a kid caught with his hands in the cookie jar, Dario's dark eyes stretched wide open. He'd somehow managed to turn a nearby potted plant over, spilling black dirt everywhere.

"My bad," he called out.

"I can't take you anywhere," Kimber groaned.

"I'll be right back," said Nicolette. "I need to get that cleaned up before the kids come out. They'll think it's botany day and get dirt all over themselves and everything else."

Nicolette waddled down the hall. Kimber guessed it was more to flirt with Dario. Good thing Jackson wasn't there, or he might go toe-to-toe with Dario in the boxing ring. Sighing, Kimber signed her name and Dario's on the sign-in sheet. A few pages covered the clipboard from the previous three days, leading her to believe the sheets were only changed every month. The tiaras had been discovered just over a year ago. She set the pen down and spied a long black filing cabinet labeled Records. If Nicolette kept flirting with Dario, Kimber might have a chance to take a peek. She tiptoed around the counter. Just as she got close to the cabinet, a voice shouted out.

"Kimber Reyes!"

Everything and anything Kimber wanted to do was

lost when she heard her name being called. The elevators closed behind a doctor in a white coat. Kimber stepped back in front of the counter and flipped her hair off her shoulders. Her eyes focused on the man and she tried to recall who he was.

"It's Vin," the deep voice said. The closer he came to Kimber, the more she started to recognize him. It couldn't be. "You know, Marvin."

"Holy crap," Kimber breathed. A flashback of memories flooded her. The good kid who'd posed as her fake boyfriend in high school now stood before her in a white lab coat, teal pants and a teal plaid oxford. Gone were the wire-rimmed glasses that had hidden his chocolate-brown eyes. Kimber reached out. Marvin wrapped his oversized arms around her waist and twirled her in the air. With each spin, Dario stalked closer and closer until he stood right beside them. "Dario, this is my old friend Marvin Smith."

"Just Vin now," Marvin clarified.

"Vin," Kimber let his name roll off her lips. "I didn't know you were still around."

With a chuckle, Vin nodded his head. "I decided to stay after I finished up my residency last year just after you and your crew had that awful bout of food poisoning."

Kimber grabbed her stomach and groaned with the memory of eating her uncle's potato salad with raisins in it.

"You kept tabs on her when she left?" Dario asked him. Suspicion drizzled from his voice. It was be weird that he would jump to that conclusion, Kimber thought. And this was funny, since he was adamant about keeping *them* at a friendship level.

Vin squared his shoulders at Dario. "Of course. Kimber's a very special lady. But you don't have to take my word for it. Ask the kids who missed seeing her come around here to cheer them up."

"But you didn't bother letting your presence known until just now?" Dario pressed on with his mini interrogation.

"Dario," Kimber interjected, hitting him in the chest with a playful swat. "Be nice."

"He's got a point," said Nicolette. She sidled up beside the doctor and elbowed him in the ribs. "I told Vin when he was around last year to say hi to you, Kimber. But he didn't think it was a good idea. Now that you're back, well, hmm."

"Well hmm, indeed," Vin said. "No one wants to a reunion over food poisoning."

Had it not been for the elevator opening and the beauty queens' excited conversation interrupting them, Kimber was sure Dario had been going to say something nasty. There was no need. Vin was one of Kimber's good friends from high school. They'd studied together, hung out together, but that was it.

Dario's inner growling ended when the tiara squad and children all caught sight of one another and met at the counter. Kimber, glad for the distraction, clapped her hands and made the introductions. The young group of girls ranged in age from four to fourteen and every single one of them wanted to try on the sashes and crowns.

"Girls," Kimber said, "I'm glad you're excited about the sashes. This week I thought we could start by making your own sashes. I want you to think about your power word that best describes you and then write *Miss* in front of it."

Kimber immersed herself with the girls and forgot everything else. This was what being a beauty queen was all about—inspiring others.

It didn't take long for Dario to decide he didn't like Vin. Sure, it was hypocritical of him to question Vin's reasons for keeping track of her after seeing her a year ago when Dario had done the same thing in Dubai. Dario had justified his secrecy by telling himself he wanted to keep an eye on her but keep his distance at the same time. She'd made it clear she had other places to go in life and he'd been standing in her way. But for Vin, Dario found it creepy. Friends, his ass. Vin had a thing for Kimber.

The entire time the batch of beauty queens talked to and fawned over the kids, Vin was watching Kimber. Dario didn't appreciate the way the good doctor's hand lingered on her back when he introduced her to the other doctors. Since Kimber and the rest of the beauty queens planned on being there for the remainder of the afternoon, Dario decided to head over to the garage at the ranch to divert his attention from Vin.

There, he puttered around with his blowtorch and a few scraps of metal, same as he had a year prior. Before long he'd constructed three small tiaras. If memory served him correctly, Alisha had a few more costume stones in her jewelry box.

Head covered with protective gear, Dario didn't hear or notice the door open until Darren banged on the table. A few red sparks flew through the air, dying before they hit the ground. Darren put his hands in the air.

"Whoa," he exclaimed. "You look like you want to hurt someone."

Not just someone. One person in particular. "What are you doing here, Darren?"

"The last I checked, Dominic put all of our names on the mortgage."

Cool air had followed Darren into the garage. The clock over the double doors indicated Dario had been preoccupied for a couple of hours. Almost time to get Kimber. Dario set the blowtorch down.

"My bad. What's up?" He softened his tone. He and his twin were similar in looks, with the same light coloring and build. In elementary school people had sworn they were identical, but the older they got, the more easily people could tell them apart.

"Nothing, really," said Darren, rolling up the sleeves of his cream-colored sweater. "I thought we could get in the ring but with the way you're looking right now, I don't think that's a good idea. What's bugging you?"

"I don't feel like talking about it. Let's get in the ring," Dario said, taking off his black welding helmet. The protective gear was that of an alien head with a demonic smiling mouth. He cradled the protective gear under his arm.

"Hell no!" Darren laughed. "Not with the mood you are in."

"I'm not in a mood."

"We're twins. I can sense your irritation," explained Darren. "Maybe we should save that energy you're working with for the Boxing Around the Christmas Ring competition. Parker Ward won last year. Says he plans on winning the Santa Belt this year."

With the aggression he felt at that moment, Dario was sure he could take the gold-buckled belt right now. "I wish him the best of luck."

"I saw the Spider out front." Darren changed the subject, probably because he knew Dario would jump in the ring with him without hesitation. "How's it running?"

"Check out the horsepower," Dario replied. "Want to go for a ride?"

Darren held two fingers up. "Two things I won't do with you when you're angry—get in the ring and drive. Not unless you tell me what's going on with you."

Just then Dario's phone buzzed. Eager to see Kimber again, he grabbed the cell from the back pocket of his jeans and read the message.

"Whoa," Darren shouted. "What's Kimber doing now?"

"Who says this has anything to do with her?"

Chuckling, Darren shook his head. "Again, we shared a womb, remember?"

Dario's response was to flip him off and then laugh. "Bastard."

"And again," said Darren, "we're twins, so you're calling yourself one too. Now, what's up?"

"C'mon and take a ride with me. I need to meet Kimber at The Cupcakery. I'll explain what's up on the way." Dario held two fingers in the air. "Scout's honor I'll drive safe."

After Dario cleaned up his mess and placed the half-completed crowns under a tarp, they sped into town, parking at Crowne's Garage, the one spot downtown where locals could get an oil change or a tune-up without driving for an hour. Dario shared everything that had been going on—from the airport until that morning.

Inside The Cupcakery, Darren tried to order two double chocolate vegan cupcakes for them. Dario corrected it and ordered a regular one for himself.

"That's cruel man," Darren said. "You're not going to eat the same as me?"

"I've been working out," Dario declared. "I knew Christmas Chaos was coming while you waited for a second helping at every meal," he chided him. They found a silver booth with hot pink seats over in the corner and waited for their coffee. He thought about how he might need something a little stronger if he saw Kimber walk through the doors with Vin. *Vin*, he thought, wanting to snarl.

"Let me get this straight," Darren said, wiping the low-fat icing off his cupcake with the pad of his thumb. "Kimber suggested that the two of you hook up while she's here and you turned her down?"

"I didn't flat out turn her down," Dario explained, biting off half his cupcake.

"You said 'we'll see.' Every kid knows when you ask a parent and they say that, it means no."

"I'm not a kid." What it meant to Dario was that he hadn't planned on jumping into bed with Kimber that morning just because she was horny. "I am trying to show her how I've matured."

"By training for Christmas Chaos and keeping her in the dark about the tiaras you've made?" Darren pulled at the top part of his now icing-free cupcake. "You could make a fortune in Dubai from your hobby. Alisha told me."

Dario cringed. The tiaras weren't for sale and Alisha knew it. "Our little sister has quite the imagination, don't you think?"

"I think you're a hypocrite to get mad at Kimber for moving on when you are the one turning her away," said Darren. "I see why you're all pent up. Yep, maybe you should stay abstinent until Christmas."

It was still early December. Christmas seemed too far away. Dario shoved the rest of his dessert into his mouth to make space for the coffee coming up. Tiffani, the owner's daughter as well as one of Alisha's close friends, bumped her hip against Dario's frame.

"Good to have you back," Tiffani said. "We should get together while Alisha's away."

"For what?" Dario asked. Darren kicked him under the table.

"Excuse him, Tiffani," said Darren. "He was raised in a barn."

Tiffani gave them both a wink before setting the mugs of steaming hot coffee in front of them. "I'll tell your sister I saw y'all. She worries."

"We're fine," Dario grunted.

The brass bell over the front door jingled. Like everyone else in the bakery, Dario glanced up at the next guest. His heart slammed into his rib cage at the sight of Kimber. He didn't think he'd ever get tired of holding his breath when she walked into a room.

"You got it bad," Darren whispered. "I feel sorry for you."

"Why?" Dario took his eyes off Kimber for a moment. He welcomed the distraction, fearing she'd walk in with Doctor Vin. "I didn't say a word, Darren."

"You don't have to say a thing. All the ladies in town are going to take one look at you and your pitiful puppy-dog eyes over Kimber and there goes your reputation as a lady's man."

The group of girls following Kimber inside began squealing at the display case of cupcakes. Dario's body relaxed against the cushions of the booth. So Vin had stayed away. Good.

"One day you're going to understand there's more to life than sleeping around with women," Dario said to his brother.

An ashen color came over Darren's face. "Says the man who's dated all the single teachers in town."

Instead of being proud of the notches on his bedpost, Dario shook his head in shame, thinking of all the time he'd wasted chasing other women when he could have spent more time with Kimber. "One day, big brother," Dario said, making light of the fact that he was four minutes younger, "you're going to fall in love."

Dario made eye contact with Kimber. Her bright smile and wave warmed his soul. He gave her a head nod.

"Oh sure, treat her like one of the boys if you're so in love," Darren said in a mocking tone that caught Dario's attention.

"I'm not. I told you, I want her to take me seriously this time around."

Another jingle of the door drew Dario's attention. Vin. Dario crumpled the wrapper in his hand. Vin broke through the line and headed straight to the register. Whatever he said to Tiffani now made the rest of Kimber's tiara squad giggle. Some of the girls went back to the display to choose a few more cupcakes. So the man wanted to buy a round of cupcakes for everyone. Whatever. Vin leaned down and whispered something into Kimber's ear. Not like he could hear, but Dario straightened up. A few moments later Kimber headed over to the booth in the corner. To him.

Dario rose to greet her. "How'd the rest of the afternoon go?"

"Fantastic. The boys came over and wanted to make sashes for themselves too. You should have stayed. You could have had one for yourself."

Darren snickered and stood up. "That I'd pay to see," he said, hugging Kimber. "How've you been, baby girl?"

"Great."

"Glad to see you back home." Darren hugged her once more. "Lookin' prettier than ever."

Kimber rolled her eyes. "Don't think that Crowne charm is going to work on me, Darren. Remember, I know you."

Laughing, Dario punched his brother lightly in the arm. "Right."

"Whatever," said Darren. "So, what brings you over to our table when you're in here with a bunch of single—"

"What's going on with you?" Dario asked, "You need a ride out of here?"

"Yeah," Kimber said tossing a glance over her shoulder. "About that. Vin's asked if I want to have dinner with him this evening."

Darren peered over the rim of his coffee mug, his eyes bouncing rapidly between them.

"Sounds great."

"Great?" Kimber asked, her mouth dropping open in disbelief.

"Yeah," said Dario, "depending on where you go. Bring me back a doggie bag?"

Kimber cocked a brow up at him. "You're sure?"

"Kimber, you're the one who said you wanted to just be friends and that you didn't want to settle down, especially not here in Southwood. I say go for it. He's a doctor too." Dario gave her arm a little nudge while deep down inside he wanted to rip Vin's face off.

"Well," she gulped. "If you say so."

Did she think telling him about a date would make him show all his cards? Nope, the old Dario would have torn through the crowd and shoved Vin's face into the cupcake display. The new responsible Dario, however, was going to let Kimber go on this date and find out on her own what a fraud the good doctor was.

"Like I said," Dario repeated, "bring me back a doggie bag."

Kimber backed away from Dario, her pouty pink mouth twisted with skepticism. "Alright then. I'll catch a ride from one of the girls. See you later, Darren."

Dario sat back down in the booth. His heart raced. He clenched his fists in anger. Darren watched with enthusiasm. In his twisted way, he egged Dario on. "That's right, just suppress those feelings. Let it all out at Christmas Chaos."

Chapter 5

"I still can't believe I'm sitting across from you at Duvernay's," said Vin.

Kimber crossed her legs under the table and tugged the stretchy black bodycon dress down her thighs. Vin had come a long way. When Kimber had gone to school with him he'd had an affection for comic book superhero T-shirts paired with corduroy pants. Now the man wore tailored suits. Her mind wandered to seeing Dario at the airport earlier this week. *Whatever. You don't need to be thinking about Dario right now*, Kimber scolded herself. She tried to focus on the man seated across from her but his puppy-dog eyes made her uncomfortable.

When they'd arrived at Duvernay's, one of Southwood's swankier restaurants, Kimber wasn't sure they'd be able to get a table. But she didn't want to embarrass Vin by throwing around her connection. Henri Duvernay was a cousin of Lexi's, and with no children of his own, he looked fondly upon Kimber and Philly as his extended family. The throng did not deter Vin, though. He strode through the waiting crowd and whispered to the hostess, and just like that, they were seated.

Kimber smiled at him over her glass of chardonnay. She'd made it clear this afternoon at The Cupcakery that she wasn't interested in seeing anyone seriously right now. Vin had said he understood and just wanted to catch up on old times with her. She had no idea why she'd built it up as more when she'd bailed on helping Dario that night. *Yes, she had.* She'd wanted a reaction from him, expected him to get upset. Not be ask for a doggie bag. Dario hadn't been the slightest bit perturbed, probably because half the women in town were falling all over themselves to get next to him. Kimber focused on her date.

"Remember the first time we came here?" Kimber asked.

"I had never been here before," said Vin. "It was great, but then again, I always had a blast. Being with your family was fun. Your uncles are great."

Before her parents passed away, they'd always wanted to project themselves as the perfect family. They went to church, participated in social functions and even joined the Southwood Golf Club, though they never golfed. They did everything all-American families did except have company over. Not that Kimber ever wanted friends over. She'd never known when her maternal grandparents would say something to or about her dad and set him off in one of his moods. When they'd passed away and her uncles moved in, things changed.

"They were something," Kimber laughed, setting her glass back down on the white linen tablecloth. Marriage had settled them down. Yet another reason to not tie herself to one person. It made her boring.

"I'm glad you agreed to go out with me this evening," said Vin.

"Of course," Kimber replied. "We're old friends."

A half smile forced a dimple in Vin's left cheek. "Ah, yeah. Besides finding out what you've been up to all these years, I am interested in this pageant you're doing for the town."

"Lexi's brainchild," Kimber clarified.

A fond smile now followed a faraway dreamy look on Vin's face, a common look for most men when thinking about Lexi. "Have you guys already selected a venue?"

"We're holding it at the theater on the town square. Why? What's up?"

"After seeing how the children at the hospital responded to your visit, I thought it would be a great idea to have it there. I could get some of the donors to reimburse your fee at the theater. If you held it in our theater, our children could come, as well as people from the neighboring communities who otherwise might not want to make the trek to the Southwood. We'd be a neutral zone."

The other communities—Samaritan, Black Wolf Creek and Peachville—all participated in a school rivalry. Kimber understood the hesitance in traveling here. The doctor made valid points. "I think that's a terrific idea, Vin. Thanks."

Proud, Vin sat back and folded his hands in front of him at the table. "This is awesome. We'll take care of the stage setup."

"You know my uncle Nate will want to be in on that."

"It is refreshing to know your family still supports each other," said Vin.

"They're alright," she said with a giggle, "Are your parents still here?" Kimber recalled Vin's mother not being much of a fan of hers when Kimber had chosen her then-boyfriend over Vin. Her lips twisted to the side at the thought of Philip, star football player at Southwood. Years ago Kimber had wanted to stand out from the pack by wearing a dress she had no business wearing. Her breasts and ass hadn't been nearly developed enough and she was barely sixteen at the time. All for that boy.

"Folks are fine," Vin said with a slow nod of his head. He went on to tell her about his concerns over making sure they could take care of themselves. "They sold their house and downgraded to a condo over in Peachville."

Kimber returned the nod. "My grandparents did the same thing. It sounds like the latest trend is to move into these senior dorms."

"I'm glad I'm able to continue to be here."

"You said you were in the emergency room," Kimber recalled. "Do you prefer working there? Is that your specialty?"

"No." Vin shook his head. "I'm not sure if you're aware, but Southwood is experiencing an outbreak of the chicken pox."

"I know," said Kimber. "Philly has them and it sucks because I wanted to spend time with her before I left."

"Back to flying across the country and interviewing beauty queens?"

Kimber beamed. "Are you following my blog posts?"

"I try to catch them here and there between my rounds at the hospital and visits with my folks."

"I'm so proud of you, Vin," said Kimber, "but it is going to take me time to get used to calling you that."

Vin flashed a grin, reminding her of the boy she used to know. "The moment I left for Hampton University, I knew I needed to reinvent myself a bit. I got rid of the box cut, got contact lenses, gained twenty pounds in muscle and let my roommate's girlfriend style me. She's the one who told me to drop the *Mar*. It was hard to get the folks here to stop calling me Marvin, seeing as how everyone from Southwood knew me growing up."

"Now you're a regular Cinder-fella." Kimber gave him a wink.

"With my very own princess too," said Vin. His hand moved across the table.

It hadn't been so long since her last official date

that Kimber couldn't pick up on the cues of a man about to make his move. The turn of the conversation was about to get more sentimental than she wanted. Kimber reached for her glass again to avoid Vin's attempt to touch her hand.

With a half smile, Vin shook his head. "Don't tell me you're still eluding relationships."

"What?" Kimber's voice went up an octave.

"I was about to touch your hand, in a friendly manner of course, and you pulled away. It's a move you've done since we were teenagers." Vin reached for his cup of coffee.

The fact that they were seated in not only one of the fanciest restaurants but also one of the most romantic wasn't lost on Kimber. Twin long-stemmed roses stood in the glass vases on every table. Flames from the single candles flickered in the cool breeze from the doors open to the outdoor seating area.

Kimber cleared her throat.

"There might be something in the medical books that we can diagnose you with one of these days. Maybe you're a commitment-phobe...or just relationship shy."

"There's nothing wrong with me," Kimber clarified. "I just don't have time for dating. I've got a lot I want to do, like traveling, and most men our age are looking for the same thing." Her mind flashed to Dario standing in his bedroom in his towel—turning down her offer to be friends with benefits. She thought about the way the water droplets trickled down his chest, over his pecs and down his washboard abs. Kimber's mouth went dry.

Vin laughed. "It's a good thing I'm a doctor. I can revive you if you pass out."

"I'm not going to faint or anything," she retorted with a smirk. "The talk of relationships makes me nervous."

"Nothing has changed," Vin said in a matter-of-fact tone.

The man was smart, good-looking and that was all in addition to his being a doctor. But Kimber wasn't feeling it.

"I told you this wasn't a date," she warned him.

"Relax," said Vin. "I understand where you're coming from. I don't have time for relationships either. It's just easier to get through the holidays when you have someone keeping you company."

Why did his words sound so familiar? Didn't she hint at the same thing with Dario? "I am not that person," Kimber assured him.

"Oh crap." Vin apologized profusely. "All that came out totally wrong."

"I think we better call this a night, Vin." Kimber signaled for the waiter to come over and asked for their meals to be packed up, then suggested to Vin that it was best they end their evening.

One of the selling points of his particular condo was less noise from the amphitheater across the street. But Dario hated that his side of the building didn't face the street. The problem with the more private side was that he wouldn't be able to see the shiny piece of tin that that Vin joker would use to bring Kimber home from their date. So what if Dario timed his evening jog for a peek at what this clown wanted to do?

It would be presumptuous of him to show up at Kimber's door and interrupt any good-night kiss. Dario clenched his fists together at the idea of anyone else's lips on hers. Nothing worked to take his mind off her—not working out, lifting weights or knuckle punches. The only thing he fueled was his muscles. It was after midnight when Dario couldn't take it anymore. Kimber hadn't bothered to call him and let him know she was home. A thousand questions went through his head.

What if the doc had her pinned down on the bed?

What if she had the doctor pinned down?

What if she tripped over the throw rug from in front of her couch and couldn't get to the phone or the door?

Dario paced the floor from the living room to the hallway. Hamilton marched right alongside him. "What do you think, Ham?"

The pig grunted up at him. Deciding the latter was a possibility, Dario grabbed his keys and fiddled with the strings of his gray sweatpants. The hell with it, he could tie them up when he was at her door. Yanking the knob, he pulled the door open and paused for a moment.

"We have to stop meeting like this," Kimber said, chewing her bottom lip to keep from smiling.

The little minx had switched from a little black dress to a short pink terry cloth robe. Dario couldn't help but recall those long, smooth brown legs of hers wrapped around his waist. He cleared his throat and observed the rest of her attire. The untied sash hung down by her legs, leaving the garment open to reveal a thin pair of pink shorts and a tank top—no bra. Dario gulped. She carried an oversized aluminum-foil swan.

"You brought me leftovers?" Dario asked, taking the dish. Hamilton begged Kimber to pick him up, which she did.

"Why do you have him naked?" Kimber asked, stroking the pink ears. "I know Alisha and I don't see eye to eye, but I know she has a few tutus around here for him to wear."

"He's a pig," said Dario with a dry sigh. "And a tutu?"

Ignoring him, Kimber tapped her chin. "I saw a Christmas one online. I think I'll get it for him."

"The condo needs to be decorated for the holidays, not the pig." Dario headed down the hallway. "It looks like you didn't even touch your meal."

"I would have only given you what I had but when I asked the waiter to pack it up, Henri came over to the table with an entire meal. He wanted me to make sure you got this," said Kimber, "and I am supposed to tell you that payback is coming."

Cute. Henri Duvernay thought he was going to get an advantage by fattening Dario up and slowing him down in the ring this year.

"Want to tell me what Henri's talking about?"

"No." Dario turned to head into the kitchen. The pitter-patter of her fuzzy slippers caused a smile to spread across his face. "You're home late from your date."

"It ended a while ago," Kimber confessed. "I took a shower."

"Cold?" Dario turned to face her, gritting his teeth in case her taunting answer was, *Not alone*.

Kimber shook her head then pulled her long dark hair forward over her shoulders. He couldn't help but notice the way the curls ended just at the swell of her breasts. "You sound like a man who is speaking from experience."

"Helps keep the mind sharp," Dario admitted. He set the food on the counter, tempted to dig into it. "So you decided to be sweet and bring this to me now, when we already had plans to meet up tomorrow to pick out stuff for the twins' guest room. Was your date that bad?"

Kimber exhaled deeply. "It wasn't a date, not like you thought, and less than what Vin thought."

"What?" he demanded.

"You didn't seem to care if I was going on a date with someone else, so don't get huffy now," said Kimber. "I told Vin from the get-go I wasn't looking for a date but it turned out he had other plans."

"And he expected more?" Dario exited the kitchen. "I'll kill him."

Kimber went after him and pressed her hand against his bare chest while she cradled Hamilton with the other. His nipples stood erect, as did other things, after just a simple touch of her fingertips. "You can't kill him. He was just hopeful there'd be sparks between us."

"And?"

"There weren't." Kimber shrugged her shoulders. "I didn't expect there to be."

Dario glanced at her arms and saw goose bumps. "You've experienced them before?"

Jutting her chin forward, Kimber nodded. "I've gotten them, thank you very much."

He wasn't going to point out the way the hairs on her forearms rose when she folded her arms across her chest. Relieved, he pressed on. "So, other than no sparks, how was your evening?"

"Interesting. Vin accused me of avoiding relationships."

The last thing he wanted to do was agree with the doctor, but the man had a point. Dario opened the foil swan. A wave of steam rose through the air, bringing the scent of a big, fat, homemade steak burger—an item not found on Duvernay's swanky menu. Henri brought the monster burgers over a summer or two ago to the gym. The fat to meat ratio was ridiculous and yet it was so damn good. Dario's mouth watered.

"Did you hear me, Dario?" Kimber asked.

"Hey, as a victim of one of your ghosting episodes, I'm not having this conversation with you."

Kimber crossed her arms. "You can't be serious. I thought we'd gotten over this."

Instead of discussing the matter, Dario picked up

the burger with two hands and began eating. Grease ran down his arms and into the rosemary truffle fries. Damn Henri.

"Dario, you know I left because I needed to get serious about my future."

Dario nodded and swallowed his big bite. "And even after I knew you landed that job on the pageant circuit, you never got back in touch with me."

What Dario liked about Kimber, besides everything, was the fact that she wasn't pretentious, especially when it came to eating food like this. Dario handed her a fry, which she took while he reached back into the fridge for two bottles of beer. He twisted the caps off before handing Kimber hers.

"So no, I'm not having that conversation with you, Kimber," he said. "We can share a meal, share chores this holiday season, but I am not going down that road again."

He lied through his teeth but he knew he had Kimber right where he wanted her. She saw he'd matured, had a job that didn't require him to be under a car all day long. Now Kimber was going to witness his self-control. The goose bumps on her arm a moment ago told him she was going to cave any day and confess how she felt about him.

"And help me discover who the creator of the tiaras is," Kimber added.

Dario stopped chewing his fry. How did he keep forgetting about that? He needed to make sure that he didn't sign in at the front desk at the hospital. For the life of him, he couldn't remember what he'd done. "Uh-huh," he said, lifting his bottle to his lips.

"I don't think it will take too much longer," Kimber went on. "I have an idea as to who it is."

Heart racing, Dario tried to maintain his cool and took a drink.

"I think it was Vin."

Beer burned the back of his throat and shot up his nose as he choked on the brew. "What?" he sputtered.

Oblivious as to why he'd choked, Kimber reached for another fry. "Don't worry. I'm going to be cool about it."

"Why do you think he's behind it?"

"There were certain things he said during dinner. Last year, Vin finished his residency at the hospital when all that crap happened with the crowns for the kids. I didn't bring it up at the time, but the more I think about it, the more I'm leaning toward it being him."

Dario drained his beer and belched. "He doesn't strike me as the kind of guy who can bend steel."

"He took a shop class in high school," Kimber said with a bit of mischief behind her voice.

"Sounds like there's more to that story."

Kimber shrugged. "I'm just saying I know he took a shop class and passed with an A."

"And you know this how?"

"Well," Kimber began with a nibble on her bottom lip, "the class was a requirement back then, and he was struggling. But he had a tutor who helped out."

"Southwood is a friendly town but why would another high school student help?"

"Oh, just because the guy who helped him pass did so to get Vin, who was Marvin at the time, to pretend to date me."

Dario wished he had another beer. "Why?"

"You've met my uncles—there was no way I was going to be allowed to date the captain of the football team." Hamilton tried pressing his snout toward her bottle of beer so Kimber set him down on the floor.

"This story just gets better and better."

"Jealous?" Kimber playfully pinched his elbow.

Yes, he thought. "Hardly," he answered. "So, what happened between you and the star football player?"

"We didn't see eye to eye about a lot of things."

"Like?"

"Like he wanted to use his scholarship and get a degree and come back here and teach PE."

Dario chuckled. "You don't like teachers?"

"I didn't like the idea of settling back in Southwood, so I broke up with him when he went off to college."

"Couples can work things out, you know," said Dario, although if she had, she might be married with a few kids by now instead of at his place after midnight. Kimber's heavy sigh told him it was a moot point. "You don't seem bothered by it," Dario noted.

Kimber shrugged his shoulders. "It was perfect timing for him to leave. Hey, let's watch TV. There's this great Christmas movie based off a book by Lacey Baker."

Avoidance. Why wasn't he surprised? "Hmph," he huffed.

"What?"

"I don't know—you were saying something earlier about commitment phobia."

The playful pinch on his elbow turned into a harsher one. Dario grabbed Kimber's beer and drained the rest of it, all while trying not to laugh.

Chapter 6

After staying up all night and talking after Kimber's non-date with Vin, and the plans for moving the pageant to the hospital, Kimber and Dario headed down to the town center—like everyone else who wanted a fresh Christmas tree.

A tree stand stood next to City Hall and was packed with customers young and old, inspecting all the limbs, needles and height of the varieties. Kimber had looked forward to this as a child. Afterward, her parents would take her to get a hot chocolate at The Cupcakery. The tradition would still stand. But they still had work to do. Dario's condo wasn't fully decorated, the pageant contestant list wasn't finalized and Kimber was no closer to ordering a tiara for Lexi.

"I think with the way y'all's balcony opens up and

has that beautiful view of the stream, this tree would be perfect," Kimber said, standing in front of the six-and-a-half-foot tree with her hands on her hips. She craned her neck to see the top. The open space in Dario's living room would be the ideal spot.

"You like this one?" Dario asked, standing close behind her.

The weather in Southwood had begun to reflect the time of year. It was never cold enough to snow, but chilly enough for Kimber to make use of her camel-colored wool jacket. Even through the thick material, the warmth of Dario's body was welcome.

"I think it's great. Look how the lower branches are high enough that Ariana and Justin won't get into them."

"Don't be too sure," Dario said stroking his chin. "They may be three, but they give their parents a run for their money at the playgrounds."

The image of a tiny Dario giving his parents hell brought a giggle to her throat. Kimber glanced upward and inhaled deeply at the sight. A few gray strands of hair stood out in his shadow on his rugged jaw. When he noticed her stare, he looked down and smiled. Without taking his eyes off her, Dario spoke to the kid. "We'll take this one."

Kimber beamed. "You sure?"

"You said it was perfect," Dario said with a shrug, "That's good enough for me. How about some hot chocolate before we meet up with the photographers?"

The change of venue had opened up the Christmas Pageant for more entrants. People did not care that they had three weeks to get ready. This was pageant territory—everyone came prepared. Dario had suggested she interview camera crews from the local area. With Lexi's early morning blessings, they'd updated Grits and Glam's Instagram page to inform their followers of where they'd be later to talk to photographers. It made sense. She wondered if this was part of the urban planning skills he'd picked up from his job in Dubai, something he'd mentioned as they'd talked until sunrise. When Dario clarified what he'd been doing there, Kimber felt silly for thinking he'd been looking for a job. Hell, he had a job—a serious job too.

"Do we have time?"

"I'm driving," said Dario. "So, of course we do. Let me finish up here with the delivery."

Kimber stepped aside to admire a few of the wreaths. She figured she needed one for her door and one for Dario too. Picking a couple with full pine-green needles and a fresh wintery scent, she took them up to the counter, not intending to eavesdrop on Dario's conversation.

"And a dozen of the five-foot ones delivered on the twenty-third," Dario said on the low before pushing a business card across the countertop with his blunt index finger. He tossed a glance over his shoulder and straightened up in a sketchy way.

"While you've surprised me with a lot about your life in the last twenty-four hours," Kimber began, cocking her head to the side, "I never pegged you as a botanist."

Brows furrowed together, Dario chuckled. "What?"

"Or forestry guy. Whatever they're called. All those trees you just ordered," she said, pointing at the makeshift counter. "I'm assuming you're going to do something special with them out at the ranch?" When a light shade of red tinted Dario's cheeks, Kimber narrowed her eyes at him. "Want to tell me what's going on?"

"Like you said, you learned a lot about me last night," Dario said, tapping the slope of her nose with his index finger. "Now, how about we head over to Peachville now and get that hot chocolate."

"Did I hear my name?"

Lilly Stringer stepped between Kimber and Dario on the straw-covered path that led back to his black Hummer. Kimber swatted long strands of bright candy cane–red hair that caught on her glossy lips when Lilly flipped it over her shoulder. Kimber wondered if Lilly taught her kids to be this petty. She probably did, Kimber thought. A few years ago, Philly had had her first taste of bullying at the hands of Lilly's sixth grader. Kimber had taken the lead after a visit with the principal did not work out. She made a deal with Lilly that if her kid didn't stop bullying Philly, she'd personally see to it that the congregation at Southwood Baptist would learn exactly how Lilly had earned her coveted position as the choir director's assistant.

It was no secret that after Lilly's divorce she'd made friends with Dario. The Crownes began to migrate to Southwood five years ago, when Dario was still in college. He came up from Miami during the

breaks and managed to make a lot of lady friends—
which was why Kimber had kept her distance from
Dario in the beginning. Though she knew firsthand
how easy it was to fall under the spell of his charm.

Dario at least offered a supportive smile and reached
around the assistant's frame. "Lil," he said, tugging
Kimber forward, "we're so glad to see you."

Lilly's dark eyes darted between Kimber and Dario.
"Really now?" She gave a half laugh, as if not believ-
ing the two of them could ever be a couple. "Kimber,
I thought you were living overseas after you didn't get
that job with MET."

But the mention of MET reminded Kimber of
Amelia's words. The station might call on her yet. She
slid her hand into her pocket to pull out her phone.
She feigned boredom by scrolling through the screen
while the two old "friends" got reacquainted. Kimber
had messages from a few of the beauty queens she'd
met in London. Instagram photos they'd tagged her
in. There was an instant message of Philly playing
connect the dots with the red pox marks on her arm.
And she had a few confirmations from this morning,
including one from a DJ who wanted to volunteer his
services to the pageant, especially since the venue
was a place he used to frequent as a kid while visit-
ing his sick sister. Kimber liked the heartfelt angle
of the story. But there were no messages from MET
Studios requesting her presence.

"We just flew in from Dubai this week," Dario
explained to Lilly.

The truth was the truth, Kimber thought smugly.

She fitted herself closer to Dari's frame, claiming him to spite Lilly's distasteful glower. For a second everything seemed so perfect between the two of them. Dario had been one of her best friends. She was sexually attracted to him, no doubt. And besides the mishap of last year, they'd never had a real fight or argument. Dario had pursued her since laying eyes on her. Was he really no longer interested in her? *Nah, never,* she thought, resting her head on Dario's chest, evoking a partial lip curl from Lilly. Kimber smiled in satisfaction.

"I see," Lilly went on quickly. "I won't hold y'all up. Dario, will I see you again this year?"

Of all the nerve. Kimber stepped forward but Dario still had hold of her arm. He bid Lilly good-bye and steered the two of them off toward the car.

"I'm not going to have your little trollops disrespect me, Dario."

"How is it disrespect if everyone thinks we're best friends? Aren't we? Unless you didn't tell me you wanted to be friends?"

Taken aback, Kimber stopped walking. "Yes, I mean…well." She fumbled for the words she wanted to say.

Dario tipped her chin. "Close your mouth or you'll catch a cold. Now, let me give you a boost into the seat."

"Are you forgetting about the offer I proposed to you earlier this week?" Kimber reminded him. He attempted to lift her by the waist to help her into the passenger's seat. She managed to press her back into his body, teasing him. She heard the inhale he took. Dario was definitely trying to resist her. Kimber tossed a smile over her shoulder in time to watch his jaw twitch. To taunt him further, Kimber pressed her backside into him too. "Why are you making things so hard?"

In one fluid motion, Dario lifted Kimber into the Hummer. She giggled as he stormed around the giant vehicle.

"And here I thought beauty queens were quiet and demure."

Her laughter died down over a choke. Kimber shook her head. "Have you just met me or something?"

"I don't know," Dario said right back. "I feel like after we talked last night and you told me about stealing a dress from Lexi's store, maybe I don't know you like I thought."

A roll of her eyes was all she needed to give him before they headed down the road. He hadn't given her an answer and it didn't slip her mind that he still wasn't responding to the reminder about her offer. At least not verbally. There were telltale signs he wanted her. It was three weeks until the pageant and Christmas. Something was sure to happen.

"When was the last time you went to Peachville?" Kimber asked, rocking back in her seat, apparently getting comfortable for the thirty-minute drive. The brown coat she wore opened at the bottom, exposing long legs fitted into a pair of skintight jeans and brown boots that stopped at her ankles. Dario knew beneath the suede shoes she wore a pair of *Elf*-inspired socks because he'd seen her come out of her bedroom this morning.

"Probably the last time we were here," he said, happy to talk about something other than Lilly.

Whatever kind of date he and Lilly had been on was in the past. He'd thought she understood good and well they were simply friends. But Lilly was also part of the Christmas Chaos regime. She and her former husband split up their holidays, where she traveled with her kids over Thanksgiving while he got the kids for the winter break. She slayed in the Christmas Cookie Crush Contest. Lines of gingerbread houses were set up as part of the obstacle course. Contestants had to march or hop over a half dozen of the houses, belly crawl under the lowest branches of Christmas trees and then climb over a log wall half-covered in holiday wrapping paper. If memory served him correctly, Darren was working on this with Kimber's uncle Nate. Nate Reyes was grandfathered in for an invite on account of the time when his wife was on assignment.

Kimber sighed. "Everything about that day seems so long ago."

"You became a world traveler soon after," Dario noted. "Is being back here making you want to stay?" Before the words finished leaving his mouth, he'd already caught the frown on her pretty face.

"Please," she grunted. "I would have thought by

now you understood I have no desire to settle down in Southwood."

"You act like you love it here."

"I do, but not enough to stay. I'm not sure if I ever told you or not but my folks weren't the happiest living here."

Hands gripping the steering wheel, Dario shook his head. "I don't believe you did."

"You know my dad was born and raised in Florida."

"Villa San Juan," Dario provided. He'd been to the northwestern island town a time or two on a delivery. "They didn't want to live there?"

"No, my mom always felt self-conscious being around that side of the family," Kimber explained. "I always thought it was because she didn't speak Spanish and didn't want to be made fun of."

"Is that why you didn't grow up bilingual?" He'd heard the stories about her uncles not listening to her unless she addressed them in Spanish. Having been raised by a second-generation Dominican and Cuban mother, Dario had learned early on to understand the language even if he didn't use it all the time.

A beat filled the space between them. "Jingle Bells" played from the radio, which was set to one of the stations that played Christmas songs around the clock.

"I speak it now," said Kimber with a slow smile. "Never too late to learn."

Dario took a deep inhale of the air. "You're living proof. How many languages do you speak now?"

"Just a few." Kimber's voice trailed off while she nibbled on the corner of her top lip.

With his right hand he counted for her. "English, Spanish, Arabic, French and Italian. What am I missing?"

"I'm picking up Portuguese," she added.

"Wonders never cease. I could use you at the conference table," Dario half-heartedly teased. The comment was in jest, but in reality, he could use a woman like Kimber beside him while making deals and compromises. Dubai was growing. But then, so was Southwood, especially on the stretch of land between it and Peachville.

Trees were being cut back to make room for the stretch of outlet stores anchored at a few gas stations and hole-in-the-wall restaurants. As they grew closer to Peachville, Dario slowed down for traffic. A festival was happening at the public school right at the border. Cars darted on and off the road. He kept a watchful eye on the way Kimber's hand gripped the side of the door and slowed his speed more.

They arrived at Bradley's Bakery. The local spot rivaled The Cupcakery with their cupcakes, but what set them apart was their variety of other pastries. Despite her protest, Dario dropped Kimber off at the curb while he found a parking space around the corner. When he approached, she was hanging up a sparkling colored flyer about the upcoming pageant on a message board at the covered bus stop.

"I didn't even realize you had that with you."

"I always come prepared," Kimber said, smiling up at him while he held the door for them to enter.

"Bienvenidos." They were welcomed from behind the counter as they entered. Everyone else in the bakery seated at the lavender-and-white checkered tables turned to greet them the same way.

"I love it here," Kimber whispered, clinging to his elbow.

The cases were filled with a variety of desserts and breads. They both agreed it would feel like cheating on The Cupcakery if they ordered any of the delicious chocolaty treats with the crushed candy canes. They focused on the display cases of cookies decorated like elaborately colorful tacky sweaters, and pastries like cannoli dipped in mini red and green chocolate chips. Five minutes later, they settled on a couple of caramel-crusted pecan croissants and two hot chocolates topped with what looked like fresh whipped cream and Oreo sprinkles.

"After we meet up with the photographers, I hope you don't mind hanging out here for a minute. There are a few shops I want to check out," said Dario, watching Kimber pick at a few nuts. Was she trying to be seductive with him? How was he supposed to concentrate with her dainty fingers slipping between her red-painted lips? He took a gulp of his hot drink and shifted to adjust himself in his jeans.

"What kind of shops?" Kimber perked up. "You know I'm down for shopping."

"A toy shop with homemade toys made out of wood like back in the day."

The afternoon sun coming in from the window caught Kimber's light brown eyes as they widened. The amber color reminded Dario of the stones he'd used for the tiara he'd made her last year. The gift had never come out of the box thanks to their interlude under the sky. He twisted his lips to the side, trying to remember where he'd thrown the box when he came home after her major rejection. He cleared his throat to stamp down the memory of his heart breaking for the first time.

"Count me in. My cousin, Kenny, prefers to watch other kids on YouTube play with toys rather than play with anything. And his brother and sister don't help. Angel and Victor will spend all day watching him watch the videos."

"Kids these days," Dario mumbled.

"Right?"

Like the bakery in Southwood, this one had a bell over the door to announce new customers. Dario flicked his wrist to check the time. Three men came in together. As when Kimber and Dario had walked in, the rest of the patrons greeted them. Kimber, with her back to the door, turned to join in the fun but she rose from her seat.

"You've got to be kidding me!" Kimber exclaimed while covering her mouth.

Curious, Dario stood to see what was going on. One of the gentlemen walking through the door stopped short so the man following bumped into him. Obviously Kimber and the first man knew each other.

Dario inhaled deeply when she darted across the floor to hug him.

"Oh my God! I didn't know I'd be meeting you!" Kimber said, pulling away but holding on to the man's hands.

A camera hung from his neck by a green camouflage strap. He stood tall at six-five. Squaring his shoulders, Dario sized him up and figured he'd go a round or two in the ring before the final knockout.

"I didn't want you to see my name and then decide not to meet with me," the man answered.

"Now why wouldn't I?" Kimber asked him. Her fingers gripped the hem of his blue Peachville High T-shirt.

Dario recalled two people from the same company contacting Kimber this morning like lightning the moment she posted on social media. More people began to enter the bakery. Kimber pulled the guy closer, out of the way.

"Oh, where are my manners?" she said. "Philip, I want you to meet Dario Crowne."

"Crowne you say?" This Philip character asked, eyeing him up and down.

"That's right," said Dario. "You know me?"

Philip shrugged. "I know Darren. He invited me to visit the ranch."

The two simple sentences told Dario a few things. Philip knew about Christmas Chaos. And Philip was single. Judging from the way the dude kept his arm wrapped around Kimber's waist, he wanted to fix the latter.

"How do you two know each other?" Dario asked Kimber.

"Remember when I told you about Vin? This is Philip, my friend from high school."

"Friend?" Philip asked, tugging Kimber's side closer to his.

Great, Dario grumbled. *This is turning out to be one hell of a Merry Ex-mas.*

"'Twas three weeks before the Christmas Pageant." Kimber held her selfie stick in the air and touched her chin, pondering her words. "Or is it 'twis, since it hasn't happened yet? I don't know, folks, y'all tell me. I'm standing here in front of the case of coveted tiaras housed here in the office at Grits and Glam Gowns off Main Street in Southwood, Georgia. We have tall ones, short ones, clip-on ones, pinned-in ones. But what we don't have are the custom-made ones anonymously left at Four Points General Hospital. If you see something, say something. I'd love to feature you on my next blog. Alright, pageant pals out there, this is your favorite on-the-scene beauty queen correspondent signing out for now."

Kimber stopped filming and headed out of Lexi's office to find her aunt giving a mother and daughter the royal treatment, as every customer received. She remembered the woman as one of the coaches at Southwood Middle School who'd insisted Kimber come to PE dressed appropriately and expected her to participate. She offered a half smile, then waved at the little girl wearing one of the complimentary tiaras Lexi had started giving away with the purchase of a dress. According to Lexi, everyone deserved to feel like a princess.

"Thank you again for coming," said Lexi, handing her customer a white garment bag as she walked the lady and her young daughter to the door.

Kimber stood behind the register in awe of her aunt's hands-on customer service, taking care of the last customer of the day. They'd been pretty busy for a Sunday afternoon. And not all of it was folks coming to Grits and Glam Gowns for dresses for the Christmas Pageant. Lexi had recently released her New Year's Eve line and women pounced on the se-quined dresses alongside mothers fighting over the reduced-price one of a kind toddler cupcake dresses for the pageant.

"You didn't have to come in today, but I'm glad you did. You can tell me how the kids are doing. If you let Philly tell it, she's in an oatmeal prison," Kim-ber said, following her aunt to lock the door and flip the sign to Closed.

Deep down she knew Lexi wanted to see how things were going with the pageant. So far Kimber had everything handled. The social media blast had brought the contestant list to forty by last night. No one had a problem with the last-minute extension. One person thanked her for giving them something fun to do on Christmas Eve. The hospital board and Nate were meeting this week to work on the theater. Sashes and trophies had been ordered. Lexi wanted to take care of the tiaras, which was fine since Kimber's quest to find the designer of the custom crowns was on hold. She still needed to meet with Vin once more.

Lexi laughed and tossed her blond hair off her shoulder. "I can't wait for Philly to win an Oscar. She's been practicing for a while now."

It wouldn't surprise Kimber to see her sister make it in Hollywood as an actress. She did have a flair for the dramatic. "Vin mentioned she is contagious until the pox are scabbed over."

"Dr. Vin?" Lexi repeated with a grin. "He'll always be Marvin to me ever since the two of you pretended to be a couple. I still recall how sweetly he looked at you last year."

"While I got my stomach pumped due to my uncles trying to cook?"

Lexi smiled and waved off the past. "Let's get some tea and you can give me the *tea*."

They headed into the kitchenette, which separated Lexi's two businesses. On one side, she owned one of Georgia's most visited boutiques for wedding, prom and pageant dresses. Music poured through the open doors on the other side of the business where Grits and Glam Studios trained budding pageant queens.

"There's no tea to spill," said Kimber. She took two glasses down from the pink painted cabinets over the sink.

"He had such a crush on you. It was so cute." Lexi took the glasses to fill them with ice from the door on the side-by-side stainless steel refrigerator. Kimber followed to grab the pitcher of sweetened tea with floating lemon slices.

"I don't think so." Kimber frowned. "Things may be different now."

"Because you can finally see how handsome he is?"

Kimber narrowed her eyes at Lexi. "What?"

"You never looked past the glasses and the geeky clothes," Lexi explained. "But I could tell the way he looked at you, he only went along with your cover plan because he liked you."

"As a *friend*," Kimber clarified. "But as I was trying to say, we did go out for dinner last Friday."

"What? You didn't tell me."

With a shrug, Kimber shook her head. The same blah feelings she'd had after the dinner washed over her. "I'm telling you now, and really, there's nothing to tell. Dario and I ran into him at the hospital in the children's ward."

The words just rolled off her lips. Dario and I. Like they were a couple or something. But they weren't. Kimber didn't do relationships.

"Wait, you were with Dario?"

"Yeah, we have an agreement. I'm helping him childproof and decorate his condo for his brother's family. In return, he's chauffeuring me around town."

Lexi rubbed her temples. "What now?"

"You sound like you're the correspondent." Kimber pursed her lips. Lexi began to laugh. Her shoulders bounced up and down. "Maybe I shouldn't sing that single version of 'Jingle Bells' to you."

"Oh, I'm still single," Kimber assured her. A chill crept through the air.

"Did you not see how cute Marvin has become? And how he's trying his new name?"

"Not interested, Lex," Kimber warned.

"Anyway," Lexi goaded, pushing Kimber's forearm. "How did Marvin get you away from Dario and how did Dario allow you to go out with someone else with him standing right there? He never liked having to share you when you came home from college."

"Why would Dario have an issue? He's made it clear he wants to be friends."

"Oh, Kimber," Lexi sighed and sat back in her chair. "I was half teasing about the Marvin part. I get that you were just a teen then. But now, honey, you're too smart to be that blind."

"Blind about what?" Kimber had looked for the signs. If Dario were the jealous type, she didn't see it.

"Kimber, you may have your uncles fooled but you know you never conned me since the day we met."

"Ever?" Kimber asked. "How about the time I took your dress or the time I ended up being here because Philly won Miss Peach Blossom at the fair and got you as her pageant coach?"

"Not funny," said Lexi. "I know more went on between you and Dario."

Heat crept up Kimber's neck. "I—I…"

"Don't go into details with me, dear," Lexi laughed. "I just want you to know that I know exactly when it happened."

"What? Shut up. No, you don't."

Lexi nodded. "Last year, shortly after Charlotte

and Richard got engaged. The Christmas party at the elementary school."

Impressive, Kimber thought.

Lexi went on. "That boy has been lovesick since the day he laid eyes on you, but you wouldn't give him the time of day."

"We were the best of friends," Kimber defended herself, crossing her arms over her chest. "He was busy hooking up with all the single ladies. He's a player. If eye daggers were real, I'd be dead right now. You should have seen the way his groupies looked at me."

"I'm pretty sure Dario was getting the same daggers. You were quite the player yourself," said Lexi.

"Oh shut up," Kimber gasped. "Not you too."

"I just call it like I see it, sweets."

"Well, you may flip your lid when I tell you who we're going to go with for the photographer for the pageant."

The ice in Lexi's glass fell against her mouth as she drained her drink. "Who?"

"Philip."

Kimber sipped on her tea while her aunt had the giggles.

"I'm glad you find this funny."

"It's like your own version of boyfriends of Christmas past."

Except Dario was never her boyfriend. It had been three whole days since she offered a perfect arrangement for them to get through the holidays and he showed no sign of being interested.

"I'm sorry. I'm sorry." Lexi wiped tears from the

corners of her eyes. "Tell me about Philip. What's he been up to since graduation?"

Kimber filled Lexi in on what she'd learned over hot cocoa the previous afternoon. Philip had been hired as the head coach at Peachville High during the football season and he worked for a local photography agency, a craft he'd learned in college. As expected, Philip never wanted to go into the NFL. What Kimber did find shocking to learn was that he'd married but was now divorced after three years, and that he had a four-year-old daughter he wasn't going to see this Christmas. Regardless of their past history, Philip's portfolio spoke for itself.

"What is it you want from him?" Lexi finally asked. "Or do I need to clarify whom I'm speaking of?"

"Aunt Lexi," Kimber whined, "why are you picking on me?"

"Put your big girl panties on. This is your doing. No one told you to leave town after what happened between you and Dario. You hightailed it right out of here."

"I waited until Christmas."

"Leaving that boy heartbroken," Lexi scolded.

Kimber sighed heavily with sarcasm. "Uh, yeah, I think he's over it. As a matter of fact, he and I are back to being the best of friends again."

This time Lexi mocked Kimber's sigh. "Girl," she cackled, "if you believe that, I've got a bridge to sell you."

If she'd been with anyone else, Kimber might have

pouted at her aunt's words, but because she knew Lexi told it like it was, she didn't. Plus, Lexi might smack her in the back of the head. "I did offer him a friendly arrangement while I'm here."

"Friends with benefits?"

Well, when Lexi said it out loud like that with an eye roll, Kimber felt foolish. She jutted her chin out while Lexi scooted away from the table. "You offered that grown man a childish game? He isn't nineteen. Dario is a mature business man with a career. He's looking for someone to settle down with."

"I don't ever want to get married." Kimber recoiled.

"Settling down doesn't mean you have to get married, but you are getting too old for booty calls."

"I didn't offer a booty call." *Not really*, she thought.

"Girl, let me get out of here and check on my babies. You need to get wise before Dario finds someone nice to be naughty with."

Chapter 7

After posting on her Sunday blog about the custom-made tiaras, Kimber heard back from the mother of one recipient on Monday when she was getting ready in her apartment. That woman's daughter had received a crown in a red-and-white box before she ended her extended stay at the children's wing. Like the father she'd heard from the previous day—same MO and no name. The designer dropped off a box of twelve the first day and then started mass-producing them for every discharge until Christmas. It was like she—or he—was a serial tiara maker.

National Letter Writing Day fell on a Wednesday that year. Kimber had plans to visit the kids at the hospital that afternoon and write letters to Santa with Lexi's junior tiara squad—the middle school–aged girls. But that wasn't until later. In the meantime, Kimber spent the morning twin-proofing the upstairs rooms at Dario's place. The morning rain kept them from venturing out. For Kimber it was a lazy day inside, getting things together while wearing a pair of gray yoga pants and a Crowne's Garage T-shirt knotted in the front. She enjoyed working with Dario.

It never seemed like it took an effort to be around him. She didn't worry about having to get dressed up or throw on makeup or touch up her hair. Dario made no comment about the messy bun piled on top of her head, as if they really were just the best of friends. He hadn't responded to her friends-with-benefits offer. Friendship. It was what she wanted, right? She was friends with her exes. Look at her with Vin and Philip. Okay, look at her and Philip. Dario was a friend. Why was this so difficult?

Lexi's words still echoed in her mind. Sure, maybe at one point Dario had developed feelings for her but he did not act like it now. Though they worked together during the day, in the evenings Dario went off on his own and didn't come back for hours—not like she checked or anything. Dates? Women? *Brothels?* There were no brothels in Southwood. Kimber irritated herself with the curiosity, especially seeing Dario yawn and stretch like he was tired. *Get a grip, Kimber.*

To distract herself, Kimber took out her phone from the pocket on the side of her leg of her yoga pants, posed in front of the bare tree and clicked it to broadcast. The red light came to life and so did she.

"Hey, pageant pals out there, this is your favorite on-the-scene beauty queen correspondent." She offered a wave to the viewers watching. "I just wanted to show y'all how far I'll go to uncover the stories behind the mystery tiaras." She waved her hand up and down the tree to fan the green needles. "I'm doing manual labor just to get to the bottom of the tia…" She stopped speaking when Dario walked behind her shot in order to get to the couch. On his way he pulled his shirt over his head then flexed his muscle for the camera. The likes and hearts floated across her screen. "Okay, see the stuff I have to deal with in order to uncover the truth? Tell me your stories. Ta-ta for now."

Kimber crossed the room to the kitchen. A few people commented on her post who had or knew someone who had the exact tiaras she talked about. After sending each person who had a story a direct message for contact info, Kimber set her phone down on the counter and headed back into the living room.

"I never thought babyproofing a house took so much work." Dario maneuvered himself into the corner of the L-shaped gray couch with a yawn. His coppery-colored skin was quite the contrast, as was his heavily tattooed frame. He was inked with various cars, engines and his mother's name and face, but Kimber's favorite was the three-pointed crown meant for his last name, right between his belly button and the waistband of his shorts. The sculpted muscles of his thigh twitched as the fabric of his black mesh shorts hiked up. One hand covered the crown while the other supported the back of his head and showed off the bulge of his biceps.

Kimber tried not to stare. Looking too hard might induce some form of drool, which was easy to do around Dario and his sexy self. Hamilton grunted as well, turning three times in his Sherpa-fleece-lined bed before plopping down for a slumber. Soft snorts filled the air.

Kimber stood at the V of the sofa to press her knee against Dario's. "We're not done yet."

"How do you know so much?" Dario complained.

"Remember, I have baby cousins," replied Kimber. She nudged Dario once again. "C'mon now. We have things to do this afternoon."

Dario sank deeper into the cushions. "My God, woman! We've installed locks on the cabinets, measured all the soft ornaments four feet from the ground, covered all the outlets and we ordered the Sesame Street Christmas sheets even though I think the baby shark ones are better. Let's take a nap." To drive his point home, Dario clapped his hands together to sing the old—and tired—"Baby Shark."

"Stop playing," Kimber ordered.

Arms still outstretched, Dario clamped his hands on top of hers. She'd known Dario was a large man. He managed to always make her feel safe. "Uh-oh… the shark has you."

"Boy, quit," Kimber laughed in an attempt to avoid the tingle of electricity bolting through her veins. She yanked her hand back. In turn, she stumbled. With quick reflexes, Dario reached and pulled her forward.

They laughed together for a moment before Kimber realized where she sat. "I should probably get up."

Dario's hands fanned against her backside. "Don't act like we didn't fall asleep the other night on this couch."

Their lips were so close Kimber tasted the vanilla coffee he'd finished off that morning. She felt her chest tremble. "Falling asleep is something completely different from this and you know it."

"Explain what *this* is."

Oh, so now he wanted to call her bluff? Kimber pursed her lips. Dario gave her a lopsided grin. "Don't play with me, Dario," she warned him.

"Because you don't want to get wrinkled up for seeing Dr. Vin? And here I thought you didn't get excited over him."

"I wouldn't wear this for him," Kimber said, rolling her eyes. Pleasantly trapped by his arm, she didn't move.

Dario cocked his head to the side and checked her out. "Good. This look is too sexy for him."

"Oh please," she groaned.

Within the gentle restraint of his arms, she adjusted the way her body rested on his. She pulled her knees into the couch, straddling him. Through the fabric of her yoga pants she felt the rise of his desire for her.

"I'm serious, Kimber," Dario said. Gone was the hint of laugh lines at the corners of his mouth. "Forget all the tiaras, makeup, sequined gowns and giant hair. Nothing is sexier than you wiggling around here in your pants and my shirt."

Kimber gulped. Dario wedged his fingers through the knot at the front of the shirt. The palm of his hand pressed against the space between her belly button and the swell of her breast. Her nipples hardened beneath the fabric. She shivered but didn't move, determined to have the upper hand in this situation.

"You've got goose bumps," Dario said, moving his free hand. His used the side of his thumb to trail a line along her upper arm. He cocked his head to the side. "Are those for me or for your date later?"

"It's cold," Kimber whispered, dismissing the fact she'd offered herself to him just the other day. Dario leaned up to press his lips against her neck. She questioned everything she'd done with him since being back, including her offer. Why did it matter who initiated what could be considered the second round of great lovemaking in her life? She needed to just go with the flow. And appreciate how easy it was to relax her body against his, especially when his tongue snaked out from between his lips. Dario's hands moved over her body, slow and seductive. Juices within began to flow at his mere touch. She curved her hips against the undoubtedly hard erection beneath his shorts then ground them back and forth.

Mind on autopilot, Kimber tilted her head to the side and kissed his firm jawline. Bristles of chin hair from his skipping this morning's shave tickled her lips. Their mouths found each other. Familiarity of touch flooded back. Dario was a firm kisser. Not aggressive but determined. Kimber cupped his face with her hands. His fingertips traced a line down her spine then around her rib cage. The move didn't tickle as much as it compelled her to deepen the erotic thrust against his cock. Just when she was at the brink of a dry-hump orgasm, Kimber's cell phone shrilled through the sexual tension hovering in the air.

"Don't get it," Dario broke the kiss to order.

"It's a regular ringtone," Kimber said. Like that made sense to anyone else. The phone rang a third time. Kimber pulled against his light restrain. "C'mon now, it could be someone calling about the tiaras."

Dario licked her neck and followed it up with a kiss just at her lower ear.

"Or M-MET calling."

With that, Dario held his hands up in surrender. Kimber slid across his lap. Her eyes caught a glimpse of the bulge tenting his shorts. What was she about to do? She felt the wetness on her panties. Her body screamed for relief or a cold shower.

A deep thump pounded between her ears. This could be it. This could be the call she'd been waiting on from MET. How ironic to be in the same position as last year. Kimber found her phone next to the remote control for the flat-screen TV hanging on the wall. Shaky fingers pressed the green talk button. The area code was local, not from Florida where MET made its home or even in the Atlanta area. "Hello?"

"Kimber?"

"Vin?" Kimber asked, staring at the number.

Dario banged the back of his head against the cushions of the couch. The feeling was mutual at this being the interruption of their interlude. Kimber tucked a stray hair behind her ear. "Hey, what's up? Is everything okay for this afternoon?"

"Yeah, I just finished speaking with Nicolette."

"Is she okay? She's not due for a few more weeks."

Vin's chuckle came over the line. "Yes, she's fine. She and I were talking about your mysterious tiaras."

"Oh really?" The moment of truth. Kimber sat down on the barstool at the counter to turn her back on Dario. A pig themed calendar hung on the wall by the utility table in the corner of the kitchen, and she grinned at the thought that Hamilton would ever sit still long enough for a photo shoot. "What do you have for me?"

"I think this is a story that needs explaining face-to-face."

"Sounds serious," Kimber said. "I could be ready and over there within the hour."

"Great, I look forward to seeing you again, Kimber."

"Same here," Kimber blurted out before disconnecting. When she turned around to tell Dario, she found herself alone in the open floor plan. Upstairs, she heard the water turn on. A little devil appeared on her shoulder, urging her to finish what they'd started while a little angel reminded her that getting the story behind the tiaras would not only give her a good segment to show MET, but also allow her to get her request in to have a spectacular tiara made for Lexi.

Oh, what the hell, she told herself, trotting up the staircase. She found the door to Dario's room open. His shorts were on the floor by his bed. Kimber cracked open the bathroom door. Since his place was customized, Dario had more luxurious fixtures than she did. For starters, the man had a walk-in shower with a ceiling head. No steam rose over the top of the door, making the glass doors clear as day.

Water darkened Dario's hair and ran down his back. His head was bent, his back turned, which gave her the perfect view of his firm behind. Dario's right hand moved down by his hip. Something guided Kimber inside the bathroom. Her bare feet sank into the beige rug by the brown granite vanity. Eyes transfixed by the gush of water flowing over every inch of him, it took Kimber a moment to realize what he was doing. The attempt to get out of there quickly and quietly failed. Kimber's hand hit something on the counter and the cup holding his toothbrush and toothpaste spilled into the sink.

"You alright there?" Dario asked.

Shoulders hunched, Kimber closed her eyes. "Sorry! Sorry!"

"Turn around, Kimber," he ordered.

Eyes still closed, Kimber spun around.

"Open your eyes," he demanded with a softer tone.

She did as she was told. Dario faced her, his full erection in his hand. Her mouth went dry. It was one thing to fantasize about it at night with her battery-operated boyfriend. It was something else to straddle it with clothes on. But now. Right in front of her, in all his magnificent glory, he was spectacular.

"Come here," he said.

Once again on autopilot, Kimber stepped forward,

close enough that when she came near the shower doors, he reached out and took her hand. The cold water on her wrist snapped her out of her trance. Dario dropped his hard member, which bounced forward, and turned the knob on the wall. Steam filled the space between them. Kimber took another step closer until her toes hit the ledge.

"Scared?" Dario taunted her.

In full bravado, Kimber shook her head. Her thumbs hooked the waistband of her pants and with the aid of her feet she stepped out of them. Not waiting another second, Dario pulled Kimber into the tiny space. Water dampened her shirt within seconds.

"Where were we?" Dario asked without waiting for an answer. His hands reached for the bun at the top of her head and took it down while his mouth reunited them.

Kimber mewed, hating the material between them. As if he understood her thoughts, Dario lifted the hem over her head, leaving the two of them naked together. His erection pressed against her belly. Kimber's hands ran over his shoulders, arms, chest and member. She stroked his length, gripping and pulling, rolling her thumb over the slick helmet head. Droplets of precum mixed with the water of the shower. Dario moaned. He knelt down before her, kissing and suckling her breasts. Thick moisture formed between her legs. She throbbed for him. Satiating part of her need, Dario spread her legs apart, hooking one over his shoulder. A long blunt finger pressed inside her. Kimber gave a little cry. How long had it been? A year? Dario spread her lips apart with his fingers, rolling her bud between his thumb and forefinger. Within seconds the sensation of an orgasm gripped her body. She held her breath.

"Let it out," he coaxed.

Kimber leaned against the shower wall. Her hands gripped the metal bar as the first wave come over her. Dario moved her leg off his shoulder to his waist. Water pooled between their bodies when he stood and slipped himself inside her. Kimber tried to balance herself on one toe, but their heights didn't match. Knowing the difference, Dario picked her up by her behind. His fingers took a firm hold of her flesh. The protective hard grip excited her. She came again while he pulled halfway out and plunged back in.

Kimber hugged her body against his and let him bounce her up and down. His legs bent enough to support her weight. Under the showerhead he kissed her once more, tasting her tongue and suckling on her bottom lip. Kimber tilted her head and offered her neck, and he obliged before moving on to her breasts. The water stopped abruptly and before Kimber understood what was going on, Dario carried her to his bed.

Both of them soaking wet, she climbed into the cushion of the four-poster bed. Kimber propped herself up on her elbows, cocking one leg up, her head to the side while he fumbled with what she figured was protection from the side drawer. Without the steam or distance, she got a better look at him and decided she might need to scoot back.

Dario shook his head with a lazy grin. "Nah, don't

run from me now." He caught her by the ankle and brought her to the edge of the bed.

Penetrated to the hilt, Kimber moved one foot to his chest. He clasped both legs and held them straight against his chest. Kimber's breasts jiggled before he reached down to hold both together with his fingers. His thumbs rotated between her nipples. Kimber's body quivered with the threat of another orgasm. How was this even possible? She tried to hold back but couldn't. Her inner walls clamped down on his driving cock. Back arched, Kimber gripped the messy sheets. Her eyes fluttered with each satisfied wave.

Dario took both her calves and held them wide open. He thrust forward and grunted with each one, faster and deeper. Still in a haze, Kimber watched his body in overdrive. Eyes closed, his lips moved like he was reading a book for a moment before his mouth dropped open, frozen almost. His whole body stopped moving. Kimber tightened her walls once more and when she did, his whole body shook. Even through the condom she felt the force of his orgasm shooting out of him. Once spent, Dario kissed her all the way up her thighs, stomach and breasts to her face.

"That was…" He was lost for words.

"Amazing," Kimber supplied for him. He collapsed onto the bed and she turned to her side, facing him. Her hands couldn't help but caress his jaw. Dario closed his eyes and smiled. Amazing how such a rugged, handsome man looked so innocent while pretending to sleep. At least, she hoped he was pretending.

"Dario?"

Dario wrapped his arm around her waist and pulled her as close as possible. The sheets were soaked. Their bodies half-dried. "I'm not 'sleep."

"Dario," she whispered. "I'm sorry I left the way I did last year."

"Sshh," he said. "I told you. That's in the past. We can't change who said and did what. What's important is that we're here now."

Kimber bit her bottom lip. "Well, about being here now. I need to get to the hospital."

"We're going to be there on time, Kimber," he said with his eyes still closed.

"No, I promised Vin I'd meet him before the letter writing starts. He has something important to tell me about the tiaras. I think he's going to confess to being the maker."

Dario's arm tightened around her waist. His face sank into the crumpled comforter. "Well hell, this we gotta hear."

"Miss Kimber!"

After signing in at the desk upstairs with Nicolette, Kimber heard her name being called. A small, frail girl in a wheelchair was being pushed off the elevator. Kimber's heart sank and soared at the same time. Christiana, the petite blond being pushed by a young volunteer, raised the hand not attached to the IV pole hooked to her wheelchair. She'd been in and out of the hospital since Kimber started volunteering there.

Setting the flower-shaped pen down on the counter,

Kimber rushed over to the precocious thirteen-year-old. "Christiana, I'm both glad and not glad to see you."

"Aw you know me and this lymphoma can't stop this love-hate relationship."

Kimber knelt by Christiana's side. She was close to Philly's age and should be spending her afternoons chatting with friends, playing video games and maybe going crazy over the latest kid line of Ravens Cosmetics. "It's back?"

"Just for the holidays," Christiana laughed. "I believe I heard you were holding a beauty pageant here and you know we had to be here for a front row seat."

"How about a front row seat as one of the special guest judges?" Kimber asked her.

Excitement lit up Christiana's alabaster face. "For real?"

"Sure," said Kimber. "You'll get a special nametag and everything."

Within the limitations of the IV, Christiana reached up and gave Kimber a hug. Over her shoulder, Kimber spied Vin coming through the doors down the hall. He wore a white lab coat over a pair of brown plaid pants.

"Are you going to do some letter writing to Santa today?" Kimber asked Christiana as she pulled back from the hug. The expected straight face looked back. "I'm guessing you're going to help organize."

"Correct," said Christiana. "I'm babysitting."

Vin came up behind Christiana and the volunteer with a deep laugh. "Don't be too hard on them today, Miss Christiana."

The young girl's cheeks turned a bright red. "I won't, Dr. Vin."

It was cute the way Vin—Marvin—evoked such a sweet response. She remembered Vin blushing during the outfit of choice portion of the beauty pageants he'd accompanied her to back in the day.

"Somebody has a crush," Kimber said once the girls were out of earshot.

A stethoscope hung around the doctor's neck. Vin shoved his hands into his pocket. "Oh please," he chided. "You would know a thing or two about crushes, since everyone around you had one."

"Apparently I don't know as much as I thought I did," Kimber mumbled. "How are you doing today, Vin?"

"I'm a lot better now," said Vin.

A warm relaxed feeling came over Kimber. She felt better, as well. Every bone in her body was left satiated. Her skin still buzzed with the sweet memory of Dario's lips. Then Vin's sweaty palms were against her forehead. His hand gripped her elbow and led her to the wall just to prop her up. Kimber wondered if she'd blacked out for a moment. Dario had been in the waiting room coloring with one of the kids and was already charging toward them.

"I'm fine," she said quickly, stepping out of Vin's concerned hold. "Really."

Dario stepped between Vin and her. His large hands caressed her shoulders. "You okay?"

"Perhaps you haven't eaten today?" Vin suggested.

"My colleague's office is right this way and I know he keeps some crackers. I can take her from here."

Vin held his hand out for Kimber but Dario wrapped an arm around her, not heeding a thing Vin said. Tucking his hand back into his pocket, Vin led them just a few feet down the squeaky-clean corridor. A camera followed them. For a moment Kimber thought it seemed odd to have such high-tech equipment but realized this was the children's ward. Their safety mattered.

No wonder she had to sign in each time, Kimber thought, leaning on Dario. "You guys, I'm totally fine. I think I just got a little heated. It is warm in here, right?"

"A little," Dario agreed.

Using a white passkey clipped to the pocket near his nametag, Vin opened the office with Dr. Ross's name card outside and ushered them in. A flat black leather couch stood against the wall under half a dozen academic degrees, all framed in black wood. A large desk with mounds of paperwork and folders stood in the center and white lab coats hung from a rack behind the door.

"Let me take your temperature," said Vin. He pulled out a thermometer for her to place under her tongue while he pressed his wrist against her forehead. All the while Dario sat beside Kimber.

"He's a legit doctor," Kimber mumbled.

"I can take you downstairs to see my degrees if you like," Vin said. "Now tell me, nod yes or no.

I know everyone over at the Reyes house has the chicken pox. Have you been around them?"

"Not long enough," Dario answered. "She was there, what? Five minutes before she and Lexi noticed the spots?"

The thermometer pinged. Vin examined the numbers. "No fever."

"I'm telling you I just got a little winded," Kimber tried to explain.

"Were you doing something to cause you to lose your breath today?" Vin asked her.

Kimber glanced up at Dario before she cleared her throat. "If cleaning counts."

"You need to be careful around the fumes from chemicals, okay?"

Nodding, Kimber sat back on the couch. "I feel so silly. Did anyone notice?"

"No," both men chorused.

"Thank God." She breathed a sigh of relief. "How about that drink?"

Vin moved across the room to the brown fridge by the closed door. "Crap, he doesn't have anything in here. Could you grab her something from down the hall?" Vin reached into his front pocket and extracted a dollar bill. "It's on me."

Dario snorted at the money. He hesitated a moment before coming to his feet. "I will be right back."

"Your new guard dog is well trained," Vin said in a teasing lower voice since Dario had left the door ajar.

"Now, now," Kimber scolded with a smiling *tsk*,

"that's not nice. Dario is just concerned, just like you."

Grabbing a stool from beside the couch, Vin wheeled it to sit in front of her. "Yes, but I went to school for this."

"And who's doing it for free?" she quipped right back at him in defense of Dario.

"Okay fine," the doctor sighed. "I'm not going to pick on your Neanderthal."

"Vin," Kimber warned. "Why don't you tell me what you know about the tiaras? Have you been following my blogs?"

"Nicolette," he answered with a shrug. "We were talking about the last time you were here with the kids and the pageant you held for the patients."

It still seemed odd that Vin was around last year but hadn't wanted his presence to be known. "And?"

"Well, I did overhear about the problems you were having with that company about price gouging at the last minute so I…" Vin's pregnant pause brought Kimber to the edge of the couch with anticipation. She wasn't sure why waiting for this revelation didn't make her as thrilled as expected. Kimber swore she heard the tick of the second hand on his watch. The gold face stood out against the darkness of his deep brown skin.

"What is it, Vin?"

"I didn't want to say anything earlier because I didn't want to make a big deal of it," he said. "I never wanted to tell anyone, I just wanted to make your day better. I'm the designer you're looking for. I didn't realize you would ever research it for your article."

And then some, Kimber thought. "Why didn't you say anything last year?"

"I was already avoiding you," said Vin. "Remember?"

The journalist in her started thinking of questions, but they'd have to wait. Someone knocked on the half-opened door. Vin came to his feet when one of the nurses poked her head inside.

"Sorry to interrupt, Dr. Vin," she said. "There is an issue that needs your attention."

Vin offered Kimber an apologetic smile. "Duty calls."

"Sure." Kimber came to her feet with the help of Vin's forearm. "We can talk later about the tiaras."

The two of them separated at the door. Kimber followed the sound of laughter down the hall. She found a group of kids, boys and girls, spread out at a half dozen tables. Crayons, paper and childproof scissors sat in silver pails, serving as centerpieces. Christiana rolled by the tables, helping the children with their letters. Some of the other pageant squad had arrived in Kimber's short absence. The only person missing was Dario.

Kimber's heart swelled with excitement just thinking his name. She studied the group of kids with her hand over her mouth. Her thumb traced her bottom lip. Something circular pressed against her back. She figured Dario had returned with her drink. Kimber, happy to see him, spun around. But it wasn't him.

"Philip?"

A camera, dangling from a neck strap, scraped against Kimber's elbow. She reached up and wrapped her arms around his shoulders for a hug. In this cooler weather, Philip had chosen to wear a thin, dark blue shirt and a pair of khaki cargo pants. "I didn't expect to see you so soon," she said.

"I thought I'd come by and take a few pictures of what goes on before the pageant's bright lights," he said. "I got this idea to put a booklet together for the contestants. It'd be nice to show my players there's more to life than being in the NFL or a rapper. I just saw your uncle at the theater. He might come and speak to the team about building things and business."

Jaw dropped, Kimber pushed on Philip's shoulder. "What? That is so cool of you."

"Well, you know," Philip crooned. "I gotta inspire kids somehow."

"You certainly inspire me," said Kimber. She leaned against the wall, positioning herself to be the first person Dario saw when he came back. What was taking so long with the drink?

Philip returned the slight push on her arm. "Maybe this time around, I'll inspire you again."

Kimber shook her head. "I'm sorry, what do you mean?"

"I mean, you know, last year." Philip pressed his hand against the spot on the wall above her head.

"Why do I feel like I'm missing something?"

After a look around and over his shoulder, Philip leaned closer. "The tiaras," he whispered close.

A thud hit the pit of her stomach. "What tiaras?"

"The ones that showed up last year. I know you're trying to find out who designed them and I wanted to clear up any confusion. I was here last year right after you exposed that pageant for fraud. Even after five years of not seeing you, I was still in my feelings about how you ended things with me. We were the it couple and you ended things cold. I wasn't sure if I wanted to see you right away, but I did want to do something nice for you."

"Oh, I already know," Kimber said with a relieved smile. It was comforting to know that Philip and Vin remained friends over the years. Vin must have gone to Philip for help. They'd probably laughed over hiding from her last year. "Vin told me."

"Vin?" Philip pulled his head back. "Who is Vin?"

"Marvin," Kimber said, stopping short of adding a *duh* at the end. "We were just talking about it."

"I don't know what the hell is going on," snapped Philip, "but he didn't leave the tiaras behind. I did. I made them in the shop at school."

Confused, Kimber shook her head. A fog began to form. What was going on here? First she spent a year wondering who created them and now she had two people confessing within the same hour? "I don't understand."

"My cousin Auggie said you were asking about them," Philip explained, "on, like, a video blog or something. He knows I like to play around with power tools and asked me about them."

Kimber recalled talking about them to the front

desk clerk, but had no idea Auggie followed her column for the blog or that he would uncover this. The plot thickened—which was good considering she spied Vin coming through the door of the stairwell. "Vin, do you mind coming here for a moment?"

Smoothing down his tie, Vin approached the two of them. His smile broadened at the sight of Philip and raised his hand to shake. "Damn, Philip Grieco, how long has it been?"

"Not long enough," said Philip. "What's the deal, man?"

Vin smoothed his hand down his stethoscope. "With what?"

"Someone enlighten me as to what's going on?" Dario demanded, coming up behind Kimber. He handed her a bottled water then stood with his left shoulder in front of her.

Kimber pulled him back a step. "Relax, Dario. We're just trying to find some clarity. I don't know what's going on here, but if both of you are true to what you're saying, y'all won't mind coming up with another one."

"What?" the men chorused.

"By the night of the pageant," she added, crossing her arms over her chest. "Or my article is going to expose a lot more."

"Want to enlighten me?" Dario asked.

"Sure. While you were gone, Vin admitted to me that he created the tiaras. And while I was out here waiting for you, Philip just sprang the news on me that *he* created them and left them behind."

Chapter 8

"This is hilarious," Darren laughed.

That weekend, Dario still could not believe the turn of events. He struggled to suppress the need to wrap his hands around the throats of the doctor and the photographer and show Kimber he was a changed man. The old Dario would have settled things up right there in the hallway, but that hadn't been the time or place.

"At least you can take out some of your frustration on the photographer at Christmas Chaos," said Darren, finally sobering up from his cackling. Dario regretted telling Darren what had been going on over the last few days.

Kimber had left bed early that morning to head off to a baby shower with some high school friends who'd promised to bring her back to her apartment after hanging out. Not that Dario needed to approve her plans. Dario's plans that morning included setting up the inside of the ranch house with his brother. They cleared out the rooms, placing the furniture in portable storage pods that had been placed behind the house so no one driving by noticed and thought they were moving. After Christmas Chaos, they usually took advantage of the empty space and repainted the walls—which sometimes was necessary if the night-long party got out of hand. Regardless of what people thought, colored icing did stain if left on the wall.

"Speaking of Christmas Chaos and this photographer…" Dario said, hammering a nail into the wood for the makeshift platform hoisted four feet off the ground. This contraption was for the jousting competition that used the inflatable giant lollipops and candy canes that decorated front lawns.

Darren, down below in the box that would eventually be filled with a soft foam mat, measured out the distance between the drop and the landing to make sure it was safe. "Um, Phil, right?"

"Whatever," Dario said over an irritated sigh. He preferred not to call him anything but *the photographer*. "He alluded to Christmas Chaos."

"Oh yeah, that's right," Darren snapped his fingers together. "He's a single dad and won't have his kids this Christmas."

The rule had been to invite disgruntled single parents, so once Dominic was married, Christmas belonged to the family. The twins just wanted to continue to have fun. But Dario pondered if this would be his last Christmas Chaos. He saw himself married and settled down by next year. After being with Kimber last week, he was one hundred percent positive they were destined to be together—regardless of what these two imposter clowns were trying.

"Man, you left the door open for these phonies by refusing to tell Kimber the truth," said Darren, getting back to the incident. Dario shot his brother a look. Darren held his hands up in surrender. "It is my duty as your older brother to tell you the truth no matter how much it hurts."

Dario went back to hammering the same nail he'd been fixated on for the last three minutes. He was losing his edge. This platform would have been built in thirty minutes a year ago, but today his mind was sidetracked and filled with how to make things right with Kimber. "I can't come out and tell her now."

"Why not? Didn't we learn as children that honesty is the best policy?"

Hammer in midair, Dario snorted. "Did you practice it?"

"Hell no," Darren laughed. "But we're not talking about me, we're talking about you and Kimber. If you want her like my twintuition is telling me, then you need to go forward and tell her. Unless you want me to step into your place."

"Twin magic isn't going to cut it." Dario hammered the last nail in and decided he was done with this for the day. "We're not kids anymore and you're…" Dario pointed the head of the hammer in Darren's direction.

Darren flipped him off. "Whatever, man, I look good. And now you get to see what you'll look like with a dad bod."

"A what?" Dario hopped down to the mat. The sky was clear and there were no predictions of rain. Wet weather didn't bode well for Christmas Chaos. After the tree throwing, he'd planned on a tree lighting service for those parents who wouldn't be with their families on the big day.

"A dad bod." Darren patted his stomach. "The ladies love it."

"I think they also love the idea of the key word in there, bro," said Dario. "The part about being a dad. Unless there's been something going on since I've been gone for the last year."

"Hell no," Darren exclaimed. "I make sure to wrap up every time."

Dario stepped closer and patted his brother on the shoulder. "Good boy."

"What about you? Are we going to have any surprises in the New Year?"

"Let me get through the holidays without her finding out about the tiaras," said Dario, pulling his sweaty shirt over his head. "Then maybe we can plan for the future."

Tonight he and Kimber had plans for a picnic in the park to watch a Christmas movie on a big outdoor screen. Dario had already had their order of Garrett's popcorn delivered to the condo to take on tonight's excursion.

"Do me a favor, will you? Saw these boards for

me." Darren picked up a couple of two-by-fours. "You know the size."

"Alright, but then I'm out of here. I gotta let Hamilton out."

"You're so domesticated now," Darren teased.

It was a good thing Dario hadn't mentioned the chicken in the crockpot. "I think you're confusing me with yourself." He laughed before heading over to the sawhorse in the driveway in front of the house. The level ground made it a better surface than the grass, plus it was in the shade.

While working, his mind focused on Kimber and her potential heartbreak over the betrayal of her old friends. Old *friends*. He scowled and sawed the wood. Those two jokers wanted a hell of a lot more than friendship. But they were wasting their time fawning over her. Kimber was his. Tonight's picnic in the park would show the whole town they were together, not as best friends, but as a couple. This excited him. Being around Kimber in this capacity made him happy. Dario would have accepted being Kimber's friend, but this was better. It wasn't just benefits. She cared. God knew he cared too.

"Damn."

Dario glanced up from his task and found a yellow convertible GTO in the driveway. Kimber paused in the front seat while the other women sat up in the car hollering out catcalls. Kimber mouthed an apology as she shook her head at her friends.

"Don't make him mad," said Kimber. "He's got a saw."

"Saw, see, whatever," said the driver. "How ya been, Dario?"

He couldn't recall her name. The only person on Dario's mind was Kimber now that she was here. And then he realized something. She was *here*. The making of Christmas Chaos was here, as well.

"What's going on, ladies?" Dario set the saw and wood on the ground.

"Oh, you know," said the girl sitting on the headrest of the back seat behind the driver, "we're just being our regular rowdy selves."

"Speak for yourself," Kimber said, reaching for the door. Dario met her and held on. She cocked a glance at him. "Let me out."

"You can't just roll up on some dude's house without a phone call first," said the girl in the car behind the passenger's seat. "Gosh, Kimber."

"This isn't just some guy, Maureen," said Kimber before flashing Dario a killer smile.

"G'on and claim your man."

Given the fact he was the man to be claimed, Dario nodded, opened the door for Kimber and took a deep, proud breath. Kimber stepped out of the car, heels first. He didn't recall seeing the little black dress and studded heels when she left that morning. This might be another outfit he'd want to see her in later—minus the little black dress.

Kimber slipped against Dario's frame. "It's been great catching up with you guys."

"Don't forget we're meeting up for Christmas Cocktails after we chaperone the dance on Tuesday."

Dario recalled the dance at Southwood Middle School. Considering it was an event for hormone-ravaged teens and preteens, the ladies deserved an evening afterward filled with some alcohol.

"Thanks, Johnetta," Kimber said to the driver.

The yellow car backed into the street and took off with more catcalls over the booming music. "Sorry about that," Kimber breathed, "and about just popping up on you like this."

Dario shrugged his shoulders. "It's cool."

"I remember you said you were coming out here today and I didn't think you'd mind giving me a ride back into town whenever you're ready to go. I can just hang out with Hamilton. Is he here?"

"No," Dario said quickly...too quickly.

Kimber smoothed a lock of hair behind her ear. "Is there someone inside I shouldn't see?"

"Of course not." Dario reached for her hand. Their fingers laced together, locking in place. "You can pop up on me anytime you want."

"Can I now?" Kimber looked up at him. Sunlight flickered against her light eyes. Their bodies faced each other. "Why is that?"

"Because you are my lady," he said. With his other hand he traced his index finger down the side of her face. Dario's heart slammed against his chest.

Kimber's lashes fluttered. "Are you calling me your girlfriend?"

"My lady," Dario clarified. "We're grown adults, Kimber."

Shoulders squared, Kimber gave her head a light shake. "I'm not planning on staying in Southwood."

"As I said, we're grown. I can travel, you can travel, and let's not forget I'm friends with a sheikh who has his own plane. We can figure that out later. All I know is this." He paused to wave his finger between his chest and the soft swell of her breasts. "This is officially happening between us."

Kimber kissed the tip of his finger. "Well damn, let's go make this official." She grabbed him by the finger and tried to lead him back to the house.

Dario let her pass him, then twirled her around in a dance move before dipping her in his arms. He kissed her lips and neck. Kimber fumbled around with her purse. "Let's capture this moment for my blog."

"There's nothing to capture," Dario said dryly. "You need to stop posting all your business on the Web." Kimber stood stock still except for her blinking eyes. His concern stemmed from the videos that had led to the fake confessions from both the doctor and the photographer. But he immediately regretted how it had come out. "Babe," he said gently pulling her into his arms, "I'm sorry. This heat is making me crazy."

Kimber eyed him suspiciously. "Maybe we need to get you inside?"

"Let's go back to the condo and celebrate."

"If you're not feeling well," Kimber argued, "you should go lie down."

"I don't want to go in there or Darren might make me clean more. I was really trying to sneak out of here." The quick excuse was enough to make Kimber relax in his arms as she smiled. He savored this moment, yet hated himself for having to lie to her. Soon. Soon enough he'd tell her everything.

Sunday night picnics in the park were a new thing in the last year and Kimber looked forward to being a part of one. All types of blankets were spread out on the grassy knoll, from old green plaids to afghans to bedsheets. Someone even brought a blow-up love seat. Kimber and Dario settled on an old dark blue quilt from his closet. Neither of them had planned it, but when he showed up at her apartment, they were each wearing black sweatpants and a white Crowne's Restoration shirt.

Dario had been sweet enough to pack an actual meal for their picnic. The chicken he'd made smelled better than anything coming off the food trucks parked along the edges of the park. And to make things even better, he'd brought her favorite caramel and cheddar cheese popcorn for dessert.

"This night can't get any better," Kimber said, looking up. Resting her body against his chest she got a view of his clean-shaven chin. She didn't need to see his face to get chills down her spine. The memory of pulling into his driveway and seeing him all sexy with his shirt off while holding a saw was forever singed into her mind. She couldn't even get mad at her friends for ogling him. Dario was hot. And right now, he was all hers. People she'd known growing up in town waved hi, stopped by to welcome her back or speak to Dario about one matter or another.

"Maybe," Dario said. He nudged her back with his knuckles, "we're about to get a visit from one of those politicians."

Through the crowd of locals, Kimber spotted her cousin with ease. Ramon Torres stood a head above everyone else. Not many mayors sported a man bun and made it look cool. The fact he grew his hair out only to donate it to Locks of Love made him even cooler. Maverick Torres sat on his shoulders using his father's bun as a steering wheel. Where the two-year-old thought he was going baffled Kimber, but either way, she scrambled to her feet to greet Ramon and his wife, Kenzie. People stopped to shake Ramon's hand or have a quick conversation with him.

"There you are," Ramon said in a deep booming voice. He and Kenzie wore matching red T-shirts with #TeamSouthwood on the front in bold letters. "I heard you were in town."

"*Hola*, Tío Ramon," said Kimber. He was her father's first cousin, close in age to her uncles, so he earned the moniker of uncle, as well. *"Hola, primo."* Kimber held her arms out for the baby and he came all too willingly.

Kenzie Swayne Reyes embraced Maverick and Kimber at the same time for a group hug. "Hey, sweetie, how are you?" She pushed her mass of curly red hair off her shoulder, taking a glance at Dario, who stood by Kimber's side. "Fine, I see," she said with a wink.

The two men greeted each other with a firm handshake. "I talk to your brother Darren all the time. I hear you're doing big things in Dubai, Dario."

"Yes, sir, trying to."

"You know the city's coming up with a regional urban planning board. I would love to throw your hat in the ring as leader of the project if you're up to it."

Unlike Kimber, Dario wanted to stay in Southwood and she didn't judge him for it, though she knew it would concern her when it was time to leave after the holidays. Rather than think about their future together, Kimber excused herself from their conversation, promising to return with a couple of beers. Kenzie followed and linked her arm through Kimber's elbow.

"I saw Amelia around here," said Kenzie. "You may want to savor your time with Maverick because once she sees him, she's going to take him away from you."

Laughing, Kimber nuzzled her chin against the baby's cheek. Maverick sat on Kimber's hip and waved to everyone they passed. "He's such a good baby," Kimber noted.

"Or good for you," said Kenzie. "You have that magic touch. I can't wait to see you with your own one day."

"No, thanks," Kimber replied. "I'm good as long as I can hand them back."

They made their way through the wave of people there for the movie. Pretty soon there wouldn't be any place for more people to sit. "How are things at the rec center?"

"Great. I posted the flyers for the pageant and got a great sign-up list of people interested in participating or helping in some way. We all like that it's going to be done at the hospital, having all been there in one fashion or another."

"Been where?" asked a feminine voice behind them.

"Amelia," Kimber exclaimed, turning around. Her grip around Maverick's waist tightened when her aunt reached for the baby. Her feelings were hurt when Maverick leaned all of his body toward Amelia's waiting hands.

"Told you," Kenzie said, elbowing her.

Amelia carried on a baby talk conversation with Maverick. "They just don't realize we have an understanding. You're always going to come to me. And I will always feed you treats." Amelia extracted a couple of red and yellow gummy bears from a baggie in the pocket of her green Florida A&M hoodie.

"Amelia." Kenzie shook her head.

"What? I'm not above bribery," said Amelia. "Kimber, have you heard from MET yet?"

Almost every second of the day, Kimber pulled her phone out of her pocket to make sure she hadn't missed a call. She had the ringer turned up high and on vibrate, just to be safe.

"You're not trying to work for them, are you?" Kenzie asked. The line moved forward.

"If they'll have me."

"That sucks." Kenzie pouted.

"Hey, *I* work for them, you know," said Amelia.

"Yeah, and when they call you for a story, you're off and running."

Amelia shared a look with Kimber. They understood the excitement of exposing a story.

"That's the fun of it," explained Kimber. "You never know what you're going to find."

"How about that mystery tiara designer?" Kenzie asked. "Have you solved that one yet?"

It was hard not to roll her eyes. Kimber had decided to not tell anyone about Vin and Philip both copping to being behind the designs. One of them had lied for sure. Hell, both of them could be lying. Kimber still wasn't sold on either one of them. The tiaras she'd seen were made with careful workmanship. They were pieces of sculpted art.

"Have you been following my story?" Kimber asked.

"I'm all about the pageant news," said Kenzie. "Who isn't?"

Bewildered, Kimber looked between them. "Huh?"

"Some reporter you are," Amelia said. Even though her aunt said it with a playful smile, a twinge of hurt tapped into Kimber's veins. "How long has it been since you've updated your page?"

Kimber blinked and thought for a moment. Not since that Wednesday when she'd started a post and Dario distracted her. "Well, ah, you see…"

"Oh, leave her alone, Amelia, she's been hiding under a rock with Dario Crowne," chuckled Kenzie.

Amelia raised a brow at Kimber. "Is this true?"

"Well…" The line moved again, and this time they were up for an order. Kimber put in for two beers. Kenzie and Amelia suspiciously declined the alcohol.

"Kimber," said Amelia, "I don't want to be the wet blanket on your parade but wasn't hanging out with Dario last year what caused you to miss the once in a lifetime internship invitation?"

Kimber wanted to add that initially it had been a once in a lifetime chance for someone else. She'd known late in the month that she wasn't the company's first choice. Kimber chewed her bottom lip for a moment and avoided Amelia's motherly glare.

"I get that you and Dario are close, but are you close enough that you're willing to risk your chance to work for MET again?"

"Maybe MET isn't her dream job," Kenzie provided. "I mean, you do both. You run a successful ice cream parlor here and you still go off on assignment. Can't Kimber have the same thing?"

Kimber nodded. "The thing is, Amelia always comes back. I never wanted to come back to Southwood." The people near them hissed in shock. She swore it became silent for ten feet around her in every direction. "Kidding, kidding," she said to the crowd of onlookers. "I love Southwood, that's why I'm back for the holidays."

"Key phrase is *for the holidays*," Amelia added. "She's getting out of this town and going places," she told everyone before wrapping her free arm around Kimber's shoulders. "Don't let them bother you. If you want to come back to Southwood later on, do like I did. Go live out your dream while you're young and ambitious."

The crowd began to talk again and everyone went

about their business. Kimber let Amelia's words sink in. She needed the reminder to keep on track.

"Everything okay?" Dario asked when she returned with their drinks.

"Mmm-hmm," she mumbled. Kimber cuddled close against Dario again. He turned her so her back was braced against his right arm. The night sky framed his head; stars swirled around him. She gave a soft sigh at his narrowed, questioning look. "Everything is fine, I promise. Did Ramon talk you into staying in Southwood?"

The rest of her family sat adjacent to their blanket and the second feature started. Maverick waddled between his parents and Amelia and Nate. Kimber always wondered if Amelia and Nate hadn't wanted children or if they'd been too busy with life. Kimber loved Amelia but she also knew Uncle Nate spent a lot of holidays alone because of Amelia's job.

Kimber thought about the women in her life, from her mother to Lexi and Amelia. Her mother had been a stay-at-home mom. Kimber wanted none of that lifestyle. She didn't like seeing her mom making sure dinner was ready by six. Lexi worked. Amelia traveled. And even though Kimber had vowed to never live in Southwood as a grownup, she was certain she'd be able to hold an even balance of motherhood and a career as long as she had the right partner.

Just then, Dario wrapped his arms around her body and kissed the top of the head. Kimber cuddled closer, knowing if she ever decided to settle down, he'd be the perfect guy.

* * *

The kid-friendly music played at the elementary school became a joke between Kimber and her friends. They'd spent the afternoon baking and decorating cookies with all the kids. Kimber still smelled like sugar and was sure she had cookie crumbs down the off-the-shoulder sweatshirt she wore. The girls had agreed to dress up in eighties-style clothing. Kimber's attire was a tribute to Madonna and to Jennifer Beals from the movie *Flashdance*. Black rubber bands crowded her wrists while three belts wrapped around the waist of her black leather miniskirt. Just like in high school, Maureen and Johnetta had managed to take over the dance floor in the gym and perform the latest dances right alongside the kids. Being away for a year prevented Kimber from knowing some of the ridiculous moves but that didn't stop her from having fun.

"I think I made up for a year of no exercise," Kimber said later, as they sat at a round table at Southern Charm, one of Southwood's few nightclubs. Another booming song came on over the speakers. Maureen wasn't tired and headed off to the dance floor leaving Kimber with Johnetta and Nicolette.

"I plan on being that active in a few weeks," said Nicolette, rubbing her belly. "I've gained, like, sixty pounds."

"You needed it," teased Johnetta. "You were all skin and bones before. You have a killer rack now."

Kimber hid her laugh by sipping her drink while Nicolette proudly shook her boobs at the table. A waiter coming over turned beet red. "She's just taking these things on a test drive," Johnetta explained.

The girls sobered up and put in an order for wings and more drinks. Talk turned into what Kimber had missed over the last year while in Dubai. She hated missing out but she had dreams. Instead of attending last year's weddings, she'd interviewed international beauty queens. She'd missed the opening of her friend Beth's homemade jewelry shop as well as the summer fair and Southwood's own beauty pageant. If she got a job in Atlanta or someplace closer, she could commute just like she had when she was in college. If she discovered a huge story behind the designer of the tiaras, she might be able to choose where she worked from. MET had satellite studios all over the East Coast.

"Hey, Kimber," Nicolette said, fiddling with the umbrella in her drink. "Were you excited to find out Vin was behind the tiaras? I think it's so romantic." She blinked her long lashes.

Johnetta rolled her eyes. "He didn't do them," she said. "My cousin did."

Kimber rolled her tall glass of Long Island Iced Tea between her hands. "I am surprised both of them stepped up for it."

"You sound more disappointed," noted Johnetta. "I thought you'd be excited. Philip has never gotten over losing you."

"Whatever," Kimber sighed. "I hadn't heard from him since he graduated and now I'm supposed to believe that a year ago he decided, out of the kindness of his heart, he wanted to anonymously design tiaras? Vin too?" Neither lady had an answer. "Don't you think it's odd that neither one of them told me about it when it happened?"

"Well…" they chorused.

Kimber finished her drink. "Exactly. But we'll see. Whoever delivers the tiara on Christmas Eve will be the one telling the truth."

Nicolette played with the fork on the table. "And what happens then?"

"I know you're not asking her if she's going to start dating one of them when the truth comes out," Johnetta said.

"She's seeing Dario," said Maureen coming up at the tail end of the conversation. "Didn't you guys see the two of them at the park together?" Maureen bumped her shoulder against Kimber's.

Kimber mouthed a silent *thank you* to her friend.

"Wasn't that y'alls official debut? They were so adorable," Maureen told the other ladies. "Everyone thinks it's cute the way the two of you, of all people, found each other."

"Everyone who?" Kimber turned to ask. "I haven't heard anything."

"Again, you've been busy with Dario."

"The pageant," Kimber corrected.

Maureen rolled her eyes and giggled. "Mmm-okay sure." She pulled out a chair to sit next to her friend. "It's okay. We all think it's cute that the two most unattainable single people in Southwood are seeing each other."

A nervous chuckle escaped Kimber's throat. "What?"

"The folks aren't wrong. You and Dario were the biggest players in town," said Nicolette. "But I do approve of you two as a couple."

Kimber pressed her hand against her chest. "I was never a player. I honestly don't understand where that's coming from."

"Philip," Johnetta said.

"The three college boyfriends you had between your freshman and sophomore years at FAMU," Maureen added. She'd spent those first two years at school with Kimber before finishing up at Georgia State. "Each time you got mad at one you dropped him."

"Life is too short to sit and argue when you don't see eye to eye," Nicolette said. "That said, if I were to leave every time Jackson and I got into a fight I'd be one lonely mama." She rubbed her belly. "But if I were you, I'd be careful around Lilly Stringer and all the other single ladies. I see them whispering in Dario's ears when you're not around."

For the first time in her life, Kimber felt a twinge of jealousy. Maybe even remorse over her actions. Distancing herself from Dario had kept them apart for almost a year. A year of lonely nights in bed. Damn. Kimber wondered what he was doing now. When she'd asked if he'd wanted to come to the dance he'd declined—saying she should hang out with her friends if she planned on leaving after the holidays. A twinge shocked her heart. Leaving after the holidays meant she was leaving him too. Didn't he care?

Over the last few days, Dario had been close with

Kimber, yet distant at the same time. They got the condo decorated and kidproofed. They didn't have to spend every second of the day together. When they weren't by each other's sides, Dario was off at the ranch or helping Darren get in shape, as if he were training for a boxing match or something.

Though he'd been known to date two women at the same time Kimber didn't believe that was the case now. When they were out and about, women did wink at him, but so did the men, as if there was some big inside joke going on. Each time she asked him about it, he avoided the question. Realizing just how many times it had happened, Kimber took back any feeling of regret for what happened between them last year.

She squared her shoulders and listened to her friends chide her about her notorious dating record. It was true, she didn't end relationships well. Maybe there was a string of brokenhearted men. And, sure, one fight or disagreement wasn't a reason for a breakup, but the difference between her and her girlfriends was that they still lived in Southwood. With Kimber's traveling lifestyle, she didn't have to stay with a man she didn't get along with. She didn't have to force herself to stick around like her mother did.

At the end of the evening, Nicolette dropped Kimber off at the front door of her apartment. It took all she had to not go over to Dario's place. He'd wanted her to have fun tonight—so he could have his own fun.

Inside the quiet of her apartment, she set her cell phone on the coffee table in front of her and curled up on the couch. The lights on the Christmas tree Dario bought her last week brightened up the room just enough to keep it from spinning. The infamous drinks had a way of sneaking up her.

Leaving the banana clip in her side ponytail, Kimber lay down on the couch in a way that would not break the clip and fell asleep, trying desperately to keep from thinking about Dario. She'd always sworn to herself she wasn't the type to settle down. She'd hightailed it out of relationships at the first spark of trouble.

There'd been at least two, three if she counted the conversations Dario had with the single ladies when they were out on the town, times when she'd felt some type of way with Dario. Him ordering her to not answer her phone. Him ordering her to not post her business on social media. She hadn't left yet. There was still a draw to him. She wasn't ready to say goodbye to him. This had been the best time with him yet. Her heart felt full of warmth when he was around. A void appeared when they were apart. She counted down the minutes to when she'd see him again. Whatever the reason, it was on the tip of her tongue.

At some point in the middle of the night she felt a set of strong arms lift her up off the couch. Through half-closed eyes she saw Dario's wink.

"Shh," he urged her. "Go back to sleep."

Weary, Kimber couldn't keep her eyes open. Dario pulled her against his chest and the next thing she realized, he'd set her on the cushions of her bed. The smell was different, though, more masculine, and her bed had turned into a four-poster. Not her bed. She was at his place. Kimber turned over and was met with Dario's hard body. He pulled her against his warmth and wrapped her up close in his arms. And she went to sleep, pushing all the worked-up fake anger away. This was where she belonged.

"I love you, Kimber," Dario whispered.

"I love you too."

Chapter 9

"So you broke into her apartment and kidnapped her?" Darren stood in one corner of the boxing ring in the gym attached to Crowne's Garage, mocking his brother's actions of the previous night.

Wise of his brother to be so far out of reach, Dario thought from his corner. He punched his gloved hands together and stretched his neck, rocking his head from side to side. "Watch it," he said through his mouth guard. "Put your hands up and your protective gear in."

Darren stretched his arms over the ropes. "Nah, I'm good."

In the few weeks they'd had to work together, Dario had seen a definite transition in Darren's frame. The abs were back and there were more defined muscles in his arms. "We have a few more days until Christmas Chaos, Darren. Your punches aren't going to hurt a wet napkin."

"Oh ye of little faith." Darren pushed away from the ropes. "I'm planning on using mind control over my opponents."

Boxing Around the Christmas Ring was the most violent event of the night. It was meant to get rid of the holiday aggression of everyone who needed more than cookie crunching or a javelin throw.

"Well, I need to work something out," Dario said, jabbing his fists in the air toward his brother.

At least the move got Darren off the ropes and into the center of the ring to escape Dario's reach. "Worried about those guys stealing your thunder, huh?"

"No," Dario said. "They can't come up with a replica of what I can do."

"All this is your fault. If only you'd just told Kimber from the beginning that it was you. Tell me something, is part of this anonymity because of Pops?"

Dario took a swing and caught his brother in the shoulder. "What?"

"Well, you know how he used to stop us from playing with dolls."

"I never played with dolls," Dario corrected. "I needed to grab Alisha's dolls to size them up when I made the dream house for her. The first time I did it he beat the crap out of me for it."

Darren stood still. His taunting smile disappeared. "I know. I'm sorry."

"I'm good," Dario said, mentally shrugging off the memory of his father's beatings. The physical blows

Dario had taken were one thing. Bruises didn't last. The taunting did. John Crowne, rest his soul now, had not been a nice man. Growing up like that had shaped Dario's mind.

"There's nothing wrong with you making the tiaras. Why are you letting them take the credit for it?" Darren asked, sidestepping another blow. "Given the fact Kimber didn't press charges after you took her from her place, I think you're golden with her."

"First of all," Dario said, sending an uppercut toward Darren's chin, "I have a key. I've had a key ever since last year when Charlotte and Richard got engaged." Darren closed his eyes in anticipation of the blow. But Dario didn't want to hurt him for real, not even for speaking the truth.

"Ohhh." Darren perked up, rolling his fists around. "What's the next step? Marriage?"

"Kimber is far too freaked out by the idea of marriage. She has her eyes on a career away from here."

Darren shrugged his shoulders. "Well, it's not like you guys didn't have a long-distance relationship before."

"We weren't together before," Dario reminded him.

"So after you bought all those tickets that summer when she manned the kissing booth, you were still seeing other women when she went back to school?"

Dario stopped shuffling his feet. "We… I…"

"We… I…" Darren mocked him.

Dario threw a punch and it landed on his brother's chin. "My bad."

Outside light spilled into the garage and stopped their sparring. Breathing heavily, they faced the door, their arms on the ropes. Heels clicked on the cement floor. Once the door closed, a curvy frame came into view. Kimber, in a green sweater dress and thigh-high brown boots, folded her arms across her chest. "The door was unlocked," she explained. "I've been calling out for you guys for a minute or two."

"Sorry," Darren said. "I meant to turn the sign to Closed. Your boyfriend here dragged me off to whip me into shape."

"Is that true?" Kimber asked, feeding into Darren's search for sympathy.

Dario shook his head and laughed. "If someone robbed the place, Darren wouldn't be in shape to run after them."

For the first time that morning Darren threw a punch, landing it on Dario's left cheek. Kimber covered her mouth with her hands to stifle a horrified scream. "Oh my God. You guys are so rough."

"It didn't hurt," Dario assured her. "He punches like a girl."

That comment got Kimber's hands on her hips. "I'm a girl. Want me to hop into the ring and go a few rounds?"

"Depends." Dario offered her a lopsided smile. "Rounds of what?"

"Y'all need to take your dirty talk someplace else." Darren attempted to get out of the ring but Dario swept out with his leg, catching his twin's foot and bringing him down to the ground.

"We're not done here," he told his brother.

"Dario," Kimber called out. "Be gentle with him."

"I'll be with you in a second," Dario hollered over his shoulder. "There's a chair in that closet over there with the Mustang engine on the door."

Kimber stood still. "There are, like, three doors with pictures of engines on them."

"The middle." Darren yelled in pain. "But you don't have to get it. I've got Dario right where I want him."

Tossing Darren around into a jujitsu submission, Dario said, "Yeah, right."

"Okay, so you remember my plan to play mind games to win?" Darren struggled to get out of the hold.

"You gotta be able to talk," Dario reminded him.

"I'm 'bout to use my last breath on you and get out of this move."

"Try it."

Darren punched at Dario's forearms. "That room you just sent your girlfriend to is where I threw that gift you made her last year and never gave her. I believe it's a one of a kind tiara made by none other than you."

Dario let his brother go with startling quickness. He hopped out of the ring onto the mat below and rushed over to the door. Kimber was already inside the closet, her hand stretched into the air for the string to the light switch.

"Hey," Dario said, trying to hold his breath.

"Whoa," Kimber exclaimed, clutching her necklace of tiny Christmas ornaments. As she turned to face him, the light came on. The string swung back and forth. "How did you get here so fast?"

"I took care of Darren already." The red-and-white-striped Christmas present was right there, front and center, with her name scrawled in his handwriting. Dario reached over Kimber's hand to attempt to push the present farther back on the shelf. The door closed behind him. She cocked her head at him, confused. "This room is dusty," he tried to explain.

Kimber pressed her hands against his chest. An arched brow rose on her face. "And here I thought you were trying to get frisky with me."

"Huh?"

"Seven minutes in heaven," Kimber said, rising on her tiptoes.

Who was he to resist a kiss from her? Her mouth fueled him with desire. "I am sweaty."

"So make me sweaty too." Kimber bit her lip and grabbed her cell phone. Her nails were painted with candy cane stripes and blurred as she set the timer. 07:00. "Something about seeing you all sweaty and manly, ohh!" She shimmied her body against his.

Dario untied his gloves with his teeth, freeing his fingers to roam her body. The knit of Kimber's dress felt soft against his rough hands. He hooked the hem up over her hips. Kimber braced her foot on a lower shelf. She wore a skimpy pair of lacy underwear beneath her dress. As a test, Dario slipped one finger into her moist center. Craving her, his knees weakened. He swore under his breath, inhaling her sweet, minty breath. Dario took her mouth once more. Kimber's nails pawed at his chest down to his stomach. Dario's cock strained in his shorts until she freed him. Her gentle hands caressed him but this interlude did not call for soft hands. He spun her around, bent her over and entered her swiftly from behind.

Kimber yelped in excitement. She moved her body back and forth and then did the ultimate move, bending over completely and grabbing her ankles. Amid the sheer pleasure, Dario tried hard not to lose his mind. His hands gripped her hips, careful not to hurt her, and he bucked until they both came. The timer went off over their panting.

"Now that's what I call seven minutes in heaven," Kimber breathed, straightening her clothes.

Dario cupped her face, kissing her lips, caressing her tongue with his. "I promise to give you more heaven later."

A week before Christmas Eve, Kimber found herself stretched out on the bed, wrapped in soft blue sheets and—even better—Dario's arms. The previous month might have been the best month of her entire life. Between the chestnut roasting, Christmas caroling, and the smooth setup so far for the Christmas pageant, all combined with getting to do these things with her best friend, Kimber didn't think things could get any better.

"I like that you wake up with a smile on your face," Dario said, pushing her hair off her forehead. A sliver of light spilled through the dark curtains where they'd been shifted apart by the wind from the ceiling fan.

Over the last few days the winter weather had settled in through Southwood, making spirits brighten in anticipation of Christmas.

Warmth from his body made her not want to get out of bed. "I could stay here all day."

"I don't mind," he replied. "What *do* you want to do today?"

Back arched, Kimber stretched her body. Sleeping naked against Dario's hard frame was tantalizing. The tips of her fingers pressed against the curves of his abs. Dario pulled her hand to his mouth and kissed the tip of each finger.

"Okay, but what do you want to do afterward?"

Eyes fluttering, Kimber tried to focus. "I need to go shopping."

"What kind? Grocery? 'Cause I have everything in here you need. Clothes? I'll have someone come over with a closetful you can choose from."

"I get the feeling *you* don't want to leave the bed today," Kimber said. Two large calloused fingertips traced circles around her tailbone. Her toes pointed then flexed before she tossed her right leg over his thigh. She half closed her eyes, amazed at how turned on she was by the heat flowing between their legs. This feeling of love consumed her. She loved him and he loved her. Kimber caressed Dario's cheek with her right hand. Was it possible to feel this happy?

"If you wanted to get out of the bed, I'm not going to stop you," he said.

Kimber moved her body and his hand clamped down over hers. "Oh really?"

"My mistake," Dario semi-apologized, "I thought you were about to roll out of the bed."

"This California king?" Kimber laughed and gave her head a shake. "But seriously, believe it or not, I do need to get up and get a move on the day."

Dario let her go and flattened his back into the mattress. "To get Lexi a present. That's right. If you could get her anything, what would it be?"

Following his move, Kimber rolled onto her back. Their hands touched and raised together in the air between them. "Since I can't trust Vin or Philip, I am going to have to rethink my gift for Lexi."

"You sound sad," he noted. Their fingers locked together and released in a dance-like move.

She sighed sadly. "I am. I thought a tiara would be the perfect gift for her. She and Amelia have been the best role models a girl could ever ask for. I mean, they stepped into this motherly role without hesitation." Kimber paused to take a shaky breath. Dario stroked the length of her index finger with his thumb, silently waiting for her to continue. "I wasn't the easiest person to get along with when my parents died."

"I'm sorry you had to endure that," said Dario. "You know I lost my dad not too long ago. He tried to make amends before he passed away but he had been out of our lives for so long by the time his apology would have mattered."

There was something bitter in his voice. Kimber let go of his hand and pulled herself up on her elbows. "I think this is the first time you've ever mentioned him."

Dario's handsome face scrunched up with thought. "I don't think so."

"It's true. I've heard Darren mention him before. He always referred to your father as an SOB."

A deep chuckle rattled in Dario's chest. "That he was."

"So, you didn't get along?"

He snorted.

"Aw, that makes me sad," she said with a pout. Still on her elbows, Kimber turned on her side to face him.

Dario's lips twitched but he didn't look at her. "My dad was quite the ass, to say the least. He left my mom when we were younger and never looked back until he was on his deathbed and wanted forgiveness."

"Did you give it to him?"

"No," he clipped. "What do you say to a man who called you a punk all your life? Or smacked you around when you cried after falling off a bike?" Kimber's heart ached as he spoke. "All my memories are of him telling me how I was going to grow up and be a weak man."

Kimber gasped. "What? Jesus, I'm so sorry."

"It's all good now."

She reached out and touched his biceps. "You're the manliest man I've ever met in my entire life."

"Besides Vin and Philip?" Dario cut his eyes to look at her before his lips spread upward into a teasing smile.

Kimber gave a little dig of her nails into his muscle. "You're funny."

"What are you going to do if both of them show up with tiaras?"

"Then I'm going to interview them and post it. Hopefully MET will see the story and remember I'm a viable candidate for a field journalist position."

Just that second her phone rang from the nightstand on her side of the bed. She gasped. Dario opened his mouth and widened his eyes in excitement for her.

"Hello?" Kimber answered without looking at the number.

"Hey, sis!" Philly's cheerful voice came over the line. "Video-chat me. I want you to see what I look like."

While she was naked, in bed with Dario? "Maybe later. Are you all cleared up now?"

"I am. Can we go shopping? You said we could go once I cleared up."

"Funny you should mention that," Kimber said. Dario's hands splayed against her backside. She tried to ignore the wanton tingle in her insides. "So, um, I, I'll come and get you."

"I'm coming in with Lexi. Will you meet me at the store in a little bit?"

"Sure." Kimber congratulated Philly for healing quickly before hanging up. She'd barely set the phone on the nightstand before Dario pulled her body on top of his. She straddled his legs but laid her breasts against his chest.

"You were saying something about giving a ride?" Dario placed his hands on her hips.

"I did," she said over a chill of excitement. "I've got to get dressed."

"I'll let you get dressed, but first…"

Kimber dipped her head and kissed his lips. No better way to get the day started than a quick roll in the sack.

"Uncle Dario! Uncle Dario!"

Young voices echoed throughout the house followed by a deep voice. "Kids, stop running."

And another voice filled the air. "Oh, look how great everything looks."

Dario swore under his breath. "We're going to have to pick this up later. Right now we have about fifteen seconds to get dressed before we're terrorized by a couple of toddlers."

After a morning of shopping, mani-pedis and double cheeseburgers, Kimber and Philly topped off their day of fun with a banana split with pecans, caramel and fresh whipped cream at The Scoop, Amelia's family's ice cream parlor. Being related to one of the owners came unlimited ice cream. During their spa treatment, Kimber had gone with a royal blue to match her sweater while Philly asked for the unicorn treatment. The unicorn colors, consisting of pastel pinks, purples and blues, now shone under the bright lights above them at the parlor while Kimber's nails stood out against the cool white countertops. Philly pushed herself around in circles in the swirling chair after each bite.

"Don't get sick now," Kimber warned her.

"You just don't understand how good it feels to be free," Philly squealed, kicking her leg warmer–clad legs back and forth. "I've been cooped up with those babies."

A few of the customers watched them and smiled fondly, probably former friends of their parents. Kimber was used to the looks from the townspeople. They were always that sweet, sad smile where they'd tilt their heads to the side, glad to see the girls were adjusting to life without their parents. Kimber blew out a sigh and focused on her sister.

"I bet you got to do a lot of reading though."

Philly had been the first of them to catch the fever for the pageant world. Then she stopped doing them and took up softball, although she'd never lost her taste for a tiara. Today was no different, other than that the crown she wore was small for her growing body.

"I read so much I was sure my eyes were going to bleed." Philly did another turn before grabbing her spoon to take another bite of her dessert. "How's your search for the tiara designer going?"

Kimber narrowed her eyes. "You've been following my blogs?"

"Always," said Philly with a coy smile, reminding Kimber of their mother. "That and I'm Facebook friends with Jenny Grieco, cousin of Philip."

"Ugh," Kimber groaned. "What did she say?" She couldn't believe she was leaning forward to hear the gossip from a middle schooler.

"That Philip regrets breaking up with you."

"I broke up with him, but whatever." Kimber

shrugged her shoulders and went on. "Did he think by saying he designed the crowns that I would get back with him?"

Philly cocked her head to the side like the other ladies did. "Aw, whatever happened between the two of you? I liked him."

"I thought you liked Dario."

"I'm mature enough to like two people," said Philly. "Dario is going to move back to Southwood at some point and I know you don't ever plan on coming back here to live."

Eyes widening, Kimber turned her lips down in a frown. "You know that?"

"I am way more aware than you'd ever guess. I see things."

"Like?"

"Like the way you are with Dario is different than when you were with any of your other boyfriends," said Philly all wise and whatnot with whipped cream on her upper lip. "I like him for that. But I also know you liked Philip." Philly slipped off her stool and pressed her hands together under her chin, then out of nowhere grabbed on to Kimber's arm. "Uncle Stephen, stop, don't kill him, he's my boyfriend and I love him."

The mocking plea caused Kimber to laugh so hard tears came to her eyes. Years ago she'd said something along those lines.

"And then he wanted you to settle down with him," Philly reminded her, "and you ripped that poor boy's heart out."

"Someone's been binge-watching teen dramas," Kimber mumbled.

"Will you talk to him?"

"Sure, when he comes up with the tiara, I'll do a whole interview."

Philly took another bite of ice cream. "Did you ever stop to think it might be Dario? Philip has access to a workshop at his school. But Dario has access to one all the time. He owns a garage."

It took a few seconds of blinking for Kimber to process the obvious answer. The image of him standing shirtless over a power saw was still burned in her memory. He had access to all types of scrap metal from the cars he worked on. "I mean, it could be him. But why wouldn't he tell me?"

"Duh," Philly said, rolling her eyes. "You have commitment issues."

"What show did you learn that from?"

"Dr. Phil."

One of the ladies watching came over to the two of them. "I'm sorry to butt into your conversation but are you guys talking about the beautiful tiaras that showed up at the hospital last year?"

"Yes, ma'am," answered Kimber. She swiveled her chair to face the woman. "Kimber Reyes," she said extending her hand.

The older woman pulled Kimber into a hug. She smelled of fresh strawberries, probably from the home-made sauce The Scoop used. "Now, I've watched you girls grow up. I taught your mother in school many years ago. She'd be so proud. I'm Mrs. Hanson."

"Thank you," the girls chorused.

"These tiaras you're looking for. I recall a couple of them being at the pageant for my great-niece who'd been in the hospital."

Excited, Kimber nodded. "Really now? Does she recall seeing who brought them in?"

Mrs. Hanson shook her lavender-tinted head of hair. "I was there before and after the show but there was so much chaos, *I* never saw anyone bring them into the bedroom where they were found."

"Do you recall seeing Dr. Vin or Philip Grieco at the hospital?" Philly, the budding journalist, asked.

"Celeste," called the woman who'd been sitting at the table with Mrs. Hanson. "They were both in Jackson's graduating class."

"Oh yes, I remember them now," Mrs. Hanson went on. "They were both there. I remember it because I never moved from my seat and I could see how the two of them were sneaking around the hospital."

Philly elbowed Kimber in the ribs. "Sneaking around because one of them dropped off the tiaras and didn't want to get caught by you."

"I'm not sure if that helps," said Mrs. Hanson. "I can call my granddaughter right now and have her bring her tiara here. Got a sec?"

Elated, Kimber's heart pounded against her chest. "For this, yes."

Mrs. Hanson stepped aside. "A few of her friends received them, as well, for Valentine's Day and Easter. Maybe everyone should wear their favorite tiara, like you, Miss Philly."

Philly adjusted her crown and smiled.

Kimber chewed her bottom lip. Something Mrs. Hanson had said bothered her. According to the conversations she'd had with Dario about the deliveries. Some were made when she knew he was in Southwood. But the others? He couldn't have been the mystery designer. And though he'd never done anything to indicate whether he was or wasn't, she'd debunked the idea before the story took life in her mind. Kimber couldn't ignore the disappointed feeling that Dario wasn't her mystery man. Somehow thinking he'd been the man behind the tiaras made the gesture feel like a fairytale romance. It had to have been either Vin or Philip.

"I've been thinking," Philly began. She stirred the sprinkles on top of her ice cream until they colored the vanilla treat a pinkish-purple color. "It would make sense for Dr. Vin to be the designer. He had access to everyone's charts when the kids were being discharged."

"Valid point, little sis," said Kimber. "I thought about it, but I also don't peg Vin as the shop-class type."

"Philip Grieco on the other hand, yes." Philly twisted her lips to the side. "Is that why you've left them out of the blogs?"

"Exactly," replied Kimber. "I don't want anyone else popping up and trying to lay claim."

"Mmmph," Philly mumbled. "Perhaps you shouldn't have so many exes."

"Little girl, I will make you walk home," Kimber joked. The girls laughed for a second, both knowing Kimber would never leave her behind. "Alright tell me, how's my makeup look for the video I'm about to shoot?"

"Here, let me help."

Most people wouldn't let a twelve-year-old fix their makeup, but considering Philly came from a background so connected to the beauty world, what with their aunts being friends with celebrity judges, reality show socialites and connections to Ravens Cosmetics, the girl knew a thing or two.

Kimber hadn't realized how quickly time was flying by until the bell over the door announced the latest visitor. A small girl walked in and stared at Kimber. It took Kimber a second to get over the spiral curls on her head.

"Felicity?" Kimber covered her mouth. "Oh my God. How long has it been?"

Felicity put some pep in her step and met Kimber halfway for a big hug. "Let's see, I've been in remission since the beginning of this year, so at least that long."

"Philly, this is Felicity." Kimber introduced them. "She was the winner of the Miss Four Points General Hospital last year."

Philly gave a wave and a quick hello.

"I'm so glad you came down here," said Kimber. They made their way to an empty booth to sit and chat. Kimber listened to Felicity, now fifteen, talk about going back to high school after dealing with her leukemia.

"I looked up the number on the shirt you wore the day you posted from that hottie's garage."

"Oh goodness. Crowne's?" Kimber's eyes furrowed together. "You called there?"

"I tried to comment live but you stopped the feed. I've been waiting for you to call me back."

"Weird. Did you speak with anyone?"

"A guy named Darren, who said he'd make sure he'd give my information to the right person."

"I'm so sorry, Felicity. I'll find out what happened."

"In the meantime, do you want to see the crown?" Felicity reached down beside her into the cross-body purse over her hoodie.

If Kimber didn't know any better, she'd swear a ray of light shone down on top of the masterpiece. The designer had known that with Felicity's hair being thin at the time, a tiara with clips or pins would not work. So the maker had fixed it so Felicity could wear her tiara as a headband with two parts. The first part she wore like a regular headband and the second part, extending forward to wear on top of her head, was the crown with all its lovely intricate parts, costume diamonds and pearls. It was a work of art. Kimber took out her phone and filmed all angles of the tiara and Felicity wearing it. If Vin or Philip had done this, they were geniuses.

Chapter 10

Seven days. Which meant it had been seven whole nights that Kimber spent sleeping without Dario. With Dario's family staying at the condo and the Reyes home being chicken pox–free, Kimber had slept in her own bed in her childhood home for the last week, forcing her and Dario into something of a dating ritual. The Reyeses and the Crownes had worked at the same table decorating cookies for the previous weekend's bake sale. Sunday dinner had been celebrated at Duvernay's. Monday evening, Dario had picked Kimber up for a date of ice skating in the park. When he'd tried to go upstairs to get her, Stephen had blocked the path. It had been a funny yet embarrassing way for her uncle to still treat her like a child.

Tuesday and Wednesday Dario had been busy with

some other project. It irritated her that he didn't spend all his time with her, but she knew that was the inner brat in her speaking. What bothered her more was the photo on the Greater Southwood Chamber of Commerce web page inviting folks to spend time in the small town for the holidays. She'd caught a few timeline photos of Dario speaking with Lilly Stringer as well as her old middle school coach and even one of Philly's former teachers. Dario's reputation as a lothario was strong and it wasn't like she in a position to gripe about exes. She had two still claiming to be the legendary tiara designer.

"I want you to show me your entire room," Dario said over his tablet. Like her, he was in bed. It was Christmas Eve morning. The sun still hadn't risen. Kimber was sure they'd spent the whole night talking, switching from phoning to video-chatting each other. From the angle she could tell he was on his back with his arm behind his head. The light of his bedroom caught the bulge of his biceps.

"Not a chance," Kimber replied. Kimber sat on her queen-size bed. The bed paled in comparison to Dario's, but it was comfy nonetheless.

The walls of the bedroom had gone through several changes over the years, from pastel ponies to Barbies to her favorite boy bands from over the years. In order to preserve every stage of her life, three of her lavender-painted walls were covered with various sized gold or black frames, all holding documents dedicated to her phases. The wall against her bed remained picture-free but it did hold shelves full of her stuffed animals. Twin black lamps lit the room as Kimber spoke with Dario.

"I could climb the trellis outside your bedroom window and you could sneak me in," he suggested.

Kimber laughed at her screen. "Don't forget, my uncles live here too. You may have to deal with them if they catch you."

Dario flexed his muscles. "I think you'd be worth the risk."

"Do you now?" Kimber teased. She sank back against her pillows and propped her tablet on her raised knees. She watched Dario lazily rub his chest and grinned.

"I see that sneaky smile you have there," said Dario. "You're just as bad as me."

"Maybe I want you just as bad," she tempted him, flicking the strap of the white camisole she'd worn for bed.

Dario sat up. "Damn girl, are you trying to get me killed?"

"Depends on what you'd do to me when you get here." Her heart raced with wicked temptation. She wasn't seriously about to have video-chat sex. She wondered if her battery-operated boyfriend in the nightstand would wake the house with its buzzing.

"For starters, I'm going to take that thin thing you're wearing that you've been using to tease me and I'm going to rip it off your body."

"Ouch."

"Never fear," Dario went on with a lopsided grin. "You just tell me where it aches."

Kimber perked up, as did her nipples. "Aches or where I want you to kiss and make it better?"

Dario's hand moved out of sight. "Kimber," he whispered with half-closed eyes. "I need to see you today."

Her cell phone, left on the nightstand by her bed, lit up as it rang.

"Don't answer that," Dario said.

As much as she didn't want to, Kimber rolled her neck to stretch out the sexually charged kinks. "I've got to. Did you forget the pageant is today?" As she angled her body to grab her phone she caught Dario slamming his head into one pillow and covering his face with another.

The call turned out to be one of the pageant mothers worrying about the space her daughter will have in her dressing room. Kimber regretted passing out her personal number. MET still hadn't called but Kimber held on to the hope they'd use her for New Year's Day. That would be the tipping point for when she should leave. Pageant prep was gearing up for contestants. Interviews were scheduled. All the things she needed to do were ticked off in her head but she didn't feel nearly as excited as she had the previous year when the opportunity came around. A year ago she'd been ready to get the hell out of Southwood. Now, love made her want to stay. She couldn't stand the idea of a long distance between herself and Dario.

Kimber turned the phone off and focused on the monitor. Dario's body rose and fell with a light snore. She decided not to wake him and disconnected the call. From downstairs, the rich scent of strong coffee made its way through the vents.

Even though they'd been preparing for the Christmas Pageant for four weeks, it still felt like Kimber was running around like a chicken with its head cut off on the day of the event. Once Lexi got her cup of coffee in her the two of them headed to the hospital bright and early. They spent the day tidying up last minute details. Nate was already there, working on nailing a skirt to the stage. Sponsors who helped financially were awarded banners, which hung from the skirts on the stage.

"Looking good, Nate," said Lexi as they entered the theater.

Kimber crossed her arms over her chest, nodding in agreement. "I'm impressed."

"I'm honored to have your approval," Nate said, reaching to rumple the top of Kimber's head.

If she were sixteen, sure. But now? Kimber stepped out of the way. "The hair," she warned him. "Don't mess up the hair."

"What's that style called?" Nate asked. He closed his tool box.

"A messy bun," Kimber replied.

Nate wagged his finger at her. "You're cute. I have to run into town. Do you want to ride with your old uncle?"

"I do need to get my dress from the condo."

"Oh no, I thought you brought it to the house," Lexi said. "I thought we'd all get ready there and take pictures. I was able to get your photographer to come over and take pictures of the family since we're all going to be there."

Nate looked between the two of them. "Isn't your photographer that poor fellow you dumped after high school?"

"Philip," Kimber provided.

"That's interesting. C'mon and take a ride into town with me." Nate waved Kimber on after they both promised to return to the house as soon as possible. "We can chitchat about your Philip friend."

"There's not much to tell," said Kimber as they walked out of the hospital to Nate's dark blue Dodge. A heavy metal toolbox rattled in the bed of the truck. "I'm assuming you heard the news about the tiaras?" she asked him, sliding into the passenger seat. Like their home when Nate first took it over, the cab of the truck was a mess. Fast-food wrappers cluttered the seats.

"Just push all that down."

The engine came to life. "I don't understand how Amelia allows you to be such a slob," she said.

"Amelia doesn't get into this thing. We're always taking her car when she's in town."

His words resonated in Kimber's ears. "Uncle Nate."

Nate was quite for a moment. The same silent treatment she was always given when she didn't address him in Spanish. *"Tío,"* she said with a huff.

"What's that, sweetie?"

"Amelia's been working with MET Studios for a

while now, right?" Kimber traced a smiley face on the dashboard with her index finger.

"Yeah, when she's not running things at The Scoop," he answered. "Why, do you want to work at an ice cream parlor?"

"Cute," Kimber said with a reluctant laugh. "I'm asking because she goes off on assignment a lot."

"Nothing new with that," Nate commented. "What's going on?"

"I'm just thinking about my future, if I get this job."

"Did you ask Amelia to hook you up with one?" Nate asked, turning on the road leading toward town.

Kimber frowned. "Heck no, I don't want her help, not that I don't love her for trying. I mean she has given me insight that MET is looking for a field journalist in the Atlanta area."

The cooler weather had thinned the pine trees to the point where Kimber could see into the new development. If memory served her correctly, this was the same area where, a year ago, she and Dario stopped the Christmas sleigh to enjoy the candy cane sky.

"You want the job?"

"Sure."

"And you'd give up your glamorous life traveling?" Laughing, Nate elbowed Kimber's arm.

"Maybe."

"And it's Dario that has you thinking you want to stay closer."

Kimber's eyes cut over at her uncle. "How do you and Amelia deal with long distance?"

"Well, for starters," he began, "we're *married*, not dating. Did Dario say something about settling down?"

For a split second Kimber thought her heart would burst through her chest. "We're seeing each other, officially."

"I saw y'all at the picnic in the park, but I mean is he ready to give up his partying ways and you yours?"

"I never partied," Kimber lied, crossing her arms over her chest. "I'm just giving myself options."

"From my understanding, you have several options. Marvin, who is a doctor, Philip, a coach, photographer, and from my understanding, the shop instructor, and then there's Dario."

"You don't have to say his name like that, like with dread," Kimber noted. "And the other two are not options, just guys who both claim to be the ones who made the tiaras that popped up last year."

"Yeah." Nate *tsk*ed. "I heard about that. Have you checked the security cameras?"

Blinking, Kimber shook her head. "I asked one of the security officers. He said they've had a new system now for about year and they loop over the tape or whatever every week."

"'For about a year' makes me wonder." Nate scratched the hairs of his goatee. "I did some work on the children's wing last year. I can check and see if they kept any of their old tapes. That will settle things once and for all."

"I am hoping when the person shows up without a

tiara, we'll find out who is the true designer and who is the liar," Kimber replied.

"I've liked the interviews you've posted, though. Great feel-good stories."

"Thanks," Kimber said. Her voice trailed off as they passed the spot in the road where it happened. The spot where her parents took their last breath.

Nate reached over to give Kimber's shoulder a squeeze. "You know they'd be proud of you."

"Maybe," Kimber said. Would they have stopped fighting long enough to notice? Who knew? Kimber thought about her relationship with Dario. Yes, she was irritated with him that he'd been busy this week, but not to the point where she felt the need to end things with him. She wondered at what point her parents stopped looking past these little irritations and started arguing. She and Dario argued, but made up. Would they ever stop making up? Was she ready to stay in town for love and find out? Kimber sighed and looked out the window.

Nate filled the rest of the ride into town with his missed lyrics of Christmas songs. Occasionally Kimber laughed. He dropped her off at her building and promised to pick her up once he grabbed his tools but Kimber finished before he did. Armed with her garment bag, Kimber started to head back to the shop but the business across the street caught her eye. The doors to Crowne's Garage were lifted and the red car Dario drove her to the hospital in was in the bay. Her heart raced with excitement at the possibility of seeing Dario, even if it was just for a minute. Quickly, she crossed the street, waving to the people she knew.

Kimber stepped over the threshold. Drills sounded from under the floor. Dominic Crowne, the oldest of the siblings, stepped out from the back office, wiping his hands on a red towel. "Kimber Reyes," he said, as if he hadn't seen her in forever. His smile made her feel welcome, like family. "I didn't expect to see you today. Everyone in town is talking about your pageant."

"Lexi's pageant," Kimber corrected with a smile. "Are we going to see you?"

"If I can get this bookkeeping situated I will. What brings you here today? Dario's out at the ranch house."

She felt her smile falter, and she quickly tried to come up with an excuse. "Oh yeah, of course. I was stopping by because the last time I was here, I dropped my necklace in your closet in the back."

Dominic raised a brow.

Heat touched her cheeks as she realized what she'd been doing when she lost her necklace. "It's um, big and kinda gaudy, but it's going to look great with this dress." Kimber patted the garment bag, hoping it would distract him from asking any embarrassing questions.

"Hang on, I'll go check."

Across the street, Kimber spotted her uncle getting back to the truck. She needed to get back too. Nate wanted to get going. She could tell because he climbed back out of the truck. Not wanting him to go to her apartment, Kimber stepped out of the garage. "Uncle Nate! Uncle Nate!"

Her uncle saw her flagging him down. Quickly, he hopped back into his truck and carefully made a U-turn right into the driveway of the garage.

"Oh, I thought you'd left for a moment," Dominic said, coming up behind Kimber. "Hey, Nate."

Nate opened the door to greet Dominic. The men shook hands then gave each other a half hug. "What's up? Y'all got time for a tune-up today?"

"On Christmas Eve?" Dominic laughed. Just then, the garage echoed with the sound of a tool hitting the cement floor.

"You sound open to me," Nate retorted. "How about I come by next week?"

"I can't make any promises," joked Dominic. "Speaking of promises, I can say that I did give it my best shot looking for your necklace but I found nothing that fit the description. I did, however, find this thing with your name on it. Knowing the scribbly writing, it's from Dario."

In presenting the package, Dominic held it in both hands and took a bow. The box was wrapped in red-and-white-striped paper. Something about it was familiar but she couldn't put her finger on it.

"Alright, Kimber." Nate clapped his hands together to get her attention. "We've got to get back before my sister-in-law has our heads on a platter."

"Thanks for checking, Dominic," Kimber called out as Nate ushered her to the passenger's side door. She slid into the seat, sad that she didn't get a chance to open it and wondered why he wouldn't just give it to her himself.

"You gonna check it?" Nate asked, bringing the engine to life.

"No. I think I'll wait until I see Dario again."

"Tonight?"

Kimber shook his head. "No, he's busy tonight. But I will definitely see him tomorrow."

"I don't need you coming with me," Dario said over his shoulder to Darren, who was hot on his tail. Before leaving the ranch, he threw on a dark green oxford and, to be festive, a Rudolph the Red-Nosed Reindeer tie. He hadn't worn a suit or tie in a month. Maybe it was the daily workouts with Darren making his upper body bigger, which constricted the material around his neck. He wasn't sure he was going to be able to fit into his clothes in Dubai.

"Hell no," Darren complained. "I'm not taking the chance that you don't come home with me to the ranch tonight. You've got one hour here at the pageant."

Time was limited. Not just for tonight, but when the start of the New Year came around, Dario needed to face his new reality. Spending these last few days playing with Justin and Ariana had been a blast. Whenever he needed to leave to prepare the ranch, the kids cried. He hated that. As their uncle, he wanted to be there for them. And seeing how much they'd grown in just a year, well, video-chat didn't do them justice. He reveled in rolling around on the floor and fake wrestling with them, the piggyback rides and sneaking ice cream even though their father told them no. Dario wasn't sure he wanted to leave. Funny, but in trying to prove to Kimber how mature he was, he'd messed around and actually become mature. Well, after tonight it was a sure thing.

Dario sighed but continued to walk down the hall and make his way through the crowds of people standing in line, waiting to either get inside the theater or just mingling in the halls. A few people tapped him on the shoulder and promised to see him later.

Christmas Chaos started in ninety minutes. Dario needed to see Kimber before he stepped into any ring and risked getting hit in the head. He'd abstained from sex all week, tortured himself without a taste of her lips. He'd be damned if he got a concussion without first laying his eyes on her.

"If you just told her the truth," Darren started, finally catching up to him.

"I'm glad to hear you're not winded from trying to keep pace," Dario joked.

Darren flipped him off without looking at him. "I don't see her," he said, scanning the crowds. "We're probably going to have to go closer. There are a couple of seats up front. But we still need to leave in order to welcome everyone. Plus, I don't like to leave all that alcohol unattended."

"It will all be fine," said Dario. "C'mon, let's go up there."

"To the stage?"

"Behind it," Dario replied. He'd spotted Kimber backstage when the curtains opened for the little kids on stage to do a song and dance. She was in a green dress. His heart beat out of control. "We've got to get back there."

"Just waltz backstage?" Darren asked, a bit of self-doubt in his voice. "You see that line of older women standing there like bodyguards?"

Dario elbowed his brother in the ribs. "C'mon, take one for the team. Get us backstage." In truth, Dario did want to see Kimber. But he also had to check out how those two clowns were going to look coming to her empty-handed on the tiara.

Blocking the door that would allow them to get backstage, a large woman folded her arms across her chest with a scowl on her face to deter any unwanted presence in the back. So far, she wasn't impressed by Darren's charm. Dario turned to make a call to Kimber to try and get her to come out from backstage to let them in. She didn't answer right away.

"Dario, my man."

Dario turned around and noticed the bun first on a six-foot-plus man before he realized it was the mayor.

"Ramon," said Dario, extending his hand for a shake.

"Good seeing you, Dario." Ramon clamped down with his free hand on Dario's elbow. "Say, have you had a chance to consider the Urban Development position at Four Points?"

"I haven't heard anything else about it," answered Dario. "What's new?"

"We're talking new, fresh off the board meeting," Ramon said excitedly. "This pageant has brought the community leaders together and we're looking to develop more between our four points. I threw your name out into the mix as a possible candidate for the urban planner position. I contacted Aamir Assadi and got him to send over your development plans for the work you've done in Dubai. I hope that's okay."

Creepy, but okay, Dario thought as he nodded his head. This week did have him thinking about staying in Southwood. This might have been the best news yet. "Great," Dario replied.

"Are you here to see Kimber?" Ramon asked, leading Dario back to where the female bouncer was either about to choke Darren by the knot of his tie or pull him in for a kiss.

"Darren, stop playing around," Dario said with a straight face, "Ramon's going to bring us to Kimber."

"See, babe?" Darren cooed. "I'm not here to try and pick up women, my brother is."

The woman let Darren go. She greeted Ramon, gave Dario a nod, then whispered for Darren to call her sometime.

"My wife told me she was backstage where the girls line up. I'm guessing you'll find Kimber there too."

The scent of every Bath & Body product filled the air. The sequins of the Christmas-colored dresses caught the backstage lighting, making the area flicker like a giant disco ball. The singing from up front made its way beyond the curtain, causing the chatter behind the thin wall to rise. Dario wasn't sure how, but he lost sight of Ramon in the wave of the next batch of girls getting ready to perform.

"I think I see her," Dario said to Darren, who was close by. Kimber leaned against the wall in an office with floor-to-ceiling windows. Her uncles were inside, standing in front of her, and the not-so-good doctor stood off to the side with a ten-inch black box in his hands. "This way."

Dario's breath caught in his throat. Glitter sparkled off Kimber's smooth, golden fawn skin. Her dark hair spilled over her shoulder on one side and down her back on the other. An image of her just like that, only in white, popped into his mind. God, he loved her. He began to pick up his step to get to his woman but crashed into another person. Bouncing back, Dario was ready to apologize to whichever budding beauty queen was in front of him, but as his eyes adjusted to the disco-effect light, they narrowed down on someone else.

"Alisha?" Dario cocked his head to the side. "What are you doing back?" Then his eyes focused on the man behind her, their family's friend, Aamir Assadi. "With Aamir?"

Chapter 11

The pageant would go down in Four Points General Hospital history. The patients in the extended ward put on a show to welcome the guests, who crowded the theater. The patients were given prime seating in the front rows where the wheelchair access was better. Not everyone attended, which left more room for the guests. Typically, pageants with children were limited to immediate family only, but families from Southwood, Peachville, Black Wolf Creek and Samaritan packed the place. Amelia's street team from MET Studios worked their magic, as did the camera crew. Lexi did her thing as emcee. Judges, real judges from each city's courthouse, presided as officials at the table.

At one point, the wing the theater was in had been

a discharge area. The loading zone had been turned into a stage and arena seating built around it with a parking deck behind. Inside, a long black curtain concealed the chaos backstage from the audience—but not necessarily the noise. Contestants from each city shared parts of the empty offices and rooms down either side of the hallway and up the stairs one level. Parents were given a buzzer that would sound off when they were to send their children to the stage. Little kids were assisted by parents. Girls fifteen and older were instructed to take responsibility for getting themselves to and from wherever they were supposed to be.

"Alright, pageant pals," Kimber said into her phone on her selfie stick, "if you're watching at home, give us your list of favorites so far. Don't forget, I'm Kimber Reyes, your correspondent at the Christmas crown competition." The group of girls she'd just featured helped her end the segment with a loud excited scream. She hugged the girls and headed into the designated office area.

Nate had helped prepare the unused observation room behind the stage. Floor to ceiling soundproof glass walls separated the hallway-slash-backstage area, which gave a reprieve from the commotion. A wire fed into the room at the monitors. In the center of the nine side-by-side stacked monitors was the main stage where Lexi stood as emcee. She introduced the next contestant for the current age group.

Someone sat in the corner and edited the angles of the last group contestant performances on a computer screen. Black Wolf Creek's representatives were definitely there to win in the seventeen to twenty-one category. All ten of the contestants were over five-eleven without their heels. And Kimber thought Peachville was sure to win in the category of cuteness. The cupcake dresses—from Grits and Glam Gowns—were hands down the most adorable. A couple of the beauty queens representing Samaritan were viable contestants, as well.

Because this was a Christmas pageant, all the titles to be won had a festive theme, ranging from Miss Candy Cane, Miss Winterfest, Miss Wintergreen and Miss Elegant Elf, to the most coveted title of Miss Christmas. Kimber stood next to the portable rack holding all the white sashes with red cursive writing for the titles. A red cloth was draped over a six-foot utility cart so that the only thing Kimber detected were the wheels underneath. Lexi didn't want anyone seeing the tiaras until the perfect time.

Christmas was tomorrow and Kimber had failed at getting Lexi the tiara she wanted her to have. That was, unless Vin or Philip came up with the right one. She was ashamed, as well, that she would not give Amelia the right present by being selected by MET, again, so they could be colleagues as well as aunt and niece. She did have a backup present for each of them—their favorite perfumes—but Kimber's heart sank with disappointment. She'd wanted the perfect gifts.

"I'm so proud of you, kiddo," Nate said stealing Kimber's attention from the backstage interactions.

Praise from her uncles brought heat to Kimber's cheeks this Christmas Eve. She even let Nate ruffle her hair for a second before ducking away from his hands. Because tonight's event had a Christmas theme, everyone behind the scenes was dressed in festive red, green and white. Knowing that, Kimber had chosen to wear one of Lexi's designs, a full-length emerald-green gown with a strapless sweetheart top.

"You did a good job here too," Kimber complimented him right back. "I can't believe this was once a pickup area."

"Ah yes." Nate rubbed his knuckles on his puffed-out chest. "The magic of a hammer."

"Lexi said she wanted you to emcee," said Stephen, walking away from the fascination of the editing process. "Why aren't you out there with her?"

"That's her thing." Kimber shook her head, pointed to the shot and watched Lexi do her thing from behind the curtains. She slipped her hand into the pocket of her dress and touched her phone. Still no word from MET. Trying not to be too disappointed, Kimber reminded herself there was still New Year's Eve to cover. If that were the case, it gave her another week with Philly. And, of course, there was Dario. She ignored the excited pulse in her blood.

"Where's your boyfriend?" Nate asked. "I had something to show him."

"I'm not really sure," Kimber answered, chewing her bottom lip for a moment. "He had something else to do tonight. He may stop by."

Stephen scrunched up his face. "But this is *your* thing. Why wouldn't he be here to support you?"

"He means fawn all over you," said Nate, chuckling while he draped one arm around Stephen's shoulders.

Living at home this week had reminded Kimber of how different her two uncles were. Stephen still believed Kimber was quite the innocent one, which was cute. Last year before going away he'd bought her a stuffed unicorn. If she had to guess, he probably still thought she was a virgin. Nate, on the other hand, had always seen through Kimber's antics, especially as a teenager, and called her out on her bull. She wouldn't trade either one of them for anything in the world. They were her family.

"Dario's allowed to go wherever he wants," Kimber assured Stephen.

Nate shook his head and added a *tsk* along with it. "I was rooting for him. He could have shown up for a minute."

A group of young pageant princesses passed by the window to line up behind the stage. Once they stopped squirming, the folks on the other side of the line were able to get through. The first person Kimber noticed was Vin. He carried a black box under his arm. When he waved, pit stains were visible on the red T-shirt he wore.

"Looks like it's showtime for you." Nate nudged Kimber toward the door. "There's another office over there," he said, pointing across the hall.

Stephen stepped in front of his brother with his

hands up. "Now, if they go in there, we're not going to be able to help our dear sweet niece with judging for herself."

"What's there to judge?" Kimber asked. "If he's the real designer, we'd know because he made it."

"You sure about that?" Stephen countered.

"Yeah, it could be a replica," added Nate.

Because she *would* know it, Kimber thought. The ones made after the original tiara were too similar to have been made by different designers. She felt in her bones that only one person had created such beauty. Before Kimber could respond, Vin knocked on the clear door.

"Hey," he said. The sound in the hall filled the room then went silent once he closed the door. "I was hoping I'd catch you before the show ended."

"Perfect timing," said Nate. "Why don't you come on in here? We're just waiting on your rival."

Vin chuckled. "Oh, there's no rivalry. Philip is always clowning around. It's no wonder Kimber broke up with him." His chuckle continued nervously. Kimber spied a bead of sweat rolling over his temple.

Why was he nervous? Did he not have the real thing? Kimber sighed with annoyance. She glanced down at her phone as it buzzed. She'd missed two calls and prayed it hadn't been MET phoning in while she filmed her segments.

The pit of her stomach quaked as she retrieved the messages. When the deep voice came over the line, she relaxed against the wall with a smile. It was Dario, wishing her good luck tonight. The voice mail went on to the next call. Kimber closed her eyes and prayed it wasn't the dream call she wanted. Not now. She needed a little bit more time before traipsing across the country or to wherever MET wanted to send her... if she got the job.

"We don't have to wait for Philip to show up with a fake tiara, Kimber," Vin suggested. "Why waste time?" He thrust his package into her hands.

Reluctantly, Kimber lifted the box. There, on top of a black velvet pillow sat a perfectly crafted tiara with wire leaves filled with sparkling faux diamonds. Her fingers traced the points where the headband and tiara were welded together.

"Incredible," she breathed. This was just like the one she'd seen in the second batch of tiaras. The finishing was smoother and the leaves curled a little more but it was still lovely. "Wow, I didn't think you had it in you," she said, looking up at Vin's waiting face as a smile stretched across it. Blood pounded in her ears. The only thing she heard was adrenaline racing.

"I thought you might like it."

"Yeah, let's hold on to that for a minute."

Philip stood in the doorway, filling the space with his height and brawn. The camera strapped around his neck dangled from a bedazzled band. Tucked under his arm was a familiar black box the same size as Vin's. Kimber shook her head.

"Good grief," she groaned. "Alright, let's see it."

Nate took the box from Philip and handed it to her.

Philip had the nerve to inhale deeply. "I hope you like it. I gave it a lot of thought."

"I'm sure you did," she mused.

Like the box she'd just opened, this one had the same feel, same weight, and damned if it wasn't exactly the same crown.

"Aw hell," Stephen said glancing into the box. "We were rooting for you. Me and Lexi were rooting for you."

Another voice filled the room. Dario, Darren in tow, stood behind a bewildered Philip. "Well thanks," he said to Stephen.

Stephen half shrugged his shoulders. "Sorry, my man, it's pretty *chaotic* in here. Wouldn't you agree about the *chaos*?"

A bridge of awkward silence passed between the two men. Kimber wanted to fit herself against Dario's frame but with Nate, Stephen, and Vin surrounding her, she couldn't move.

"Don't you like it?" Philip asked, stepping into the office more. "I know you wanted to give one as a gift to Lexi, but I thought this suited you more."

"It's beautiful, Philip," Kimber sighed, "I was just telling Vin that when he showed me his."

Philip grabbed the box in Vin's hands. "What the fu—?"

"Hey now," said Nate, wagging his finger. "There's a lady in the room."

That coming from her uncle was priceless and she would remind him about this moment when the time was right. Kimber looked back and forth between the two men. "I need both of you to tell me what is going on."

Again, the door opened and closed. Lexi breezed in, talking at a fast pace, going on about the pageant. "Oh fantastic, the tiaras arrived," Lexi said, spotting the cart. "I told her to put them in here and leave them covered. You guys haven't looked, have you?" Lexi stood in front of the cart with her hands on her hips. She turned at the waist to look at her audience. "So, what do you say one of these big strong men helps me bring these tiaras out to the stage for crowning? Oh, Kimber, you've got to see these." In one swift move Lexi pulled off the covering. "Have you ever seen anything like this before?"

Kimber blinked in disbelief. Vin gasped. Philip finally let out his curse. Nate and Stephen swore, as well. At the door, Dario scratched the top of his head and Darren gripped the doorjamb and laughed.

"I actually have seen something as beautiful," Kimber finally answered Lexi. She grabbed the boxes from Vin and Philip's hands. "See?"

"She promised me a quiet transaction." Vin cringed and at least had the decency to look ashamed.

"Kimber," Philip began to explain, "I handpicked this one of a kind tiara for you. Do you know how much I bid on this?"

Confused, Kimber sighed. "So neither of you took the time to handcraft a tiara. Instead, you two ordered these. Like, offline? You both make me sick. I've wasted all this time searching for the designer, which you both clearly weren't."

Lexi breezed across the room to inspect them. "So." She set her hands on her hips. "I guess it's safe to say Alisha Crowne's secret is out."

"Alisha?" Everyone chorused, except for Darren, who stopped to let go of the door and grip his stomach in a belly laugh. Dario elbowed him.

"Alisha was behind these?" Her enemy. The woman who hated her most in the world, created these beautiful tiaras? How long had Dario known? Kimber cast a glare at him. "Why did you let me make a fool of myself all this time when you knew good and well who made these?"

"Kimber, this isn't what you think," said Dario. "Let's go somewhere and talk."

"I'm fine where I am."

"Guys," Lexi cut into the tension. "I've got to get these things out. Vin, Philip, why don't the two of you help me?"

It was probably the safest thing for them all to leave the room right now. Kimber felt so stupid. Of course, Alisha would have something to do with this. Her brothers owned a garage. She had easy access to a welding machine. She had plenty of time. And the other obvious piece—she had connections to the jewelry Kimber had found in Dubai. After Vin and Stephen left with Lexi, Kimber covered her face with her hands and screamed into her palms. "I am such an idiot."

"No, you're not," Dario said. "Would you all give us a moment to talk?" he boldly asked her uncles. To her surprise, they listened and moved out the door, taking Darren with them.

"I can't believe you let me walk around for the past month interviewing girls, talking to the public about trying to find the designer when you knew all along." Anger filled her. Embarrassment flowed through her body. No wonder Darren was in hysterics. He'd known the whole time too.

Dario made a move to touch her arm, to calm her down, but she just pulled back, hitting her elbow on the wall, which caused her to drop her cell phone. She bent to get it, but he stopped her, holding her by the curve of her elbow. His fingers traced the throbbing spot. "I need to explain something to you." He braced his other hand against the wall by her head, half trapping her.

In defiance, Kimber crossed her arms for distance. "I thought you'd given up your childish games, Dario."

"I have," he said. "Don't give me that."

"So much that you let me…"

"Run around town," Dario finished for her. Any other time his charming smile might have given him a second chance but this time it didn't work. Kimber thought about her mother. How many chances had she given her father to charm his way back to her?

A standard ring tone filled the distance from the ground.

"Don't get it," Dario demanded.

"You mean like the all the other times you tried to get me to not the answer the phone? Was that because you didn't want me to find out who the designer was?"

"Kimber, if you just want to argue rather than talk things out…"

She crossed her arms over her chest. "Did you forget? I don't argue." Then she pushed him by the chest to bend over and get her phone. The screen said Unknown Caller. Funny how quickly things changed. She prayed the call was for her.

"Kimber." Dario had the nerve to growl out her name.

With her eyes on him, Kimber's thumb switched the call to Talk. "Hello?"

"May I speak with Kimber Reyes?"

"This is she."

"Hi, Kimber, this is Rory Montgomery."

Heart soaring, Kimber spun around to face the monitors. She steadied her breath. "Hi."

"Kimber, I apologize for this last-minute call but if you're still interested in doing a piece for the MET Network, we're looking for a reporter to cover a segment in Atlanta. Would you be able to make it by tomorrow morning?"

"I absolutely can."

"Great," said Rory with a sigh of relief. "I have all your information on file. We can take care of the paperwork at our satellite office there."

"No problem." Kimber tried to remain calm. "Thank you so much."

"Do you have any questions for me?"

"Is it okay if I ask what happened to the correspondents on your list?"

"Chicken pox," Rory chuckled. "So, we literally need a fresh face for the cameras."

Kimber listened to the last-minute details from

Rory. Her credentials would be sent to the office. Her assignment would be emailed to her and her hotel tab would be picked up by the station. Kimber turned back around and found the room empty. Dario was gone. She thought she saw the top of his head going through the crowd. Despite being angry with him, Kimber wanted to share her news with him too. She yanked the door open.

"There you are, you twit," Alisha snapped. She stormed into the room with such force Kimber stumbled backward.

Irritated, Kimber rolled her eyes. "I don't have time for you, Alisha. But congratulations on your tiara line. They are beautiful," she added with a sarcastic smirk. "Now, if you don't mind stepping aside, I need to find…"

"My brother?" Alisha scoffed. "Ain't no way in hell I am letting you near him. You're just going to hurt him, and I'll be damned if I let him run off for another year because of you."

"What are you talking about, Alisha? Dario got a job in Dubai. In his field of study," she added.

"A job he could have done anywhere but he wanted to be as far away from you as possible."

At their first reunion at the airport Dario had been distant with her. She'd had a feeling it was about the way she'd ended things before they ever got started but he'd said he was over it. He'd seemed fine all this time. Paranoia set in. Was this his plan all along? Did he seek some sort of revenge against her? No, she argued inwardly. A man who made love to her like he did was not in it for a game. "You don't know what you're talking about, again. Now move."

Not budging, Alisha stepped into Kimber's way. "No. I'm not done with you. You need to know the truth so you can stop playing with people's hearts and time. Dario left here because of you. You chased him away by calling him immature. You said he needed to grow up and quit playing with toys all the time. Do you know how incredibly insensitive that was? Do you know what my father did to him for playing?"

An ache gripped Kimber's heart at the memory Dario had shared with her. She could never imagine what would drive a father to strike his child no matter what. "We talked about your father."

"But did he tell you how he beat him? Belittled him for doing things like making cars for my dolls, building homes for them, welding things for them? Even as a kid he would always do whatever he could to keep the kids from picking on me by making sure I had the coolest stuff ever."

Something in Alisha's words settled in with Kimber. The welding. The skills. He would have had access to the hospital and the rooms when walking in with her. He freaking had access to a garage to work with Alisha on them.

"Well, give the beauty queen a trophy," Alisha said dryly. "Is it clicking yet?"

"Dario helped you make the crowns," Kimber deduced.

"Jesus, woman. Are you daft?" Alisha scowled at her.

The doors opened. Sheikh Aamir appeared and stepped inside. The noise behind him settled down. Kimber wondered if the hushed tones from the four-man security team posted outside the office had anything to do with it or if most of the girls were now out front by the stage waiting to hear their names being called. Kimber cast a glance at the monitors and realized it was the latter.

"What my love is trying to explain…"

My love…? Kimber wished she'd thought to flip on her camera as she watched the royal's hand secure its place on Alisha's waist.

"Alisha believed in her brother's talent, as did I, and was smart enough to mass-produce his designs. Hence the tiaras we flew in tonight."

Alisha's body softened against the six-foot sheikh. "Dario's going to kill me, but oh well. You needed to know. He may have wanted to keep his anonymity, but I am tired of him walking around thinking he needs to impress you."

"Sweetheart, we've talked about your anger issues," Aamir spoke close to her ear.

"If the two of you will excuse me." Kimber side-stepped the two of them and headed out the door. To where, she had no idea. She stormed down the hallway in the opposite direction of the crowning ceremony. Angry tears formed in her eyes.

Nate bumped into her as she rounded the corner. "Whoa, where are you going?" Upon seeing her fighting tears, he grabbed her and pulled her into a safe hug.

"I've got to get out of here," Kimber said, trying

to hold back her emotional breakdown. How was she supposed to believe anything from Dario ever again? What did it matter? There was no point in talking. This was over. They were over, she told herself, to the painful feel of her heart breaking.

"The last time you," he said as he raised his hands for air quotes, "*got out of here*, you were gone for a year. I don't know if I can eat your uncle's cooking alone for that long."

The joke made Kimber smile. "I gotta leave. I can't stay."

"Why?" Nate let her go to tip her chin toward him. "Why do you feel you need to leave every time something gets tough?"

"Because." Kimber's voice croaked. Her bottom lip trembled. "Because I don't want to end up in a relationship like my parents. Before you and Stephen got here, they were horrible. They argued all the time. I don't know why they stayed together. I never wanted to be like them. Trapped here in Southwood and resenting the person that made me stay."

"Oh, Kimber," Nate breathed while holding her once again. "I can't believe that's what you've been thinking about your folks. Ken and Betty may have argued some—"

"A lot," Kimber added, stepping back.

"Maybe they did, but trust me, if my brother had wanted to leave, he would've. The same for your mother. She was one of the strongest ladies I've ever met. Couples argue. Couples stay together because they want to, not because they have to. There's a difference."

"You think they loved each other?"

"Passionately. You know us Reyes men, we go big or we…"

"Go home?" Kimber provided.

"We go bigger. Especially if she's worth it."

Cheers sounded from down the hall. The pageant was coming to an end, as was her relationship with Dario. She hated missing it. Her training in her journalism classes had taught her to be a professional and not let the camera see what was going on in her personal life, but not now. Not tonight. She just wanted to go home and pack. Kimber pulled away from her uncle and started walking. "I gotta go."

"Did you and Dario work things out?" Nate asked, walking with her.

Kimber shook her head. "I mean, I know he snuck the tiaras into the hospital. And I think he is the one who made the first tiara, if what Alisha said is true."

"So, you don't want me to show you the footage I found?"

Her heels skidded to a halt. "What footage?"

Nate extracted his phone from the front pocket of his slacks. "I told you I'd find out about the footage from last year. Here's a clip of the exact day Dario brought the crowns in to the hospital. Can you imagine the frustration he felt getting overlooked by you?"

The sound was off, but she recalled the exact outfit Dario wore. The pageant had been earlier that day. The sleeves of his Santa suit were still intact. How had she not questioned him about that huge sack of gifts? He set a red-and-white wrapped box down and disappeared from frame. A few moments later he walked back in, with Kimber. Kimber watched, feeling the egg all over her face. She didn't need the sound to remember how she'd asked everyone who came into the room if they knew about the box of tiaras. She never once asked him. Instead, on that day, Kimber had accused Dario of being immature and not having any goals in life other than playing with his expensive toys in the garage.

"Dario's been quite the player around town," Nate said all of a sudden. "Hey, it takes one to know one, but I have seen a difference in him. And I also saw his face when he left the office tonight. He looked like a man broken. And who could blame him? He had to sit around for the last month and listen to those two jokers say they created the tiaras."

"He could have told me."

Nate nodded. "I am sure he has his reasons. Being a big buff guy like myself," he said as he flexed his biceps, "it's hard to admit to the world you're part of something gentler, like creating dainty tiaras."

"So you believe he helped."

"You can only follow the trail in front of you, Kimber. What does your gut tell you?"

"It tells me I need to have this conversation with Dario," Kimber replied.

"Great. You can take my truck to go see him."

Kimber half laughed. "You want me to drive?" She snatched the keys he dangled in front of her. "What's the worst that could happen? It's not like I can do any further damage to it."

"Cute, Kimber. Cute," Nate called down the corridor after her.

"Oh, by the way," Kimber said, turning back. "Tell Amelia I'm pretty sure I'm going to get the Atlanta job at MET."

Chapter 12

With her skirt gathered in her lap, Kimber drove down the road toward the Crowne's ranch-style home. The family allowed small aircrafts to use their track as a landing strip, but the number of cars parked seemed impossibly too many. She drove by familiar cars from some of the folks in town. Had it not been for the small aircraft parked carefully on the side of the road, Kimber would have sworn she was at a college frat party.

She found a spot on the grass across the street from the house and pulled in at an angle. The tail end stuck out, but she was confident no one else would drive down the road. Everyone else in the world was here or at Four Points General it seemed.

Before her heels touched the driveway, Kimber's

insides thumped with the booming music coming from the house. The front door opened, and two guys helped carry a third man outside. The man being assisted bled from the nose.

"Best night ever," the bloody guy said.

Kimber sidestepped them and slipped into the house. Or, at least, she thought it was the house. The interior had been changed from a cozy home to an apocalypse center. The furniture was gone. Spray paint covered the walls. In one corner of the room a Santa Claus piñata hung from the ceiling. One blindfolded woman was beating the thing with a bat while other women cheered. The place reeked of alcohol. The sign above the tub filled with what Kimber assumed was Jell-O read Bobbing for Elves. Through the congealed mass she could see little pointed hats on plastic elves. Darren ran through the house, shirtless, screaming in a battle cry. "The champ is ready! The champ is ready!"

Before Kimber found out who the champ was, a loud male voice came over a speaker system.

"Women's Christmas Gauntlet starts in ten. After that, Boxing Around the Christmas Ring starts in fifteen minutes."

A guttural cheer erupted throughout the house. Darren stopped running once he spotted Kimber. She supposed her attire stood out from everyone else who was dressed in some form of tacky shredded Christmas sweater or shirt. Catcalls came from a group of women down the hall, catching her attention. Emerging from the dark hall came Dario. He wore a pair of red Rudolph boxer briefs and a red silk robe. His bare thighs were oiled, as was his chest. When he realized Darren had stopped moving, Dario glanced around the room and made eye contact with Kimber. Her heart lurched with intrigue but mainly disappointment.

"Kimber?" Dario asked, pulling the hood off his head. "What are you doing here?"

"I thought I was looking for something, someone," Kimber said with a sigh. This was the Dario she'd met years ago. Wild. Crazy. Reckless. "But I don't…" She swallowed past the lump forming in her throat. "I don't think I'll find what I'm looking for here."

Kimber turned to leave. Once she closed the front door behind her she half expected Dario to come after her. *Foolish girl*, she thought, wiping the tears away from her eyes. Blinded by them, she crossed the street to the truck and slammed the door. She needed a moment to collect herself before driving. A set of fireworks sounded off in the air in red, white and green. Even with the windows closed, she heard the chants of the guests.

"Christmas Chaos! Christmas Chaos!"

The words made her recall something her uncle Stephen had said. He kept alluding to chaos with Dario. Did he know? It didn't matter, she told herself with a shake of her head. A white firework above the car lit the inside. She spotted the red and white box Dominic had given her that morning. In the preparations for the day, she'd forgotten about it. She leaned over to grab it from the floorboards of the passenger's side and tore off the paper. The bulky wrapping was totally Dario's doing. She lifted the fold and took out a familiar box. There, set on a doll-sized pillow was a tiara. A custom-made one with coppery metal twisted into heart shapes and topaz jewels welded into the centers of them. Her fingers traced the fused spots where the metal met. A note slipped from the pillow. With a shaky breath she read the scrap of paper. "A prototype of a one of a kind tiara, for a one of a kind lady, who has my one of a kind love. Love, Dario."

Kimber scrambled to get out of the car. She kicked out of her heels, lifted her skirts and ran back inside the house. Lilly Stringer stopped her. "Where do you think you're going?"

"Move, Lilly. I need to see Dario."

"Didn't you just have a chance?" Lilly cackled and looked behind her for support from her friends. "Dario's done a good thing around here for us single folks, Kimber. Christmas Chaos is what we look forward to every year when we can't be with our kids."

The titled events made sense now, Kimber thought. Everything was geared toward trashing Christmas. "Look," she started to say, "I'm not here to stop anything. I just need to see Dario."

"You gotta play to see the champ," said a burly woman with red and green frosting on her face.

Dario made his way to the ring with Darren rubbing his shoulders, hyping him up. His opponent was Philip Grieco. This night couldn't have ended on a better note. The day had already been crappy enough.

He thought he'd gotten rid of Philip and Vin when they'd exposed themselves as frauds, but somehow, he became the villain in this Christmas tale. His sister had hijacked his designs and had been selling them online. And then his lady, who he'd thought had ended things at the hospital, just caught him in his biggest lie yet.

The boxing ring he climbed into stood at the back edge of the property. Benches placed around it were filled with onlookers who didn't want to get dirty but made a charitable donation to watch tonight's big event. The empty seats in the front two rows belonged to the winners of the other big events, including a spot for the winner of the obstacle course, which was about to take place.

"Use your anger tonight," Darren said, rubbing Dario's shoulders. "Think about how that dude tried to take away everything you worked hard for."

What he'd worked hard for was for Kimber to see him as a mature guy worth dating. He'd ruined that with his lies. Maybe he'd let Philip get in a few good punches. He deserved them. Screaming brought Dario out of his funk. The crowd in the seats stood so they could see the field. Dario and Darren leaned against the ropes and watched.

There, out on the track, he spotted a body in a green gown belly crawling under the row of Christmas lights in the bed of crumbled Christmas sugar cookies.

"Is that Kimber?" Darren asked.

Dario hopped out of the ring to the ground. He

watched his woman army-crawl the course, out-run her opponent and then hop on the platform to battle one of the single mothers from Peachville in a candy cane joust. Kimber took the woman down in seconds and continued the obstacle course leading to the ring. The crowd cheered for her.

Dario, though confused at what the hell she was doing, fist pumped the air when Kimber dodged the glitter bombs thrown at the competitors making their way down the long run. Kimber held the bottom of her dress in her hands. Her legs and feet were covered in an array of goo. But she was a full ten feet ahead of the other ladies when she hurtled across the silver-garland finish line, right into his arms.

"Are you crazy?" Dario heard his voice. He didn't realize he'd been screaming in a cheer for her that had left him hoarse. "What are you doing?"

"I'm going big," Kimber panted. "Did I win?"

"Yes, you won." Dario dipped her back in his arms. He pulled the strands of tinsel from her hair. Mascara ran under her eyes. Cookie crumbs were smeared across her cheek like blush and her skin sparkled with glitter. He wasn't sure she'd ever looked more beautiful.

"But did I win you?" Kimber asked, her breathing beginning to straighten out.

"You always had me, Kimber. Always." Dario dipped his mouth to her sweet lips and kissed her. The surrounding crowd cheered for them. "I love you, Kimber."

"I love you too."

Epilogue

A Christmas station played children's holiday music on a loop at the crack of dawn Christmas morning. Wrapping paper flew everywhere. Coffee percolated in the kitchen. This was the scene of real Christmas chaos in the Reyes household. Amelia and Nate sat on the love seat in the sunken family room. Stephen sat in the chair while Lexi perched on the arm of it with her husband's arm wrapped around her waist. The three smaller children squealed in delight at their gifts. And Philly, who'd decided she wasn't too cool to get excited at the presents, squealed right along with the kids.

Kimber sat on the couch and took in the view, not sure what next Christmas would bring. Beside her, Dario held her hand.

"What time are you guys leaving today?" Amelia asked them.

"After we have breakfast with Dario's family," answered Kimber. "We'll be in Atlanta for a week."

Amelia smiled in delight. "My colleague. I'm so proud of you. Best Christmas present ever."

"Speaking of," Kimber said, chewing on her bottom lip. "I am sorry for the perfume, Lexi. I had no idea you knew about the tiaras."

"I wanted you to discover on your own," said Lexi with a nod. "And I love the perfume."

"Actually," said Dario, clearing his throat. "Kimber did get you something else." He reached down into the duffel bag by his feet and handed Kimber a box. "Go ahead. You basically designed it."

Kimber wasn't sure how much joy she could get in one day. She and Dario were spending the next week together in Atlanta. After the holidays he planned on taking a job with the Four Points Urban Planning board and last night he'd driven her to the new subdivision just outside of Southwood to the perfect house he wanted to buy for them.

After lifting the lid of the box, Kimber covered her mouth and gasped. Dario had designed a tiara for Lexi. The metal was a blond color in homage to Lexi's hair, and at the peak of each crest of the crown was a blue mother-of-pearl sphere.

"The metal is Muntz," Dario explained.

Kimber rose to hand Lexi the tiara.

"I'm glad to see you wised up," Lexi said while hugging her. Kimber patted her back then turned around to face Dario.

He'd moved off the couch and got to one knee while presenting a box to Kimber. Her heart raced. Out the corner of her eye she spied Philly filming them. Nate leaned forward in the love seat while Amelia bounced up and down excitedly, smacking Nate's arm. Dario opened the box. A square-cut diamond greeted her. Dario took the ring out and held it between his large thumb and index finger.

"Kimber, before we start this adventure in Atlanta, I want to make sure you know..."

"Yes," Kimber interrupted him.

"He didn't ask the question," Stephen clarified for her.

"How much I love you," Dario continued. "You've been my best friend, held me to the highest standard and you've been the brightest spot in my life."

"Yes," Kimber repeated.

"Kimber," Nate warned. "Let the man speak."

Every fiber of her body screamed with excitement. "I already know the answer."

Dario offered her a lazy smile. The twinkle in his eyes drew a return grin. "I'm not stopping or leaving this house until you answer my question. No way I'm sitting quietly by, ever again."

"What's your question?" Kimber asked, trying to keep a straight face. She wanted to cry, scream and hurry up and celebrate with a kiss.

"Kimber Reyes, will you marry me?"

"Dario Crowne, of course I will."

* * * * *

We hope you enjoyed these soulful,
sensual reads.

Kimani Romance is coming to an end, but
there are still ways to satisfy your craving
for juicy drama and passion.

Starting December 2019, find great new reads
from some of your favorite authors in:

Drama. Scandal. Passionate romance.

**New titles available every month,
wherever books are sold!**

Harlequin.com

The coffee shop was still busy enough that they had to queue for their
drinks, but they managed to find a table.

"Thank you." He gestured toward his espresso.

His wallet had been in his hand, but she had sidestepped neatly in front
of him, her soft brown eyes defying him to argue with her. Now, though,
those same brown eyes were busily avoiding his, and for the first time since
she'd called out his name, he wondered why she had tracked him down.

He drank his coffee, relishing the heat and the way the caffeine started
to block the tension in his back.

"So, I'm all yours," he said quietly.

She stiffened. "Hardly."

He sighed. "Is that what this is about? Me giving you the wrong name."

Her eyes narrowed. "No, of course not. I'm not—" She stopped,
frowning. "Actually, I wasn't just passing, and I'm not here for myself."
She took a breath. "I'm here for Sóley."

Her face softened into a smile and he felt a sudden urge to reach out and
caress the curve of her lip, to trigger such a smile for himself.

"It's a pretty name."

She nodded, her smile freezing.

It was a pretty name—one he'd always liked. One you didn't hear much
outside of Iceland. Only what had it got to do with him?

Watching her fingers tremble against her cup, he felt his ribs tighten.
"Who's Sóley?"

She was quiet for less than a minute, only it felt much longer—long
enough for his brain to click through all the possible answers to the
impossible one. The one he already knew.

He watched her posture change from defensive to resolute.

"She's your daughter. Our daughter."

He stared at her in silence, but a cacophony of questions was ricocheting inside his head.

Not the how or the when or the where, but the why. Why had he not been more careful? Why had he allowed the heat of their encounter to blot out his normally ice-cold logic?

But the answers to those questions would have to wait.

"Okay…"

Shifting in her seat, she frowned. "'Okay'?" she repeated. "Do you understand what I just said?"

"Yes." He nodded. "You're saying I got you pregnant."

"You don't seem surprised," she said slowly.

He shrugged. "These things happen."

To his siblings and half siblings, even to his mother. But not to him. Never to him.

Until now.

"And you believe me?" She seemed confused, disappointed?

Tilting his head, he held her gaze. "Honest answer?"

He was going to ask her what she would gain by lying. But before he could open his mouth, her lip curled.

"On past performance, I'm not sure I can expect that. I mean, you lied about your name. And the hotel you were staying at. And you lied about wanting to spend the day with me."

"I didn't plan on lying to you," he said quietly.

Her mouth thinned. "No, I'm sure it comes very naturally to you."

"You're twisting my words."

She shook her head. "You mean like saying Steinn instead of Stone?"

Pressing his spine into the wall behind him, he felt a tick of anger begin to pulse beneath his skin.

"Okay, I was wrong to lie to you—but if you care about the truth so much, then why have you waited so long to tell me that I have a daughter? I mean, she must be what…?" He did a quick mental calculation. "Ten, eleven months?"

Don't miss
Proof of Their One-Night Passion
available December 2019 wherever
Harlequin Presents® *books and ebooks are sold.*

www.Harlequin.com

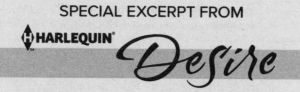
"That's it, Peterson Higgins, no more. You've had three servings already," Myra said, laughing, as she guarded the pan of peach cobbler on the counter.

He stood in front of her, grinning from ear to ear. "You should not have baked it so well. It was delicious."

"Thanks, but flattery won't get you any more peach cobbler tonight. You've had your limit."

He crossed his arms over his chest. "I could have you arrested, you know."

Crossing her arms over her own chest, she tilted her chin and couldn't stop grinning. "On what charge?"

The charge that immediately came to Pete's mind was that she was so darn beautiful. Irresistible. But he figured that was something he could not say.

She snapped her fingers in front of his face to reclaim his attention. "If you have to think that hard about a charge, then that means there isn't one."

"Oh, you'll be surprised what all I can do, Myra."

She tilted her head to the side as if to look at him better. "Do tell, Pete."

Her words—those three little words—made a full-blown attack on his senses. He drew in a shaky breath, then touched her chin. She blinked, as if startled by his touch. "How about 'do show,' Myra?"

Pete watched the way the lump formed in her throat and detected her shift in breathing. He could even hear the pounding of her heart. Damn, she smelled good, and she looked good, too. Always did.

"I'm not sure what 'do show' means," she said in a voice that was as shaky as his had been.

He tilted her chin up to gaze into her eyes, as well as to study the shape of her exquisite lips. "Then let me demonstrate, Ms. Hollister," he said, lowering his mouth to hers.

The moment he swept his tongue inside her mouth and tasted her, he was a goner. It took every ounce of strength he had to keep the kiss gentle when he wanted to devour her mouth with a hunger he felt all the way in his bones. A part of him wanted to take the kiss deeper, but then another part wanted to savor her taste. Honestly, either worked for him as long as she felt the passion between them.

He had wanted her from the moment he'd set eyes on her, but he'd fought the desire. He could no longer do that. He was a man known to forego his own needs and desires, but tonight he couldn't.

Whispering close to her ear, he said, "Peach cobbler isn't the only thing I could become addicted to, Myra."

Will their first kiss distract him from his duty?

Find out in
Duty or Desire
by New York Times *bestselling author Brenda Jackson.*

Available December 2019 wherever
Harlequin® Desire books and ebooks are sold.

Harlequin.com

Looking for more satisfying love stories
with community and family at their core?

Check out **Harlequin® Special Edition**
and **Love Inspired®** books!

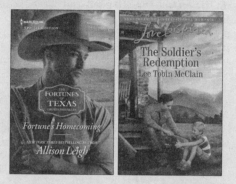

New books available every month!

Love Harlequin romance?

DISCOVER.

Be the first to find out about promotions, news and exclusive content!

Facebook.com/HarlequinBooks

Twitter.com/HarlequinBooks

Instagram.com/HarlequinBooks

Pinterest.com/HarlequinBooks

ReaderService.com

EXPLORE.

Sign up for the Harlequin e-newsletter and download a free book from any series at **TryHarlequin.com.**

CONNECT.

Join our Harlequin community to share your thoughts and connect with other romance readers!
Facebook.com/groups/HarlequinConnection

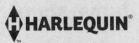

HARLEQUIN®

**ROMANCE WHEN
YOU NEED IT**

HSOCIAL2018